THE MOONS OF JUPITER
RESURRECTION

BY APRIL ADAMS

San Diego, CA 92101

First eBook Edition: February 2014

ISBN: 978-0-9844003-4-8

Cover design by Drop Dead Design

For For my Fledglings,
Amberle, Alex, Kevin and Noa.

TABLE OF CONTENTS

ONE

Captain Condliffe took his place in the bridge, settling into the oversized silver swivel chair as his crew moved with urgent purpose. Like his crew, he wore pale, pearlescent coveralls with the IGC patch sewn onto the front over the left breast. The only sign of his rank as Commander were the simple, fringeless epaulettes on his shoulders.

The young Captain was taking reports, watching monitors and listening to the Dragon all at once. The Beryl Dragon had not seen so much activity since her eggs had manifested and Condliffe knew that it would be a long time before things settled down again, if they ever did.

The Commander leaned back in his chair, rubbing his chin thoughtfully. He needed a shave. A few more hours and he would be looking as bad as Jovak. He ran a hand through his hair and, feeling the dark curls envelop his fingers, realized a haircut was in order as well.

Shave and a haircut...two bits, he thought, nervously distracted.

The war with the Chimera, so uneventful save for a few skirmishes over nearly one hundred years, was now escalating with the force and power of an avalanche.

The Beryl Dragon, *his* Dragon, had recently been attacked even though the assault had been thrown back quite easily. A Chimeran Battle Cruiser had dropped into their star system only weeks ago, gen-braking and releasing a number of ill-equipped fighter jets that had launched a horribly disorganized attack on the Dragon.

Condliffe had ordered a counter offensive and dispatched half a dozen fighters from the Beryl Dragon's jet bay. The Chimeran fighters had evaded the IGC jets for as long as they could, taking pot shots at the Dragon before they were chased off like a ragtag band of mosquitoes.

It was over almost as soon as it had begun and the event had coincided with an internal attack on the Opal Dragon on the other side of the galaxy. Captain Condliffe thought the whole incident seemed a ruse, a feint to discover a weak spot or their Standard Response Protocol.

He had spoken just yesterday with Commander Blaylock, the Executive Officer of the Opal Dragon, and had voiced his concern that the recent strikes might have something to do with the Third Year Dragons manifesting their eggs.

Blaylock had dismissed the idea at once and was certain that it had to be something else causing the escalation. The Copper Dragon as well as the Silver Dragon had also borne eggs but had not been assaulted, and the Opal Dragon had been attacked even though her eggs had hatched over two years ago.

Still, Condliffe wondered. He had a nagging suspicion that the eggs were involved somehow but he did his best to dismiss the idea, trying to write it off as being over protective of his Dragon's offspring.

The Beryl Dragon had manifested her eggs two standard years ago, the living starship producing the eggs deep within her belly, the part of her body that was still most organic. The rest of her was more metal and machine.

Doc Kuri, the head of the Dragon's medical staff, had put in the call to the Captain twenty-four months ago - after confirming with the Engineer that the two ovoids in the viscous hydrogen of the Dragon's lower abdomen were indeed eggs.

Condliffe had immediately left the Navigator in charge of the bridge and rushed to the engine room with his heart thrumming and his Executive Officer, Commander Slater, right on his heels. The belly of the Dragon, its bottom-most chamber and stifling hot, was a maze of machines and upright field columns that contained most of her organic matter.

The Captain found the dark-skinned doctor along with two of his staff and Mr. Jovak, the Dragon's Engineer, conversing excitedly. Jovak was a tall and lanky human with pale skin, deep-set eyes that were a blue-gray color, and golden blonde hair. As always, he needed a shave. Commander Slater threw a scowl at the man but the look went purposely unnoticed.

The doctors and the Engineer stood in front of a tremendous column of organic matter contained by a thin but powerful Vespra Field. The field was clear, showing the opaque silver of the Dragon blood mixed with clear liquid hydrogen. The syrupy matter swirled in the column like a slow moving cyclone.

Condliffe's eyes flicked about, determining his exact position in the ship, and knew in a second that the column before him led up to the Ventricle, the chamber that contained the Dragon's starfire heart.

Jovak stepped aside for the officers and Kuri ran an infrared waft over the column, illuminating the viscous hydrogen inside. He stopped when he reached two oblong shapes, dark spots inside the silvery slush.

"There they are," he breathed, almost singing the words.

"They look like rugby balls!" Condliffe exclaimed, surprised. He could hear Jovak snicker and the doc flashed a smile of even white teeth. Condliffe smiled in the distracted manner of a man just told that he was going to be a father. "I mean, I can't believe how small they are!"

Kuri nodded. "They will round out and grow quite a bit in the next eighteen months, to about the size of a two-man space pod. Then we will extract them. After that the Hatchlings will finish maturing within the eggs for another six to nine months."

"Shouldn't we just keep them in there until they are ready to come out?" Condliffe asked, unable to pull his eyes away from the dark spots suspended in the silvered hydrogen. Kuri shook his head.

"The wet environment slows down the process – they might not hatch for two or three years if we did that."

Dr. Hayden, one of the ship's medics, wore the same distracted smile as the Commander. "They like it too much in there," he said. He was having a hard time taking his eyes off the shapes as well.

The Captain finally drew his eyes away and turned to his Executive Officer. "Begin the evacuation of the aircraft in the starboard Fighter Bay," he commanded. "Put as many as you can in the port side bay, and contact IGC Military Logistics to redistribute the remaining jets and equipment."

"Yes, sir!" The XO replied quickly, his constrained excitement no less than the Captain's. After a nod of dismissal from Condliffe, he turned on his heel to hurry off and hand down his orders, but not before throwing a dark look at the Engineer. "And you need a shave, Mr. Jovak."

The Engineer ran a hand over the strawberry-blonde scruff along his jaw. "I'm on my way," he assured.

The Captain, also scowling at the man, turned back to the dark spots within the column of hydrogen slush, his face softening.

Eighteen months, he had thought. *Could they really get that big in a year and a half?*

He found it hard to believe, but the Doc was right - they could and they did.

The two eggs had grown more round and quite large and then had been extracted through the Vespra Field by the Engineer and then carefully carried from the belly of the Dragon with a field manipulator and placed in the Fighter Bay that everyone had already begun to call The Womb.

The Womb was an enormous space, large enough to house an entire platoon of fighter jets, as it would need to be to house the Fledgling Dragons as they grew into Draconae. The hangar had been divided into sections to let IGC crew install even higher security measures while the Engineer, along with the Dragon's medical staff, worked to settle the eggs and make them secure.

The eggs, to everyone's surprise, were practically colorless. Every other Dragon egg that had manifested from the Third Generation Dragons had been a pure bright color, one for each spectrum of the rainbow. The eggs of the Beryl Dragon, however, were dark gray. One was so dark that it was almost black.

"What do you think it means?" Condliffe had asked the XO and the Engineer, pushing away the nervousness that he felt as the eggs were being transported to the Womb. Both had shrugged.

"Maybe Dragons see more colors than we do," Commander Slater had suggested.

Mr. Jovak offered his thoughts almost absently as he guided the eggs with the manipulator. "Maybe they represent Alexander's Band," he remarked, his blue-gray eyes keeping sharp watch on the distance between the eggs and the walls of the corridor, which wasn't much. The eggs were large, taller than the Engineer, and nearly as wide as the hallway through which they were passing.

Something else occurred to the Captain and he wrapped a hand around the elbow of a nearby elfin midshipman with sand-colored hair and pointed to the great rounded eggs that the Engineer was floating down the corridor. "What colors are those?" he asked.

The midshipman's almond-shaped eyes went round with surprise. "Sir?"

Captain Condliffe held the elf's elbow as he walked along, keeping up with the crew moving the eggs. With his other hand he gestured impatiently ahead. "It's not a test," he told the elf.

"Just tell me if those eggs look like plain black and gray to you."

"Errr, well, the black one looks studded with aum," he replied as they walked, not quite sure what the Captain was after.

"Aum?" Condliffe asked, searching his own memory. "That's a color in the Elvin spectrum, right?"

"Yes, sir," the elf said. "Very close to gold."

"And the gray one?"

The elf peeked around the body of Doc Kuri. "It looks like it is studded with nac."

"Which is close to the color silver," Condliffe murmured, recalling a lesson he had been given years ago on elfin eyesight.

"That's right, sir."

"Thank you, Deaven," the Captain said, releasing his arm and hurrying ahead so not to miss anything.

"You're welcome, sir," Deaven replied as the Commander strode briskly away, equally pleased that he could help and mystified by the Captain's odd behavior.

Condliffe watched with fascination as the eggs, plain to his eyes but no less precious, were set and settled into The Womb. He ran a hand over each, feeling the rubbery, pebbled surface under his palm. The shells were soft but more than a meter thick to allow the embryos continuous growth.

Due to their drab colors, the dark eggs had been nicknamed Coal and Stone - though Jovak's remark had been picked up by others and as a pair they began to be referred to as Alexander's Eggs.

At the time of their transport to the Womb and in the days that followed, they had been given much attention. Everyone, no matter what their rank or job upon the Dragon, was eager to see the progeny. All members of the crew would visit and coo over them as if they were newborn infants.

As time passed, the crew aboard the Dragon returned to business as usual with their traditional crisp, military, precision. Only the ship's medical staff kept a constant watch upon the eggs, monitoring their temperature, size, and internal statistics. Occasionally a curious crewmember or small group of them would stop by to see if any exciting developments had been made.

Days and weeks and months passed and there had not been any changes or much excitement to speak of - until just a week ago.

Seven days previous, the medical staff had determined that

the eggs had reached their maturity. The shells were starting to harden, a sign that most of the nutrition stored in the casings had been used. The Hatchlings would soon reach maturity and emerge from their shells.

"How soon?" Condliffe had demanded of Doctor Kuri, nearly bursting with excitement and pride.

The doc had shrugged and rocked his head back and forth as if he were giving a visual estimate on the sale of a used aircar. "Kept under the same conditions? More than a week from now, but less than a month," he responded. "If we immerse them in a saline fluid we can delay the process up to six months, maybe nine."

The Commander smiled. "That won't be necessary."

Commander Condliffe had notified the InterGalactic Council and the IGC Operations Director had put in the call to the Jordan Training Center. Just last night they had arrived – freshly scrubbed and hollow-eyed from years of training. Seven cadets of the best and most highly trained pilots culled from all the civilized galaxies, each one near ready to rupture with hope and terror.

The Captain and the Executive Officer had dined with them, engaging the cadets in conversation and eyeing them curiously, eagerly wondering whom among them would be selected by the Fledglings to be the Jordans of the Beryl Dragon.

Two of the cadets were female – one with skin as pale as milk but as rough as sand. Condliffe wondered if that was a natural occurrence or a result of the training to which she had been subjected. The other had dark skin, darker even than Kuri's, and tightly braided black hair. She had a quick laugh like Kuri and quick eyes like his XO, Commander Slater. Condliffe took an instant liking to her.

He had been surprised to find that one of the male cadets was a Zealot. Commander Slater had unabashedly asked him about his feelings on killing other beings and then, even more abrasively, asked how he felt about the Zealot Chimeran Commander that most referred to as the Boy Vicar, or more often, the Vicar of Blood.

The young man had fixed his gentle brown eyes on the Executive Officer and responded solemnly that the Chimeran were an abomination and he did not consider their demise as actual murder.

"As for the one they call the Vicar of Blood," he added, "he was denounced by the One Church, as I am sure you know." The cadet then smiled at Commander Slater and told him that his own course had been decided by The One and that the One Lord, who had seen him through thus far, would see him through for the rest of the journey.

"How in the hell did The One get you past Malherbe?" Slater had asked, meaning the ill-tempered Master Sergeant at the Jordan Training Center. The question pulled a chuckle from everyone, including Condliffe. He too, had been subjected to the brutal NCO and remembered him all too well.

Like all the other cadets, the young man had introduced himself only his by initials – BW. He had smiled benignly at the Executive Officer and his question. "The One gave me the strength to persevere, and closed my ears to his abuse."

Commander Slater gave a low whistle. "In that case there may be something to your religion," he admitted thoughtfully nodding. "The only thing that kept me going was the hope that I would get to kill the bastard someday."

Everyone had laughed heartily at that, even the transport crew that had joined the cadets and the officers for dinner at the Captain's request.

The transport craft that had brought the cadets from the training center on the moon of Lido was now docked with the Dragon. It started having trouble with its field generators on the way in and the transport crew had been working frantically in an effort to fix them as quickly as possible.

The Dragon, however, was headed for Spaceport Nine Jupiter and Condliffe had insisted that the craft stay docked until the rendezvous. Space travel was too risky with glitchy generators.

Now, in the simulated light of dawn, the Commander ran his hand down over his stubbled chin and up through his slightly shaggy hair and wished he hadn't insisted. The trans crew might have been safer taking their chances.

Hell was breaking loose on the other side of the galaxy.

The Opal Dragon had been drawn and all Condliffe could do was watch and wait. With the would-be-Jordans tucked safely inside the Womb, he listened to reports from his Navigator and from the secure broadcast monitors. He kept one ear open to the IGC coms but, most of all, he listened to the Dragon. His Dragon.

Though they were separated by over two hundred solar systems, the Beryl Dragon could feel her sister's wrath. She could feel the anger blossom in the starfire of her own heart for Opal's Fledglings and their humankind; separated, torn, tortured and furious. Beryl, too, longed to shed her metal skin and bring down destruction on those that would do hurt to her kindred, but as of yet there had been no call.

Her sister did not call to her for help. Nor did Condliffe, who she thought of as her human-Dragon-childmate, command to intervene though she could feel the desire in his heart. She could feel his tension and his indecision, and she knew that he too was waiting for the order to attack. Had her sister called, she would override any commands by her child-mate, Condliffe. Likewise, should Condliffe command her, she would not wait to be called by her sister Dragon.

The young Commander drummed his fingers on the arm of his chair, in the same mental quandary as his Dragon. He was waiting for the call for help, or for the Dragon to make the decision to intervene for them. They shared a mutual uncertainty and she could feel Condliffe vacillate for the same reasons as her own – they feared the endangerment of the precious cargo they carried.

There was something else, too, that made her hesitate. There was a nagging ache in her belly and she did not know the cause. Something wasn't right inside her, in the huge empty spaces the humankind had carved out for themselves. She tried to understand what it was and when she did not, she could only think that it must be the combined feeling of distress from the entire crew.

In her mind's eye she could see her sister exploding into the atmosphere of some lonely moon and melting an entire coordinate of moonscape into basalt and ash. She was killing those that had hurt her children, but there seemed to be no counter from those she and her sister called the Otherlings.

The Otherlings were neither human nor elf, but something that their kinds had created. She had heard the word the Condliffe-child-mate had used for them: Chimera. The Chimera Otherlings had turned on their creators and made war, but this was the first time in nearly a century that they had been able to cause real harm.

All eyes were trained on monitors, all ears on the coms. There were several holos over the bridge dash showing the destruction being brought down by the Opal Dragon and everyone that wasn't moving double-time about the room watched, fascinated.

The Beryl Dragon watched as well, but with her own senses rather than the holos. She too was tensely fascinated, the nagging ache inside her temporarily forgotten. Until the ache became a sharp pain, stabbing and terrifying.

Fire! she cried out, though Commander Condliffe was the only one that could hear. *Danger!*

The Captain had jerked simultaneously with her terrified warning and doubled over in his chair with an excruciating pain in his left side, (*my starboard side,* he thought wildly) and was immediately surrounded by his crew. His blue eyes, wide with terror, sought out his Executive Officer.

"I'm here," Slater assured him, dropping to one knee so that they were eye to eye. "What is it?"

"Who's guarding the eggs?" Condliffe whispered hoarsely.

The XO shook his head, puzzled. "The Jordans are there with them, the medical staff, the Engineer..."

The Captain's face spasmed in a grimace of pain. "And not one of them is armed!" He pushed himself out of his chair and ran from the bridge without giving a single order.

Slater's eyes flicked to the belts of his surrounding crew. "Denley!" he called to the Gunnery Lieutenant.

"Yes sir!"

"You have the con," he commanded. "Nav and Coms stand fast - anyone else wearing a sidearm come with me!" With that, he turned and fled after his Captain.

Captain Condliffe ran hell-bent down an artery, skidding to a halt on his feet before an open tube lift and jumped in, palming down the rounded inside wall. The air current took him down two levels before he palmed it off and took off running down another corridor.

Too slow! he agonized. *Too slow!*

The Dragon, also in agony, urged him on. *Hurry!*

He pushed his legs as hard and as fast as they would take him. Never in his life had he run with such intensity. Finally, when his legs were burning and his knees felt as if they were going to give, he dodged into the side corridor that opened up into The Womb. The area soon expected to be renamed Fledgling Bay.

Condliffe cried out and fell, crumpling to the steel floor of the enormous hangar. His momentum carried him, sliding on his knees across the silvery surface a few more feet before his limp body came to a miserable halt.

Only moments later nearly thirty officers and crew, those from the bridge and those that had been gathered along the way, came crashing into the bay behind their Executive Officer to come to a scorching stop, piling up behind where Captain Condliffe had collapsed upon the floor.

"Jesus!" Slater whispered, his mouth and throat going dry at once.

It was a massacre.

At first Commander Slater couldn't help but take it all in with a single glance, a nightmarish scene of staring eyes, wounds, burns, heaped bodies, crooked limbs and smoking flesh. Blood was everywhere; spattered over the lifeless faces, splashed on the walls, pooling on the floor.

The would-be-Jordans had been cut down, mostly by laser fire from the looks of it. Scorch marks marred the usually smooth silver inner wall of the bay. But two had been gunned down with live rounds and two more – the ones closest to where the Captain knelt staring in shock - lay in spreading lakes of blood with their throats cut wide open.

They must have been the first ones to go down, Slater thought. *The infiltrators would have certainly tried to take out as many as they could as silently as possible so an alarm could not be raised.*

Slater noted that one was the dark-skinned female cadet with tightly braided hair that he had thought a sure pick for a Jordan. The other had been the abrasive blonde-haired male pilot that the Captain had thought would be the other. Now they would never know if they had been correct in their cheerily presumptive guesses of the night before.

Two more had been inflicted with knife wounds, probably the next that had been assaulted, before they had drawn attention and their assailants had shot them. They lay clumped in a pile of smoking flesh and blood.

The rest of the kills were cleaner, and included the medical staff that had been on duty. One had just given Slater a physical less than a month ago. The XO felt a wave of sickness wash through him and knew that they had been next, since they had access to coms and could raise the alarm. After that it must have just been target practice for the infiltrators.

Everyone stared in sick abject horror at the scene before them.

"We're gonna need more Jordans," a mid-shipman whispered irreverently, though not unkindly.

"What for?" Captain Condliffe whispered back.

Slater's head snapped up and for the first time he saw what wasn't there to see. The terror of the scene had taken all his attention but now he couldn't believe that he had missed it. Alexander's Eggs, Coal and Stone, the enormous elongated globes that had been safe and warm within The Womb for the past year, were gone.

Condliffe finally turned his head, looking up at those clustered close behind him. When his searching eyes found those of his Executive Officer he grabbed the pale shimmering cloth of Slater's trousers at the knee. "The transport crew," he said.

Commander Slater, wide-eyed until a furious scowl took shape on his face, pushed past the others and ran from the bay shouting orders into the comset that was hooked over his ear. Second Coms Officer Attel, at the coms board in the bridge, replied with an affirmative.

Yes, the transport had left and already rendezvoused with a carrier. Since he had not been notified to the contrary, Attel assumed they had been able to fix their generators and were headed back.

The Executive Officer cursed Attel, and his mother, as he ran for the bridge and ordered every jet in the Fighter Bay to launch and pursue.

Captain Condliffe still knelt in what was supposed to be Fledgling Bay within a matter of weeks, his knees at the edge of a spreading pool of blood. The officer that was ingrained within him took inventory as he looked around the massacre. Each note his mind took made him feel more sick than the last.

Seven bloodied and burned corpses of pilots, the best the JTC had to offer. Three medical personnel. One with more time and experience than Condliffe could begin to comprehend, another that was barely out of his internship.

And one missing Engineer.

The Captain's eyes searched the scene, hoping. He was gratified when he saw the spot where the Engineer had put up a fight. Though it was obvious he had lost, it told the Captain that it was not a member of *his* crew that was responsible for the horror he was now witnessing.

In the lake of blood spilled from the fallen male cadet on his right, was a long trailing smear where the undoubtedly limp body of the Engineer had been dragged. If offered Condliffe little comfort.

His Engineer, along with Alexander's Eggs, the eggs of *his* Dragon, were now in the hands of the Chimera.

TWO

The figure on the bed shifted slowly, the pilled blanket that may have once been black twisting and bunching in a slow tidal wave of cheap cotton.

She felt heavy. Compressed. She could see bright light through her eyelids and her first thought was that she might still be bound to a bed in a hospital and the light was coming from the fluorescents.

God, how she hated hospitals. And fluorescents.

Squinting, she cracked her eyes open and saw that the light was sunshine streaming through a window full upon her face, bright and rosy. She moaned and turned her face away.

She could feel someone close to her, moving in response to her sound. When the voice spoke it was as warm as the sunshine. Also, like the light upon her face, it had a peculiar quality, like a gentle weight.

"Johanna? Johanna? How are you feeling?"

She tried to laugh but all that came out was a hoarse gargle. Her throat felt like an ancient and rusty hinge. She tried to swallow but only succeeded in making a sound like sandpaper being pulled across a rock.

A cup of water was held to her lips and, though she normally despised help, she opened her mouth eagerly. The water was cool and welcome as it poured into her mouth and dribbled down her chin.

She tried to sit up but again felt as if she were being held down by restraints. She looked down her body to find that, instead of restraints, she was covered with a blanket that was thin but felt achingly heavy, as if it were made of lead.

"Scarl," she croaked, letting her weight drop back onto the pillow.

"Hmm?" The voice asked, leaning closer. "What was that?"

"Scarlett," she said, her own voice thick and heavy, like the light and the air. "My name is Scarlett."

The voice that was close to her laughed softly.

With tremendous effort she rolled over, turning away from the voice and the light, and did not fall back asleep as much as she was pushed down into it.

★

Commander Blaylock, the Executive Officer aboard the Opal Dragon, had outwardly remained calm, shielded by an iron hard military discipline. Inwardly, he was seething with fury.

The XO had wanted the Red Jordan stripped of her rank and locked in the brig. Knowing that was impossible, he would settle for her to be locked in a mental institution. And forever might not be long enough as far as he was concerned.

The Captain of the Opal Dragon sat with his Executive Officer and his Engineer in the soft pale chairs in a sunken area of the bridge nicknamed "the pit." Calyph, the Engineer, was a blue-eyed, sandy-haired elf and, though not an officer, was an important member of the crew and the Captain knew that he had an emotional attachment to Jordan Scarlett.

"It's not her fault," Captain Brogan had told the small group gathered there as other officers and crewmen moved tirelessly about the rest of the bridge. The last week had been tragic for the crew of the Opal Dragon and as the crew worked upon her restoration, they pushed themselves past the point of exhaustion so as not to have to think about the loss of the Emerald Jordan and the tenuous state of Jordan Scarlett.

Jordan Blue attended the meeting in body only. With her eyes and mind far away, she stood with her arms folded across her chest and her face turned away, her lithe body leaning against the velvet back of a chair. Platinum blonde hair was pulled away from a narrow face that bore a double jagged scar on the right side. One streak of puckered flesh fled from red lip to pointed ear and another, smaller ripple, shot down across the line of her jaw.

Though she had always worn a blue flight suit to accent her sapphire-colored eyes or a silver flight suit to complement her bluish-silver Fledgling, she now wore one of black - her personal sign of mourning. The number eight was stitched in silver and blue thread on the upper left arm of the shimmering black Mylar suit that clung to her slight form like a second skin.

Every other officer and crew member, dressed in their usual pale coveralls with the IGC patch over the left breast, wore a simple black armband in deference to Jade, the Emerald Jordan who had taken his own life to prevent the capture of the other Jordans of the Opal Dragon.

Captain Brogan placed an elbow on the arm of his chair and his thumb under his chin, letting two fingers rest against the cropped silver hair just behind his temple. That hair had been silver for a long time, impeccably trimmed over a face that was still ruggedly handsome, but Calyph had noticed that the thick thatch of silver hair had begun to turn white. The irises of the Captain's eyes, already pale, also looked decidedly lighter.

"Doc Westerson saw it coming and warned us," Brogan told them. "I should have taken stricter measures."

"Take them now," Blaylock advised. He was handsome as well, slim though more compact, with dark hair, a hooked nose and fierce dark, hazel eyes. "She needs to be in a hospital, in a secure ward, so she can't hurt herself or anyone else."

Brogan sighed heavily. It would tear him apart to institutionalize Scarlett but he was afraid it might be his only choice. The loss of Jade was still tearing him apart – he couldn't emotionally bear to lose Scarlett as well. He glanced up at Jordan Blue but the half-elf fighter pilot had nothing to offer.

"Excuse me, sirs," Calyph said. "May I say something?"

Brogan smiled and held out his hand, palm up. "Please."

Blaylock winced. *Always the indulgent father,* he thought. He shifted his gaze from the Captain to the elfin Engineer with an air of forced tolerance and a scowl of irritation.

Calyph cleared his throat. "I think putting Jordan Scarlett in a hospital is probably one of the worse things you can do to her."

Jordan Blue turned slightly and regarded the Engineer with a chilly gaze. Commander Blaylock looked as if he had just been doused with water, completely surprised and dangerously angry.

"And just what do you suggest?" he demanded. "You can't let someone with SM simply run amok, especially one that has access to the most powerful weaponry in the civilized galaxies and beyond!"

Calyph shifted in his seat and cleared his throat again, undeterred. "Scarlett needs to have her feet on solid ground, that was Doc Westerson's most crucial directive. But she needs to be around people, around living things, around someone who can help her. Not locked up and isolated. It would make her cra... worse."

Crazy, was what he almost said. But Scarlett's glass was already half full of crazy. The officers knew, but not the crew. Most just knew that the Jordan was sick. Either way, it would not have been polite to say just how sick she was.

Jordan Blue arched an eyebrow at the Engineer and it was obvious that even the Captain was suppressing some amusement. A touch of a smile was carefully tucked between his lip and cheek.

"Well?" Blaylock prodded. "Don't keep us waiting."

Calyph took a deep breath. "There is a moon in the Fifth Sector of the MWG. It is one that was actually terraformed based on my home planet." Brogan nodded to indicate that he knew of the place while Blaylock twirled his hand, impatiently urging Calyph to continue. "Anyway, in the southern hemisphere is a brim-town called Kayos. A few klicks to the east lives a monk. I think he could help Scarlett."

The entire bridge seemed to go still. Though no one would have dared to be actually listening in, stewards paused midstride and the conversation between the Navigator and the Coms man halted in a jagged and unfinished sentence.

Jordan Blue straightened slightly, as if feeling the silence caress her back.

It lasted only a second. Then the usual clicks and static from consoles and monitors resumed their chatter and a room of people that had been momentarily slowed in motion returned to their activities at their normal speed.

Calyph watched as Blaylock leaned forward with slightly bulging eyes and planted his hands on his knees. For a moment the Engineer thought the Executive Officer was really going to let him have it. But instead of shouting, Commander Blaylock threw back his head and laughed uproariously.

Calyph looked about the bridge, expecting the room to go still again, but the officer's laughter did not seem to be disconcerting to anyone but himself.

The XO laughed and laughed, while the others in the pit watched first with surprise and then with growing amusement. Brogan's fingers came down to drape across his mouth and Jordan Blue's sapphire eyes tightened in a grimace of amusement before they looked away once again. The Executive Officer laughed till he had tears streaming from the corners of his eyes.

"You're going to get Scarlett some religion?" he finally managed, choking on his laughter. Calyph shook his head.

"He's not that kind of a monk..."

"Martial arts?" Blaylock demanded hopefully, his dark eyes gaping at the Engineer. "Please tell me that he is the type that will hit her with a stick when she mouths off." He went into more gales of side-shaking laughter.

Calyph shifted in his seat. "No, actually... he... has a farm."

The officer howled and Calyph could only stare. He had never seen the XO lose his military bearing, not even for a second. Blaylock was so known for his cold and calculating nature that he hardly seemed human. Calyph's blue eyes darted about nervously.

The Captain was more restrained though his amusement was obvious as well. Even Blue had a smirk on her face, though her eyes avoided both the officers and the Engineer. Calyph didn't know if the smirk was because of Commander Blaylock's outburst or the idea of Scarlett being sent to a farm. Probably both.

"Enough," Brogan finally told his Executive Officer in a gentle tone and his next in command did his best to compose himself. The Captain looked at Calyph and nodded, encouraging him to continue.

"Well," Calyph told them, "he rehabilitates animals." Commander Blaylock covered his mouth with his hand but otherwise restrained himself. "Mostly horses," Calyph continued quickly, "that have been injured."

Captain Brogan's brows drew together over his pale eyes. "What makes you think he could help Scarlett?" he asked.

"He helped a metallurgist that I know, I prefer not to say who. But this monk, Elaeric, was able to help him overcome a mental block that had been keeping him from accessing his abilities properly."

"Is he a Zenarchist?" Brogan asked, piqued.

Calyph nodded, reluctantly. "And you should know that he was involved in the Seven's singularity."

Brogan again planted an elbow on the armrest of his chair and he stroked his lip thoughtfully, his eyes far away.

"I think the environment is just what Jordan Scarlett might need," Calyph said. "And I think Elaeric could help her."

"Can we put a button camera on the monk?" Commander Blaylock asked from behind his hand. The Captain frowned and made a shooing gesture at his officer. The Executive Officer stifled a giggle.

Jordan Blue still stood with her arms folded and her face turned away, leaning against the back of a chair. Brogan glanced at her but it was obvious she wanted no part in the discussion. He sighed and turned back to the elfin Engineer.

"I'll speak to Doc Westerson immediately," he told him. "If he clears the plan, can you make the arrangements?"

The Engineer nodded emphatically. "Yes, sir."

Brogan rose from his chair and the others stood quickly. Even Jordan Blue straightened to attention and turned to face the Captain as he leaned forward and grasped the Engineer by the shoulder.

"Thank you, Calyph. I think you are right, and that this will be the best thing for Jordan Scarlett."

Calyph bowed his head and, as the Captain turned to leave, Commander Blaylock leaned towards the elfin Engineer like a conspirator.

"If she has to milk a cow," he said from the corner of his mouth, "I want to see it."

Calyph smiled nervously, unnerved by the strange behavior of the usually stoic Executive Officer. Blinking rapidly, the Engineer gave his head a little shake to clear his mind after the XO had turned away.

Then he left the bridge to send a holo to Elaeric. Jordan Blue's cool eyes followed him, but only for a moment.

 THREE

The vanity was a grandiose monstrosity. It was ridiculously large and complex, more industrial than feminine, like a carnival hall of illusions with unframed sections of glass angled in wild directions. It looked like a miniature space wreck of glass and metal that had been rebuilt by clumsy and uncaring hands.

A special alcove had been built into the bedroom to house it and the mirrors, all of different shapes and sizes, diffused and returned the golden light of the bedroom in so many directions that it seemed to radiate with a luminosity all its own.

A figure sat before the glowing myriad of mirrors, fastening a necklace around her slender throat. The piece of jewelry was a heavy gold chain of wide oval links, each as big as her thumb, which brought out the golden strands in the mostly brown hair that hung down her back. She wore matching earrings, each a large gold link that brought out the gold in her bright brown eyes.

The only other piece of jewelry she wore was on the index finger of her right hand. At first glance it appeared to be one large ring, but a closer inspection would show that it was actually three small silver rings, each with diminutive carvings in the bands and each set with a golden topaz.

The first ring was carved with tribal diamond shapes and the topaz was diamond-shaped as well. The second ring had an oval shaped topaz and was carved with a repeating pattern of ovals, dots, and lines. The bottom ring was engraved with curlicues and set with a round topaz akin to the golden dome of a fortuneteller. Like the vanity, the stones on the rings gave off a luminous golden glow.

The woman leaned back, regarding her reflection. There was movement everywhere as a hundred reflections moved, but the woman only looked at the one directly in front of her.

"Well, Faith?" she asked.

The reflections, including the one she was regarding, did not respond but simply returned her even stare, gazing from a roundish face that was plain but not unattractive, and universally infamous.

The woman known as Faith de Rossi, the Chief Executive Officer of the GwenSeven Corporation and all of its affiliates, rose from the plush bench chair that faced the vanity. The bottom of her white caftan swirled around her feet like a dress. She eyed a wide gold arm cuff on the glass counter of the vanity that provided her a com-link with her security but, knowing she wouldn't need it, chose a wide gold belt instead.

She was planning to meet her sister in the living room, since it seemed the most seemly place for sisters to sit and talk with one another. Also, because there was a bar in the living room. Since it had been months since their last meeting, she knew they would have much to say. She would need a drink. Or three. Maybe six or five.

Faith ran a hand through her gold and brown locks and, with a final glance in the mirror, left her bedroom and walked down the hall towards the living room.

The living room itself was a great expanse of three-inch thick and diamond hard polished black granite, topped with plush white sofas that sat upon thick sherpla skin rugs. Smooth white leather chairs flanked the sofas and stood in pairs about the room. A great curved glass wall looked out into the deep of the night sky.

Faith owned the largest villa in the city with the most expensive view; a grand vista of nothing. No mountains, no lakes, no rolling hills. Nothing but deep black space and stars so bright she could distinguish their type by their color.

She had first seen the villa while it was nearing the end of construction. Faith had been ushered out on a private craft from Callisto to the very new satellite city that hung just outside the orbit of one of Jupiter's largest terraformed moons.

From there, the urban housing agent had deftly maneuvered a small viewing craft to the outskirts of the suburbs at the most southern tip of the floating city.

The agent, in an expensive tight skirt suit and equally tight and expensive hair coiffure, chatted away the entire time in an annoying but ignorable manner about city developments. When Faith saw the villa her throat made a strange wheezing sound, like a sigh in reverse.

The satellite city was close enough to the gas giant to afford the protection of its magnetosphere but far enough from it to be excluded from its atmosphere – safe from solar winds but left to hang in perpetual night.

To Faith, the development looked like an alien flower turned upside down. Slender metal stalks connected the large ovoid villas to a central community hub that dangled from a thicker metal stalk that was attached to the city itself.

"That one," Faith said pointing to the lowest pod, then just a half-built skeleton of steel. The agent smiled and tapped her stylus on her acrylic pad. She knew Ms. de Rossi could afford it, could afford anything, or else it would have been one of her sub-agents toting her around.

"Very nice selection, ma'am. We should schedule..." she started but Ms. de Rossi dismissed her with a wave of her hand.

"It needs to be at least five thousand square feet of living space, if it isn't already," Faith told her. "And by living space I mean the middle level. The top and bottom levels will need to be gutted, from what I can see here. My security detail and PA will see that it has everything I require." The agent nodded and made notes with her stylus.

"And I want the craft dock on the top, not the side or the bottom."

The agent made a sucking noise with her teeth and gave her an apologetic shake of her head. "They don't do that due to..." she started but Faith cut her off without so much as a glance in her direction.

"Make it happen."

The agent pressed her lips together and nodded, scribbling notes. There wasn't a chance in hell she was going to let this commission go.

"My PA will schedule an appointment with you for all the legal docs and to go over everything I will need."

"MasterPlan handles all customizations," the agent said. "I will give their number to your PA, along with anything else you may require."

Faith nodded absently, never taking her eyes off the strips of metal that would one day be her home.

Her personal assistant spent half a day with the agent and four full days with MasterPlan, going over every detail needed to finish the residence. When MasterPlan denied their request for the special glass for the under-floor, saying that it was unobtainable, both the glass and the workers trained to handle it were portaled in to build what was requested.

The head of security for Ms. de Rossi spent three days with MasterPlan making specifications, and came out at the close of every phase of construction to make certain everything went in properly. Faith herself spent a day with them at the end. She trusted her assistant implicitly, but there were things that even the person who ran her life did not need to know, and security measures that she would personally ensure.

Faith stared at the stars through the one-way glass wall as she thought of the months she had waited for the villa to be complete. Though work kept her busy, it had been nice to have something entirely different on her mind for a while.

Faith turned and walked from the living room window towards the bar but her PA was already there, pouring her employer a drink from a dark green bottle. Penny, her personal assistant, was wearing one of her sensible brown suits; the skirt sensibly long, her brown hair in a sensible brown tie. When she turned around, her brown eyes looked out through a pair of smart looking frames.

Penny was still very young - or was taking something to stay that way. Faith smiled as her assistant handed her a tall flute of golden champagne.

"Thank you, Penny."

Penny smiled and started to say something when a soft ping came over the podcom. "That would be your sister," she said politely. "Shall I show her in?"

"Of course."

Faith walked back towards the wall of windows, the hem of her white pants skimming along the glassy surface of the black floor. Looking out into the starry expanse she sipped the golden liquid from her glass. The effervescent fluid filled her mouth and left a trail of bubbles going down. Faith closed her eyes, relishing the sensation. She had tired of many things over the years, but champagne was never one of them.

"Sister!"

Faith turned to see her sister, Charity, sweep into the room and down the foyer stairs to the living room. Charity wore a long, loose, silver dress lined with gold cloth. Her golden hair was tied back with a silver scarf and she wore a necklace of bulky, uncut emeralds around the curve of her throat.

Each ear, surgically rounded like those of her sister, had four polished emerald studs that brought out the green of her eyes. It was the first time Faith had seen her sister with green eyes and she found them quite becoming.

Charity had a rather small entourage with her, for once, but Faith hardly took notice of them. Charity always had a number of people in her wake but this time only a pair of young men had accompanied the younger de Rossi woman along with two of her personal assistants.

At first glance, Faith took both men to be part of Charity's security detail - but a second look told her immediately that her initial assessment had been wrong.

The first man was undoubtedly security, tall and lean with a smart suit all in darkest blue along with a com-link tucked into his right ear. He was strikingly handsome, so much so that one might suspect him to be manufactured, but Faith knew a human when she saw one. He may be highly jacked, but still a human.

He stood perfectly still, his hands clasped in front of his belt, sharpened senses already having taken in every element of the room upon entering. His eyes for the most part stayed fixed upon Charity, leaving her only to occasionally dart about the area before settling on her once again. He was no cause for a double take.

Faith's gold and brown eyes went the other young man and felt her hand tighten around her champagne glass. There was no mistaking the construct for a human. Not for her. She knew every make and model.

The one that stood in the foyer was lean and muscular with a tan-olive complexion, hazel eyes and a thatch of black hair over black brows. He wore gray pants and a black shirt that, while not tight, did nothing to hide the build underneath. He looked about the room with a dreamy curiosity. His face was perfectly formed, with high cheekbones and full lips that parted in smile that was a bit dopey. He looked like he was fresh from a cannabis party.

Faith was staring at the young man, unable to help herself, when her ebullient guest embraced her.

She greeted her sister with a quick, compulsory hug and a peck on the cheek.

"You look wonderful!" Charity gushed.

"As do you," the older sister countered reflexively. She turned, searching for her PA. "Penny?" Faith began, but Penny was already at the bar pouring a drink for Charity. Charity waved a jeweled hand at her. She wore a triplet set of rings almost identical to the rings that Faith was wearing, though hers were set with emeralds and she wore two on her left index finger and one on her right.

"No, Penny, I'm drinking Varti these days."

With her back the guests, Penny was able to hide her smile and the fact that she was already pouring the Varti. She brought it to Charity and politely raised her brows at her employer, waiting.

Faith gave a quick nod to her PA. "Would you please take..." Faith paused and looked at her sister.

"Aide," Charity prompted.

"Aide and..."

Charity turned around, surprised. "Oh! And...her assistant."

Faith regarded her sister with a tight smile and eyes bright with amusement before turning back to Penny.

"Would you please take Aide and her assistant into the kitchen and see if they would like something to eat?"

"Of course."

Geary, Faith's head of security, appeared from seemingly nowhere to lead Charity's bodyguard to a secure area in a room above where his charge could be watched on a monitor, but not heard. Geary had blue-gray eyes like cut steel and his dark hair was flecked with silver and cropped close to his scalp. He had once been the platoon leader of an IGC Special Commands Unit. He was of average height and unassuming build, but moved with a feline speed and silence that belied his somewhat average appearance.

Faith suspected that he was fucking Penny, though she could not have cared less. As far as she was concerned, he and Penny were both the best at what they did and whatever they did on their own time, precious little time that they had, was their own damn business.

As Charity's guard left with Geary, Aide remained where she was and politely cleared her throat. Charity glanced at her and then followed her gaze to the dopey young man still standing in the foyer.

"Oh!" Charity exclaimed, laughing. "How could I forget?" Charity motioned to the young man still waiting. His hazel eyes caught the movement of her hand and he turned his face to her and smiled.

Glancing about in dreamy curiosity as he descended the steps into the living room, he walked to where the two sisters stood and stopped when he was almost between them. The room filled with silence and the young man looked from one sister to the other and back again.

"And this is?" Faith finally prodded. Charity's smile was languid and sly.

"A gift, of course."

Faith felt the hinges in her jaw loosen and a breathless chuckle came from deep within her abdomen. Abashed, she looked at her sister. "You're giving him to me as a gift?" she asked. Charity nodded, her smile lecherous.

"A very well made gift, if you ask me."

Faith laughed and shook her head, clearly at a loss for words. Charity watched her, amused yet intent.

"I've never actually owned a construct," Faith confessed, her voice low and husky and slightly breathless.

"I know."

The young man watched them talk, his eyes going from one to the other, the small and slightly dopey smile still on his face.

Faith tried to swallow, but found her throat too dry. She tried to clear it instead. "You, ahem, got him from our factory?"

"Of course!" Charity admonished, placing her jeweled fingers over her heart. "You didn't think I would give you a cheap knock-off, did you?"

Faith shook her head as she admired his face, unable to pull her eyes away. "Charity, this isn't the time."

"It's past time."

"I have so much going on, so much still to do...»

"Aawww!" Charity's face drooped in mock sympathy. "Poor Faith! No time for love?"

"There are too many things I need to take care of, things that need to be finished."

Charity smirked. "You know what they say about all work and no play..."

"That you get to rule the universe?" Faith asked with a smirk that mirrored her sister's, though she did not take her eyes off the young man in front of her. He had a narrow chin with a trace of a dimple, but it was the color of his eyes that held her fascination. She sighed. "He is one of a kind," she admitted quietly.

Charity's smile was indulgent. "Not another one like him."

"And his placement?"

"75-75 EQIQ.»

Faith knew immediately what sort of construct had that ratio. A shiver went up her spine. She smiled and shook her head.

"Charity, I don't know if I am ready for this," she began, but looking at him – the set of his jaw and the color of his eyes – her heart stilled her mouth and robbed it of discourse. She realized that looking at him stopped everything within her that wanted to continue in a logical direction.

Her sister held up a hand, cutting her off. "It's time." When Faith gave her a doubtful look she sighed. "If it helps, think of it as research." Faith trembled with nervous laughter but her sister persisted. "I'm serious. You've been doing nothing but logistics for almost a hundred years. When was the last time you had a hand in R and D?"

The young man looked back and forth between the two as they talked, seeming for all the worlds both oblivious and content.

"Not since I worked on the last prototype," Faith admitted, her eyes traveling over his body, taking in every detail.

"And when was that?"

Faith's body shuddered with a convulsive chuckle. Her white sleeves swirled around her. "A long time ago."

"In a galaxy far, far away."

"You're unconscionable!" Faith laughed.

"But correct."

"We've made a lot changes since then."

"You oversaw and approved them all."

"From a compute screen."

Faith drew air deep into her lungs and looked at the male construct. He *was* beautiful. Perfectly sculpted from head to toe. She reached out and ran her fingers down his arm and he smiled at her.

"Are muscles back in?" she asked absently.

"They're all the rage, again."

"Everywhere?"

Charity laughed. "Everywhere we're selling. What's the difference?"

Faith's eyes flicked to her sister's, suddenly suspicious. "Have you...?"

Charity waved off her question with a look of mild disgust. "It's tacky to play with someone else's toy. Especially one that you plan to give as a gift."

The construct caught Faith's hand as it traveled down his arm and kissed the back of it softly. Another nervous laugh escaped her lips, followed by a sigh, more delighted than resigned. "Very well," she agreed. "In the name of research."

"If that helps."

"Does he have a name?" Faith asked.

"His tag said 'Jasyn.' But, of course, you can call him whatever you like."

Faith bit her bottom lip to keep her smile from splitting her face in two. "No, I like Jasyn. Penny?"

There was a whisper of nylon and Penny was at her side. An inclination of the head accompanied by raised brows was given a simple nod in reply. After so many years together, it was all the communication needed.

Penny motioned to Jasyn and had begun to lead him down a hallway accompanied by Aide and Aide's assistant when Faith called out to her.

"Penny?"

The PA turned as she waited for instruction. "Yes, ma'am?"

"Take him to Geary, first."

Penny nodded and turned to Charity's assistants. "Aide, you know where the kitchen is?" she asked.

Aide nodded. "I do."

"If you would please make yourselves comfortable there, Cook will fix you anything you would like and I will meet you there in a few moments."

Aide nodded and headed for the kitchen with her assistant.

"I had Chaz run a sweep on him, already," Charity assured her sister as they watched Penny lead the handsome figure back up the foyer steps before she held out an arm, inviting the construct to precede her into the circular lift at its center.

Faith watched them go with mild amusement, her lips turned up at the corners. Her gold and brown eyes were trained upon the man's body and the way his muscles moved beneath his clothes. "I'm glad you had the foresight," she said, almost teasingly. "But

I'll have Geary run another. You know how I am about security."

"Do I ever!" Charity laughed.

★

Charity moved to one of the sofas, kicking off silver sandals to sink her feet into Faith's sherpla skin rug. Faith moved to the bar to refill her glass while her sister stretched out on the couch like a prized cat.

They talked for hours though their words were short and sentences clipped. They communicated in that special way that only people who are closely bound with one another can. Two like minds that travel down the same road, where words are only nudges for direction.

They talked first of family, as always. Hope was still lost, a fact that did not come as a surprise to either of them. Grace was fallen, Constance the same. So cliché but so familiar that any news or news of no change was as cozy as a soft pair of socks.

"And the little one?" Charity asked. "Did she make it through that nasty ordeal?"

Faith nodded though her eyes were distant. "Yes."

"How well?"

Faith shrugged. "Well enough. "Have you been to see mother?"

"Yes."

"And?"

Charity shrugged. "Same as always."

"And the old man?"

"Still alive," Charity said, her face a mask of disgust. "God only knows how, the way he abuses his body. Ugh! You should see him, Faith. He's disgusting."

"I know."

"I don't know why you never had him killed."

Faith raised a finger away from her glass as she took a sip, indicating that she had already considered the idea and had dismissed it. She lowered her glass, resting the bottom of its stem on her thigh.

"Because she loves him," she offered Charity as an explanation. "God only knows why, but she does."

"Don't you think she would be better off without him?"

28

"Of course. Everyone does, except her. But I don't know what it would do to her. So, as long as she is around, he will be too."

"At least she has Constance," Charity mused. Faith still seemed a bit dreamy. "When do you meet with the council?"

Faith's brown and gold eyes came back into sharp focus and she looked at her sister. "Day after tomorrow."

"Are you ready?"

"Of course. How are things on your end?"

Charity waved a hand as she drank from her glass, an indication that her end was just fine.

"Your...gift?"

"Safe at the castle. And yours?"

"Safe."

"Do you think she will?"

Faith shrugged. "We'll see."

"And the girl?" Charity asked, changing tack. "Any luck?"

Faith shook her head. "Not yet."

"You still think she will?"

Faith nodded. "I have a feeling about her."

They were silent for a while, both musing over their clipped discussion and sipping from their glasses before returning to other matters.

They talked about the company and discussed plans, both long and short term. Charity scolded her sister for working too much and told her that she needed to take time off, to which Faith hid her face in her champagne and waved her sister off with a hand naked of rings. She had heard it a hundred times. Finally, the conversation turned to gossip about the social circles in which they traveled.

Time spent together, along with numerous cocktails, made goodbye hugs longer and accompanied by promises not to let so much time pass before meeting again. Personal assistants and security guards appeared to wrap things up for the night.

Faith offered to let Charity stay the night, though she knew her sister would decline. Faith's extravagantly furnished villa was Spartan compared to the sumptuousness Charity was accustomed to traveling in, much less living. The younger de Rossi's common conveyance jet was even larger and more luxurious than Faith's villa. Faith despised the craft, though not for its opulence.

While not technically a corporate jet, Charity's enormous spacecraft was nonetheless emblazoned with an equally enormous G7 along the side in shining gold and silver - which exasperated the hell out of her sister who thought it a terrible security risk.

"Do you think people would not know it was mine if I didn't have the logo on it?" Charity had asked when Faith pressed her about it. Faith had sighed and given her a resigned shake of her gold and brown locks of hair.

"I suppose not," she had conceded. Her sister was right, everyone in the seven galaxies knew to whom the craft belonged, it was impossible not to recognize.

The space faring mansion was complete with a reception parlor, dining rooms, and bedrooms that included one for Charity that housed a closet as large as any clothing store known in the seven systems. The craft itself was so large that it could not dock directly with Faith's villa but had to dock at the city's spaceport. From there, Charity took one of the craft's transport tenders with a minimal crew to her sister's home. Faith was mildly assuaged that the massive jet also housed an adequate security detail.

After fond farewells, endearing cheek kisses, the hissing of airlocks, and departure of craft – Faith was able to breathe a sigh of relief. She loved her sister and loved seeing her when she did, but it could be so exhausting. She walked through her bedroom without so much as a glance at her surroundings, pulling off her clothes in her dressing room and slipping into a short camisole of gold silk.

She cleaned her face and teeth and was almost in bed before she saw there was someone in it.

"Jesus!" she whispered hoarsely, stepping back so quickly that she almost fell. Jasyn sat up between the copper colored sheets, wearing nothing but a pair of black undershorts. "You scared the shit out of me!" she accused him, laughing softly once the shock had passed.

"I'm sorry."

It was the first time since his arrival that he had spoken. His voice was poignant, slightly deep but very smooth. It struck a chord within her that resonated throughout her entire body.

The metal shell around the outside of the villa had closed for the night, save for a few centimeters where the wall met the ceiling. From there a faint reddish glow bled into the otherwise darkened room. It shed a soft glow over his tan skin, making it a rosy molten gold. Shadows edged the muscles of his arms and chest.

Faith cupped her right elbow with her left hand and ran the smooth nail of her right thumb over her lips, thinking. As beautiful as he was, she was still very unsure. She could not help but analyze her emotions, trying to identify what she was feeling.

It's not fear, I'm sure of that. At least, I think I'm sure. Faith chuckled nervously and felt a silly elation mix in with her other emotions. *Trepidation? Is that it? Maybe some fear after all? It's just that... it's been so long.*

Jasyn pulled back the covers for her, silently encouraging her to get into bed. Faith stayed where she was, undecided.

"Do you ever speak, without being spoken to first?" she asked.

"I can, if you want me too." He looked as if he was about to say more, but remained silent. Her eyes narrowed at him.

"What is it?" Faith asked.

"Ms. de Rossi told me it would be better if I didn't say too much. At least, not for a while."

Faith laughed. "I am Ms. de Rossi, too. Did you know that?" Jasyn nodded but looked as unsure as Faith felt, his full lips pressed together in a thin line. "We're sisters," she continued. "Do you know what that means?" This time the nod was quicker, more sure.

"You are in the same family."

"Yes, but we not the same person. I'd like you to say what you feel. Don't be afraid to tell me what you are...thinking." He smiled and pushed back the bedcovers.

"I think you should come to bed," he whispered.

Faith stayed frozen a moment longer. The construct looked at her, his carefully crafted hazel eyes seductive and inviting. A beautiful stranger in her bed, yet she knew every line of his face and knew the exact colors that were used to make his eyes. Her thumbnail slid across her lips.

Isn't this what you wanted? she asked herself. *What you have been wanting for so long? Yes,* she answered, *but I didn't think it would be this way.*

He smiled at her and she realized that was all that she needed.

She slipped into the bed next to him and pulled a copper-colored pillow under her head. He pulled the shimmering covers up just enough to envelop them both to the waist, his lips parting in a shallow smile to show perfect, white teeth. He propped himself up on an elbow and looked at her as if he was seeing her for the first time. He smiled nervously.

"I'm not really sure how to start," he confided quietly. Faith's smile was warm. She took a deep breath, as if ready to take a deep plunge.

"Why don't you start by kissing me," she breathed, "and we'll see where it goes from there."

After a moment of hesitation, his head dipped down and she closed her eyes, letting their lips find one another with a soft magnetic grace.

He pulled back from her almost immediately, his face a mixture of surprise and confusion. She watched him carefully, not sure what was wrong. He bent to kiss her again, and this time he did not stop.

Faith kept her eyes closed, finding that it was easier that way.

With her eyes closed, she could pretend that he was really the man she loved. Her first love - torn from her by principle, kept from her by the damnable war that had ravaged her family as well. The only man she knew she would ever love.

As his passion increased she could feel an unholy darkness moving within her, taking over her soul and making her own body respond.

Then suddenly, like magic, she felt herself transported across the gaping and jagged mouth of time. She was taken back across the days and the years and the decades. Then they were *his* lips she felt upon her lips, and *his* hands she felt upon her body. She moved underneath him, underneath his body and underneath the years, moving beyond time, feeling herself becoming urgent, insistent.

At the last moment she barely had the sense to bite her lip, not to keep from crying out, but to keep herself from crying out his name.

FOUR

When Scarlett opened her eyes again it was dark. The voice she had heard before now had a face and at first it was all that she saw. For one alarming moment all she could see was a green, bald, disembodied head, floating in the darkness.

"You're early, aren't you?"

The green face tilted up to regard the Jordan. "I beg your pardon?"

"Aren't you supposed to come at the end of the story?"

"I sense that you are making a joke of some kind, but I do not understand. Would you care to explain?"

Scarlett shook her head. "Forget it."

As her eyes adjusted she could see that it was a man, indeed bald, but not disembodied. He was simply sitting cross-legged on a chair and looking down at an acrylic on his lap that was glowing green and illuminating his face.

The man leaned over and touched a panel on the wall, raising a light while still keeping the room dim. In the glowing circle shed by the light, Scarlett could see mostly down to the end of the bed she was in, a bedside table with a pitcher of water and a glass, and a little man wrapped in pale green robes.

He was small and elfish, with dark almond-shaped eyes, though his ears were round at the tops – and Scarlett had never seen a bald elf before. Nor had she seen one with golden brown skin. He was altogether peculiar.

"How are you feeling, Scarlett?" He pronounced her name slowly, as if he was tasting it, and the tone of his voice changed, as if he were talking to a small child or indulging an invalid in a harmless joke.

"Thirsty."

He motioned to the pitcher of water on the nightstand though he made no move to get it. Scarlett pushed herself up in the bed and reached for the pitcher. She paused, breathing deeply with her hand on the handle.

"It's the gravity, isn't it?" she asked, but continued before he could answer. "I'm on a high gravity planet, aren't I?" Her face tightened into a grimace of disgust. "An *elfin* planet. A god-forsaken planet in some god-forsaken part of the universe. Sent here to be punished, or to get better, or both. Swept under the stars anyway, at least for the time being."

She sighed and hefted the pitcher, which felt *very* heavy, and poured herself a glass of water. She looked at the golden man, sitting cross-legged on his chair. He smiled, showing square teeth that were slightly yellowed at the gum line.

"Yes," he said.

Scarlett heaved another sigh and drank the water. It went down her throat in profound, cooling waves. She put the empty glass back on the nightstand next to the pitcher and frowned at the seated figure.

"Yes? Yes, what?" she asked. The little man smiled at her.

"Yes."

Scarlett groaned as she lay back down onto her pillow. "Punishment," she grumbled. "I'm being punished."

The small figure leaned forward and dimmed the light, bringing darkness back to the room.

When Scarlett opened her eyes again the room was bright with morning light. She squinted against the heavy glare and, as much as she didn't want to, pushed herself up into a sitting position, forcing herself to look around.

The room looked like any that would be found in a small country cottage and was even smaller than it had seemed in the dark. The single bed and nightstand were pushed against a plaster wall under a large wood-framed, four-paned window. Against the wall she was facing was a narrow chest of drawers topped with a slightly warped mirror. There was a single wooden door with a tarnished brass knob.

The little man was gone, along with the chair and the water, making Scarlett first consider that it might have been part of a dream. She decided she wasn't that lucky.

Scarlett stood up and was overcome with wave of dizziness. She stumbled to the dresser and laid her hands on its wooden surface to steady herself, waiting for the spell to pass.

As it did she looked up into the mirror and at her warbled

reflection, made strange by the imperfection in the glass. The image that peered back at her looked more like a scarecrow than a fighter pilot.

Her face was gaunt and sallow, the strong arms she remembered were turning into fleshy sticks, and her once lustrous dark hair was a matted mess of dull corkscrews.

"Jesus," she whispered. "What happened to me?" She remembered what Doc Westerson had said, right before she laughed in his face.

You have SM, Jordan, he had told her, his voice firm but his demeanor cautious, as it should have been.

Scarlett had barked out harsh laughter, as if proving him right. The sound had the grating cackle of an old crone.

Space Madness. She still couldn't believe it. For one thing, it sounded silly. It was something they would say as children, in low voices, drawing out the words while waggling their fingers at one another. For another, she had always believed herself to be in total control.

It wasn't until she found herself on the dark side of a moon, bleeding from her nose and mouth and one of her ears, questioning herself – *questioning her own reality* - that she began to doubt how in control she might be.

It had been Calyph that had saved her. He was the first one to break the silence that had spun out in the blood smeared vehicle garage on the moon of Leoness. The Opal Dragon had been drawn to her children and was unleashing platinum fire on the unfortunate souls and scenery of the newly terraformed moon.

The outside air was pregnant with the echoes of the Dragon's distant but furious screams, while in the hangar of ground vehicles the only sound was the panting breath of the two Jordans as they each fought for sanity and control.

Calyph had been the first to speak. His voice was soft and tentative but it carried through the echoing space.

"I know why she is eight," he had offered.

"What?" Scarlett demanded. Her face was a mess. She had bitten the inside of her cheek as well as the side of her tongue as Blue had goaded her and pushed her to the brink. Her body shook uncontrollably as she tried to hold on to something real, her sanity unraveling like dry, useless rope. Blue's accusations flooded her with a sickening sense of *unreality*. The Crimson Jordan began doubting her own actuality, began to actually consider that she might not be a real person at all but one that had been manufactured, a *construct* for love of God.

Blood was running from the corner of her mouth like drool from an idiot. Her intense rage had also given her a bloody nose that she wiped roughly at with the back of her hand, smearing her face with gore. One ear was bleeding as well, a result of the sonic boom that the Opal Dragon had drawn in her wake as she tore into the atmosphere of Leoness.

"Dragons all tend to favor certain elements," Calyph said softly, "and each one has a higher elemental trace content than the others. The number corresponds with the periodic table of the elements. For Blue and Cyan, it's oxygen, represented by its atomic number...eight."

Scarlett rocked back on her heels as if she had been slapped. She felt the hinges of her jaw loosen and used the last of her will to keep it from hanging open.

Blue looked up from where she was crouching on the tarmac. Her sapphire colored eyes were glassy and her grin made her look slightly mad.

"And what would that make your element, Scarlett?" she asked. "Sulfur. Brimstone. Gunpowder." Her small body shook with silent, mirthless laughter. "How appropriate."

"It accounts for your colors as well," Calyph added.

Scarlett shook her head. "Sulfur is yellow."

"Not when it is ionized," he told her. "It creates a red hue. It doesn't necessarily reflect your nature. There's a possibility that because you are from Io you might carry trace elements within your body."

Blue snorted. "My money is on her nature."

"What about the other egg?" Scarlett asked. Calyph cocked his head, not sure what she was after.

"What other egg?"

"The Silver Dragon manifested two eggs – one of them is blue. They can't both be eight."

"Oh. No, it won't be eight. There are actually two blues in the rainbow. Jordan Blue and Cyan are the lighter shade. The other egg is actually indigo, which is darker. It will wax more towards nitrogen and be number seven."

Blue shuddered. "Almost as bad. She would have accused me for working for someone else entirely," she said, jerking her head in Scarlett's direction as her bottom dropped down on the tarmac with a tooth-rattling thump.

The Blue Jordan rested her forearms on her knees and let her head droop down between them. She felt impossibly exhausted - physically, spiritually, and emotionally.

"But that doesn't explain the bio on her mother," Scarlett argued. She felt as if everything was unraveling from every end, and just when she thought she had everything figured out. "She was sure she is one of six."

"I am," Blue said without lifting her head. The fingers of her left hand lightly touched the platinum band around her right wrist. The look in her eyes was one of infinite sadness as her fingers ran lightly over the smooth metal before moving away again.

Calyph shrugged. "It was a micro-bio," he said softly. "It wouldn't have detailed information. I can get a full bio from the troll when we get back on the Dragon."

"What about me?" Scarlett whispered. Her voice sounded far away, and not even her own. It was the voice of a frightened child. "Why is there so little that I remember?"

Blue muttered something that Scarlett couldn't hear. The Red Jordan tried to find a scathing remark but the only thing that came from her bleeding mouth was a small moaning sound. Her stomach turned and she felt as if she were going to be sick. The open space in front of her, lined with vehicles and reeking with the smell of smoking flesh, began to swim before her. Her face, smeared with drying blood, looked up at the ceiling as she felt her knees buckle. She felt herself slipping. Slipping down and slipping away.

She was vaguely concerned about her head whacking the concrete floor but was too weak to even put out a hand to break her fall. The last thing she knew was the feel of Calyph's arms going around her, catching her as she went down.

Now, with the gravity of the planet weighing heavily upon her body and the gravity of her situation weighing heavily upon her mind, Scarlett looked at the apparition in the warped mirror, trying to remember what had happened next. She thought that she had slept for the next three days, though she could recall moments when she acted quite lucid.

The forced lucidity had been caused by her determination to hang onto Fledge, to stay with him. Those moments had been followed by fits of rage where she had to be sedated. Scarlett was glad that most of those images were blurry.

Though Space Madness still sounded ridiculous, the face staring back from the mirror made it quite believable. She looked like a creature that had crawled from a swamp. The baggy cotton shift that hung about her diminishing frame was no help.

"Well," Scarlett said to the reflection, "we'll remedy that right away. And everything else, for that matter."

She pulled open the top drawer of the dresser and took a quick inventory of its contents. There was a hairbrush and a parcel of underclothes, all hers. They turned out to be the only items that had come with her to wherever she now was.

The next drawer held two cotton peasant blouses and a pair of linen pants. The other drawers were empty. They obviously didn't want her to have many of her own belongings. There was nothing modern, nothing technical, and definitely nothing extravagant.

She was probably lucky to have any personal items at all, though it might have not been luck. In all likelihood it had been Calyph, trying to provide what comfort he could for her.

Something else occurred to her and her eyes flashed back up to the mirror. She quickly turned her head to see the two garnet studs in the top of her right ear and then turned her head back the other way to see the platinum one embedded in her left.

She let out a deep breath, not aware that she had been holding it in for the past few seconds.

"At least they didn't have the wherewithal to take those out," she muttered, wondering if they had gone unnoticed, forgotten, or were just considered unimportant or too difficult to remove.

Scarlett returned to the top drawer and pulled out the assemblage of underclothes that had been secured together with a swath of linen tape. They were gray cotton and completely utilitarian - as were any military issued clothes. They were definitely not something she would wear for a romantic evening, but they were hers and for that she was grateful.

She pulled a single pair of underwear from the collection, smiling at the idea of Calyph packing them for her. *How he must have blushed!* Scarlett thought, picturing the color rising in his cheeks and all the way to the tips of his pointed ears.

As she pulled a bra from the bundle there was a heavy clunk as something dropped back onto the rough wooden panel of the drawer bottom. Scarlett reached down and fished it out. As her hand closed around the cold metal she could feel hot tears welling in her dark, crimson-flecked eyes.

She opened her hand and looked down to see a winged crest in worn brass and fading enamel attached to a black ribbon with a silver clasp. Scarlett breathed deeply, pressing the crest to her lips as she fought back tears.

I owe you one Calyph. Again.

She held the enameled emblem in a tight fist, the black ribbon spilling between her fingers. She tightened her grip until the brass wings began digging into her palm painfully and the threat of tears began to retreat. With a grateful sigh, she tucked it back beneath her bundle of undergarments and closed the drawer.

Scarlett pulled on the linen pants that had been left for her, which were too short, and one of the cotton blouses. A look at the mirror showed she looked more like a scarecrow than ever, her limbs sticking out of the ill-fitting clothes.

She retrieved the hairbrush and pulled it through the snarls of her hair. It helped, but not much. What she really needed was a shower. Not to mention a few good meals and some better fitting clothes.

The thought of a good meal made Scarlett's stomach rumble painfully. She glanced about the room and spotted a pair of banged-up red wooden clogs by the foot of the bed. With a look of disgust, she slipped her feet into them. They were chipped and dented, but fit surprisingly well.

Moving slowly and a bit jerkily in the high gravity that seemed determined to pull her down, she went to the room's only door and tried the knob, having less than a second to consider that it might be locked. It turned easily and opened onto a hallway. One side of the hall was dark and ended with a closed door. Another closed door was across from hers. The other end of the hall was open and bright. She didn't need a sign or a steward, the way was clear.

The short hallway opened onto a tiny kitchen with a sunny nook that held a small table and three wooden chairs. The little man was at a wood burning stove, putting on a pot of water.

He wore a belted blouse, loose pants and soft shoes, all made of the same soft, sage-green material. Earlier, Scarlett had thought he must be part elf because of his somewhat slanted eyes and slight build, but now saw that he had a broad round face, and rounded little ears. He turned as soon as Scarlett stepped into the room.

"Well!" he exclaimed, pleased. "If it isn't Johanna Scarlett!"

Scarlett winced and shook her head. "It's just Johanna, but no one but my family calls me that. Preferably Scarlett. Or Jordan."

The little man looked surprised. "Jordan? I was not aware you had three names."

"It's not a name, it's a rank. Like Captain or Lieutenant."

The small man leaned back, his sage-colored clothing undulating with his movement, and regarded her with his wispy dark brows raised over his almond-shaped eyes. "Is that so? And who gives you such a rank?"

"The IGC. But the training is grueling and, even if you make it, you need to be chosen by a Fledgling Dragon."

"Ah! You must tell me about this training."

Scarlett gave him a wry smile. "It's not something I'd like to relive."

The little man bobbed his head as if he understood, but with cordial disappointment. "I am being rude. I have not introduced myself. I am Elaeric."

"Pleased to meet you," Scarlett offered, though her tone was more flat and resigned than friendly.

"Are you hungry?" he asked. She brightened considerably.

"Starving."

"Splendid! You fetch the eggs and I will cook us a feast."

Scarlett leaned forward, her eyes wide. "Excuse me?"

"There is a basket by the door." He motioned to a woven straw basket sitting next to a small pail on a bookcase by the kitchen door. Scarlett gaped at him and then chuckled, shaking her mess of dark hair.

"I'm not here to do your chores," she told him with equal measures of haughtiness and disgust.

Elaeric smiled. "And I am not here to wait on you. It is only the two of us, and breakfast should come before lunch. Or would you rather milk the goat?"

Scarlett's look of horrific shock melted into a scowl. She snatched the basket off the rickety bookcase, her hunger outweighing any argument she could offer.

"Fine. Where are the eggs?"

It was Elaeric's turn to look surprised. "In the chicken coop, of course." He held out a hand to the door but Scarlett opened it first and, throwing him a glare, stomped outside. The clogs were already biting into her ankles.

The light outside was bright and rosy. Scarlett threw her gaze about the sky, squinting against the light of the binary stars. One was a white dwarf, the other a red giant. The well-traveled Jordan knew at once where she was, or at least had a good suspicion. The heavy gravity pull and rosy light of the binary system made it fairly obvious.

Scarlett groaned and looked around. She was surrounded by rolling grasslands, though there were tree-covered mountains far to her right. The farmhouse she had just exited was a small stone and timber cottage with a vegetable and flower garden, edged by a few fruit trees with wide, spreading branches.

A fenced chicken yard with a henhouse stood on the far side of the vegetable garden. Scarlett wrinkled her nose, smelling its heavy stink on the morning breeze. Beyond the coop was a small barn sporting a fresh coat of cheery green paint.

Facing the cottage, across the dirt path that led to the barn, was a fenced meadow containing a chestnut mare with a spot of white on her nose and splashes of white on her lower front legs. Seeing Scarlett, the mare dug her hooves into the earth and charged at the fence between them with her head down and nostrils flared. The horse stopped at the last second, only centimeters from crashing into the rail fence, hooves churning up the grass and digging grooves into the earth. It snorted and jerked its head, glaring at the Jordan.

Scarlett gave it a long look and a twist of a smile before she headed for the henhouse. She passed the garden and paused outside the whitewashed door of the wood-paneled coop. She could her the quiet mutter of the chickens as they clucked softly inside. She pushed open the door of weathered boards and was assaulted by the fetid smell of the darkness inside.

"Ugh!" Scarlett quickly pulled her head back out into the heavy sun, trying not to gag. Elaeric was just leaving the cottage, humming jovially with a pail hanging from a wiry arm. She took a breath of clean air, as clean as it could be this close to the coop, and stuck her head back inside, quickly looking around before pulling it back out.

"Where are the eggs?" she called. Elaeric stopped as if struck.

"There are no eggs?" he asked, clearly distressed. "Nothing at all under the hens? *Any* of the hens?" Then it was the Jordan's turn to be distressed.

"*Under* the hens?" Scarlett's look was one of horror. "You want me to stick my hand...?" A smile began to spread over Elaeric's broad face and Scarlett turned away before he could say anything.

Determined not to appear any more foolish than she already had, she pushed opened the rickety door and stepped inside.

She was immediately overcome by the gloaming darkness and the heavy smell. Her eyes adjusted after a few seconds. Her nose did not. Sunlight streamed in through the cracks and holes between the slats of the henhouse. The floor was thick with droppings and Scarlett was glad for the first time that she didn't have her own boots on.

Six hens sat in boxed nests nailed along one of the walls, placidly clucking away at each other in the manner Scarlett associated with the female group of any species. Scarlett took a deep breath and made a face, as much to the smell as to what she was about to do.

"You filthy animals!" she hissed under her breath. "You smell like hell!" The hens went on clucking as if she wasn't even there.

Scarlett paused before the first nested bird, her face scrunched into a mask of acute distaste. Then, before she could change her mind, she gently plunged her hand under the chicken and into the nest. Expecting the warmth but still startled by the incubatory heat and gentle puff of feathers dusting the back of her hand, Scarlett carefully groped about until her hand closed over what felt like a warm smooth stone and pulled it out. The hen shifted her feathery bulk but otherwise did not seem to mind – it just went on gossiping with her neighbor.

Scarlett looked at the egg in her hand with mild surprise. "Hmph," she remarked, looking at the hen. "That wasn't so bad."

She put the egg in her basket and repeated the process with the other hens on the top row of boxes with the same result. Again with the first on the bottom row. The second hen on the bottom row, however, had no egg. Scarlett shrugged and stepped over to the box with the last chicken with her hand already stretching out, eager to be done with the nasty chore, and snatched it back, quite startled.

To start with, the said chicken was enormous. At first the Jordan thought that maybe it was a turkey, or some other strange poultry she had never seen alive. It wore a thick mantle of mottled black and gray feathers and had a splash of bumpy red skin about its face and along the bottom of its sharp beak. Its body (or maybe it was just the feathers, Scarlett couldn't tell) hung over the sides of its nest - obscuring the box completely.

But what brought Scarlett up short was that the beast was looking at her. The other hens never stopped their mindless throaty chatter, constantly tipping and bobbing their heads like a theater box of village idiots full of cheap liquor and equally cheap gossip.

This particular chook was completely silent and completely still. Then, it began pop and jerk its head as if to get a better look at the intruder in her house, staring at Scarlett with a single black eye that looked like an angry dollop of oil, full of hate. Full of something else as well - something Scarlett recognized and had been quite acquainted with all her life. Defiance.

The corpulent hen glowered at the Jordan, not just angry, but full of challenge. Daring her. Scarlett grinned and reached down and thrust her hand into the mop of downy feathers.

Before she could get her hand beneath the bird, much less begin her diminutive search of the nest, the chicken's head snapped down and pecked the back of Scarlett's hand with the ferocity of a rabid dog.

Scarlett cried out and snatched her hand away. "Dammit!" she cursed, examining the back of her hand. There was already a plump of blood welling up in the small hole that had been pecked out of her skin. She looked back up, glaring at the fat bird.

The hen popped and jerked her head like a wary boxer, never taking her angry black eye off of Scarlett.

The Crimson Jordan, Intergalactic Starfighter and jet-setting pilot that had been so recently reduced to ill-fitting peasant clothes and henhouses, leaned towards the bumpy red face that glared back at her.

"You do that again," Scarlett hissed, "and whatever I find under there is going right back up the chute it came out of!"

The Jordan thrust her hand under the downy feathers of the fat beast, its black eye still and watching her now with something akin to amusement. Scarlett fished out an egg, triumphant.

"Ha!"

She placed the egg delicately in her basket and with a flip of her dirty hair trounced out of the hen house, victorious and resplendent in linen and clogs.

★

Breakfast consisted of the gathered eggs, strips of fried ham, toast, and coffee sweetened with goat milk. Normally Scarlett would balk at the meal, especially the eggs. It wasn't that she had never eaten eggs, she had eaten many and from birds that ranged from common to exotic. But never before had she eaten eggs that she herself had just plucked warm from the nest.

Under normal circumstances she would have been reluctant or even disgusted, considering that just minutes ago her food had been under the ass end of a group of unruly live birds that smelled like holy hell. Now, she was too hungry to care and wondered if she had even eaten in a week.

She thought it most likely that she had been fed through a tube when she was quarantined aboard the Dragon but she couldn't remember and for the moment didn't give a rat's ass. Her saliva glands were out of control and she thanked Elaeric with more sincerity she thought herself capable of when he set the plate down before her.

Scarlett ate four of the eggs, two strips of ham, two pieces of toast, and drank two cups of coffee. Elaeric sat with his silken garb swaddled tightly around his body and watched her with interest as he delicately ate his egg.

"I thought all monks were vegetarians," Scarlett remarked between mouthfuls of food. Elaeric smiled, showing his strong but aging row of teeth.

"And what makes you think I am a monk?" he asked. "Is it my eyes?" he queried, opening them wide, making their almond shape more round. "Or is it my color?" he asked, tilting his face to indicate the pale golden tone of his skin. "Is it my hair?" he asked, bowing his head to give her a better view of his bald scalp.

Scarlett laughed and washed down a mouthful of toast with her coffee and poured herself another cup, shaking her head.

"None of those things," she told him, "though they are all horribly cliché. It's your ungodly expression of inner glee. Like you are always laughing on the inside."

Elaeric laughed aloud, delighted. "You are more perceptive than I thought, but you are wrong. Yes, I am laughing on the inside, as you say. But, no, I am not a monk. My robes may be cliché, but I saw no need to change a style of dress that I had become most comfortable with, and certainly no need to surgically change my eyes." He leaned forward conspiratorially. "Though I will confess, these are not the eyes I was born with."

"Really?" Scarlett asked, arching a dark brow. "What happened to the originals? Old age?"

Elaeric grinned. "Lost 'em in a bet."

Scarlett snorted. "Were you ever a monk?" she asked before stuffing her mouth with toast.

"I was."

Scarlett nodded emphatically and gave a great swallow. "I knew it. Why did you give it up?"

Elaeric leaned towards her again like a thief in the night. "Women!" he confessed with a hoarse whisper.

Scarlett chuckled, despite a mouth full of coffee and wagged a finger at him. "That is both an empty as well as a loaded answer," she accused once her mouth was free of its cargo.

Elaeric smiled and changed the subject with brusque ease. "Only five eggs today?" he asked. Scarlett nodded, her mouth full of toast again. "Bottom middle?" Elaeric inquired, indicating the chicken whose nest had been empty. Scarlett nodded again, washing her food down with a swig of coffee.

"I take it this is not the first time?"

Elaeric shook his head slowly, looking a trifle sad. "Eighth day in a row. I fear she may be past her time."

For that, Scarlett had no answer. She had been raised in a city and now lived aboard a spacecraft. At least she *had* been living there.

"So," she asked, mopping her plate with the crust of her toast, "how long do they intend to keep me here?" Elaeric regarded her with mild surprise.

"Keep you here? You may go home any time you like."

Now it was Scarlett's turn to be surprised and her heart leapt with a sudden surge of hope. "I can?"

"Of course. You are not a prisoner! You are, however, on medical leave. You have the power to return home anytime you like. But returning to work will not be allowed until your Captain sees fit."

Scarlett sat back, thoughtfully chewing the last of her breakfast while Elaeric related the decisions to send her to her present location and who had made them.

★

After breakfast Scarlett helped Elaeric scrub the dishes and then followed him outside. The chickens had left the coop and were pecking about the yard. Elaeric picked up a small sack of grain and tossed a handful into their midst. He held the bag out to Scarlett who gripped a fistful of the seeds and tossed it to the chickens.

The hens went crazy for it in their calm plucky way and Scarlett wondered what it was that gave humans joy to give food to birds. She walked slowly through their midst, keeping a wary eye on the fat black and gray feathered fowl, half expecting it to chase her, but the beast apparently had no interest in the Jordan.

After feeding the chickens Scarlett followed Elaeric to the meadow fenced in with the split wooden rails that held the chestnut mare. The horse rushed the fence, as she had earlier that morning, snorting and stomping, full of aggressive anger.

"Do you know what this is?" Elaeric asked.

"It's a horse," Scarlett answered. "I'm not a simpleton."

Elaeric smiled as if he may have other ideas. "And what is the horse?"

"A four-legged beast of burden."

"Is that all you see?"

Scarlett frowned. "What are you after?"

Elaeric waved a hand as if to shoo away the questions. He placed a silk-slippered foot onto the bottom rail. "She is beautiful, yes?"

"I'm not a horse expert," Scarlett replied, her tone mildly sarcastic, "but yes, she does look like a fine animal."

The horse was long legged and lean, plated with rippling muscle beneath her sleek brown coat. The mare stomped and jerked her head, flipping her rust colored mane with an air of defiance.

"She reminds me of your chicken," Scarlett said.

"Really?" Elaeric asked, surprised. "She makes *me* think of *you*!"

Scarlett laughed, though she took his meaning clear enough. "Well, she obviously isn't a farm animal. Not your average beast of burden. She doesn't even look like she would let anyone ride her."

Elaeric put his weight onto the bottom rail of the fence, pulling himself up and throwing a leg over the top rail. "Right now, she would not," he agreed.

"Why is she here?"

"She is here for the same reason as you - to heal."

Scarlett gave him a wry smile. "A horse with space madness?

Now I have heard everything." She pulled herself up onto the fence next to Elaeric, though not with his easy grace. The gravity would take some getting used to.

Elaeric laughed. "No. She was a prize racing horse, but she was injured. They brought her here from Amos."

"She's not from this planet?"

"No. A horse from here would never grow so tall. The gravity disagrees with her as much as it does with you." He reached out a hand to stroke the mare's nose but she jerked her head away from his hand. "But it will make her strong again," he continued. "That, and some careful teaching."

"What happened to her?"

"A fine race horse she was. Like a slip of silk in the wind. But a broken leg broke her spirit. Even she knew that she would never race again." He reached out again to pet the horse again but again she jerked her head away. "It is a hard thing," he murmured, "to be denied your passion."

Scarlett thought of Fledge and felt a lump rise in her throat like hot dough. She decided at that moment she would do whatever it took to get back to her Fledgling Dragon, chickens and clogs be damned.

"Do you see her field?" Elaeric asked, sudden and curious.

Scarlett looked at the meadow and shrugged. "Of course."

Elaeric followed Scarlett's eyes and shook his head. "No. Her *field*," he repeated, making circular motions with his hands around the body of the horse.

"Ohhh, you mean, like an aura?"

Elaeric nodded emphatically but Scarlett shook her head. "No."

"Hmm."

"What does it look like?"

The small golden man perched on the fence and pursed his lips, twisting them to the side of his mouth. "It is supposed to be red, but is filled with gray smoke and black anger - just like yours."

Scarlett stepped down from the rail and regarded Elaeric with her own twisted but knowing smile. "I can read you like a book, my new friend." Elaeric beamed at her, pleased – but said nothing. The Red Jordan sighed. "So, I am I supposed to heal the horse, or is she supposed to heal me?"

The monk smiled, showing his even square teeth.

"Yes."

FIVE

Faith had just finished getting ready when Jasyn awoke. She saw him stir as she rose from her bench in front of the vanity, dropping a long linked-chain necklace over her head and adjusting it so that it fell down between her breasts. She wore an impeccable white suit and white heels.

She walked over to the bed as he sat up and looked around, eyes still sleepy. Faith knew he must be tired. His amorous attentions of the previous night were repeated. Twice.

Though she had been happy to be woken both times, she had the feeling that he hadn't slept much at all.

"Good morning," she said, sitting carefully on the edge of the bed.

"Good morning."

She felt physically incapable to stop smiling while she was looking at him, and almost as unable to look away. Even as she had gotten dressed she had kept stealing glances at his sleeping form under the rumple of golden covers.

He waited patiently, quietly, his own smile small and a bit shy in the artificial morning light. Faith sighed.

"It's going to be a busy morning," she told him. As if to emphasize her words, the bedroom door opened to admit her personal assistant Penny as well as Mari, her housekeeper.

Penny wore a smart and snug brown dress with a tailored brown jacket and a wide black belt. A pair of glasses with black frames and small rectangular lenses was perched on the bridge of her nose. Mari wore a looser and longer brown dress with cap sleeves and a white apron.

"Is it alright for Mari to start packing?" Penny asked.

"Of course," Faith said without turning or taking her eyes from Jasyn. "You'll let her know what I'll need?"

"Of course."

Faith crossed one leg over the other and put the palm of her hand down on the bed to lean closer to Jasyn without toppling over.

"I'm getting ready for a trip," she told him, "so I will be pretty busy today. I want you to make yourself at home. Rest or sleep as much as you want, then get cleaned up and have some breakfast. Penny will see that you get some new clothes."

"Where do you want them?" Penny asked, coming in from the dressing room at a brisk walk, an acrylic held deftly in one hand while she pecked on it with the other.

"His clothes? My closet. Have Mari move all of my evening gowns into one of the guest rooms."

"Is there anything specific you would like for him?" Penny asked without looking up, her fingers moving quickly on her tablet.

"Anything from Fredrick's will do, for now. And get him an acrylic."

Penny stopped typing and looked up at her employer over the tops of her rectangular lenses. "What should I put on it?"

Jasyn had been looking back and forth between the women as they spoke but Faith had kept her eyes fixed on him. "Nothing," she said. "Open a vertical account for him and show him how to use it. Let him pick whatever music, movies, books or games he wants."

"Any other applications?"

Faith's smile widened. "Whatever he wants." Penny hurried from the room to get started. Faith reached out and put her hand on the blanket over the shape of Jasyn's knee. "I'm going to be busy today but we'll have an early supper tonight before I leave. Okay?"

Jasyn's smile was shy but genuine. "Okay."

★

The day was hectic but not any more than what Faith had expected. Though Penny fielded most of her calls, there were some that she simply had to take. She was going all the way to the Flower to meet with the Patricians of the InterGalactic Council, including the Director of Artificial Intelligence. It was a trip she didn't make often and there were many who wanted to meet her personally while she was there.

Opposite her living room, on the other side of the round foyer, was her office; a vast space of polished wood and polished metal. A high backed chair covered in golden suede sat behind a three-sided mahogany desk that was topped with a few flat screen acrylic monitors. One section of the desk was inset with a table–holo. Two fashionable chairs of dark brown faced the desk, backed by deep couches upholstered in distressed leather.

There were people coming and going from the villa in a near constant stream and Faith met with a few of them in her office, but spent the majority of the afternoon ensconced in her bedroom.

What she was doing in there, Jasyn had no idea. He knew she had already bathed and it was obvious that she did little to her face or hair, not that either warranted much attention in his mild opinion.

He doubted she could be sleeping because when he did see her, she was in a continuous state of motion. She possessed a quiet restlessness and was never still, even when she was standing in the same spot.

After he had risen, he spent a piece of time figuring out the shower and the dryer in the bathroom adjoining Faith's bedroom. After he had dressed in the only clothes he had, Penny had come into the room and ushered him into the kitchen for breakfast. She had disappeared while he had eaten, leaving him to watch the cook as she bustled about the kitchen and Mari as she appeared and disappeared.

The entire female staff flitted about, seemingly bound by the same state of restless motion as their employer, though not with the same state of calm.

As soon as he had finished eating, the cook scooped his plate and utensils up and Penny swooped in with her acrylic tucked under one arm to usher him into the living room.

"Hold still," she told him as she held up her acrylic and used it to snap a picture of him while she called out directions. "Hold out your arms. Good. Now turn around. Good. Now come sit down," she said, motioning to one of the white chairs near the clear wall of windows that looked out into space.

As Jasyn sat down he saw Faith enter and stride across the room, speaking into a small golden comset hooked over her right ear. Jasyn's eyes followed her until she disappeared into her office. Penny sat in the chair next to him and picked up a thin rectangular box from a side table and slid a manicured thumbnail into the seam at the bottom. She tilted the open box and a new acrylic slid out into her palm. It was more or less the size of a dinner plate and looked like a pristine rectangle of glass with smooth edges.

"This is called an acrylic," Penny told him. Jasyn smiled at her. She showed him how to turn it on and, after typing on it for a minute to set and employ the applications, showed him how to log in to the account she had just created for him. "You can hold it this way, or this way – it doesn't matter – the screen will turn and adjust either way. See?" She turned it from vertical to horizontal, demonstrating. Jasyn nodded.

Penny pulled the side table from between their chairs so that it was in front of them and laid the acrylic down so they could both see the screen.

She showed him how to change screens, how to access the stores he was allowed to use, and how to buy music and movies and games. Penny almost told him that it wasn't a holo pad, so the movies and games would be flat, but figured he wouldn't know the difference.

"Can you remember all that?" she asked. She spoke slowly with her chin down and brows up as if she were addressing a small child. Like a child, he smiled and nodded. Penny, with a long and dubious look, turned off the acrylic and laid it back on the table. "Show me."

Jasyn, with a dubious look of his own, picked up the acrylic and turned it on. After studying the screen for a moment he was able to log on, hesitantly pecking out the letters of his name and the numbers that Penny had given him.

Though he was slower than Penny, he was able to perform everything she had shown him. He handed it back to her, grinning.

"Very good!" she exclaimed, bobbing her head encouragingly.

Faith entered the room again, still talking to her comset. Jasyn's eyes followed her as she paced back and forth across the foyer while she spoke. She paused and a restless foot tapped and tapped as she cupped her right elbow with her left hand, her right thumbnail grazing her bottom lip as she listened to the comset.

As soon as she started talking again she turned and disappeared into her bedroom, the door closing behind her. Jasyn looked back at Penny.

"Does everyone have an acrylic?" he asked her.

Penny gave a small shrug, her shoulders tight in the tailored jacket. "Just about. Anyone who can afford one, that is."

"Does Ms. de Rossi have one?"

Penny shook her head.

"Why not?"

Penny smiled. "Because she has me."

Her own comset chimed and she tapped it, looking away from Jasyn as she listened. "Good. Can you send him down, or should I send Mari?" There was a short pause as she listened. "Fine, thank you." She touched her earpiece, cutting the link. "Your clothes are here."

She stood, tucking her acrylic deftly under her arm as she strode away. Jasyn tucked his own under his arm and followed her.

The foyer was a round, raised platform in the center of the villa floored in the same black granite as the living room. In its center was a circular glass lift wrapped with a spiral staircase leading both up to the top level and down to the bottom.

The elevator descended, holding a man in a yellow uniform and cap, his arms laden with wrapped parcels and boxes. The curved glass door slid open and he stepped out onto the polished stone floor.

Penny took Jasyn's acrylic from him and motioned for him to take the packages. Once his arms were empty, the courier pulled an acrylic from the back of his waistband.

"Sheesh!" he exclaimed to Penny. "I wish your security guy would let me bring down a field manipulator." He handed Penny a plastic stylus and held the acrylic pad out to her.

She smiled at him, plucking the stylus from his hand. "That wouldn't be very good security now, would it?" She signed for the delivery, trying not to touch the warm pad with her hand.

"I don't know," he sighed, taking back the stylus. "It's pretty standard."

"Not for here, but I'm pretty sure you know that." She batted her eyes behind their square black frames and he gave her a conciliatory smile.

"I suppose." He entered the elevator and it rose up, leaving her alone with Jasyn.

"Come on," she directed.

"Where?" he asked. He had to crane his neck around the parcels piled in his arms to see her walk down the hall. He followed as quickly as he could.

"To try those on." She led him down the corridor to a door. Across from Faith's personal quarters were three guest rooms and Penny took him into the first. "You can put those down."

Jasyn tried to set them on the bed carefully but they tumbled all around, a few falling to the dark carpet. He picked them up and added them to the pile on the bed.

"There's a full length mirror over there," Penny said, gesturing across the room. "Try everything on. If there is anything that doesn't fit, put it back in the box. Everything else, just leave on the bed. I'll have Mari hang them up in Ms. de Rossi's closet for you."

Penny turned and left, pulling the door closed behind her.

Jasyn watched the door for a few seconds to make sure it wasn't going to open again and then turned and began opening the packages. He wasn't sure what clothes went together but he tried them on and they all fit surprisingly well, even the shoes.

There were two items, one shirt and one pair of pants, that he thought looked ridiculous so he put those back in the boxes. He finished by putting on a clean set of clothes and leaving the ones that he arrived in on the bed with the new ones.

Dressed in a fresh shirt and pants, hoping they were an acceptable combination, Jasyn opened the door and stuck his head out. There was no one in the hall. He went back to the living room where Penny and Geary were talking. The conversation ended abruptly as Jasyn walked in, obviously interrupted.

Jasyn gave them a timid smile as Geary straightened and walked brusquely away from Penny. The security man gave the construct a glance devoid of interest as he walked to the glass lift and rode it up.

"Did everything fit?" Penny asked.

Jasyn nodded. "Just about." Penny gave him a look that was half quizzical and half suspicion. "What do I do next?" he asked.

"Dinner won't be for a few hours. Why don't you try out your new acrylic?"

Jasyn bit his lip, considering. "Would it be okay if I look around?"

Penny measured the request in silence before nodding her head. "I suppose that will be fine. You may not go into doors that are closed, and you may not go upstairs – security is strictly off limits. Other than that, feel free to explore."

Jasyn did just that, wandering curiously. The villa was enormous, though it did not have many rooms and only a few hallways. The first thing that he noticed was that the home was round and constructed like a pie, with the raised foyer in the very middle and the access lift and winding stair at the center.

He walked down the hallway that bisected the width of the circular residence. Faith's bedroom suite was on one side, taking up nearly a quarter of the pie. The door was closed but he had a pretty good idea of what was inside. He also knew he would have more time to explore that later.

On the other side of the hallway, opposite Faith's bedroom quarter, were three sumptuously appointed guest suites with private bathrooms. He walked back down the hall and glanced into the wide space of the living room. Penny was talking to someone new but did not bother to look in his direction.

He turned and, even though the door was open, went timidly into Faith's office. He took in the immaculate span of polished metal and burnished wood, deep chairs and gleaming compute surfaces, with a single sweep of his hazel eyes.

This isn't where she really works, he thought suddenly. He had no idea where the thought came from and it felt slightly disconcerting.

He left the office and walked down the hall, briefly looking into the kitchen where he had eaten breakfast. The room was a faultless spread of tiled floor, marble countertop, plastique wood cabinets, and appliances of stainless steel that had been polished until they shone like mirrors.

The cook was bent over a granite block rolling out dough. Her round face popped up and smiled at him.

"Hungry again already?" she asked.

Jasyn smiled and shook his head. "No, thank you. Just... exploring," he told her, using Penny's word.

Cook grinned. "Been downstairs yet?"

Jasyn shook his head.

"Humph." She gave him a wink and went back to rolling dough with a quick shake of her head, still smiling.

Jasyn tilted his head, waiting for her to say more. When she started to hum to herself rather than speak, he crossed through the kitchen to the last unexplored room on the center level of the villa. It was a large dining room.

The wall he passed through, the one abutting the kitchen, was adorned with antique paintings and guarded by a sculpture on either end. A long table of dark, polished wood was surrounded by high-backed chairs and topped with three vases full of fresh cut flowers. The wall to the right opened onto the living room and, like the living room, the far wall was a great curve of glass.

Jasyn wandered back into the living room, completing his circumvention of the villa. Penny was facing the window and speaking to the comset hooked over her ear. He quietly passed through the room and mounted the few steps to the rounded polished platform in the center.

After a curious glance up the winding staircase to the forbidden section, Jasyn took the steps that led down, twisting around the circular glass elevator. With his attention focused on watching his footing, he did not look up to see the room until his foot hit the last stair. When it did, he recoiled.

His first terrified thought was that he was about to step off into space. With a dizzying rush of vertigo, his mind quickly assessed the fact that there was no vacuum and no lack of oxygen.

Jasyn stared wide-eyed as his mind processed what it was seeing.

The rounded bottom of the villa was a pool, encased entirely in a hyper-diamond shell more transparent than glass. It stretched out before him like a sparkling black lake filled with twinkling stars. The ceiling was mirror, reflecting the timeless night of space and its sparkling pinpricks of light.

He took a tentative step down onto the black stone floor, so finely polished that it reflected the stars that were reflecting from the ceiling. It disappeared into the water only a few steps away, though it took a few moments for his eyes to determine stone from glass and water from air.

The effect of the room was that of being held suspended alone and unencumbered between the stars of the galaxy. Jasyn knew that immersing oneself in the pool would be like swimming through the womb of the universe.

He knelt by the edge and dipped his hand into the water. It was surprisingly warm. On impulse, he brought his wet fingers to his mouth and touched them to his lips. He could taste salt.

As his eyes adjusted to the darkened space he now saw that the pool, stretching out more than thirty meters in front of him, took up only half of the deeply rounded room. Behind him was more polished black stone floor, equal to that of the immense pool on the other side.

On the black marble were molded glass chairs, lounges, and

small tables. In the stretch of darkness punctured by the bright flicker of stars, there was another blur of darkness that he finally made out to be stacks of thick, black towels.

Turning his attention back to the sparkling lake, he noticed a soft, lambent, glow that came from the far end of the pool like an eclipse around a black hole. He didn't know if it was for light, heat, or to simulate a star or other heavenly body.

The dark-haired construct backed up and sat on the bottom steps of the staircase, marveling at the room and thinking about the woman who had ordered its construction. The woman who had ordered his own construction.

*

When Jasyn came back upstairs it was almost lunchtime. Cook made him a sandwich of cut bread, vegetables, and some sort of sliced meat. He ate it in the kitchen at a small table against the wall, along with a plate fruit she had prepared for him. He sipped from a tall glass of water and watched her move between cupboards and drawers and food – chopping and mixing and preparing. She was like Faith, in her own way, a controlled dervish in a constant state of movement.

Jasyn observed her while he ate until her movements became so foreseeable that he could predict her next move, then the one after that, and the next after that. Just as he was getting bored, she was joined by a gangly young man, who she introduced as Bowe without looking at either of them.

Bowe gave Jasyn a nervous smile and went about his work assisting Cook, pulling out bottles and spices for her and quickly stowing them away when she was done. He moved deftly and continuously, always giving Cook a wide berth. To Jasyn, they looked like the polar ends of a pair of magnets trying to dance.

Smiling, he thanked Cook for lunch, to which she gave a nearly imperceptible nod without slowing in her work, and he went to the living room. It was quiet and empty, eerily so after the morning rush of activity. He could still hear people moving around the villa but for now he was alone. The glass wall was an enormous band of star-studded black, haunted by perpetual night.

Jasyn picked up his acrylic and settled down into a wing chair. He turned the device around in his hands, examining the sides. He glanced at the bumps and indentations that were for micro cards, universal positioning pins, microphones and pen cam software, before turning it upright and skimming his fingers along its glassy face.

Beaming like a child with a secret toy, he turned it on and began exploring it the way he had explored the villa. Tentative at first, he began to discover what was built into the device. As his comfort and confidence grew, he began with childish delight to learn what was available to him on the Galactic Web.

Within an hour Jasyn was uploading and running programs. He tried to keep some of his attention tuned in toward his surroundings, noting the comings and goings of bodies and clips of passing conversations, but before he knew it the lights in the walls of the villa began to dim into twilight. It was replaced by an ambient lighting that began to glow from the ceilings and floors.

Jasyn glanced up to see Bowe setting the table in the dining room for an early supper for two, just as Faith's bedroom door opened to release a burst of movement and sound that moved like a quiet storm of cream-colored snow and technological politics.

Faith, impeccable in a swirling white dress with her hair pinned into a nimbus of brown and gold and framing a face tight with concentration, Penny in crisp brown taking furious notes, Mari trotting along while chattering instructions at the young man transporting the luggage, and Geary sidelining it all.

Faith spotted Jasyn and her shoulders, pulled so high with stress that they were reaching for her ears, dropped immediately. She turned from her original course towards her office and came straight to him, her icy exterior seeming to melt a little more with every step.

Jasyn stood up, letting his acrylic fall onto the cushion of the chair. Faith smiled, her comset a golden hook over her right ear, expelling a jabber of noise. She pulled it off and tossed it onto a couch, the jabber rising to a heated cacophony as if telepathically sensing the loss of its listener.

"You look fantastic," she told him sincerely, admiring the new clothes as much as the body she knew was underneath. "Are you ready for dinner?"

Jasyn took both of her hands in his own. "I'm ready for whatever you want," he replied. Faith grinned and led him by the hand into the dining room where Bowe had dimmed the ambient lighting and was pouring red wine from a black glass bottle into crystal goblet atop a slender stem.

Faith held out a hand, indicating his seat, but Jasyn pulled out her chair for her and waited for her to sit. Faith laughed softly as she sat down, suddenly feeling shy. Jasyn sat down next, his expression one of barely contained delight. Bowe, wearing a crisp white jacket, waited patiently nearby.

"What would you like to drink?" Faith asked. Jasyn smiled.

"Water is fine."

She motioned to Bowe and he filled Jasyn's glass with water from a green bottle. Faith held up her glass, and hesitated for just a second. "To the future," she said decidedly, though her voice was soft. Jasyn held his glass back.

"To *our* future?"

Faith smiled. "To our future," she agreed.

Bowe came back from the kitchen, carrying two plates and looking apologetic. "Cook has most of your meal right here," he told them. "Per your request."

Faith nodded at him and spread a cloth napkin across her lap as he gingerly placed the plates down before them. "Unfortunately I don't have much time this evening," she told him, her tone apologetic.

Bowe nodded as if this was a regrettable case but a common occurrence before he exited back into the kitchen.

Faith took a delicate bite from her plate and ate it without tasting it. She was too busy watching Jasyn as he put a bit of vegetable into his mouth and chewed slowly, obviously not knowing what to expect.

I wonder if it is nice, Faith thought, *to have each and every experience be something new, or if it would be terrifying.*

It had been so long since anything had been new to her, she thought that even a little terror might be nice. Then she realized that a little terror was what she *was* feeling, and that it was indeed quite nice.

Jasyn ate a bite of the cooked grains on his plate, taking his time to savor the texture and the taste. Faith knew that it was more than he was used to as a construct in prep, though she figured that no training or programming could have prepared him for what he was experiencing.

It was doubtful that companionship for the Chief Executive Officer of GwenSeven was on anyone's mind at the factory or at the prep center. Bought love for the creator would seem a ludicrous idea. Jasyn could hardly believe it himself, but he intended to make the most of it. He knew he had a job to do. He meant to execute that job to the best of his ability, and enjoy it to the extent of his capacity.

The construct carefully picked up the serrated blade from his place setting and cut into the artfully grilled piece of meat on his plate. With a daring and expectant expression, he cautiously put the cut portion into his mouth. His smiled at Faith as he began to chew but his expression quickly turned to one of shock.

The meat, delicately salted and seasoned, seemed to melt in his mouth like a piece of ice in the sun. Faith watched him with open amusement. Jasyn swallowed what was left and exhaled sharply.

"This is really good," he told her enthusiastically as he cut another larger bite and forked it into his mouth.

"That's because it's organic," Faith told him.

Jasyn froze. "You mean," he asked through a mouth full of half masticated steak, "this is real meat?"

Faith nodded as she finished her own bite and took a sip of the blood-colored wine in her glass, her eyes glittering. Jasyn resumed chewing - slowly, wary at first, then with more vigor.

"It's good," he confessed, helping himself to another bite of steak with renewed enthusiasm. Faith watched him with pleasure.

"I wish I could stay with you tonight."

Jasyn quickly swallowed, a frown creasing his brow. "Why can't you?"

"Work," she said, as if it explained everything.

"How long will you be gone?"

Faith's shoulders twitched in an approximation of a shrug. "Two days. Maybe three, plus travel time. All in all I won't be gone for more than a week." Jasyn looked concerned, though he kept eating.

"What should I do while you are gone?" he asked. Faith flinched.

"Is there anyplace you would like to go? Anything you would like to do?"

Jasyn put his fork down, his expression serious. "Penny said I shouldn't go upstairs. Is there anywhere else?"

Faith shook her head and took a sip of wine. "You can go wherever you want." She set her glass down and propped an elbow up on the table. She smiled at him as she traced her bottom lip with a thumbnail. "You just have to know that there are a lot of people looking out for me. Give them the space they need and they will do the same for you. Geary will be coming with me, but his second, Tom, will have a small security contingent here. I'll have him show you around."

"Is there an outside?"

Faith laughed. "Yes, there is an outside, but you can't go directly outside the villa without a field pack. Though if you mean more places to explore and walk around, I will have someone take you to The Hub. The Commons are there - it's the center of the development – there are lots of parks, shopping, and...I don't know what all else. Above that is the City, though I don't know if there would be anything there that would be of interest to you."

Penny stepped into the room and held her acrylic primly down in front of her skirt, waiting silently. Faith wiped her mouth with her napkin and stood. Jasyn rose, pushing his seat back and walked to her side of the table.

Faith meant to take his hand but he surprised her by slipping his arms around her waist and pulling her close and kissing her. His hands slipped up her back, holding her tight in a silent plea for her to stay.

She wanted to stay, so badly that for a moment she actually considered the notion but then quickly dismissed it. She broke the kiss and laid her face against his.

"I'll be back as soon as I can," she whispered, her eyes closed. She let her hands drop, running down the sides of his body as he kissed her again. She disengaged herself from his embrace as gently as she could, giving him a quick but final kiss. "I'll see you soon," she promised, then turned and left him in the semi-darkness of the room.

Penny fell in step behind her and as they passed through the living room Geary and another security man fell in behind the two women.

Jasyn took a few tentative steps so he could watch them go. They all entered the circular lift in the middle of the foyer and up they went to the dock and the craft that waited there. Faith, her mind already a galaxy away, never looked back.

SIX

JP closed the book and ran his slender fingers over the smooth leather grain of the cover. The leather had been worn softer than felt and smoother than silk. It was the only book that he carried that had real paper pages. Pages that were as thin and frail as the shed skin of a snake.

The Chimeran Commander had thousands of books in his library; syn-pap, ultra-glass, acrylic, holo, and even a number of parchment scrolls from every corner and civilization in the universe. He even possessed a collection of Golgoth Lainyes that he acquired about the same time he had obtained his Battle Cruiser.

This particular collection ranged from their civilized (or what passed for civilized to a Golgoth) history to modern technology. The wide array of massive tomes were bound with hide and latched by copper fastenings that had tarnished over the years, leaching green discolorations onto the hide.

The inside of the Lainyes appeared to be full of blank pages, since the Golgoths kept their learning strictly for select individuals in their upper castes, and without the correct DNA of the reader, the pages would remain blank. JP, however, also had a collection of amputated Golgoth index fingers to go with the books. With the help of a specially made metal harness he could wear one of the large scaly digits between his own index finger and thumb as if it were one of his own. A translator contact in his left eye would allow him to read the foreign text at his leisure.

The book on his lap, however, was the only book that he always carried and the only one that really meant anything to him. It was the Millennia Bible of the Cassar Zealous Faith, also called the One True Faith. JP's held all four testaments; The Old, The New, The Secret and The Spoken - the last was often referred to as the Elfin Addendum as it was the elfin account of God and the messiah, passed down orally for more than a thousand generations.

JP was different from the other Chimera in more than just looks, but his appearance was indeed strikingly deceptive. His heart-shaped face was that of a lad anywhere between fourteen to eighteen human years, just on the fringe of losing the roundness of a young boy and on the verge of becoming the angular face of a young man.

He had bright blue eyes and neatly combed auburn hair. There was a spatter of freckles on his porcelain skin that often had the ruddy complexion of a youngster just coming in from a snowball fight.

His devout righteousness along with his angelic looks were the perfect camouflage for what many would consider the most dangerous Commander in the Chimeran military.

JP had started his life simply as BG-Syn. His first and only owner had named him John Pierre but JP had left that name behind long ago and now only went by the initials. He had once been nicknamed "Pious" by a woman who he usually thought of as "that Godless jezebel, Charity de Rossi."

JP wore a royal blue cassock with a high white collar, devoid of any epaulettes or insignia that would designate him as an officer much less the Commander of the Battle Cruiser *Resurrection*. His only adornments were the symbol for infinity stitched in white thread on his left sleeve and a silver ring bearing the same symbol on the third finger of his left hand.

He wore his officer's chain, a sequence of linked figure eights, under his cassock-style coverall. All officers wore a similar necklace made of gold or silver, depending upon their rank. JP's was platinum, as was the chain for all Commanders.

His quarters on the Battle Cruiser were fashioned after the monastery where he had spent nearly half his life. Though made almost entirely of composite and plastique, his rooms had the appearance of hewn white stone and aged timber. The only light came from the faux wax candles. Coming in from the outer corridor of steel and fluorescents, the effect could deliver quite the shock if one was not accustomed to it.

On this night JP had been reading the Old Testament, his favorite, and the account of Noah and God's wrath upon the humans that were so filled with sin that they had to be destroyed.

Like all Cassars, JP believed in reincarnation. The Commander liked to think that he was Noah incarnate, or possibly Charlemagne or Constantine. Unfortunately, like all constructs, he had next to no imagination. But JP knew his history, and knew that history was bound by the circular law of the universe to repeat itself.

The story of Noah never failed to fill the Commander with a great sense of righteousness. JP felt that, like Noah, he had been chosen by God to save his people – those that were worthy of being spared that was – and, in JP's opinion, that number was not large.

After the Great Flood, God had sent Noah a rainbow as a sign of promise. And now, as the Chimera amassed their strength and the tide of war was finally beginning to change, The One had sent another rainbow.

The Dragons, the mighty living ships and the great unassailable strength of the IGC Military, for two thousand years had been living representations of metals and stone: iron and silver and copper - onyx and pearl and the like.

But in the Year of the Fourth Dragon, which was not actually a number of standard years but simply the fourth chit of the human-elfin timeline that marked the gestation of a new generation of Dragons, the eggs that the Dragons had manifested were colors.

True, JP knew that some were calling them the Gemstone Fledglings, but he knew better. The spectrum made it undeniable - red, orange, yellow, green, blue, indigo and violet. Everyone in the seven galaxies was calling it the Year of the Rainbow.

JP thought of it as the Year of Promise.

Three of the eggs had hatched just over two years ago and the Fledgling Dragons were just beginning to grow in size and power, but they did not concern JP. Another Commander would handle the Fledglings. JP was after the eggs.

The boy-faced Commander drummed his manicured fingertips on the soft leather grain of his Bible, avoiding the dark splotch that marred the otherwise perfect surface.

The Drawing of the Opal Dragon had been a mess, but not a loss. Well, not a total loss.

Bjorn and his band of hedonistic miscreants had been laid low –blasted and burned to ash like the sinners of Sodom and Gomorrah. Bjorn, like Lot, had escaped with his life by leaving and not looking back.

Due to the fact that the licentious Commander had somehow had the sense to leave his ship, *The Macedonian*, on the far side of the moon, it had been spared. For that, JP was mighty glad and grateful to The One. Battle Cruisers were not easy to come by.

The main objective had been achieved. In the confusion and

concentration of the fight, the eggs from the Beryl Dragon had been acquired. For JP, objects (such as equipment, ships, or say Dragon eggs) were always acquired, never stolen. Stealing was a sin.

The most severe casualty, as far as JP was concerned, was Rohn Stojacovik, the Executive Officer of *The Macedonian*. Stoj had been a stellar officer and a key player in the revolution since the beginning. He had, at the very least, kept Bjorn in check. The Cause would suffer and had great reason to mourn his loss.

JP crossed himself in the memory of Stoj before he traced a circle in the air with two fingers and said a silent prayer for his soul as a knock came at his door.

"Come in!" he called.

The door opened to admit a small woman with a narrow face and dark hair pulled back into a comely bun. She wore a plain gray coverall with a white round collar, the lazy eight symbol for infinity stitched onto her left sleeve in blue thread. She pushed the door open with her hip as her hands were occupied with a tray.

"Good evening, sir," she greeted, placing the tray down on a side table next to the chair where the Commander reclined with his Bible on his lap. On the tray was a plate with the Commander's meager evening meal, a thick slice of unleavened bread and two chunks of pasteurized cheese, one white and one yellow. Next to the plate was a goblet of mulled red wine.

"Thank you, Larissa," he offered warmly.

Larissa blushed. "Is there anything else I can bring you tonight, sir?" she asked, her demure eyes carefully darting to and from his piercing gaze.

"Do you know when the transport is expected to arrive?"

"Within the hour, sir," she reported, quickly daring to meet his eyes with her own before looking down again.

"Will you come and let me know when it arrives?"

Larissa smiled broadly, feeling honored. "Certainly, sir! I'll be here before it has even docked."

"Thank you, Larissa."

Her eyes darted around the room, trying to decipher if there was another need he might have that she could meet. The quarters were comforting, inviting and soothing. And the Commander's presence alone filled her with both peace and joy. She wanted to linger but knew it was neither polite nor proper.

"Is there anything else for now?"

"Not now, Larissa," he told her. "You have been more than kind."

Though she did not want to keep him from his supper, his benevolent smile spurred her to brave a question. "May I ask what you are reading about tonight, sir?"

The Commander's smile broadened. "I was reading the story of Noah."

Larissa frowned, looking thoughtful. "I remember that story," she said, nodding her head as her brows furrowed. "May I ask you a question, sir?"

"Of course." JP crossed his legs and tilted his head, curious.

"What I don't know," Larissa confessed, twisting her hands together, "I mean...what I can't remember...is that...were Noah and his wife the only two people left? Did they have to start all over like Adam and Elle?"

JP shook his head, a small smile at the corners of his full lips. "No, it was only with the animals and the birds that there were two of each kind. Noah was allowed to bring his family."

Larissa cocked her head. "So how many were there, sir?"

JP smiled beatifically. "Eight."

Larissa beamed at this revelation as if he had shared a secret and bowed to the Commander as she backed through the door, closing it softly as she left. She walked slowly, her head down to hide the blush rising in her cheeks.

The One taught that people were sinful creatures, in mind and body, and had to live pure lives in order to cleanse their filthy souls. Larissa was quite aware of that and knew she would serve the One to purify her soul till the day she died. But she also knew that if it were up to her to repopulate the galaxy, she would want it to be with none other than her devout and dashing young Commander. As she started down the brightly lit corridor, a series of alerts sounded over the open com-system. On any other ship the sounds would have been beeps. On the Chimeran Battle Cruiser *Resurrection*, the sounds were bells.

In the stillness of his cabin, JP blessed the wine and then laced his hands together as he prepared to give thanks for his meal of bread and cheese. He had no sooner closed his eyes and bowed his head before there was another knock at his door.

"Come in!" he called, though he did not raise his head from his prayer.

Larissa came back in, her mouth already open to speak but seeing JP she quickly closed her mouth and eyes and bowed her head as he prayed silently. When she heard his soft Amen, she echoed the word and looked up at him, her dark eyes blazing.

"The transport is on approach!" she exclaimed before he could ask. Seeing the look of pleasure that spread across his face, the look of *rapture* that appeared to be only for her, made her feel that if she were to die at this moment, she would die happy.

JP carefully set the tray aside and stood, smoothing down his cassock. "Let's go meet them. Shall we?"

Larissa bowed, holding the door open for him and then quickly falling in behind as he passed her and walked briskly down the corridor.

Many of the crewmembers were already on their way to the docking bay, also walking briskly. No one ever ran aboard the *Resurrection* unless it was an absolute emergency. The Commander would not allow such unseemly behavior aboard his vessel.

JP strode down the brightly lit corridors of his ship, finding it hard for the first time not to run himself. Decades of planning and fighting and conspiring and more planning and fighting and planning were finally going to show results.

The IGC would no longer be the indisputable strength of the galaxies. The rainbow would belong to the chosen. There would no longer be battles so small and irrelevant to be named "skirmishes" with the condemnation and contempt of the InterGalactic Council. JP himself would ride a Dragon, brandishing a flaming sword like Michael, hewing down those in his path with death and destruction.

Like Moses, he was going to free his people from the yoke of subjugation. Even more, he would bring those that were not his people out from under the cloak of ignorance to walk in the light of The One.

His mind danced with righteous visions as far as his limited imagination would allow. He would grant amnesty to the Catholics. He would end Golgoth slavery.

Still, he couldn't help but seethe, *May the One help any of the de Rossi's if I ever get my hands on them. And I will. The One is always just.*

Besides, that cog was already well oiled and turning.

"Lord, forgive me," he whispered.

Larissa, nearly trotting to keep up with him, heard his words and felt her heart expand in response.

Every crew member, dressed in dark gray coveralls marked with the Chimeran symbol on the sleeve and the with same white round collar at the neck, stood aside and bowed as he walked by. The fresh-faced Commander was deeply respected and revered by all aboard his ship.

JP turned from one corridor into another. Within a minute he had reached the Battle Cruiser's docking bay. The guard, tall and lean and angularly handsome, stood smartly at attention as the Commander neared.

"The transport?" he queried of the guard.

"Inside, sir."

JP beamed. "And the pilots? The Engineer?"

"They were escorted to the med-bay, sir. They had sustained a number of injuries in their escape from the Beryl Dragon. The Engineer was still unconscious."

"May The One bless them for their efforts," JP said earnestly and the guard bowed his head in agreement. "Has the transport been opened?"

The guard shook his head. "No, sir. We thought it best to wait for you."

"Excellent. Has everything been made ready?"

"Yes, sir."

"And Commander Petrov?" he inquired regarding the whereabouts of his Executive Officer.

"On his way from the bridge, sir."

The Commander paused, anxious to open the transport and get the eggs into the chambers that had been specially prepared for them but knowing it would not be proper to do so without his second-in-command by his side.

Patience, he told himself, just as he caught sight of Commander Petrov at the far end of the corridor, striding briskly towards them.

"There he is," JP remarked. "Let's not wait any longer."

The guard bowed again and stood aside for the Commander and the Lady Larissa. Commander Petrov fell in behind the two, not far behind. Once he passed, the guard turned to follow them into the docking bay.

The transport, hijacked from an IGC craft plant a year ago, had entered through the network of pulsing gold veins crisscrossing the gaping mouth of the Battle Cruiser's conveyance bay. The nitrogen membrane kept the molecular air contained and pressurized while allowing aircraft to pass through. The vast bay was a hangar for transport craft, shuttles, and even land vehicles, though those were few.

The Commander and Larissa skirted two land rovers with track wheels more than three meters high. Petrov, tall and lean with white-blonde hair and ice-blue eyes, caught up with them as they rounded a row of six phera crafts lined up next to a company-sized shuttle ship. The hangar guard followed close behind.

As they strode around the back end of the shuttle, the rest of the bay opened up before them to reveal the space had been saved for the craft that was now there. It was a utilitarian transport and anything but aerodynamic. A hulking mass of titanium plates and steel rivets sat on the tarmac of the bay, steam seeping from the bottom like the breath vapor of some square and squat metal beast.

A considerable crowd had gathered. Every soul aboard the Battle Cruiser *Resurrection* that was not on direct duty had found their way to the docking bay and waited as close as they dared to the transport and their excitement was palpable.

JP hurried around its bulk to the back of the craft where, six months ago, his mechanics had scooped out an allowable, if dangerous, amount of field generators and the entire galley to install a special compartment. A large, warm, and wet shock chamber that would safely house unhatched Dragon eggs.

JP beckoned with his hand at the tall guard that had escorted them into the bay. The Chimeran guard moved to the side of the transport, motioning for two junior crewmen to open the bottom hap-latch on the back of the transport,

Moving in unison, the crewmen pulled the bolts along the bottom of the compartment. There was a hiss of air as the seal was broken. JP stood stock still, flanked by Larissa on one side and white-haired Petrov, who stood half a head taller than him, on the other. His lips moved as he murmured a prayer.

Larissa wanted to see what was within but could not pull her eyes from the flushed face of her Commander. He looked like a boy on Christmas morn, nearly bursting with excitement at not only the thought that he was about to get everything he had asked for, but everything that he deserved as well.

Together, the crewmen lifted the door hatch. Though the L-shaped cover was seven meters of thick and riveted steel, it rose easily on the pneumatic hinge, hissing like an angry reptile. Vapor poured from within like fog spilling across a moor.

Larissa's chest heaved as she watched the face of the young Commander, and then her breath hitched uncomfortably as his expression changed, albeit ever so slightly. The transformation was so minute that only someone watching him closely – and someone that knew him well – could decipher the change. And the perilous danger that it implied. Larissa swallowed and held very still, only moving her eyes to see what abomination the transport had brought.

As the vapor cleared the Commander's blue eyes widened as they played across the shock chamber and the soft prayer that he been uttering died on his full lips. Then his eyes sought out the guard that had escorted them into the bay. The guard, like Petrov and Larissa and everyone else present, looked at their Commander with an expression akin to terror.

"Call Medical," JP instructed, his voice barely above a whisper. "See if our guests are being treated there." He turned back to the transport, his bright eyes traversing the compartment as the guard made the call on his comset. A squawking reply came back to over the comset and the guard cleared his throat nervously.

"Sir, they haven't made it there yet."

"Find them."

The guard moved to leave, but not fast enough for the Commander. "Run!" he hissed at the man before turning to everyone present, his hands balled into fists. *"RUN!!!"* he shouted, his fury echoing throughout the bay. *"FIND THEM!!!"*

The crowd broke like water dropped on a hot griddle and everyone but Larissa and Petrov bolted like panic-stricken animals, dashing madly in every direction.

The coverall-clad Chimeran woman, numb with distress, was unable to will her limbs into movement. She stared at the trails of vapor coming from the wet shock chamber with the Commander and the Executive Officer. All of her earlier feelings of dying happy were now gone. They were replaced by the feeling that she might die very soon, and in a very horrible way – without absolution from The One nor from the man she loved.

She could only hope that he would be the one to spill her blood and cleanse her soul. She was confident that he would. Certainly a lot of blood was going to be flowing, and soon.

The compartment was empty.

SEVEN

Sean ran pell-mell down the sidewalk, his blonde hair whipping behind him and the gray messenger bag that held his acrylic bumping wildly against his hip. The bag was made of a heavy canvas and had a line of green holographic alien skulls just above the double seam of black thread.

He came to a skidding halt in front of the metro stop just as the tube was pulling into the cradle of curved concrete. The door slid open silently and Sean found a seat easily since the car was mostly empty and clean to the point of sterility. He was anxious to get home, which was a first for him – and anxious to talk to Grandpa, also another first. He had some questions and he had come to realize that his Grandpa was always the one with the answers, oftentimes the answers that no one else would give him.

Sean shifted his bag over to his other hip and watched the green landscape slide by. It still filled him with wonder.

A shiny new acrylic was tucked neatly inside the new ac-bag and both had accompanied him to his new school. At first, Sean thought that his parents were giving him the high profile items as some sort of peace offering after they had made him move and go to a new school, but later he realized they were saving him the embarrassment of having horribly outdated gear.

Sean had been furious and fought tooth and nail, as Grandpa would say, about the move to the Upper Klick. As far as he was concerned, there was no reason for them to move – no reason at all. Just because his Aunt Jo got some wild hair up her ass about living someplace not good enough for *her*, when she didn't even live with them in the first place, the rest of the family had to up and move.

Sean was at a spot that even he knew was an important stage

in his formative years. He was a teenager for Chrissake! He had worked hard to assimilate into a suitable clique of guys like himself before high school. Being a freshman was going to be hard enough. Going in without any friends was going to be horrific.

Of course Mom and Dad didn't care where they lived – they would still have the same job, maybe at a different location, but they would have all the same friends. Jeanette didn't care because she had nothing but shit between her ears.

But he was a person too, wasn't he? Didn't his feelings matter? Didn't he get a say in how he wanted to live his life? Wouldn't it hopefully be among peers with whom he had found a niche and in a life where he was already envisioning a future?

After three sleepless nights he finally summoned up the courage to say these things to his father. His father was at first understanding, even sympathetic. But as Sean drew out his plea he soon realized that his father was holding back laughter. It finally burst forth in not-so-sympathetic chortles of hilarity.

"I'm sorry," his father apologized, covering his mouth with one hand. "I know how you feel son, I really do, and I don't always like it myself. But we are a family and we have to do..." and here his father giggled, *he actually fucking giggled,* before sucking in a quick breath, "what we have to do," he breathed out. He seemed to regain a bit of control and told his son, "we are a family, and we stick together." His father's control then wavered as he bit down on his bottom lip, trying to stifle some crazy mirth from within. "Perhaps," he offered with raised brows, "you can tell your Aunt Johanna how you feel, the next time you see her." He held it together for a moment longer, then his mirth broke free and he went off into a storm of laughter. He attempted to rein it in and tried to comfort his son but did a poor job at both.

Sean finally dismissed him as crazy. Why not? Half the family was certifiable. And his dad was right. If his *father*, Johanna's *older* brother, didn't have the balls to stand up to his *little* sister – then Sean knew that his own pubescent testes were probably not up to the task either.

He loved his Aunt Jo – she was fun, famous, a total badass and most often brought presents for no reason. But there was something else inside her too, something that Sean was now old enough to see.

Behind that quick smile were eyes that went fathoms deep and held no mercy. Sean had seen her get angry a few times and was once there to see her lose her temper entirely. He wasn't about to piss her off.

Sean felt a bit disgusted at his father, whom he considered castrated by his own sister, and ashamed at himself for not having the guts to stand against her either. For a shockingly long few days he had thought long and hard about the Chimera, and had empathized with them.

This must have been how it was for them, he thought, the realization bright and strangely painful. *Waking up to realize that you are not your own boss. Even less - to have no rights and no say whatsoever in your own life. What to do, say, or even wear. It's like being a teenager – or worse, if that is possible. At least I know that in a few years I will have those rights, as painful as it is to wait. Those poor bastards had no hope.*

Sean's anger was both useless and fruitless. As it all turned out, the move was the best thing that ever happened to him.

For years and years his Aunt Johanna had always simply moved them up a single level or two to keep them in the upper middle klicks. This time, probably tired of having to arrange the moves so often, she moved them all the way to upper suburbia. Simply put, all the way to top.

It was a whole new world, literally, and not just for Sean. The newest klick had been constructed within the last standard solar year and everything on it and in it was brand new. The podments, the parks, the grass – even the atmosphere was new, since the people in upper suburbia got to breathe it first before it was recycled down into the lower levels of Three Mile City.

The buildings that Sean had always lived in before had been huge, growing, crowding complexes holding anywhere from twenty to two hundred podments. The one they were in now held only four, but it was the biggest podment they had ever had and Grandpa was in the same building in one of the smaller units.

But the real shocker for Sean was school. At his old school there were very few people who knew anything about his family and even less that cared. He was a small fish in a big pond and literally disappeared in the crowd. But here it was another story. Here, he was *fucking famous.*

On the first day at his new school Sean painfully endured the first few hours while everyone stared at him - not knowing if it was his clothes, his hair, or what. He sat uncomfortably through his morning classes, trying not to squirm physically like he was mentally. Then at the lunch break he found himself suddenly surrounded by other kids, all asking him questions at the same time.

Was he really Sean Mattatock?

Yes.

Was he really the grandson of Joseph Mattatock, the Fighter Captain from the Amliss Attack, the famous battle that changed the war?

Yes.

Was he really the nephew of Johanna Mattatock, the Jordan of the Red Fledgling called Scarlett?

Yes.

Someone urged him to sit down at a lunch table and there was a great deal of pushing and shoving to get to sit at his table, and even more so to sit next to or even close to him. His blue eyes looked around in disbelief as he ate, mostly food that was given to him, politely declining a great deal of the offerings. Someone gave him a Zip Soda to go with the sandwich had brought. Others gave him Golon pocket candy and a girl with short blonde curls gave him a pair of cookies with the assurance that they were baked with real flour, whatever that was.

More questions poured over him and his head turned back and forth as he tried to answer them all. As lunchtime drew to an end, Sean was suddenly invited to houses, to parties, to clubs. All of the guys wanted to be his friend and all of the girls looked at him with wide, shy eyes.

Sean decided that the next time he saw his Auntie Jo, he was going to rip off her flight boots and kiss her feet.

Still, then and now, he wondered why she always got to call the shots.

He grabbed his ac-bag as the metro car slowed, pulling up to his stop. He jumped out of the momentarily stilled tram, bolted over the white sidewalk, across the grass and through the park. He had some questions and had a pretty good idea where he could find some answers.

When he got to the pod he found that Grandpa already had an audience, since his little sister got out of school a half hour before he did. Heaving a sigh, Sean dropped his bag by the door and his body down on the rug next to Jeanette, listening and waiting.

★

The crest was an ancient emblem in brass and enamel with the Mattatock coat of arms worn so smooth that it was almost beyond recognition. It had been passed down through the family for countless generations and everyone knew that it had traveled all the way from Earth.

Stephen Mattatock had given it to his son James before the family left for Io, one of the first moons of Jupiter that the humans had terraformed and settled. He had handed the crest to his son and told him that when the hammer of war came down again, as it always did, that he was to be a pilot.

"I know our family has always been an Army family," he had told him in voice gravelly with age and nicotine, "but being on the ground is no place to be in a war, take it from me. You take to the air, and teach your kids likewise. Always have a pilot, always have a protector."

Stephen's brother, Shawn might have argued differently. He had fought in the same war as his brother, though on a different continent. He did not witness the horror of the trenches, but he had seen many a pilot shot down. There were antidotes for nerve gas (he himself had carried two epi-pens full of it during the years he served) and a bullet hole, in most places, could be bandaged. But when a jet was shot by a missile, which he had seen plenty of times, there was no antidote for it and no amount of bandages would put a pilot back together, assuming you could find all the little pieces.

But James did as his father told him and for a thousand years the Mattatocks always had at least one fighter pilot, even in times of peace. That person carried the crest and had the honor to be considered the protector of the family.

Somewhere along the line the crest had been restored; re-engraved by a laser and topped with a fresh layer of enamel. A pair of brass wings had been added, one on either side of the coat of arms.

HuCenturieslater, worn smooth once again and restored once again, the crest belonged to Joseph Mattatock. He was an ace at flying, as his father had been and his father before him. No matter what the advice had originally been founded on, the advice from an Army vet that had lost half a leg and two fingers (two fingers from the nicotine cancer and half a leg from a fifty-millimeter hot round) proved to be good. The Mattatock's were natural born pilots. After ten years of service to the IGC as a fighter pilot, Joseph moved on to teach at the Academy.

He had all of his children flying simulators before they were ten and, by the time John was in his teens, all three of his kids were flying fighter craft. Though Johanna had the most natural talent, young Joe Jr. quickly became the best fighter – most likely because his older brother and sister continually ganged up on him.

It was natural to expect that Joey, though he was the youngest, would be the one to take the crest and the guardianship of the Mattatock family.

In 3888, in the Year of the Third Dragon, when the GwenSeven constructs declared autonomy and war, Joe Senior resigned from the academy and reenlisted. Joe Junior was right there with him. His father, already a Senior Lead Captain, made sure they were assigned to the same platoon.

John, Joe's oldest son, finished out the classes he had needed to become a flight instructor and took a job teaching fighter pilots at the IGC academy on Io. He had met a beautiful girl and they were thinking about getting married. Johanna, though she had a natural talent for flying and a penchant for fighting, was off drinking her way through college despite the fact that she already held three degrees.

The following years for Joe Senior and Joe Junior were busy but uneventful. Most of their time was spent training the newer recruits on flight runs but all of the action they ever saw was on simulators.

The Chimera, what the group of rebel dyers called themselves, were horribly disorganized and couldn't seem to figure out how to proceed with the rebellion they had started. The IGC did not even deign to call it a war but simply considered it an uprising of defective mechanicals that needed to be hunted down and terminated.

On the fourth moon turn in 3988, Joseph took his then current team of fighters on a test run past Callisto in response to a distress signal coming from the space freighter, *Amliss*. The run would make history, turn eyes and hearts towards actual war, and set the future of the unified galaxies on its next course.

For Commander Mattatock, the run – which was completely routine and below his pay-grade, would also be his last.

★

Johanna walked down the hallway under the glare of the

fluorescents, her steps brisk and businesslike. She glanced at a holo plaque on the wall to make sure she was going in the right direction but her steps never slowed.

She pushed open a double door and wrinkled her nose at the smell. The antiseptic air was cold and sterile. She hated hospitals. How anyone ever got better in such a place was beyond her.

She moved quickly through a busy area that must have been triage; nurses pushing floating stretchers, people rushing around, doctors being called over intercoms. Checking the holo plaques as she went, her long strides took her past a deserted cafeteria and into an eerily quiet wing of the hospital.

Johanna passed through a single swinging door and stopped. A row of molded plastic chairs with metal legs was bolted against the wall. Grandpa sat in one. Her brother John sat in another next to his wife Rebecca. Her swollen belly sat on her lap like a great round ball under her calico dress and her blue eyes were wide and frightened.

They had all been facing a closed door in a private wing of the hospital and their heads turned as one as she walked in, except for Sean. Sitting quite still and holding his mother's hand, his head was already turned to the swinging door as if he had been expecting her. He looked at Johanna with the same wide blue eyes as his mother. The chubby four year old had the same soft, golden-colored hair as his mother as well, like hay at harvest.

John stood and embraced Johanna, looking every bit her twin though they were ten months apart. Until she felt her brother's arms around her, Johanna had steeled herself against any emotion. Now she could feel the tears threatening and her throat was hot and dry.

She gently pushed him away and looked at the closed door. Behind it, her father was holding onto his life with a tenuous grasp.

"There's an IGC officer in there right now, debriefing him," John said, his voice low. She looked away, unable to meet his dark eyes. She spoke only one word, her voice barely above a whisper.

"Joe?"

John turned his own face away to avoid her dark eyes, even though she was not looking at him. "They have sent a unit to recover his body, what remains of it anyway, if they can. The others as well, along with any debris that can help them figure out what happened."

Johanna felt her throat constrict painfully, cutting off her supply of oxygen. It felt as if she had tried to swallow a ball of hot lead. Her mother had died when she was very young, too young for it to leave her feeling anything but disheartened and confused. Now, for the first time in her life, Johanna wanted to fall to the ground and sob - but now wasn't the time. She looked at the three still seated, every eye watching her and John in bated silence. The tension (and the terror, yes she could feel Rebecca's terror) was like a live presence in the quiet hallway.

Being the oldest, and the last grown male in the family, it was naturally expected for John to take the crest, and the burden of war.

The silence was broken by a monotone page over the hospital com requesting a Dr. Wester to report to the ICU.

Johanna looked at Rebecca, one hand laid protectively over her swollen belly and the other holding Sean's chubby fist. There were tears on her face, but they were tears of fear, not of mourning.

Johanna pushed her brother away and turned towards the closed door. He caught her by the arm and held her tightly.

"Johanna!"

Her face snapped back towards his, the movement quick and sharp, glaring at him though it was not in anger. It was just her nature. He shook his head slowly from side to side, as if it pained him to do so.

"No," he whispered.

"Don't be a fool, John!" she hissed. He winced as if struck. Her dark eyes flicked to his pregnant wife and young son, then she held his dark eyes with her own until he slowly released his grip. She offered him a ghost of a smile. "Besides," she told him, "you always were a shitty pilot."

She turned to her father's room and pushed open the door.

"And I'm telling you it was an ambush!" Joseph Mattatock's voice was strong, even in his weakened state, filling the soundproofed room with its vehemence. "They came streaming from behind that IGC freighter like water breaking around a dam. How was no one aboard the *Amliss* able to see them until it was too late? It was a goddamned turkey shoot! We didn't have a chance!"

Johanna closed the door behind her and the IGC officer, wearing a suit instead of a uniform, turned quickly.

"This is a confidential briefing, young lady," he instructed, his voice sharp.

"Go fuck yourself!" Johanna retorted.

The officer, dark-haired and on the younger side of middle-aged, looked as if he had been slapped.

Probably hasn't heard that in awhile, Johanna thought, unable to keep the smirk off her face. Her father, wrapped in pL membrane bandages seemingly everywhere except for his eyes and bearded chin and obviously in pain, stifled a bemused smirk of his own.

"Forgive my daughter," he said, "she is very...ahem, headstrong."

The young officer glared at her with hazel eyes that were dark and fierce, his lip frozen in what was almost a snarl, unsure as if encountering an unwanted but potentially dangerous animal in his pantry. Johanna leaned towards him menacingly, looking as though she might take a bite out of him.

"Buy him some more time," she told him, "or your time here is done."

After a moment of weighing her words and the look in her eyes, the man's lip came down and he nodded before turning back to the man on the bed. He laid a hand on her father's shoulder, his thumb resting along a bare strip of skin between the layers of pL membrane cloth and the man's graying beard.

"Thank you Joe," he said, nodding at the injured man and giving his shoulder a squeeze. "You've done the IGC a great service."

Joe winced, his face a tight grimace of pain, but managed to give the man a nod. The young officer straightened and turned to leave but Johanna caught his arm in a forceful grip and he looked at her in angry surprise.

"Hasn't he been given anything for the pain?" Johanna demanded in disbelief.

The man relaxed slightly, dislodging his elbow from her tight grip. "He refused it. He said he wanted to be lucid." He gave her final glare and left the room.

As the door swung closed behind him she turned back to her father, scowling in apparent displeasure.

"Don't be mad, Johanna," he said, trying to soothe her anger. "I had to be able to talk to him. And to you."

Her countenance softened as she pulled up the chair next to her father's bed and sat in it. She reached out and grasped his hand. He squeezed her hand but she could already feel the strength draining from it.

"You knew it would be me?" she asked, a smile poking at the corner of her mouth and the tears hot behind her eyes.

"Of course I did."

Johanna felt her heart swell with pride and loss.

"You know what you are taking on?" he asked.

She nodded, fighting tears and the damned hot lump in her throat. "I do. I'll take care of our family."

"And don't just be some damn grunt!"

Johanna smiled and the tears spilled down her cheeks. She wiped them away with the back of her hand. "I'll be the best, Dad. I promise."

Her father turned away and she thought he was finally going to request something for the pain but instead of picking up the remote for the nurse, his hand groped about the top of the bedside table. She heard a soft clunk as his hand landed on the item he was looking for and then a scrape as his fingers closed around it. With obvious effort he turned back to his daughter and pressed it into her hand.

"Give it your all," he told her, "or give it up."

They were his last words.

His life vanished so abruptly that it took a moment for Johanna to realize that he was gone. The shock settled over her like a shroud as she waited for another sound, another word, one last piece of advice or love. There was no hitching of the breath, no last gasp, no squeeze of her hand as he searched for the right last words to say. There was nothing left but the hum and tick of the hospital equipment. The last of everything had already come and gone.

Stunned, she reached over and closed the glassy, dark eyes that looked as shocked as she felt. She kissed his cheek and held tight to his bandaged form.

"I will, Dad. I promise."

Again, she wanted to fall down and sob, but again now wasn't the time. As it turned out, there was never the time.

She stood up on legs that were shaking and left the room. As the door opened into the hallway the four that were seated there rose as one.

Johanna's numb gaze traveled across what was left of her family. "He's gone," she told them, trying to fill her voice with strength rather than disbelief. John's eyes went wide with shock.

"But the doctors said..." he started, protesting vehemently, but Johanna stopped him with a shake of her head. He spoke again, this time softer, almost pleading. "They said the damage he suffered was grievous, but not likely mortal."

Johanna shook her head again, slowly this time, apologetically. Her brother's shoulders sagged and a strange gurgle came from his throat. Rebecca's hand was holding his and he raised it to his lips before letting it go. He gave Johanna's arm a fierce squeeze as he passed by her and into the room to see his father.

Rebecca sat back down and pulled Sean onto what was left of her lap. Sean edged around the roundness of her belly so he could lay his head on her shoulder.

Grandpa took Johanna by the hand and led her to a chair.

"Tell me everything," he said, lowering himself into the seat next to hers.

Johanna swallowed hard and recounted everything that had happened.

Despite a less than spotless memory, Grandpa told it word for word, except for a few expletives he thought unnecessary, to the children.

*

"That explains it," Sean said from his spot on the rug, his palms splayed on the floor behind his hips and leaning back to let his weight rest on them.

"Explains what?" Jeanette asked, her dark ringlets swaying around her tiny, heart-shaped face.

"Why she's the boss."

"She's not the boss," a stern voice said from behind them. Sean and Jeanette turned to see their father closing the door to Grandpa's podment, a good-natured smile on his face, a green sack of groceries tucked into one elbow.

Grandpa smiled, showing a row of uneven teeth, some of them broken and a few of them missing. His blue eyes were a bit watery but extremely proud.

"Then how come she moves us around and always tells us where to live?"

His father arched an eyebrow at him. "Are you complaining?"

Sean averted his blue-eyed gaze, fixing it on Grandpa's door as he shook his head, looking sheepish. "No."

John Mattatock crossed through the podment with a knowing smile and put the sack on the table in Grandpa's kitchen. "We move around because it is safer for us, having a high profile IGC officer in the family. We respect your Aunt's wishes because we respect what she does."

"Because she serves as the protector of our family?" Jeanette asked.

"That's right," her father agreed, looking back into the living room with a grin for his daughter before fixing a stern eye on Sean. "But that doesn't mean we kowtow to her. She had been pushing your mother and I for years to move to the upper burbs, it was just this time that we finally relented."

Sean gaped at his father. "*She* wanted us to live here this whole time? And *you* didn't?" He couldn't believe it. His father pulled plastic bottles full of milk and juice from the sack and put them in Grandpa's fridge.

"Your mother and I didn't want you kids raised in high suburbia."

"Did you get me some of those rolls I like?" Grandpa called out.

"Croissants? Yes," John called back.

"What about the cream filled doohickeys?"

"Nope. 'Becca says you're on going on a sugar restriction unless you agree to get your teeth fixed."

Grandpa frowned and pouted like a scolded child but Sean was still in shock about their past living conditions – they had been fine, yes, but nothing compared to what they had now. He stared at his father as he walked back into the living room to join Grandpa and the children, holding a cold aluminum can of Aleket in his hand.

"Why?" Sean asked. "Why wouldn't you want to live here?"

"Your mother and I didn't want you to be spoiled," he said, dropping down onto Grandpa's sofa. The couch was short and mushy and covered with a pilled pinstriped dark green cloth. "Think about it, son," he said, popping open the Aleket and taking a long drink. "Do you think you would appreciate all this if it was all you had ever known?"

Sean took a moment to consider this and knew immediately and begrudgingly that his father was right. Things that all his new friends took for granted constantly amazed him. He was always so thrilled by everything going on, while everyone else never seemed satisfied and always wanted more. He often found himself making an effort not to gawk like a country bumpkin at things they found old and boring.

"What about Mom?" Sean asked. "She's so..." John Mattatock

smiled and took a swig of his ale as he watched his son search for the right words. "...so, set in her ways," he finished lamely. "I can't believe she'd let someone else tell her what to do."

John looked at Grandpa but the old man's smirk told him he was alone on this one, especially if he had not brought him his éclairs.

"You're right on that account, son," John agreed. "Your mother is as headstrong as your aunt, and normally she would never let anyone tell her where she was going to live and where her children were going to go to school." Jeanette swung her legs around and sat up so she could listen better. John frowned, not sure if his words were right for her ears, then decided that she should know too, as young as she might be. "But every time the secure com line in the pod rings, or every time there is a knock at the door, your mother doesn't have to worry that it is an IGC officer telling her that her husband won't be coming home. That means a lot to your mother, and to me."

A heavy silence fell as the children absorbed the enormity of his words. After a moment Sean finally broke the stillness, though his voice was unnaturally low and quiet.

"Are you ever worried that you will get that call, or that knock, for Auntie Jo?" he asked. His father snorted and took another drink of his ale.

"No. She's too smart to get killed and too mean to die. I feel sorry for anyone who tries to take her on." He shook his head and grinned into the aluminum can as he upended it into his mouth.

Grandpa had a good cackle at that one, throwing his head back as he laughed. He obviously agreed.

"Are you having dinner with us tonight?" John asked.

Grandpa looked thoughtful for a moment, his mouth puckering in and then out. "I'll be fine. I still have some of that stroganoff that Rebecca made. I want to finish it off before it goes bad."

"Alright." John hefted himself off the sofa and went to the kitchen and placed the empty Aleket can into a round hole in a cabinet where it was promptly sucked away to be recycled. "Come on kids," he called. Jeanette and Sean gathered their things and followed him to the door.

Sean gave Grandpa a wistful look over his shoulder as he walked out and saw the old man wink at him. His questions would have to wait, but at least he was sure that Grandpa had the answers. And he had a funny feeling that Grandpa was waiting for Sean to ask those questions.

FROM
THE DREAM JOURNAL OF HOPE

I dreamt that I was barefoot. I was walking through grass that was wet and came up to my ankles, scratching and wetting them. I was not in a field but in a yard that abutted a parking lot topped in asphalt and beyond were plain concrete buildings with outdoor metal staircases and small windows that meant it could only be a hotel. Or motel. I never know which is which – something about outside doors.

My footsteps took me towards a group of people, people that I knew but could not place – from the lab maybe, or maybe just ghosts of my past. Or future. As I neared, the group broke up and walked away. Leaving only you.

You wore worker pants of heavy blue denim and a plain white t-shirt. It was the first time I had seen you in anything other than a lab coat, either over a suit or your civilians, and I was surprised.

In one hand you held a long kitchen utensil and I realized that you were cooking something on a round grill over an open flame. In your other hand you held a round aluminum can of bright blue.

As I approached I could smell the sharp and inviting aroma of cooking meat and I could hear it sizzle with each lick of the dancing flames. You turned and peered at me – your blue eyes curious and hawk-sharp as always. Your narrow face was stubbled with beard, also a first.

"Is that soda?" A voice queried and I recognized it as my own.

"Yes," you said, offering me the bright can. "I brought it back from New Tokyo on my last visit to Indasia."

I took the proffered can and raised it to my lips, tilting it so that the deluge of dark and bubbling fluid ran into my mouth. It was sweet, so sweet, and filled my insides with its jubilance. Slightly breathless, tasting your syrup upon my lips, I handed the can back to you, our fingers brushing.

"Thank you," I said.

"There are more in my room if you would like one."

My heart warmed at the thought of you wanting to share with me. "Really?" I asked. "Are you sure?"

"Sure," you said as you turned back to tend the grill, flipping

over pieces of meat. "The key is in my pocket."

Eager and without thinking I stepped up behind you and reached around in search of the key. Belatedly I realized our proximity. I could feel my breasts pushed flat against your back and I became acutely aware of my hips pressed against you as my fingers traveled over your hip to find your pocket.

Worse, I could feel the same acute awareness in your body in the way it had gone taut against mine.

My hand missed your pocket and traveled down over the denim-encased muscle of your thigh. Realizing my mistake, my wayward fingers hastily made their way up again, slipped into your pocket and closed over the flat card that was your room key when you dropped the utensil you had been holding...

why is he cooking with his right hand? I thought furtively

...and dropped your arm until your hand closed over my wrist, holding my fingers against your thigh.

Unable to pull away and unable to stop myself, I pressed my body against yours, my forehead between your shoulder blades as I tried to control my racing heart and uneven breath.

"W...wh...what room is it?" I asked, stumbling over my words as I searched for something to say.

My stuttering seemed to break the spell and I was able to turn away, taking the key with me, but you turned as well, more smooth than quick, and caught me, snaking an arm around my waist and holding me tight.

"Seven or eight?" I asked and your grip on me tightened.

I could feel your breath on my neck and the stubble of your beard grazed the back of my cheek. "It doesn't matter," you whispered in my ear. "They are connected."

Knowing I was snared, surrendering to it, I held my body close against yours as I turned, tilting my face up to kiss you, my mouth eager for yours as the dream dissolved around me like pearlescent wind and melting ice.

8

The horse ran easily, its sleek body cutting through the westerly breeze. It cut into the earth as it ran, its hooves tearing up the ground as its body cut through the air and tore across the horizon. Clods of grass churned from the damp earth were spat from its hooves as it ripped through the countryside with its rider bent low, clinging to its smooth, muscled neck.

The horse was a ruddy chestnut mare with a rust colored mane and tail, fetlocks splashed with white that matched the white stripe on her nose. The rider, her body taut with excitement, clung to the mare's neck and urged her on.

Faster, the rider thought. *Stronger. You are strong. Don't be afraid.*

As if hearing the thoughts of the rider, the horse responded in near exultation. Legs stretched and reached and muscles rippled. The wind became a roar and then a battle cry in their ears as they flew across the landscape, hooves hardly seeming to touch the ground in their self-made race.

The horse and rider made a single silhouette against green rolling hills and distant blue mountains. The silhouette crossed a meadow with long stretching strides, jumped a thin creek, and approached a narrow road at a parallel run, breaking from the solitude of the country to join those headed for the town.

The rider pulled up before they took the road, slowing the mare in an effort not to scatter the thin steam of travelers on the dusty lane. Hooves now dug deep, cutting the wild run down to a wild prance as the pair took to the road with the others, the chestnut horse dancing politely into their midst.

There were a few others on horses or mules, and a few on carts being pulled by beasts of burden, but most were on foot. They smiled and nodded at the rider and a few touched the brims of their hats in greeting. All gave her a wide berth.

Scarlett smiled back, the wind whipping her dark hair away from her face. Both her hair and face had regained their normal health and luster, though she still wore an outfit of ill-fitting country garb that she could have very well done without.

Oddly enough, of all the things she had to bear with her current living conditions and so called "healing," the clothes were the worst. Her bedraggled wardrobe of second-hand clothes had been a source of consternation and the ultimate degradation as far as Scarlett was concerned.

She had sat with Elaeric countless times through a countless number of meditations as he insisted on teaching her how to breathe, though she insisted that she already knew quite well how to breathe. She did most of her chores without a fight. Well, at least without too much of a fight.

She squared off every morning against the monstrous hen with the glaring, inky black eyes for her stupid egg. The back of Scarlett's left hand was now covered with scabby divots, some almost completely healed, some fresh. Not a day went by that the fat feathered bitch didn't get a piece of her.

She absolutely refused to milk anything. A furtive grope under the poultry was one thing. Squeezing teats was quite another.

Master Elaeric had the utmost patience. He had borne all of her ravings and tantrums with a calm that Scarlett found maddening at times. In the universe she had been accustomed to over the course of her previous life, the angrier she got the faster people moved. But her anger here was wasted on Elaeric -worse; it seemed a source of intrigue for him.

On the times that Scarlett did get angry, she could feel the pressure within her building and building, so much so that in the past it had often triggered a bloody nose for her trouble. Now she was suddenly confronted with someone who, instead of scurrying away with a fear for his life to do her bidding as he sensed the building pressure and therefore impending doom, would instead lean towards her with an anticipatory sort of glee, like a child awaiting a fireworks show.

Scarlett figured that analogy was probably more close to the truth each time and, when her tantrums failed to produce results, she finally gave them up, feeling ridiculous.

One victory she felt she had scored in her favor was with the acquisition of the pants and boots she now wore. Granted, Elaeric relented more because he knew her cotton pants would be worn through within a week of serious riding and clogs would just fall right off her feet.

To her credit, she had made great strides over the past eight weeks. She had learned to breathe and, in turn, she had taught the mare to breathe. Something she would have found both impossible and absurd in her former life.

Elaeric never ceased to amaze her with ideas and ideology that she had found downright kooky in the past.

One morning, after their breakfast and meditation, as they were hoeing weeds from between the rows of green beans in the garden, something occurred to her.

"So how did *you* end up here?" she asked, taking small chops at the earth with her hoe, churning out the weeds.

"Do you think for some reason that I am not here by choice?"

Scarlett could hear the smile in his voice.

"I don't see any other monks around here."

"You don't see any now," he told her.

"I see you."

"No more monk," he said, indicating himself.

Scarlett shook her head and her dark curls swung about her face as she drove her hoe into the dark earth. "You were a ZA," she said, her tone mildly surprised. It was more of a revelation than a question.

"Always initials, abbreviations and acronyms," Elaeric tsked. "Is that a young thing or a military thing?" he asked but when her only answer was a grin, he continued. "A member of the Zen Anarchy you ask? Yes."

Scarlett finished churning the weeds out of one row and started on the next. "There was a big hubbub about your group and your fields, right about the time the Rebellion started," she remarked, trying to recall the history she knew. It wasn't much. The IGC taught her a lot, but she could always see that everything was slanted in favor of their point of view and, as far as she was concerned, everything before the Amliss Attack had always seemed inconsequential.

"Hubbub?"

"The fields you were working on, were they the type of field you asked me about on my first day? The kind that surrounds things?"

"Yes and no, but I think you have different ideas. I think you are asking about auras, no?"

"I guess. Do you really see them?"

Elaeric paused his work and looked at her quizzically. "How much do you already know of auras?" he inquired.

Scarlett straightened and shrugged. "I know of them."

Elaeric waved a dismissive hand. "Which is to say, you know nothing." He motioned to the cherry and plum trees that bordered the vegetable garden and made his way towards the shade under their spreading branches.

Set aside for them upon the dark earth was a wooden pitcher of ice and water with thin slices of lime, sweating with condensation. Next to the pitcher were two small wooden cups. Scarlett filled them both and offered the first to Elaeric. He accepted it with a grateful bow of his head as he gathered his mustard-colored robes about his sparse frame and seated himself amongst the roots of the trees.

Elaeric smiled and spoke earnestly. "Everything in the universe, down to each atom and each *part* of an atom, is a vibration," he told her.

Scarlett nodded. "I'm with you."

"Each person - each plant, each rock – has its own unique vibration that causes an electromagnetic field, as well as a photonic field. These fields that surround objects and people and animals are their auras."

"Yeah, but how do you see them?"

Elaeric chortled softly and drained his cup. "How do you fly a jet? " he asked, holding the empty vessel out to Scarlett. "You learn!" he exclaimed. "You practice!" She filled the wooden cup with a smirk at the edge of her mouth and he nodded, his face pinched and earnest. "But more than learning to see, you must learn to *understand* what you see." He looked at the Jordan. "Do you know of the chakras?"

Scarlett shook her head. "Heard of them," she admitted before tipping her head from side to side. "Which means I know nothing of them, I know."

Elaeric nodded as if he were encouraged by this admission. "The chakras are the *dana*, the *wheels*," he paused as his mind searched for the right word then suddenly his face lit up. "The *gates* to the auras," he finished.

Scarlett refilled her own cup. The day was getting warm and, although there were no maldrove trees in their proximity, the air was getting dry. "Go on," she urged, feeling the sweat trickle down the back of her neck.

"There are seven main chakras along the center line of the body," Elaeric told her, drawing himself up and motioning with his hand, "from the base of the spine to the top of the head. They embody the spiritual energy on the physical plane."

Scarlett smirked at him and shook her dark head. "It sounds like you're trying to mix science with religion."

Elaeric shrugged. "For some there is no difference between the two. But everything has its own aura, its own spiritual signature. Take yours, for instance."

Scarlett arched a brow at the once-monk. "Red?"

"Yes, red," he said smiling. "It means you are strong-willed, passionate, competitive and sexual. You are driven to survive, and quick to anger."

"No shit," Scarlett remarked with dry sarcasm. "Try something not so obvious." In her mind's eye she could see Jade and her lip trembled at the thought of the fallen Jordan. "Tell me about the green chakra," she urged, but as the words left her mouth the Red Jordan could feel her throat tighten.

Elaeric nodded sagely. "The heart chakra," he said, tapping his own chest. "The person whose aura is green is ruled by love, strives for balance, and is self-sacrificing."

"That's enough," Scarlett whispered hoarsely, looking away, her voice already thick with emotion. Elaeric's words shot into her heart like fire-hardened barbs, they were so accurate in the description of the lost Jordan. Jade had been all those things and more. And, just like Joey and her Father, he was lost to her. Mustering control, she brought her focus to her breath, to the air around her body, and drained her cup. "Let's finish with the weeds before it gets any warmer," she suggested, standing up and brushing the dirt from the seat of her cotton pants.

Elaeric stood and placed a hand on her shoulder. "You are learning to see," he confided. Scarlett gave him half a smile and a short nod. She was indeed learning to see. It didn't mean she liked what she saw.

Even more, she was learning control.

For her efforts and achievements she was rewarded with a pair of badly used (and horribly short) suede riding pants and a pair of heavy boots with rundown heels. They were old and hard and scuffed all to hell, but at least they hid the bottoms of her too-short pants.

The mare whickered, bringing Scarlett's attention back to the road. She guided the mare around the carts and the travelers on foot, towards the medieval stone and timber structures that comprised Village East.

Today was market day and the high, stone walls of the small city-town were surrounded by rows of tents and stalls, their garish silk tops and banners snapping in the breeze.

Scarlett rode the mare between the rows of country and village folk selling their wares and produce and then through the open east gate in the stone and mortar curtain-wall that surrounded the town. The wall, Scarlett had learned, was just for show. Kayos had never been threatened and, if an enemy were to arrive at the city gates, it would most likely have the technology to blast the whole medieval fabrication to ash.

The town proper was a labyrinth of shops and homes, inns and bakeries. They surrounded a group of buildings and rounded towers that made up the local seat of government. There were ancillary buildings for IGC officials as well as for two other races in the united galaxies that were not actual members of the InterGalactic Council.

The sprawling city-town was divided into eastern and western sectors that were nearly identical in appearance though it was obvious to the Jordan that the west side was more advanced and technically developed.

"They are *not* more technically developed," Elaeric had corrected on their first trip to Village West. "The East just prefers to live a lifestyle that is more honest and simple. Do you think I eat with chopsticks because I do not know of the fork?" He waved a hand at the foolishness of the notion. "Some people simply choose to embrace what others do not, and most seem to find it more comfortable to keep them separate."

Scarlett had simply watched with longing as they rode by a wattle and daub building that was a holo café on the inside.

"If they want the technology, then why do they live here in this, this..." now it was her turn to wave her hand in a motion of distaste and befuddlement.

Elaeric had laughed gently. "Because they like the life here, they like the clean simplicity of it all. However, there are some things that people prefer not to live without in this day and age."

Scarlett, nodded, beginning to understand. She knew that Elaeric had an acrylic, and remembered the first night she had awoken to see his face illuminated by it. She had seen it one more time since then, though he was careful to keep it tucked away from prying eyes. He had electricity and running water (thank God) but, like the others that inhabited everything east of Kayos, preferred to live off the land.

In addition to holo cafés, apothecaries, and tech bars carefully disguised to look like medieval taverns and smithies, Village West had a rickety wooden train station with electromagnetic tracks that was the terminal for a monorail that ran west to the nearest spaceport.

From a bird's eye view it was as if Village West was stretching into the future while Village East reached out for the past.

Scarlett made her way to a stable on the outskirts of the town and reined the mare in, bringing her to a prancing halt. She threw a leg over the neck of her courser and slid from the saddle with fluid grace.

She gave the mare's shoulder a vigorous rub and was repaid with a good-natured shove from the animal's nose. Thick, velvety lips searched out Scarlett's own neck and playfully nibbled at her hair. Scarlett laughed and shoved back at the horse. The horse stepped sideways and threw the human's own body off balance and whickered a chuckle of her own.

A young boy with a dirty face and a mop of equally dirty blonde hair came trotting out of the stable to take the horse. Scarlett fished a small coin out of a leather purse tied to her belt.

"Rub her down," she told the boy, handing him the coin. "Make sure she has fresh hay, and a bag of oats, too." The boy grinned, his head bobbing up and down as he led the horse away.

Scarlett watched them go, grinning as well.

It felt strange to be paying with metal coins after nearly a lifetime simply using a credentials card. Stranger still, Scarlett never would have thought, not in a million years, that she would be wearing riding leathers and cotton blouses instead of flight gear.

Shaking her head in amusement, Scarlett pulled a wide scarf from her belt and tied the ends together. She slipped her right arm through the circle she had made and let it hang from her shoulder like an empty sling.

Scarlett walked through the cobbled village streets and left the outer wall on the edge of town to the stalls and tents that had been set up along its perimeter. She walked slowly, smiling at the people and inquiring about their wares, touching goblets and shields and other objects for sale or barter.

Weeks ago, Scarlett had despised Village East and the people there. They represented everything that disgusted her to the point of madness. They were slow, backwards, and generally simple and jovial – all things she hated. But as she began to meditate, nearly by force, she learned to breathe. She learned tolerance. She slowly, very slowly, began to acquire patience.

It wasn't long before the townsfolk became tolerable, then acceptable. Soon after that she found them amusing. There were even some that she had even begun to look forward to seeing on her bi-weekly trips to town; the stable boy with hay-colored hair and Rene, the baker at her favorite café. Her newfound outlook on the life around her had changed the way she looked at people, herself included.

And the farmer's market just outside Village East did have excellent produce, which was what she was after on most occasions. It did not take her long to find the stall that sold the best fruits and vegetables and Scarlett took an instant liking to the man that worked there, Arwa.

It turned out that Elaeric was quite the cook, if he had the right ingredients. Scarlett had never eaten so much organic food in her life, food that had actually once been living, and never had she thought she would enjoy it so much.

For as long as she could remember, food had simply been fuel. She put it in her body to keep it going. She didn't care if it was simulated carrots or grown coffee – it went in, it came out, it did the job.

Now, food had become a culinary discovery. Scarlett knew that Elaeric's cooking was simple but well balanced. A piece of fish, onions cooked in butter, greens with a splash of vinegar. But in every bite she could taste the white rush of the river, the earthy taste of the soil, the heavy sunlight that had infused everything that she put within her body that nourished her every last cell.

Village West, which cleverly cloaked the life she had loved so much, was full of sim-meats and carbohydrate substrates. She had gone there with Elaeric once to buy a memory pin, and had looked longingly at the sim-strate cafés. Now, the thought of them made her nauseous.

Scarlett wove through the wandering country folk, they nodding and smiling in apology if they bumped into her - as they invariably did – and her nodding and smiling in response. Scarlett felt a jolt of pride knowing that she had come a long way from her former self, but she harbored no illusions about how far she still had to go.

Eventually she found the stall that she was looking for; under slim poles of stripped birch that held up a roof of blue silk with white stripes, were slanted tables laden with root and vine vegetables. The vendor was a whip of a man with deeply tanned skin and dark, flashing eyes.

Scarlett had quickly learned where to find the best produce via word of mouth along with trial and error, but probably would have bought from Arwa had his vegetables been simply mediocre.

She waited patiently as a woman argued over the price of the tomatoes.

The woman was covered in dun-colored robes, including a wide scarf over her head in the same color. The only parts of her that were visible were her scrawny hands and pinched face. Her thin lips had a rainbow's arc but not its joy. It was a sour mouth, one resigned to eat the lemon rinds of life and spit out its bitter seeds.

"These tomatoes are too expensive," the woman complained. "They get more expensive every week!"

To Scarlett, the man behind the table looked more like a horse trader than a farmer. He wore long white linen robes and had a narrow face with a black slip of a mustache and pointed goatee. His black curls were cropped short and his black eyes held a mischievous glint. He saw Scarlett and winked.

"Madam," he offered the woman apologetically, spreading his hands. "The tomatoes are the same price every week. They are only a cetno more than farmer Whey's, and they are twice as big!"

The woman must have known this - Scarlett saw her there twice every week and, no matter what time Scarlett arrived, the woman was always there right before her. The babushka continued to haggle nonetheless.

"But I want to buy tea this week," she argued. "If I pay that much just for tomatoes I will have none left for tea!"

"But Madam," the trader offered, nearly pleading, "if I give you the price you are asking, I will have to give the same price to everyone. I will go broke!"

The woman snorted. "Extortionist!" she shouted, waving a skeletal arm cloaked in loose skin. "You will never go broke – you make more than anyone here!"

The argument wore on. Scarlett smiled and looked away,

breathing slowly. Mindful, she took calming breaths, letting everything unfold around her. She took a deep breath through her nose, taking in the smells of the market.

Scarlett was amazed at the way her senses were responding to her meditations, to her awareness of the world around her. She could hear the woman argue with Arwa without listening to their words. Her brain registered "sound" and let the words blow around her like dandelion spores being carried on a breeze.

Noting the sound, she let her focus drift to the air entering her nostrils.

In one breath she could smell the earthy bouquet of the vegetables, and the bodies of the people around her. She picked up the heady aroma of the spice vendor only a few stalls away and something else...something else that she couldn't quite identify but that quickly sent a tremor up one side of her body.

Scarlett closed her eyes, the corner of her mouth twitching up into a smile of curiosity. There was the metallic tang of blood and fish in the air, but the butcher stalls and fishmongers were much farther away - up around the curve of produce stalls and almost all the way at the northern end of the village.

She turned her face in the other direction. The scent she was picking up was more of a fragrance, warm and sensual. And familiar. She opened her eyes, startled. She looked around, gathering her bearings, and smiled at the argument still going on in front of a table heavy with gourds.

Scarlett leaned towards the arguing babushka, noting the tingle on her right side that ran from her hip all the way up to her underarm, but not dwelling on it. "His tomatoes are the best," she assured her. "And worth every cetno."

The woman drew away from her as if she had said something dirty, scowling at Scarlett and then glaring at Arwa, as if she suspected they were in cahoots somehow. Finally, with a sigh like she was being forced to shovel someone else's dung pile, she handed Arwa two coins and took her tomatoes, eyeing him and Scarlett with open suspicion.

As soon as she had trundled on her way, Arwa clapped his hands and held out his arms as if to embrace Scarlett over the table of pumpkin and squash.

"My darling Scarlett!" he boomed, flashing her a smile of large teeth so white that they stood out in brilliant contrast to his brown skin. "You have rescued me! How can I ever repay you?"

Scarlett flashed him a brilliant smile of her own. "You can sell me your tomatoes at half price," she suggested, or maybe your turnips." Arwa clasped his hands over his heart as if he had been shot.

"But Scarlett," he argued, like he had with the woman before, "if I sell to you at only half the price, I will have to give the same price to everyone. I will go broke!"

Scarlett laughed and selected a few of the small, round blue pears that she knew Elaeric liked and placed them in her scarf-bag.

"I thought, maybe..." Arwa continued, "that perhaps you would let me take you to dinner tonight?"

Scarlett shook her head, smiling. "And miss a meal cooked with your produce? Not a chance." She added a purple onion to her bag.

"A drink then!" he coaxed, grinning. "We can talk produce, if you like. You know, I am a very good judge at knowing when fruits are ripe."

Scarlett laughed again, knowing all too well what he was talking about. "I don't think so, Arwa."

"But you are missing out on produce you have never tried before! I promise, you will not be disappointed!"

"I'm sure I wouldn't be," Scarlett professed, selecting three large tomatoes. She dug a large brass coin from her purse and handed it to Arwa. He took it, his shoulders slumping in exaggerated defeat before he brightened again.

"A gift then!" he declared, selecting an item from the table laden with squash. "Something to take my place tonight, eh?" He gave Scarlett a lecherous smile along with an obscenely large red zucchini.

She laughed and snatched it from his hand. "Shame on you!" she scolded, shaking the zucchini at him. "But thank you." She tucked away the produce and flashed him a smile before she sauntered away, leaving Arwa sighing after her.

Scarlett shook her head and wandered a while longer through the market stalls, admiring cut stone jewelry and longingly running her hand over bolts of silk. On her way back to the stable she stopped to purchase a jar of salt from the Corsan Sea and again felt herself become awash with feeling, a warm tugging that pulled at her skin, brought on by that certain smell.

She closed her eyes, sure that it was something in the stall.

She could smell the freshly ground Grevin pepper most distinctly. Its hot, heavy smell filled her nose and tickled the flesh of her nostrils, making her want to sneeze.

Her nose also detected dozens of other smells that came from the rows and rows of spice jars - some delicate and others quite pungent and biting. Spices from every reach of the planet and a few from beyond - more than she could identify.

No, the smell wasn't coming from the spices. It was outside somewhere, and it was calling to her. Scarlett opened her eyes and shook her head, thanking the Spice Grevin before heading back toward the town wall.

The sun had reached its zenith and her stomach was starting to rumble. She found herself a seat on the slate patio of her favorite outdoor café and ordered a brioche and a cup of coffee.

Though Master Elaeric was a master in the kitchen, he was no baker. The only bread they ate was from an occasional loaf gotten in town or from a neighbor. It meant a little fresh bread with dinner and a day or two of morning toast. It sometimes left Scarlett craving carbohydrates.

And meat. The only meat Elaeric cooked was cured pork or a small fish. Ham or bacon with breakfast, and the rest was just tiny bits mixed into a load of cooked vegetables or soup. He used it more as a flavoring device than a meal. Scarlett hadn't had red meat since before she had ended up in Elaeric's cottage.

She had wondered, aloud to Elaeric a few times, if her blood was going to be iron deficient. He assured her that she was getting everything she needed. Because she felt fine, better and healthier than she probably ever had been, she didn't argue about it too much.

The waiter brought her brioche and coffee, along with cream and a lump of sugar. Scarlett thanked him and dropped the sugar into her coffee and stirred in the cream.

At least there's coffee, she thought, happily. *Thank Jesus there is always coffee.*

Scarlett was pretty sure that had she been without coffee the whole deal with Elaeric might have been off and she quite possibly would have opted to be institutionalized. She knew that even mental patients were given coffee if it wasn't medically dangerous.

She sipped at the hot liquid and watched the people around her. The entire place was an anachronism, and the people that once disgusted her were now a fascination.

The planet, which wasn't a planet at all but instead a fabricated moon that had been created by the elves and then terraformed by the humans, was created for people who wanted to live in a simpler time. A time long before computers and robots and living ships that traveled between the stars.

A place where things were made of wood and stone, and people grew their own food or sold hand-made goods in exchange. They traveled by foot – their own or those of the hooved variety. Most had running water and many had electricity; Elaeric had electricity in the cottage but only used it for lights and a small refrigerator as far as Scarlett knew. He cooked on a woodstove. She knew of no one that had any sort of climate control or machines to wash dishes or clothes.

For Scarlett, the corker was that it was not cheap to pack up and move to another planet and set up a new life. It was extremely expensive and only those that were quite wealthy could afford this simple lifestyle.

At first it had confounded the Jordan that anyone with a good deal of money would want to live as though they had very little, but after a time being among them, like she was now, she could understand.

There was a strange absence of anxiety. None that she could see in anyone she met. No stress, no pressure, no strain. People were not angry with a slow computer, or a virus, or a connection speed. They weren't frustrated because they couldn't get a satellite signal for their acrylic.

There was no shortage of the latest fashion, because there was no fashion at all. No one feared poverty or lack, though most had spent most of their money to get the new life they now had. No one competed for jobs or any sort of social status. So many of the disappointing and thwarting annoyances of life had been removed from the equation and were no longer an issue, much less a problem.

If something broke it was mended, usually with the cheerful help of a neighbor. If a beloved friend, or father, or even a family pet passed away – they were mourned and let go. There was no legal suit to find cause or blame, no revenge to be extracted.

The weather was planned, the economy rudimentary and stable. What was there to worry about? Even if the majority of the citizens of Kayos and the rest of the moon had spent their savings to get there, they most likely still had the money or the means to leave it if they so chose.

Though there were some, quite a few in fact, that had a much harder time letting go of the past – or the future, depending on one's point of view – and felt the need that some technologies were just too hard to live without.

They reminded Scarlett of vegetarians who ate fish and, sometimes, chicken. Especially if it was simulated and not organic because then, hey – who were they hurting?

The west side of Kayos housed those that felt that electricity was a necessity, holographic vision and video a must, and getting rave drunk in a techdicso that looked like a medieval tavern a weekly treat.

Those on the east would laugh and shake their heads at the westerners, not understanding how they could come so far and yet still be so tethered to a different life.

"They are children," Elaeric had told her when she asked about the westerners.

"Do you mean that literally or figuratively?" Scarlett asked. She had noticed that the demographics of the west constituted a much younger crowd. Some that were new to the world had the hardest time letting go of their luxuries, along with children of the easterners who snuck or fled to the other side simply to have a good time.

"Both," Elaeric told her. "It takes wisdom, and that usually means a lot of time, to learn that you can live more with less."

"But you have an acrylic, don't you?"

The monk's narrow shoulders rose up high, an exaggerated shrug under his yellow silk robe. "I am not a hermit!" he had exclaimed.

Scarlett took a long drink from her steaming cup and fished a coin from the small leather bag tied to her belt. She leaned forward, arms resting on the table, and examined the coin. It was a heavy bronze disc with the head of horse on one side and a shining sun on the other. It had been minted on the other side of the planet with alloys and lasers and probably within the last year or two, yet it looked worn and perhaps centuries old.

The coin was one of many that Elaeric always made sure was in her leather bag when she went on her errands for him. There was always a little extra for her, not nearly enough to buy a new set of clothes or even a new heel for her boot, just enough for a little snack. She supposed she could start hoarding them, but figured it would take an eternity, or feel like one, before she had enough for a decent set of clothes. The little niceties were worth more in the long haul.

Scarlett sat back in her chair, absently rolling the coin over and over between her fingers, watching a fishmonger mend the wheel of his cart. A man passing by on a shining black stallion stopped and dismounted to help him.

The strange feeling wafted over Scarlett once again as she finished her drink, though she couldn't smell anything this time that was out of the ordinary. She felt the tingle and this time it ran through her entire body. She frowned and wondered if it might be from the coffee.

It doesn't matter, she thought. *It's getting late.*

She brushed crumbs from the brioche off of her shirt and left the coin on the table before heading for the stables with her produce from the market.

The stable boy brought the mare out and held her steady while Scarlett fastened the bulging scarf to the horn of the saddle. She pulled a small copper from her purse and tucked it into the boy's hand as she took the reins from him.

"And that's for you."

"Thank you!" he gushed, the mop of hair and dirty face bobbing and bowing before running off.

Scarlett rubbed the mare's neck, admiring the shiny coat and sinewy muscles. She was about to utter praise to the animal when she was once again overcome with that peculiar feeling. It washed over her and this time the smell was close enough for Scarlett to recognize.

The Jordan clutched at the saddle to keep from staggering.

She should have known the smell in an instant, but Scarlett hadn't been able to place it since it was so out of context. Mingled with the aromas of the town and the market, the people and the animals, not to mention the warm, heavy air, the scent had been masked. Had she imagined that scent in the midst of the sterile metal of space, she would have known immediately.

The Jordan closed her eyes and put her forehead against the courser's warm neck. She tried to fill her nostrils with the smell of horse, of hay, of sweat – trying to will away the impossible.

Breathe, she told herself. *Just breathe.*

The warmth surrounded her like a second skin and seemed to gather at her groin like a heated coil. The sounds of Kayos – the cafés, the stables, the market – all seemed to fade and become far away.

She wrapped her hands in the mare's mane, holding tight. She knew whose voice it would be before it broke the muted foreground with its compelling baritone sound. And when it did, it made the heat in her groin flare and ache.

"Hello, Scarlett."

Slowly, carefully, the dark haired Jordan released her hold on the mare and turned from her horse to look up into gimlet green eyes of the Chimeran Commander, Bjorn van Zandt.

NINE

The ride home from the FG was intense and the tension aboard Faith's aircraft nearly crackled with dangerous electricity. The meetings had not gone as Faith had expected. It was an occurrence that had not happened in over a century and the eldest de Rossi sister was fuming.

As far as she was concerned, the demands that those on the AI Board at the InterGalactic Council were making were absolutely preposterous. Barin Trey had wasted her time and it had all been to no avail. Instead of sleeping or relaxing on the trip back to her villa, like she normally would, she had spent most of her time in the main room of her craft having heated conversations and sending messages over her comset through clenched teeth.

Penny was careful not to disturb her, but watched her carefully trying to anticipate any need she might have. She made sure there was always a glass of water by her hand, a plate of cold food nearby every few hours, and a steward ready with a bottle of champagne and a very large chilled glass.

When they arrived at the villa, Penny motioned for Mari to draw a bath for Faith and take her a glass of champagne. Faith strode through the villa, oblivious to the staff that wisely gave her a wide berth.

She stormed into her room, so angry that she felt that if she could breathe fire, she would. She had hoped the journey home would give her time to cool off, but it had only given her time to build up a real head of steam.

She dropped onto the bench seat in front of her vanity and pulled her hand down across the right edge of the mirror. The many reflective surfaces flipped and changed and some dissolved to reveal a simulated backdrop of the Andromeda galaxy. Others flipped to show a glowing screen of incoming mail or a shifting view of live cameras. The table of the vanity darkened to a black glass surface with a touch screen grid and ghost pad.

Faith was furiously punching numbers on the grid and ignoring the numerous holo-mails in her inbox that had piled up it the last seventy-two hours. She heard Mari come in and start her bath. She would be back in exactly seven minutes to turn it off with a glass of champagne. Faith needed it. Probably the whole bottle.

She had flown all the way to the artificial galaxy that bridged her own with Andromeda for live meetings with the IGC's Artificial Intelligence Limitations Council. Barin Trey, the Prime Council Director, had shut down nearly all of her applications with gracious nonchalance.

Faith clenched her teeth as she pounded the keys of the ghost pad, sending him a uni-message. She knew that his actions were not dictated by logic, but because of the power he liked to hold over her. The arrogant bastard probably thought it made him more desirable, and maybe to some he was. He was often referred to as the most eligible bachelor in the Seven Systems and had many prominent women, young and old, after him. Faith had no idea why.

He had asked Faith, a number of times, to accompany him on trips that were slanted more towards intimacy rather than business. Faith had declined politely every time. He had once, after they had both indulged in too many drinks at an IGC party, told Faith what a powerful couple they would make.

Faith, feeling a little tipsy herself, had come close to telling him that he didn't know what real power was. She thought of the power that GwenSeven could bring down if she wanted. It would be like knocking pins from a bridge. She thought of that power now, sitting in front of the GwenSeven Mainframe, fuming.

Stupid bastards! she thought. *They have no idea. Even as blatant as we have been in the past two decades, still they don't see.* She pecked out and sent a few more messages, all in text. She didn't want anyone to see the state she was in via a holo.

All the way to the Flower! And for nothing! She was so angry and absorbed in her fury that she didn't hear anyone approach her, and nearly screamed when a hand fell upon her shoulder.

"Jesus!" she hissed, as she spun around to see Jasyn standing there with his hand pulled back as if burned, looking scared and confused. "You scared the shit out of me!" she accused, though she didn't look angry. Jasyn only cocked his head to the side a bit, smiling cautiously. Faith recovered a bit of her composure and laughed nervously. "What the hell are you doing?"

"Waiting for you," he said, as if it was the most obvious thing in the world. Faith sighed and turned back to her vanity. The silent frosty image of Greater Andromeda hung to the left edge of the glassy black screen of the GwenSeven Mainframe. Faith looked at his ghostly reflection standing over her as he reached out and laid his hand on her shoulder again. This time she reached up to cover his hand with her own.

"Waiting for me, huh?"

"You haven't played with me for weeks," he said, trying not to sound accusing or petulant and doing a miserable job at both.

"Played with? For weeks?" Faith pressed her lips together, trying not to smile.

"Even a vacuum cleaner knows when it isn't played with," he told her.

Faith turned around on her seat so she could face him again, taking his hand and holding it between hers. All of the anger she had been feeling faded away and, as she looked into his eyes, all of the tension followed.

"First of all, I have only been gone a couple of days, not weeks," she said smiling, "Next, you don't play with a vacuum. It's a tool, not a toy, and does not possess awareness." Jasyn bit his bottom lip. Faith didn't know if it was to keep from saying something or if it was because he was trying to decide if he fit into either of the two categories she had just suggested. She stood up, letting him help her to her feet. "You are neither," she told him, touching his face. He smiled.

"I still want you to play with me," he whispered, taking her hand and kissing the tips of her fingers.

Faith smiled. She couldn't believe that she had forgotten he was there. Part of her knew she should feel terrible, even ashamed, but she felt it impossible to feel anything but wonderment when he was looking at her. She cocked an eyebrow at him.

"You want to play?"

His cautious smile widened into a grin. "Yes."

"Very well." Faith turned at the waist so she could reach back towards the far right side of the mainframe. She ran her hand up the side of the glassy computer screen and it whirled and shifted again until it reformed into the many mirrors of the vanity.

She reached out and dimmed the lights but when Jasyn pulled her close to kiss her, she pulled away. Instead, she helped him shed his clothes and then pushed him down into the reading chair next to her bed before undressing herself.

When Mari came in to shut off the bath with a glass of champagne on a tray, Jasyn was in the reading chair with Faith straddling him. Her employer had nothing on except for a gunmetal colored sheet, wrapped around her hips.

Faith froze as she heard Mari enter and turned her face the slightest bit to the right. She could almost feel the woman's shock as she left the champagne at the edge of the tub and hurried from the room. Faith smiled and turned her attention back to Jasyn. His eyes had never wavered from her face.

Later, after they had moved from the chair to the floor and then from the floor to the bed, Faith stayed up watching him as he slept. She ran her right thumbnail along her bottom lip, feeling torn between two worlds. The guilt that she had forgotten him, something that was hardly felt when she was looking into his eyes, was now a feverish chill that swept through her.

How could I forget? she thought, dismayed. *What has happened to me? How cruel have I become?*

She thought of all the years of rebellion and revolution, decades of war and bloodshed and deception and lies. Of her long fight to reunite her family. She speculated on her love for the one she had lost and shuddered against the body next to her.

She finally lay down and draped an arm over his sleeping form. Faith closed her eyes and prayed silently that the love she had once known would be reborn.

★

She awoke to Jasyn's smile.

"Good morning," she offered, still sleepy.

"Good morning," he replied, slipping his arms around her. "You're not going anywhere today."

"Penny will let me know my schedule," she answered before she realized that his last words were not a question. She looked at him quizzically.

"Nowhere without me," he said, kissing her deeply.

It was nearly another hour before she got out of bed and when she went to breakfast in the dining room, instead of being dressed in a sharply fashionable suit, she was wearing a bathrobe.

Penny tried not to stare in disbelief and had to physically avert her gaze by turning her head when Jasyn followed her employer into the room, also wearing a robe. When she looked back he flashed Penny a smile of white, even teeth. The PA opened her mouth to speak but found that she had no words to fill it.

They crossed the living room to the dining area beyond. Jasyn held Faith's chair as she sat down and took his own seat as she shook out a linen napkin over her robe-covered lap. Bowe bustled in and poured them juice, assuring them that breakfast would be out in just a few moments.

Penny cleared her throat. "Ma'am, today you..."

"Will be spending the day with Jasyn," Faith finished. "Reschedule everything else." She ignored her assistant's half-open mouth and smiled at the man across the table. "What would you like to do?"

"Can we go shopping?"

Faith laughed, surprised. "Shopping?"

"Yes. I got to visit The Commons while you were gone. There is a lot to see and do up there." He unfolded his own napkin, laying it across his own robe-covered lap. "I saw something I would like to get for you," he added.

"Very well," Faith acquiesced as Bowe placed a steaming plate of poached eggs with wilted spinach and hollandaise sauce for her down on the table. Jasyn received an identical plate and a small board of fresh sliced fruit was placed on the table between them. "We'll go shopping."

Penny, rendered speechless for only a short moment, bowed and excused herself to go make the necessary arrangements. Astounded as she was, she did feel a stab of delight to be able to deliver the news to Geary and see the look on his face. His hands would be more full than her own.

Faith and Jasyn finished breakfast together, then showered and dressed together.

This is better, Faith thought as she fastened a choker of fine gold links around her throat. *I need to do this. I need to let go.*

Dressed in a cream-colored pant suit and appropriately matched walking shoes, she left her bedroom arm in arm with her stunning, if manufactured, companion to find Penny and Geary waiting by the lift.

Geary held out a hand, inviting them to precede him into the elevator. Penny followed her employer and her companion before the compact head of security stepped in and took them up and up and up.

Faith and Jasyn stared at each other the entire ride like, in

Penny's mind, a couple of silly teenagers. She glanced at Geary but his steely blue-gray eyes were fixed on a spot directly in front of him.

Faith, as her eyes went over Jasyn's face from brow to jaw line, wondered how long it had been since she had visited The Commons. It had been a long time, she knew that, and that she had only been there once just to see what it held.

The entire community of the very wealthy and elite that lived in Callisto Villas was held suspended in space and protected by the magnetic sphere of Jupiter. Unlike the planet's many inhabited moons, a livable atmosphere did not surround the Villas. Instead, the entire space colony was inverted and completely contained, more like a spaceship held static by its orbit.

Like a great blossom of steel, it hung 100 kilometers outside the orbit of Jupiter's densely populated moons of Callisto and Europa. The villas made up the petals. They joined together at a wide circular base called The Commons, an enclosed area of sunny parks and walks dotted with shops and boutiques. The stem of the giant metal flower was a spiral of more shops, stores, restaurants, and spaceports.

The round floor of Faith's elevator ascended 50 meters and then slid sideways to join the bottom stem of the colony before rising again all the way to The Commons. Faith exited the lift with her hand tucked away into the crook of Jasyn's arm, out onto the artificially sunny promenade.

"Wow," Jasyn commented, looking around. "There's a lot less people here today than there were when I was here with Tom."

Faith smiled. "That's because of me. Geary had everyone who didn't have a Class-A clearance escorted from The Commons for the time being." She gave a slight nod to a middle-aged couple strolling through the rose garden.

Jasyn stared at her. "Does he do that everywhere you go?" the construct asked, wondering how the man could possibly pull it off, especially with such short notice. It had not been much more than an hour since breakfast.

Faith laughed softly. "No, but if he can, he does."

Jasyn noticed that, along with the substantially diminished crowd (not that it had been the least bit crowded before) as they walked along followed by Penny and Geary, other men in impeccable suits fell in behind them and a few walked a few meters in front of them. Jasyn leaned his head closer to Faith.

"Do they always follow you this way?"

Faith smiled. "Yes."

"Do they have to?"

Her smile became a grin. "They keep me safe."

Jasyn's brows drew together. "I would keep you safe." He looked at her, his features pulled tight. "I wouldn't let anything happen to you."

Faith felt her breath hitch in her throat, but she was careful not to let it show. She could feel the smooth round bicep of his arm under his shirt and she tightened her grip on it. "I know."

They walked down a paved path between creeping ground roses, their prolific blooms white and bright. Beyond was a row of knee-high green hedge, backed by a larger hedge of red roses. Beyond the hedges were rolling green lawns.

As they approached a row of shops they passed another couple that was pretending to admire something in the store window while stealing sidelong glances at Faith and Jasyn. Faith acknowledged them with a smile, knowing the exultation the couple would have describing the encounter to their friends.

"Here!" Jasyn exclaimed, pulling her towards a jeweler's boutique. He stopped suddenly and grasped her shoulders. "Will you wait here?" he asked.

Faith nodded. "Certainly."

Jasyn looked behind her towards their escorts. "Penny?" he called.

The PA stared at him for a second, surprised. "Yes?"

He let go of Faith and walked towards the door of the jeweler, motioning for Penny to join him. When she did he dipped his head towards her and kept his voice low. "Will you help me buy something for Faith?"

Penny smiled and nodded. The handsome construct grinned and she followed him through the door.

The jeweler, a small man with a fringe of gray hair above his ears and a similar fringe of gray hair on his upper lip, clasped his hands together as he saw Jasyn.

"Ah!" he exclaimed. "You came back!"

"Of course I did," Jasyn told him, smiling broadly. "I said I would if I could."

The old jeweler, who originally thought that the young man was full of shit when he had told him he was the companion of

Faith de Rossi, was now hardly able to keep from jumping up and down.

Penny gave the glass cases a quick once over through her smart rectangular black frames. "That one," she instructed, tapping on a glass case with a manicured fingernail and indicating a chain necklace made of large gold links.

The jeweler's eyes darted to Jasyn, who frowned.

"Can I get her this one?" he asked, pointing to another necklace. It was a chain similar to the one Penny had selected, one with oval links that were alternately gold and silver.

Penny frowned. "It's the same *type* that she usually wears," the PA advised, "but she usually prefers gold."

Jasyn nodded. "I know," he replied, hesitant at first. "This one is different. That's why I want to get it."

Penny shrugged. "Suit yourself." She motioned to the jeweler to wrap up the purchase and handed him a credentials card after he had carefully boxed the necklace.

Jasyn tucked the box into the pocket of his coat and escorted Penny from the jeweler's shop with a barely suppressed grin.

The jeweler himself could not suppress his own grin the slightest bit. He knew that once word got out of the necklace, bought by Ms. de Rossi's companion for Ms. De Rossi herself, sales would go through the roof. Eagerly, he rubbed his hands together before he picked up his acrylic to order a dozen more. After a second thought, he ordered two dozen instead. And raised the price on the holo tag.

"Well?" Faith asked Jasyn, brows raised. He hesitated and made a face, smiling and scowling at the same time.

"I wanted to wait, but I can't."

He pulled the jeweler's box from his pocket and, holding it out for her to see, opened it. Faith peered at it, curious and pleased.

"I know you like to wear this kind of necklace," he said quickly, "and you like gold better...but I thought this was kind of like us," he told her. "I mean, the different colors of the links. They are the same, but different."

Jasyn cocked his head, unsure of how she felt because it looked like she had tears in her eyes. "It's perfect," she told him, her voice husky. "Will you put it on me?"

Jasyn smiled, reassured, and pulled the chain from the box and fastened it around Faith's slender neck. When he was done she turned and pulled him down and close so that her lips could find his. The kiss was enough to make Penny avert her gaze. Even Geary's constantly moving eyes gave them a few seconds of privacy.

"Thank you," Faith whispered.

Jasyn smiled, surprised and shy at her show of emotion but reluctant to disengage from her embrace. "You're welcome," he whispered back.

Faith clung to him for a moment, then loosened her grip enough to turn, though she kept her arm securely around his waist. They walked through the shopping district that way, holding tight to one another.

They had lunch at an outdoor café while Faith gave him a mental sketch of what she did on a usual basis. Jasyn listened and fed her bits of food when he had the chance. He was clear to show when he was bored by her musings on work by rolling his eyes or letting his head loll about on his neck as if he was falling asleep.

Though he showed little interest in her work, he asked her lots of questions about other things, wanting to know as much about her as he could. He wanted to know where she went when she left for days on end and with whom she was spending her time.

Jasyn asked about her family, where they were and if she was close to them. He asked about Penny and Geary and if Charity lived the same way as Faith, to which Faith laughed harder then he had ever seen her laugh and he wondered why since she gave no explanation.

Little by little, and very carefully, Faith opened up to him. Sharing what she could, but saving her deepest hopes and fears for another time – should the time come. She hoped it would.

They decided to head home when the light in The Commons started to fade into an artificial twilight.

"Would you like to have dinner in a restaurant?" Faith asked.

"Whatever you want to do," Jasyn told her.

"Would you mind if we ate at home? I should probably try to catch up on work a little bit." Faith felt an edge of guilt for asking but she also felt just as much remorse for skipping out on an entire day's worth of work. She figured she was damned if she did and damned if she didn't, but Jasyn simply shrugged, not seeming to mind.

"I like Sari's cooking."

Faith regarded him with an arched brow. "You're on a first name basis with my cook?" she asked, pleasantly surprised.

Jasyn nodded. "I think she's trying to make me fat."

Faith laughed. "She just likes to cook." She leaned her head on Jasyn's shoulder as they walked through the garden on the way back to the express elevator that would take them home. "I'm glad you are getting to know everyone. Are you comfortable at the villa?"

"Yes. Everyone has been very nice."

Faith raised her head to look at him. "You sound as if you are surprised."

"I do? I don't mean to. I mean, maybe I am, a little."

"Well," Faith told him, "if anyone is anything less, you let me know immediately."

Jasyn smiled. "I will."

Geary drew in his security net as they neared the expressway. Jasyn could see more of the security team this time as they closed in and thought that Faith was about as secure as she could get. That made him feel strangely happy but even stranger was his own desire to keep her safe.

Once in the elevator, the security faded away, leaving just Geary and Penny to accompany them personally to the villa. Penny spoke only to inquire about what time they would like their evening meal and if they would like anything special.

Faith looked at Jasyn with raised brows as they descended the lift.

"I think anything together *would* be special," he said.

Faith smiled and turned to Penny. "One hour," she told her PA.

Penny tapped the comlink on her ear and muttered only a few words into it before clicking it off again.

Faith went straight to her room when they reached the villa, her fingers entwined with Jasyn's. When they were alone in the bedroom she let go of his hand and faced him. "Are you sure you don't mind?" she asked, indicating her return to work.

Jasyn kissed her on the cheek. "You know you don't have to ask me. But no, I don't mind." He picked up his acrylic and settled into the wing chair by the bed.

Faith smiled at him and went to the monstrosity of mirrors that was her vanity. She pulled her hand down across the right edge of the mirror, the rings on her right index finger clinking softly against it and reflecting the rosy light of the room as she sank down onto the velvet-cushioned bench.

The mirrors flipped and changed. Some disappeared into an image of the Andromeda galaxy. Faith tapped a few surfaces that showed live camera angles, cutting off the feed or redistributing it to recorders. Her fingers danced across the now black glass tabletop as she answered mail.

She had only been working for a few minutes when there was a knock on the bedroom door.

"Come in," Faith called without turning from the mainframe. The door edged open just far enough for Penny to be heard from the doorway.

"Ms. de Rossi?" Penny called. She had never been hesitant before about walking directly into the room, but Mari's account of what she had walked in upon had the PA's heart thumping with trepidation.

"Yes?" Faith answered, her fingers tapping away at the ghost pad.

"There is a call for you from Mr. Trey."

Faith stopped typing, her fingers hovering over the glassy surface of the vanity. "Barin?" she asked, feeling slightly stupid. As if it would be some other Mr. Trey.

"Yes, ma'am."

Faith sighed and stood up. "I'll take it in my office." She went to Jasyn and leaned down to give him a peck on the cheek. "I should be back in a few minutes, but if the call runs long I promise to be on time for dinner."

Jasyn smiled at her. "Okay."

Faith strode from the room and Penny followed, closing the door behind them.

Jasyn looked at the closed door, a puzzled expression on his face. He looked at Faith's vanity. It was still computer moded. She hadn't switched it back to the crazy maze of mirrors. He frowned at it for long seconds before looking back down at his acrylic and loading a new game.

# ONE ZERO

After his shower, Grandpa shaved with the electric doohickey he had gotten last Christmas and pulled on a pair of denim jeans over his undershorts. He chose a crisp blue shirt with short sleeves from his closet and put it on over a clean white undershirt, doing his best to ignore the way his fingers trembled as he fastened the buttons.

He combed his white wispy hair, what was left of it, and brushed his teeth wondering why he bothered. Like his hair, there weren't many left and the ones that had stubbornly remained were in poor shape indeed.

Habit, he supposed.

Grandpa walked carefully through his new podment. It was larger than the last but the furniture was the same - for Grandpa the term "same old, same old" couldn't be more accurate. But because the new pod was bigger than the last, actually bigger than any he had ever lived in, the furniture had been shifted around a bit to fit the room. The new location of the old coffee table caused him to bark his shin on it one morning last week, opening up the skin on his leg and leaving a large, welted bruise.

"Thin skin, thin shin," he sang under his breath, not put out in the slightest. Being old was rarely easy, and he had been old for a long, long time.

He carefully traversed the living room and went into the kitchen with a small smile that showed his few teeth. The new kitchen had an actual nook for his table and windows that let in sunshine, making the room bright and cheery. He had lived on the lower and middle klicks of Three Mile City for so long with only artificial light that he had forgotten how invigorating real sunshine could be.

Makes me feel young again, he thought, his thin chest swelling with pride as he pushed the buttons on his coffee maker. But the swelling hitched to a stop as he noticed that his fingers were not just trembling, but shaking.

The coffee maker had been one of the little mechanical advancements that Grandpa had not shunned. After complaining about it, and endlessly grousing as Sean and his father had fiddled with it, the thing had been able to make coffee just the way he liked it and with nearly no wait at all.

As the machine ejected a hissing stream of hot coffee into the mug he had left under the spout, Grandpa opened the cupboard that held his pills. Most were just vitamins that John or Johanna had gotten for him – synthetic herbs that were supposed to do one thing or another that he didn't give a rat's ass to remember.

Grandpa pawed through them with a gnarled hand till he found one that actually had his name on it. Having his name on it made it different. It made it worth something. Having his name on it meant it was *prescribed*.

He held it up to the light and was not surprised to see the bottle was mostly full. Grasping the bottle in one hand he tried to pry the cap off with the other but the cap didn't budge. He tried twisting it until his hand was sore. Still nothing. For a moment he considered sticking it in his mouth and using his teeth. Then he threw back his head and cawed laughter at the ceiling of his kitchen.

Instead, he put the bottle on his kitchen table and retrieved his coffee with a shaking hand and sat down to drink it, determined not to spill any on his clothes.

Usually he would take his coffee into the living room and watch the news on the pane of glass that John insisted was the television, or at least as close as he could get to one. Today Grandpa stayed at the table, looking out the kitchen windows. He didn't want to slosh hot coffee on his rug. He had been given the rug by his father and it had sentimental value – though he couldn't quite remember what exactly the sentiment was. Regardless, he was loath to ruin it with a coffee stain.

Of course the shaking bothered him. It would bother anyone. Shaking was rarely a sign of good health. What concerned Grandpa the most, however, was that it might mean that his body was really breaking down for good. Not being able to control your own hands was a lot more serious than losing hair and teeth. It could be that his time was finally drawing to a close.

Grandpa was old. Very old. And he was not afraid to die. He knew he had probably been cheating death for a century or more. What worried him was that there would be no one to take his place when he died.

Of course the Mattatock name would live on. There would always be children and grandchildren and even at least one daring soul to stand as the protector of the family. But his job was different. He had stood as witness since what felt like the very beginning. Who would bear witness once he was gone? Who would pass on the story of their family and their universal entanglement?

Grandpa had a fleeting hope that it might be Sean, though he thought it more likely that the boy would take up the crest if Johanna did not have a strong-willed child of her own. The boy showed a surprising amount of promise.

At a time when most young make the break from childhood to become young adults, they drift away and refuse to listen to a damn thing the actual adults tell them. It seemed that Sean, however, had started on that course but turned from it at the last second. He was becoming more drawn in as he got older and actually interested in what Grandpa had to say. And the move to a plush lifestyle had not spoiled him and made him a brat, but simply more aware of everything around him.

Grandpa sighed. There was a chance, but the chance was slim. Many children had shown promise over the years, but none had panned out for the job. That was why he had been the one to stand witness for long.

Or maybe I'm just too stubborn, he thought. *Or too prideful, thinking that I am the only one, but I don't think that is it. I think that there was still something I was supposed to do, or someone I was supposed to see, but I can't remember.* He huffed and took another sip of his coffee. *Can't remember. Some witness.*

The coffee seemed to help the shaking, so Grandpa made himself another cup along with a breakfast pastry.

Jeanette, he pondered. *Maybe. She loves to listen, and would probably be an able storyteller as well.*

But Grandpa doubted he could tell her everything she needed to know. Not yet anyway. He didn't think she would understand everything. And besides, she was still so innocent. He would not take that from her if he could help it.

Grandpa stayed in the kitchen all morning, drinking coffee and looking out the large windows of the nook.

The kitchen looked out over a moat of grass around the podment to the park beyond. The park was a rolling sea of green, tree-lined paths between waves of hills scalloped with wide-open expanses for kids to run and play, though only the very small seemed to appreciate it. There were silica pits with play hovercraft and composite play structures from which to climb and swing.

After more coffee, the leftover half of a pastrami sandwich from the fridge, and what seemed like an infinite number of trips to the commode, Grandpa could see children of different ages walking and running on the sidewalks. School was out.

Grandpa was trying to figure how long it would be before Sean got home, knowing the boy had extracurricular activities, including numerous memberships to what the boy had called "gaming circles." Whatever the hell that meant.

He was still trying to add up how many hours or minutes it might be when the front door to his podment slid open and his youngest grandson was standing in the doorway, blonde hair hanging over his blue eyes. Grandpa had long since given up on grumbling about a man's privacy.

"We knock, but you never hear us," Jeanette had told him with her round dark eyes, once when she had appeared suddenly in his living room and he had groused about it. Grandpa supposed that was true.

"Hi Grandpa," Sean called as he came in, flicking his blonde hair away from his face. He was surprised not to find Grandpa in his usual chair. He knew all too well that the oldest living Mattatock was a creature of habit.

"Well hello there, stranger!"

Sean tilted his head to peer into the kitchen and, spying Grandpa, joined him in the breakfast nook. "What are you doing in here?" he asked.

Instead of answering, Grandpa pointed to the bottle of pills on the table. "Can you open that?"

Sean picked up the bottle and examined the label. "No," he said without even trying the cap. Then, to Grandpa's surprise, the boy turned and dropped the bottle down the trash chute. "No one can. The pills are expired."

"So?"

"So it's a G-scrip bottle. Once the pills expire, the bottle seals itself. I'll have dad get you a new scrip."

Grandpa sighed heavily and crossed his arms over his thin chest. "I'm not sure they were the right ones anyway."

Sean frowned and dropped his ac-bag onto an empty chair. He

placed his hands on the back of another chair and leaned towards the old man, his young brows drawing together. "What's wrong Grandpa?"

Grandpa closed his mouth, setting his jaw stubbornly. He felt a sudden bout of petulance and decided that he might not want to share what was n his mind. His lips pooched out over his nearly toothless mouth. Sean pulled out the chair he was leaning on and sat in it, fixing Grandpa with a look of patient exasperation. Grandpa looked away, realizing that he was just being a coward.

"I think I'm dying."

"What?"

Grandpa looked back at the boy, annoyed. "You heard me! I think I'm dying!"

Sean looked around the room, not sure what to say. He was shocked, yes, but why? Who knew how old Grandpa was? Two hundred years old? Three? He had once told Sean that he had known the Dyer Maker. That had to put at least three centuries under his belt. But still, Grandpa had been around so long Sean supposed he had just assumed that the old man would live forever.

"What makes you think you're dying?" he finally asked.

Grandpa fixed his jaw again but relented almost immediately. "I've got the Jimmy hands."

"The *what?*"

"The shakes!"

Sean gaped at him for a moment and then laughed loudly, looking relieved. Grandpa scowled at him.

"What in Sam Hill is so funny?" he demanded.

"Christ, Grandpa!"

"Don't blaspheme!"

"Sorry," Sean apologized, still wheezing a small laugh. "But you scared me. I thought you were going to say you were coughing up blood, or maybe it was your heart, or you were passing out or something."

Grandpa cocked his head, suspicious. "I suppose it could be worse," he admitted. "But you don't think it's serious?"

Sean shrugged. "It could be, but most likely isn't. Do you shake all day? How hard? You seem to be pretty normal now."

Grandpa was thoughtful for a moment. "It's the worst in the morning. Better after my coffee."

Sean's brows drew together as he thought. "Shaking is a result of a neural malfunction, usually due to a deficiency. If you haven't had a stroke or been diagnosed with anything, you could just be short on some nutrients, especially the way *you* eat." His blue eyes gave Grandpa a glance of disapproval.

"Are you serious?"

"Of course."

Grandpa fixed him again with a suspicious stare. "How do you know all this?"

"I'm taking a pharmacology class."

"I thought you were only in high school!"

"I am. It's a Freshman Elective."

Grandpa blew air out through his pursed lips in a near whistle. "When I was your age we took shop class," he said, his bleary blue eyes becoming unfocused and distant. "I remember when we got to rebuild an air car. We got it to run, but it would only hover on one side. I was able to get in and drive it around the quad with the right side scraping the pavement and sending up a scree of sparks." He cackled softly at the memory and his watery eyes looked back into the long ago. "But Edgar! Edgar was so fat that when he got in the whole darn thing came slamming down and almost rattled itself to pieces!"

Grandpa's head tipped back and he cawed laughter. He stayed with the memory a moment longer, his cawing dying into cackles, before coming back to his grandson. "You're here early today."

Sean shrugged. "I skipped the Sphere Games."

"I thought those were your favorite!"

"They are. It's...a long story."

"Afraid that I might croak before you can tell it?"

Sean shook his blonde head, grinning sheepishly. "No, it's just that no one is winning right now."

"What do you mean no one is winning? Somebody has to win."

Sean's shoulders sagged. He had no idea how to explain open gaming to Grandpa, or hacking. It had taken him a whole afternoon last week to explain how the Sphere Games were a set of interactive war games on strategy and astrogation that culminated in a simulated jet fighter. Today he didn't feel like explaining, especially since some hacker that everyone was calling 'The Skipper' had decimated him in the games.

"It's hard to explain," Sean said, feeling lame.

"Is that so?" Grandpa asked. Sean nodded and Grandpa let the subject go. He would be the first to admit that he had no idea how the gaming circles worked, even after Sean had tried really hard to explain it to him last week, or last month, he couldn't remember when. "And today your sister has what? Piano lessons?"

Sean shook his head. "Dance class."

Grandpa's eyes gleamed. "So you have me all to yourself. You got something you want to talk about?"

Sean shifted in his seat. "Yesss..." He had wanted to talk to Grandpa about this for some time, but now that he had the chance he wasn't sure. It felt so weird looking at him across the table, practically eye to eye.

"Well? Out with it, boy! I don't know how long we have and I have things to tell you as well."

"What is it that you want to tell me?" Sean asked.

Grandpa's brows drew together slightly. "Not today," he said. "I have to think about it a little before I start, maybe even write things down if my hand will let me. I don't want to forget anything. Anything that's important anyway!" He cackled at his last sentence, knowing how shady his memory had become.

Sean frowned. "So when you said you didn't know how much time we have..."

"That's right. I meant I'm not sure how much time *I* have."

Something suddenly occurred to Sean. Lots of old people swore they were dying all the time. Usually the doom and gloomers and hypochondriacs that lived in fear or constant need of attention. Others, Sean had learned in school, knew when their time was up. Grandpa seemed more of the latter, less of the former.

"Are the shakes the only things that are bothering you right now? Is there anything more serious?"

Grandpa considered the question. Was there anything else? He thought there might be, and felt he should be truthful with the boy, but he honestly couldn't call to mind anything else.

"Not that I can think of," he admitted.

Sean looked at the old man, noticing for the first time not just how damned old he was, but how frail. His few wisps of hair, the clouded eyes, the slight frame covered with skin so spotted and thin that Sean could see that it broke open at the slightest bump. He was suddenly afraid of losing him.

"Are you taking any medicines right now?" he asked.

"Nope."

"Do you mind if I look through your cabinet?"

Grandpa's thin shoulders pulled up under his crisp blue shirt. "Go ahead."

Sean got up and slid open the cupboard in the kitchen where Grandpa kept the pills he didn't take. He immediately began taking inventory and cleaning house, tossing out over half of the bottles.

"Useless," he muttered, dropping a plastic pill jar down the trash chute. "Garbage. Useless. This one's good," said putting one of the bottles down on the counter before he pulled out the next from the cupboard. Sean stopped and turned, holding up a plastic purple cylinder, his brows arched high up over his eyes. "Where did you get these?" he asked.

Grandpa shrugged.

"Do you know what they are for?"

Grandpa shook his head.

Sean chuckled as he dropped the bottle down the chute. "Well, you don't need them. I hope."

When he was finished there were three bottles left on the counter. Grandpa recognized them as some of the more recent vitamins that John or Johanna had bought for him. Or so he thought.

"I want you to start taking these every day," Sean instructed, lining them up on the shelf over the coffeemaker. Hopefully seeing them out in the open would jar the man's memory to take them. "Take one of each every morning with your pastry."

Grandpa nodded obediently. "All right."

"I'm going to get you a few more vitamins, and some new pills. Pills that will...help your shaking. Will you take them?"

"Yes."

Sean's shoulders sagged with relief as he relaxed and sat back down.

"Wasn't there something you wanted to discuss?" Grandpa asked.

The boy nodded, unexpectedly nervous. He swallowed and plunged ahead. "One time, back at the old place, when you were telling me and Jeanette about the dyers and the Pantheon, I mentioned that they were also sold for companionship."

This time it was Grandpa that shifted in his seat. "Yes?"

"You told me that was a discussion for another time. I figured because it was something you didn't want Jeanette to hear." He figured it also might be something Grandpa didn't want him to hear either, but he wanted to know.

"That's true." Grandpa was still considering if it would be right for the boy to hear, but was curious to know what he was after. "Why don't you get me a glass of ice-water, first? It seems we're going to be talking for a spell."

Sean got up and got a glass from the stainless steel cupboard and held it in the freezer niche as the ice clinked into the glass. "From the fridge?" he asked.

"Of course!"

Sean opened the glass-fronted refrigerator and pulled out the tall pitcher and poured the clear liquid into the glass. "You know the water from the tap is perfectly safe up here," he said, closing the fridge and handing the glass to his Grandpa.

"Why take the chance?" Grandpa asked, accepting the glass with a smile that showed his chipped and broken teeth, making Sean suspicious once again that Grandpa's water wasn't really water. He made a mental note to check sometime.

Sean cleared his throat as he sat back down. "GwenSeven still sells most of their original model types, right?"

Grandpa took a sip from his glass and looked up the wall to where it met the ceiling, trying to coax back the memories. "I suppose. They just don't make them to their original specifications."

"For instance?"

"For instance, they still manufacture people for various jobs like security, or as bodyguards, but they are not as highly trained. The two of the First Seven that were trained as bodyguards had unsurpassed skill, making them quite deadly. Now the IGC won't allow such extremes and I don't think GwenSeven would want it, not after the blood bath it caused."

"The boy vicar?"

Grandpa nodded. "And some others."

"And GwenSeven was shut down for a few years after the rebellion."

"Yes," Grandpa said, nodding his head, "most thought it was for good. People were very angry and wanted someone to blame."

"So why did they open back up? People weren't mad anymore?"

Grandpa's thin shoulders went up again in a shrug. "Mad or not, people don't like working and yet they grumble if they have to pay someone else to do their work. They've spent centuries trying to stamp out slavery only to find ways to condone it in their own collective conscience."

Sean drummed his fingertips on Grandpa's kitchen table. "So they just started making people again, and simply toned down their skills?"

"Among other things."

"Other things being their intelligence and emotion."

Grandpa sipped his drink and nodded. "Of course. That was part of the deal if GwenSeven wanted to reopen their doors."

Sean chewed his lip. Grandpa was an unending source of information, and asking him questions was easier than spending a day doing research on his acrylic. Even then, sometimes the information he was after couldn't be found on his acrylic. That didn't make it any more comfortable to ask Grandpa some things.

"Is it about the sex?" Grandpa finally demanded, seeing the boy's discomfort.

Sean laughed. "Kind of, but not really." Grandpa frowned and took a long drink from his glass. "Don't worry," Sean assured, "I don't want any gory details."

Grandpa cackled softly and wiped the condensation forming on the bottom of his glass on the thigh of his jeans. "Then get to it!"

"I've been doing a bit of research on constructs..."

"For school?"

"Not really." Grandpa nodded as if it was what he had expected as Sean continued. "One thing I've noticed is that the price of the construct differs, according to their model and what they are being purchased for, which makes sense. But the price of a Companion Construct is astronomical."

"And?"

Sean cleared his throat. "Is it because of the sex?"

"What do you think?"

"I'm not sure. It makes sense in a way, but I know that there are companies other than GwenSeven that sell constructs for that, and they are much cheaper. So much cheaper that it's a little scary."

"It is scary," Grandpa told him, his voice earnest. "And in no way do I ever want you purchasing that sort of...company."

"Don't worry," Sean quickly assured him. He wasn't sure what he'd do with a *real* girl at this point, though he kept that information to himself. "Then why are the ones made by GwenSeven so different? They're so expensive that there are only a very few of them made each year."

Grandpa tipped his shaven chin up and ran his knuckles under it as he thought. "Well, Companion Constructs are tricky. They need to be smart enough and sufficiently emotionally intuitive to be able to meet wants and understand feelings, but not to the extent that they will figure out what they themselves are." His eyes fell back on Sean. "Do you remember when we talked about EQ?"

"The emotional quotient. Yes."

"Well, Companion Constructs have the highest EQ of any model – the highest that the law will allow. Did you know that?"

"Yes. I remember reading that somewhere."

"Then what does that tell you?" Grandpa asked. "If they have the most EQ of any model?"

Understanding spread quickly across the boy's face. "That they are the most dangerous," Sean said, his voice barely above a whisper.

Grandpa nodded and sipped his drink.

122

# ONE ONE

It was on her very first day at the cottage that Elaeric led Scarlett down the hallway to the door that was across the hall from her bedroom. He opened the door for her, holding out a hand to invite her inside. Curious as a cat, Scarlett walked into the room and looked around.

The first and only thing that struck her was the light.

The room was spotlessly clean and, other than two square cushions and a tall, green houseplant in each corner, bare.

Rose-gold shafts of sunlight streamed in from the windows and puddled on the wooden floor and she stared at it, mesmerized. There was something about that sunlight, other than its color, that struck Scarlett as strange, though she couldn't put her finger on what it might be.

"Please," Elaeric offered, holding out an inviting hand once again. "Sit," he urged. Scarlett gave him a blank look.

"On the floor?"

Elaeric's head bobbed encouragingly. "Please."

"Do I sit on one of the pillows?"

"If you think you need it."

The corners of Scarlett's mouth turned down and her smoldering gaze met the eyes of the monk as if in an unspoken challenge. She pushed the pillow aside as she sat cross-legged on the polished plank floor.

Elaeric shrugged and sat upon one of the pillows so that he was facing Scarlett. He wiggled to get comfortable.

"Is this supposed to be some kind of test?" Scarlett asked, scowling at him.

"Not everything is a test, Johanna. But, in everything there is a lesson. Does that make sense to you?"

"All too well. And call me Scarlett."

"Very well. Close your eyes Johanna Scarlett."

Scarlett shook her head in exasperation but didn't correct him as she closed her eyes. She popped one open again almost immediately, to see what Elaeric was doing. He had settled down comfortably onto the cushion and also had his eyes closed.

"No peeking," he told her without opening his eyes. Scarlett closed her eye, blowing an impatient breath out through her nostrils.

"Your first lesson..."

"How many lessons are there?" Scarlett interrupted.

"An infinite amount."

"Christ," Scarlett said, opening her eyes. "Are you going to try to enlighten me?"

"Not Christ," Elaeric corrected, opening his almond-shaped eyes. "Elaeric," he said, tapping his chest. "And I cannot enlighten you. I can show you the path, but you must walk it yourself."

Scarlett groaned. "I'm a fast learner," she assured him. "Isn't there a shortcut I can take to avoid most of this crap?"

"A shortcut?" Elaeric laughed. "A wormhole to enlightenment?" He laughed harder, holding his small belly, then suddenly stopped. "Yes."

Scarlett watched him in silence. "Well?" she demanded when he offered nothing more. His brows shot up in surprise.

"Oh!" he exclaimed. "You want me to tell you?" Scarlett's shoulders slumped and she rolled her dark eyes in exasperation as he laughed again. "No," he said. "Now close your eyes."

Scarlett closed her eyes.

"Now what?"

"Now, you breathe."

"I *am* breathing," Scarlett said impatiently, opening her eyes.

"You are snorting in air, like the horse outside, but you are not breathing. I want you to *breathe*." Demonstrating, he took in a deep draw of air through his nose and, after a few seconds, blew it out slowly. "Now you try."

Scarlett closed her eyes and shifted her weight, trying to make her butt comfortable on the hard floor. It wasn't going to happen. She took a deep breath through her nose and let it out.

"More."

Scarlett took a deeper breath, filling her lungs for as much as they could take and then letting it all whoosh out.

"Eck!" Elaeric scolded. "You sound like you have been pulled from the depths! You are not diving for snuba! Let the air fill your belly, not your lungs. The air should cleanse you, not wring you out. Too many more gulps of air like that and you might pass out on the floor!"

Though the idea of unconsciousness appealed to Scarlett, she did as instructed. After a minute of breathing by trying to fill her belly with air she found herself calmer, but as impatient as ever.

"What now?" she asked.

"Now you breathe. I don't want you to think, just breathe. If thoughts come to you, I want you to push them away, gently, and keep breathing. If you hear sounds, acknowledge the noise as sound and then get back to breathing. Do not become impatient if your mind wanders. Just give it that gentle shove and come back to your breath."

This is going to be as boring as hell, Scarlett thought.

"Do you think this is too difficult for you?" Elaeric asked as if he had been listening in on her thoughts.

"No," Scarlett told him, drawing the word out with childish sarcasm.

"Good."

So Scarlett sat on the hard and uncomfortable floor thinking, trying not to think, and trying not to think about thinking. It was more difficult than she expected, much more difficult, but she got through it.

What surprised her most was that when she got up she felt clear - clearer and cleaner than she had for a long time. The feeling stayed with her well into the afternoon.

The next day she approached their time for meditation with a bit more optimism and curiosity to see if it would happen again. She could not, however, keep from asking Elaeric why it was called meditation, since the word meditate meant to think about something while here they were not supposed to think of anything at all.

Elaeric had given her one of his toothy smiles and said, "you'll see."

Again, she left the small room feeling peaceful yet lucid and the feeling stayed with her all throughout the day. And, though the voice in her head was as snippy and sarcastic as ever, she found herself paying attention to the smallest of things - the grain of wood in the table, the taste of a very fresh peach, the air so quiet that she could wear it like a blanket – not that she would admit to any of it.

At the end of the first week, Scarlett began to notice some things about herself, her habits and behaviors, along with some slight changes within her. It was a little creepy but very intriguing.

The first thing she noticed was her dreams.

Scarlett had never paid much mind to her dreams before, never remembering much of them to begin with. They were simply a jumbled mass of disconnected thoughts and outrageous visions that dissipated almost immediately after she woke.

Now, her dreams were vivid and sequential, like watching a brilliant holo movie with a shadowy but determined story line. The cast was almost always comprised of people she knew or people she had met, though there were strange faces thrown it at odd times. And the dreams themselves varied from wild (like the ones in which she flew, not by ship but where she herself was flying over hills or cities) to the mundane (like gathering morning eggs or meditating with Elaeric).

Either way, the dreams were as clear and compelling as if she were really there. And she remembered them all with perfect clarity.

When she asked Elaeric about the phenomenon he had simply nodded as if it were to be expected.

"Meditating teaches you to listen to your subtle voice, your subconscious voice. The window you open with your practice during the day becomes a door in the night through which you can pass."

Scarlett gave him a thoughtful harrumph. "Anything else you'd like to enlighten me on today, Master Elaeric?" His wizened face bobbed up and down.

"Try not to judge in your practice today. Do not judge the breeze for blowing in the window to disturb you, and do not judge yourself for noticing the breeze."

Scarlett gave him another harrumph but tried to do as he suggested. For her, not judging turned out to be harder than not thinking.

That night she dreamt that she was walking through a cave of ice. The walls of the cave were a soft white that seemed to glow with dormant life and carved like the sides of an eroded canyon with lambent deep fissures of glacier blue. She reached out a hand to touch the glistening ice and her fingers came away cold and wet.

Everything was so clear that she could see the gooseflesh that stood out on her arms and the intermittent wisps of fog created by the breath from her lips. She took a few cautious steps and could hear the crunch of snow beneath her boots.

She looked down and was surprised to see that not only was she wearing flight boots, but a flight suit as well – though it was not her own. A Mylar flight suit in a bright, shimmering, blue covered her body. Scarlett looked down her shoulder at the sleeve of the suit but no number was stitched there.

Even more surprising was the way that she felt, as if a power were rising within her, expanding. Like her spirit was growing too large for her body. She felt invincible and the effect was intoxicating.

"Where am I?" she wondered aloud, not expecting an answer. But an answer came.

You are in a dangerous place, a voice told her. The voice was soothing, deep but gentle. Almost a rumble.

"It doesn't seem dangerous," Scarlett remarked as she looked around, though her soldier's training put her on an instant alert.

It is a place where you are not afraid to be yourself. Where you shun other voices, even the ones inside your own head. Where you are strong in yourself, fearless for a few passing moments.

"Why can't I always be this way?" Scarlett asked. "Why can't I always be unafraid? It is what I trained for – what I always wanted to be!"

Because this is where your deep-seated anger, from your latent fury to the strange resentment you harbor for your very existence – meets your consciousness face to face and the voices quell one another. Even when you are not angry at a particular something or someone, there is always anger within you. Your anger lies buried deep inside. It is a danger – not just to others, but to yourself as well.

"I feel that anger," Scarlett said softly. "I can feel it even now. Not the way it usually is – rising or burning or bursting to break free – but just a soft breathing, like a dragon living underneath my skin. Underneath my heart. So quiet that I never even knew that he was there."

There was no response from the voice and now she shivered with the cold, her breath a vapor. Scarlett touched the top of her left ear, feeling for the stud that would activate her field, but there was nothing there. The skin was smooth and unmarred.

She looked down at her right hand and saw a platinum band around her wrist. At first, she thought it was the same band worn by Jordan Blue. But as she looked closer the band grew and thickened, becoming a shackle. She turned her hand and saw that the shackle had once been attached to a chain. Three links still hung from the platinum cuff and threw the white light of the cave back in radiant splinters.

Scarlett made her way through the cave, shivering now and then, her boots crunching on the snow. She walked towards where the light was the brightest and soon she saw the opening. Standing in the entrance to the cave was a small female pilot with pointed ears. She had white-blonde hair that topped her head in a shining pompadour that gathered at the nape of her neck and fell over her shoulder blades in three large curls.

She turned her face and Scarlett could see a ragged double scar that triangulated out from the woman's red lips. One scar went up over the cheekbone to just under a sparkling blue eye and one scar shot down over the line of her jaw.

It was Jordan Blue, but she wasn't decked out in her usual blue attire. She was wearing red. A shimmering Mylar flight suit in deep crimson covered her body. She eyed Scarlett standing inside the cave of ice.

"It's awfully clean in there," Jordan Blue remarked. "Don't you think?"

The dark-haired Jordan opened her mouth to answer but Blue was gone in a blink of bright light.

Scarlett closed her eyes against the flash of light and when she opened them again she was lying in her bed in her room at Elaeric's cottage, rosy morning light pouring through the window.

Though the covers were up to her chin, she shivered with cold. She touched her arm under the blanket and felt the ripple of gooseflesh as it melted back into her skin.

Scarlett pulled her hand from under the blanket and looked at her fingertips, expecting them to be cold and wet, but they were dry. She lay awake in her bed, thinking about the dream. What she thought about most was the voice inside the cave. It had been a female voice, Scarlett was sure of that, and one that was not entirely new or unfamiliar. Still, she couldn't place it.

She thought that perhaps it was her mother's voice. She didn't remember much of her mother, she had died when Scarlett was still a child and had been gone for over a hundred years. Most of Scarlett's few memories of her were visual, aided by the photographs that she had seen of her.

There's no way I could recognize her voice, is there? I don't remember what it sounded like. Scarlett sat up and swung her legs over the side of the bed. *But my subconscious might,* she thought. *My subconscious would never forget.*

The voice was on her mind as she went through her morning routine, and she was so lost in thought that she hardly felt the fat chicken take a nice chunk of flesh out of the back of her left hand, though she subconsciously noted that the chicken did not look as typically smug.

On her third day at the cottage Scarlett had tried to gather eggs with her field activated. And though she was delighted that it worked, even more so that it kept the ungodly stench out, it did not work out as well as she had hoped.

To keep the monster's beak from poking her, the field only had to be set at a single factor, which made the membrane around her mostly impermeable. It was enough to stop a knife or a short-wave laser pulse, but not a bullet or a plasma round. However, it deterred not just what might be after her, but also what she was after.

It meant that handling the egg was like trying to hold an oiled mouse in a silicone glove. The giant bird jabbed at her hand to no avail, and with noticeable dismay, but the egg squirted from her field-gloved hand like an over-sized watermelon seed. It made a wet and unceremonious crump on the shit-splattered planks of the hen house.

The smugness previously unattained by the thwarted chicken now flourished and the beast held her head high, twitching it back and forth. Scarlett had stifled an angry scream and glared murderously at the hen before stalking out. She came back later with two buckets of water to wash down the floor. Elaeric never asked why and she didn't try to use her field again while gathering eggs.

Scarlett pondered her dream over breakfast, wondering what it meant and trying to place the voice that had spoken in the cave.

Seeing her lost in thought for the morning, Elaeric remained silent but watchful. He knew the power of introspection. It wasn't until lunch, after their time for mediation, that she spoke.

"Master Elaeric?" Though she had begun using the title as a joke, she now used it in earnest and he never objected. She had the feeling it was a title he had held before.

"Yes?"

Scarlett paused, as if seeing something new for the very first time. "I am a very angry person."

Elaeric grinned, pleased that he could use one of Scarlett's own colloquialisms.

"No shit."

★

"Anger," Master Elaeric told her later after they had cleaned up the kitchen, "is the result of an unmet expectation. It doesn't matter if it is mere annoyance, or outright fury, it all stems from the same place – not getting what you expected. If you can change your expectation, you can change how you feel."

"What about the past? I can't change the past so how I am I supposed to change how I feel about it?"

Elaeric smiled. "You can change how you feel now. Even now, you can decide that you had expected some things, even if it was not the case back then. For instance, the goat kicks over my pail, spilling the milk, and I am angry. But I tell myself that I should have expected it, since I left the pail behind his hoof. My anger at the goat is gone because I have changed my expectation. I reprimand myself to be more careful next time and life goes on." He spread his hands to show how simple it was.

Scarlett smirked at him. "My hang-ups aren't about spilled milk."

"Aren't they?" Elaeric asked with a sly look. Scarlett scowled at him and he laughed, laying a reassuring hand on her arm. "It should make your task easy, having hindsight, because now you know for sure what to expect because it has already happened. Why don't you try?"

It sounded both simple and ridiculous, which in Scarlett's short experience with the monk told her that he was probably right. Dubious, she went to the meditation room for the second time in the same day – a first for her - and planted her butt on a cushion.

Sunlight, clean and pure, streamed through the glass panes of the window like rosy hued bars of gold and again Scarlett was struck by the knowledge that there was something odd about that light, though she couldn't for the life of her figure out what it was.

She took a deep breath and closed her eyes.

She knew what thoughts she wanted to dredge up, but it was long moments before she could bring herself around to do so. Her willful mind wanted to wander back to the sunlight, clean and clear and warm. Instead, she gently pushed her mind the other way.

Instead, she thought about darkness. The darkness of an empty podment. A pod for one that before had recently been for two. She had sat in that dark podment and let the anger grow within her heart.

Now, after weeks of meditation, she saw that the anger she had felt that dark night in the podment just a few years ago had already been there. It had been there long before he had said that he was leaving. Galen's departure had merely thrown fuel on the fire.

Because you had already lost two men you loved? Scarlett thought. *Is that it? Do you fear abandonment? Even though the first two did not leave by choice?*

Scarlett shuddered and drew a deep, shaky breath.

One thing at a time.

Scarlett thought back to the night Galen had left, of herself sitting alone on the edge of the bed. She had been holding a piece of paper, which was odd, since paper was rarely used any more, but it bore the official seal of the IGC. It had been her acceptance to the Jordan Training Center.

Scarlett shifted her weight and visited the memory of the heat rising within her. She had not intended for them to continue their relationship after she left for school but the fact that Galen had left *her*, and left so suddenly, made it feel like a slap.

At the time, she had expected that it would be her to leave him. Certainly not the other way around.

She reached into the past and tried to turn that hurtful surprise into knowledge.

Why did I expect him to stay? She wondered. *He knew I was gong to get accepted to the Jordan Training Center, we both knew it, and I had certainly made it clear - though I never had the guts to say it outright – that I never thought a long-distance relationship would work.*

I expected Galen to leave me, she told herself. *I might not want to have admitted it, but it had been coming and I didn't have the backbone to make a clean break. The passion had been gone a long time. Like a coward, I put it off – planning on simply walking out the door for the JTC and never coming back. I was a fool not to see it – no, I was blind not to see it, blinded by my pride.*

The acceptance filled her mind and seemed to travel throughout her whole body. It suddenly felt as though a snake, whose existence she had never even known, unwound its constricting hold from around her heart.

Scarlett's eyes opened wide with shock. "Jesus!" she whispered, feeling a rush of feeling that bordered on elation. She had expected that it would take hours, possibly days, of meditation to accomplish anything close to what she had just experienced.

My god, is it that easy? It's just that easy?

She closed her eyes again.

I expected him to find someone right away, she thought, though it did not feel right. The thought was too forced and the feeling was not relief but a bitter edginess. *I guess it's not* that *easy,* she decided.

Scarlett shifted her butt on the cushion and adjusted her thoughts a bit. *I expected he would eventually find someone, how could I not? He was beautiful and brilliant and incredibly caring, something that at the time I secretly believed was a weakness. He had to find someone that needed him. It was in his healing nature. Blue needed him. Needed him more than I ever could.*

The newly discovered snake, the one that had so recently been disengaged from her heart, slithered away.

Scarlett opened her eyes again and snagged a deep breath in great hitching gasps. She couldn't believe how she felt. Light. Free. Strong.

She realized she was trembling and gave her body a shake, like a dog shaking water from its coat. She tilted her head one way and then the other, stretching her neck, then rolled her shoulders back.

She knew what she was after next. Many things had haunted her during the course of her life but there was only one thing that had shaped her anger and bitterness into the woman she had become.

Scarlett drew in a long nervous breath and then, once her eyes were closed, she puffed out her cheeks and let it out.

She was almost afraid to think it, to even try, but she did.

I knew that eventually Dad would see combat. I knew even then that the life expectancy of fighter pilots could be short and cruel. I expected Joe to be with him. I knew it was coming. I knew all along.

A great burning rose in her throat and Scarlett screamed out in anger, filling the room with her fury but not cleansing it from her soul. Her hands reached down and she grasped the cushion she was sitting on with hands that had turned into claws. The muscles in her arms stood out, her nails digging into the fabric as she tried to control the rage that tore through her body.

Maybe some things couldn't be changed; maybe others would

take more time. Either way, she could not accept or change how she felt for her father and brother. Maybe she didn't want to.

She released the cushion and buried her face in her hands but, even now, she couldn't cry. The fire inside had burned away the tears that any another person may have shed. The anger was still too much. This anger was not a snake, it was the crushing weight of a giant stone. One she was not sure that she could lever off of her heart.

Scarlett sat that way for a while, feeling both exulted and frustrated, before she got up and left the cottage to go on a long walk. She searched her soul that day and every day after. Her progress was erratic, and she was still prone to temper tantrums, but it was progress nonetheless.

Day by day and little by little, Scarlett had begun to release the small angers that had clung to her soul like ugly barnacles. She ignored the Golgoth in the room, as the saying went, but the small stuff she realized was, well, small stuff.

After Scarlett began to make headway with herself, Elaeric had encouraged her to start working with the mare.

"I don't know anything about horses," she told him.

"But you are learning to meditate. The best way to retain and grow your knowledge is to teach what you have learned."

"You want me to teach the horse how to meditate?" Scarlett laughed. "Just when I start thinking you might be as crazy as you look, it turns out that you are even crazier!"

Elaeric smiled benignly. "Sit in the meadow and breathe. You breathe in, the horse breathes out."

"You have got to be kidding me."

"No kid. Go."

Dubious as ever, Scarlett did as he said. For almost a week she spent afternoons in the meadow, cross-legged and eyes closed, breathing deeply. At first, she felt like an idiot. Then she realized it wasn't much different than the meditation room, and there was nobody to see her anyway.

One afternoon she was deep into her breathing, only vaguely aware of the world around her, when she felt someone shove her.

"Hey!" she growled, opening her eyes to see the mare. The horse had been standing over her but now, startled, trotted away. The horse snorted in a manner that sounded like laughter and stopped a few meters away.

Scarlett watched the mare with suspicion, but when she didn't move, the Jordan closed her eyes and focused again on her breath. A few minutes later the horse returned to put her nose against the Jordan's back and give her another shove. This time Scarlett let her body be moved, and kept her eyes closed. She could hear the horse stamp the ground only a few feet away.

Experimenting, she drew in a deep breath, filling what seemed like her entire body, and held it. The mare blew a great gust of air out through her nostrils.

Scarlett laughed, unable to control her mirth. "That crazy bugger!" she laughed, startling the mare. The Jordan stilled herself and repeated the process and got the same result. She did it again. And again.

Within a week of their inward and outward struggles, breathing together in the meadow, the horse began to stand right next to the Jordan. On impulse, Scarlett reached out and touched the mare's leg. She could feel a tremor run through the animal's entire body, but she did not move away. A month later, though not without a few bites and bruises, Scarlett was riding her - with more joy than the Jordan had thought possible for herself.

She had found great joy in the past while flying with Fledge, especially as the bond began to tighten and their hearts began to merge. But even that was mostly through the cold black of space, the silence so great that it was often deafening.

Riding the horse was not just the difference of night and day; to Scarlett it was much more. The feel of the horse, the powerful flex of her muscles as she ran, the wind in her hair and the smell of root and tree and earth that filled her nostrils was the most thrilling experience the Jordan could fathom.

Scarlett found that she loved to explore – from the faux medieval town to the rivers, hills, and country environs. It made her think of a childhood that had long been forgotten, even though her own had been one of metal and machinery, not of pastures and trees. The mare seemed to enjoy it just as much, filled with her own power and the joy of an all-out run. She seemed to heal almost along the same lines as her new mistress.

Scarlett gradually released her stranglehold on the past, started to feel appreciation for the present, and then slowly began to hope for the future.

The present and future that the Jordan was most concerned about had to do with Fledge, and how he was getting on without her. She felt a tremendous amount of guilt for the people she had hurt, but now believed that she could work through it. Once she did, she intended to reunite with her Fledgling Dragon.

★

Though she was changing, Scarlett was pleased. She was no fool and she saw her anger for what it was and always had been – protection when danger loomed and strength when weakness threatened. It drove her to succeed in everything she sought. It had been both weapon and shield. But now, with her newfound knowledge of herself and of the universe around her, she felt strong. Pure. She felt that she could shed the heavy burden of the anger she had cloaked about her body and soul. She no longer saw the need.

Not until she looked into the gimlet green eyes of the Chimeran Commander.

Rather than his Chimeran Blue coveralls, he wore simple, soft clothes of fine brown linen and tanned suede. Instead of softening his appearance, the clothes made him look even more arresting. His sharp features, along with his blonde hair and bright green eyes, stood out in striking contrast.

Looking into those eyes made her feel weak from her neck to her knees. Worse was his smell, so clean and so sharp that it made her want to lean towards him. And his voice – it made her feel hot all over.

She hooked a hand under the saddle belt and pulled herself back, leaning against the mare. She tried to fill her nostrils with the smell of horse but it was only a faint undercurrent to her senses.

"I thought you were dead," Scarlett said, looking away from his blonde hair and shining eyes as he smiled at her.

"You destroyed yet another one of my jets," Bjorn admitted, "but not me. You probably saved my life, keeping me from returning to that hangar on Leoness. And I am glad to hear you say that you thought I was dead, not that you hoped I was dead."

"How did you find me?" Scarlett asked.

Bjorn laughed, his white teeth flashing in the hot sun. "Scarlett!" he scolded. "I am a Commander of the Chimeran Military and a leader of my people. There is no one in this universe that could stay hidden from me."

"Leader of your people!" Scarlett challenged in an amused tone, finally meeting his gaze with her own. "You're awfully full of yourself."

Bjorn laughed. The sound was deep and reverberated

throughout her entire body like the vibrating string of a musical instrument. "Scarlett, my darling, you know so little about the war in which you are fighting."

"I don't happen to be fighting at present, in case you haven't noticed."

"I have noticed," Bjorn admitted, his voice deep. Scarlett could feel a wave of heat roll through her body but kept perfectly still. "And it is something I would like to discuss with you."

He reached out to touch her arm but Scarlett drew back, though not quickly, pushing her weight against the mare.

"Despite my present circumstances," she told him, "I have no interest in you. You should just leave."

Bjorn laughed again and this time Scarlett could feel her groin go hot, and wet. "There is something different about you Scarlett," he said, looking her up and down. "And not just your clothes. I can't imagine from what goat monger's grave you dug up those rags, but you still manage to make yourself sexually regal."

"You should see my clogs," she told him, her voice flat.

Bjorn clucked his tongue. "I know this planet prides itself on some sort of imagined history but, Scarlett!" He reached out and touched her blouse and this time she found herself unable pull away.

Breathe, she told herself. *Just breathe.*

"They do have nicer clothes than this," he told her, running his hand down her cotton sleeve and then cupping the joint of her arm. Her elbow disappeared into his hand and she gently pulled it free. "Even riding clothes," he told her, "if that is what you prefer. In fact, they have trousers that are just the *legs* of pants that fit over your actual pants, can you believe that?"

"They're called chaps," Scarlett told him, smiling.

Bjorn leaned toward her in a conspiratorial manner and gave her his wolfish smile. "I would like to see them on you with no actual pants underneath."

Scarlett laughed for the first time with him in her proximity. "You are incorrigible!" she scolded, but Bjorn did not miss a beat, nor the encouragement of her laugh. He stepped forward and wrapped a hand around her hip.

Scarlett's laugh caught in her throat and she stared up into his bright green eyes. *My god,* she thought, *he's too perfect. His eyes, his face, everything about him. He may have been perfectly sculpted, but sculpted he was. You can't forget that.* It took all of her strength to turn her face away, but she did. *It's how he was made,* she told herself. *It's not you. They made him to make you feel that way.*

"Why don't you have dinner with me?" Bjorn asked. His voice was low and husky and Scarlett could sense the reaction she was having on him. It surprised her to realize she had a similar effect on the Chimeran.

At least it's not just me, she thought.

"No," she told him. "I need to get home." As if to emphasize her words the mare whickered, edged away and then edged back into her, giving her a hefty shove.

"Please?"

Scarlett cocked her head. The word had been said in earnest, but she could tell by his expression how foreign it tasted to him. Like her, he was probably not used to having to ask twice. "No," she repeated, this time in a firmer tone.

Bjorn gave her a smile that was forlorn but he nodded. "I will be here for another four days. I have dinner at the Huit Chalet on the southwest side every night at seven." He caught Scarlett's chin in his hand and turned her face towards him. She kept her breath steady through force of will. His normally mischievous eyes were steady and serious. "Even if my company does not appeal to you, there are some things that you need to hear, things that you need to know."

Scarlett stared at him, not knowing what to think or believe. He looked like he might say more, or possibly lean down to kiss her, but instead he simply let go and walked away.

It took a long moment, but Scarlett was able to collect herself and pull herself up and into the saddle. When she did she realized that her knees were shaking.

She clucked her tongue and carefully guided the horse through the people coming and going from the town walls. The mare could sense the turmoil in her mistress and it made the horse jittery, dancing and picking her way through the crowd. When they had cleared most of the meandering townsfolk on the road home, Scarlett spurred the mare and rode like hell, leaving the road smoking in a plume of dust.

After the mare had worked herself into a lather, Scarlett pulled up and slowed her down. She was still shaken, but her mind had too many things to turn over before she got home. She dismounted and led her courser into a field. Her dark eyes sought out a thick line of deep green trees. Elaeric had taught her that it meant water. Sure enough, a stream tumbled its way through a bed by their gnarled roots.

Scarlett released the horse and watched the sun arc down towards the horizon as the mare went to the water and drank her fill.

What did he mean – there are things I need to know? About what?

Scarlett knelt by the stream and splashed a handful of water on her face. She tried to peer at her reflection but the water was moving too fast and all she could make out of her face was a rippling shadow. Despite the chill of the water, Scarlett could still feel where he had touched her chin. She raised her arm and rubbed the area with the back of her hand.

Maybe there's nothing and he's just trying to get the better of my curiosity.

The mare raised her dripping mouth from the stream and gave Scarlett a nudge.

"What is that supposed to mean?" Scarlett asked the horse, rubbing her nose. "You think I should go find out?"

The horse gave her another nudge and Scarlett laughed as she fastened her hands onto the saddle, stuck a scuffed boot into a stirrup, and swung herself up.

"I think you're just telling me that you want to get home," she said, leaning down to rub the mare's neck. "So do I." Scarlett turned the horse back to the road and let her canter at a leisurely pace all the way back home.

When she reached the cottage, the red sun had set and darkness was seeping into the ruby twilight. Elaeric met her in the yard and helped her with the scarf of produce.

"My!" he exclaimed, his yellow robes flapping in the breeze. "Extraordinary day! You get back nigh after dinner *and* we have a visitor!"

Scarlett, who had been loosening the saddle belt on the mare, stopped short.

"Visitor? What visitor?"

Elaeric cocked his head, looking surprised. "Why, he was a friend of yours - I thought you must know!"

Scarlett shook her head but said nothing as she went back to unsaddling the horse. When it was off the mare she threw it over her own shoulder and led the horse to the barn where she could be rubbed down. Her mind was a jumble of questions but she turned away from them.

When the mare had been taken care of for the night Scarlett turned her loose in the meadow and went back to the cottage. Exhausted but hungry, she dropped down into a kitchen chair. Elaeric had a dinner still warm for her. She buttered a piece of fresh bread while the monk sat across from her, waiting patiently. Scarlett, however, had also learned a bit of patience – even with herself.

"From the lady with the fence?" Scarlett asked, indicating the bread. She had helped Elaeric split rails and raise a small fence for a widowed neighbor. They were gifted with an occasional loaf of bread and, once, a peach pie.

Elaeric shook his head. "From your visitor." Scarlett paused momentarily in her chewing and then resumed as Elaeric continued. "He brought a box from the bakery. There are biscuits for breakfast, and even a brioche."

Bjorn, Scarlett thought with a shiver. *He was watching me*

"Have you ever heard the phrase 'beware of men bearing gifts?'" she asked.

"Of course. That is why I let you have the first piece of bread."

Scarlett laughed and waited for Elaeric to offer something more but he remained silent. *He's enjoying this, the little bastard.*

"My visitor," she finally said. "He was tall? Blonde?"

Elaeric nodded. "Yes. And most polite."

"Of course." She thought of her next words carefully. "And did you sense…anything about him?"

Elaeric eyed her, a trace of a smile edging his lips. "Such as?"

Scarlett sighed and pressed her lips together, not wanting to say it but knowing the monk wasn't going to help her out. "Did you sense anything evil about him?"

Elaeric looked shocked. "Evil? Why no! He was most polite! He left you a gift, in fact."

"He *what*?"

"Left you a gift. A box. I put it in your room."

Though Scarlett wanted to dash off to see what Bjorn had left her, she chewed her food thoughtfully. She tried to think of what she was after - translated into something Elaeric would understand. Then it hit her.

"What was his aura?" Scarlett asked suddenly. "Did he have an aura? What did it look like?"

Elaeric looked surprised but obliged her. "Why, it was red - just like yours."

Scarlett felt a small groan escape her lips. When Elaeric had first told her of auras, the chakras, and their colors she had been a bit skeptical about them. After a quick lesson, the monk had quickly, and quite painfully, convinced her that they were both real and accurate. The fact that Bjorn's matched hers made her feel worse, not better.

Though she felt as if she had been kicked, Scarlett continued eating in the most normal manner she could muster. When done and with what felt like an excruciating slowness, she washed the last of the evening dishes, thanked Elaeric, and retired to her room.

There were two large white boxes on her bed, tied together with a scarlet ribbon.

Beaming like a child on their birthday, Scarlett untied the ribbon and opened the boxes – already having a good idea of what might be inside.

The first box contained a pair of riding boots made of hand tooled black leather, inlaid with crimson. She kicked off the overly large boots she was wearing and pulled on the new ones. They fit perfectly. She admired them for a few seconds and then pulled them off and set them down at the edge of her bed.

The second box contained clothes.

There were two pairs of riding pants – one made of the same blue denim canvas that Grandpa always wore and the other was smooth black leather.

I should be glad that neither are chaps, Scarlett thought, chuckling. There were also three silk shirts, all cut too low and much too fashionable to have been made on the east side of Kayos.

Two were crimson and the other was blue.

Scarlett's first thought was of her recent dream of wearing a blue flight suit, but that had been a sparkling ocean blue. The shirt in the box was a carefully selected and much deeper royal blue.

Chimeran Blue, it was often called these days.

Scarlett pulled it out of the box and held it to her face, inhaling deeply. It had the sharp, clean smell of the green-eyed Chimeran Commander.

Alone, Scarlett let her knees buckle this time and collapsed in a heap upon her narrow bed. She stared at the ceiling and tried to let her thoughts drift without clinging to anything in particular. Without realizing it, she fell asleep with the smooth blue cloth against her chest and rumpled under her chin.

ONE TWO

Faith gave Jasyn, who was laughing at her, a playful shove. He feigned toppling from his seat in the jet and she smacked at him, still laughing. Everyone else on Faith's personal craft politely ignored them, going about their normal business in preparations for reaching the villa.

The days had become haphazard. Faith worked chaotically to accomplish her occupational tasks and to meet the demands that had been placed on her (most of them by herself) while working hard to allow Jasyn to become part of her life. Faith knew, more than anyone, that an artificial being didn't signify a lack of real feelings. And Jasyn was proof.

He always tried not to show any disappointment when Faith had to leave for business, but still fell short when it came to hiding his feelings. His happiness in her presence was always obvious and his smile was becoming more sure and less shy, unless there were people around with whom he was unfamiliar.

On the craft, the small space tender that Faith used for short commutes, were the staff members that Jasyn teasingly referred to as 'the usual suspects.' They were the ones that worked as the crew on Faith's personal spacecraft as well as her usual personal and security detail. Increasingly comfortable around them, he grasped Faith by the shoulders and gave her a playful shake.

"Somebody has to shake some sense into you!" he told her, ignoring the glare he got from Geary.

"Don't be ridiculous!" she told him, laughing. "Nothing has any meaning unless *I* give it meaning!"

"You tyrant!" he accused.

"Tyranny has nothing to do with it," she assured him, laughing.

Faith couldn't remember the last time she had such a good time and was still having fun, too much fun perhaps, when the call came. She was still giggling like a girl when she noticed Jasyn's face had become serious. She followed his gaze, turning to see Penny and Geary waiting patiently for her attention. Geary stood just behind Penny with his hand over the mike of his comset.

"Yes?" she asked Penny. Jasyn reached over and laid his hand on her leg. She resisted the urge to close her eyes, relishing the feel of his fingers around her knee.

"Ma'am, I have been informed that your sister has arrived at the villa. Would you like her to be allowed in?"

"Oh!" Faith exclaimed, surprised. "Of course!"

Penny nodded to Geary who turned and walked away, speaking into his comset as he addressed the security team at the villa.

Faith was delighted. She hadn't expected to see Charity until the party and that wasn't for another month. She couldn't believe that her sister would take the time for a visit right now but she was glad. There was a lot she wanted to speak with her about and knew that she probably wouldn't get the chance for more than a few words at the ball that Charity hosted every year.

Most things that Faith had to deal with, especially regarding the IGC and their constantly changing laws regarding artificial intelligence, would bore Charity to tears. Faith, however, was anxious to discuss other matters with her sister, things that she only felt comfortable discussing within the safe confines of the villa.

And the girl, Faith reminded herself. *You must remember to give her an update on the girl.*

She put her hand over Jasyn's and gave it a squeeze. She tapped her foot restlessly as the craft docked with the villa. Eager to see her sister, she was on her feet as soon as the seal on the craft hissed, waiting with forced patience for Geary to lead the way out as he always did. Once inside, she edged around him and strode into the circular elevator, practically pulling Jasyn along behind her.

Faith descended onto the villa's foyer with Charity's name on her lips, ready to call out to her, but then stopped so suddenly that Jasyn bumped roughly into her. Just as rapidly, he had an arm around her waist to keep from knocking her over as her eyes swept across the breadth of the room.

The villa's shield was open to show the star-studded sky and the living room was brightly lit. And empty.

Mari came bustling in as Penny and Geary both descended into the main room of the villa behind Faith and Jasyn. Mari's hands were clasped in front of her apron and her expression was of calm distress.

"Your sister is downstairs, Ms. de Rossi," she informed her employer, her knuckles pale as her hands twisted together.

Faith felt a chill run up her back and Penny glanced sharply at Geary. The PA had been with Faith long enough to know not only her employer's family history, but her family's habits as well. And Mari's demeanor left no doubt. She glared at the head of security, for the first time thinking that he might be as dense as all men.

"Tom cleared her," Geary affirmed, his voice low, but the PA's glare carried enough meaning for him and he put the pieces together in an instant. He looked in consternation at the lift, torn between whether to up or down.

"Geary," Faith said quickly, "it's fine." His blazing eyes told her that he did not agree.

"Do you want me to bring her up?"

Faith shook her head, emphatic. "No. I'll go down."

After looking for a moment like he might implode, her head of security turned and forwent the elevator and took the left spiral staircase, bounding up the stairs two at a time.

Faith turned to Jasyn. "Go into the bedroom and shut the door." He blinked at her in surprise as she turned away. "Tell Geary to turn off the lower level cams and mikes," Faith told her PA as she looked the staircase on the right side of the circular elevator, the one that circled down. Penny stood frozen, unsure, and Faith shot her a sharp glance that relaxed into an expression of mild amusement. "It's alright," she said, reassuring her. A wry smile creased her face. "After all, Tom cleared her." Faith started to move away but Penny called out, stopping her.

"Ma'am?"

Faith looked back to see her PA holding out a gold cuff.

Faith hesitated for a second and then took the cuff and fastened it on her right wrist. "Thank you."

She turned and peered down the winding staircase as Penny motioned to a bewildered Jasyn to get going. The construct paused, looking at Faith, but she was gazing down the staircase like she was about to jump into an abyss. Penny prodded him in the ribs and he turned and headed for the bedroom, throwing glances over his shoulder as he went. Faith took a deep breath, calming herself as she descended the stairs.

The second that her brown and gold eyes had swept across the living room to find nothing and no one, Faith knew exactly who had come to call.

Charity would not go downstairs, Faith knew. Her sister said that the vast room of darkness and stars gave her vertigo, and the creeps. Besides, the bar was upstairs. Constance was with Mother and Grace was in the Outer Banks. Hope was lost.

Besides, there was only one of her sisters that would feel comfortable standing amongst the stars, wasn't there?

Faith calmly descended the stairs and her shoes found the glassy black floor with a click-clack as she stepped onto the cold marble and her eyes searched the room, trying not to linger on the capacious pool that stretched out into the darkness.

Faith took a few steps around the staircase, her eyes traveling across the star-studded room that seemed open to the void of space beyond. Seeing nothing at first, Faith thought that Mari must have been mistaken and that there was no one on the lower lever. She swept the room again with her gaze and this time she saw her.

The lithe figure was dressed in a shimmering black flight suit. To Faith it looked as if a sliver of the eternal night from outside had broken off and reassembled itself on the near side of the glass. Even her shining hair seemed to absorb the darkness while at the same time reflecting the starlight. She stood close to the glass wall, staring out into the black with her back to the staircase, her arms folded across her chest.

Faith nervously toyed with the rings on her fingers, wishing she had a glass of champagne in her hands, or something stronger. She resisted the urge to nervously clear her throat.

"Hello Noel," she said.

"Hello," Jordan Blue responded, though she didn't turn around. "This place is strange," she remarked after a long silence. "There is something familiar about it, though I've never been anyplace like it. There is a smell here, a warmth that is oddly comforting. I don't know what it is."

Faith twisted her fingers, her mind racing as she watched the Jordan's shimmering black suit throw off specks of light.

"I'd heard you'd taken to wearing black."

"I'm in mourning."

"I heard. I'm sorry for your loss."

The Jordan huffed but still did not turn. Faith knew about the death of Noel's lover, Galen, as well as the demise of one of her fellow Jordans.

"Whose loss do you mourn the most?" she asked.

There was another long moment of silence before Noel answered. "My own."

Faith was taken aback by her sister's answer and a startled silence followed. She cast her eyes about the darkened glass room, carefully avoiding the pool.

"I'm glad you're here."

"Are you?" Noel's tone sounded both surprised and amused, if only slightly.

"Of course. Why wouldn't I be?"

Now she turned. Her face was pale and thin, illuminated by her bright blue eyes and ravaged by the scar that ran in jagged red lines across the right side of her face. She smiled crookedly.

"My dear *sister*," Noel sneered. The way she said it made Faith's heart stick in her chest. "Don't act like we have ever been close. We've hardly ever seen each other."

Faith lifted her chin. "You may not have seen much of me, but I've seen plenty of you. I've been with you a lot more than you know."

Jordan Blue's eyes narrowed in suspicion, making her scar pull taut and shiny. "What do you mean by that?"

Faith shrugged. "I came to see you quite a bit when you were younger. Almost every week when you were really young, only slightly less when you were still too little to remember. Elem and secondary. Saw you at parochial and flight. I went to all of your graduations. I even visited the Lido moon and checked in on you a few times during your Jordan training." "You did?" That was a surprise. Noel had never suspected that anyone in her family gave a second thought as to what she was doing.

"I did."

"Why didn't you ever speak to me?"

Faith walked over to a lounger and sat on the edge of the black leather seat, crossing her legs. The Jordan's wide blue eyes, one natural and one a perfect copy made of hyper optic glass, followed her. "I didn't know what to say, or how you would feel about me. Like you said, it's not like we were ever close. But I was watching over you."

The blue eyes narrowed again, this time in anger, and when she spoke her voice was low and accusing. "You hired Galen to watch me."

A small smile played at the corners of Faith's mouth. "Is that what this visit is about?"

Jordan Blue tensed, her flight suit shifting and tightening about her form, the thin black fabric rippling and casting back the reflection of the stars. She had come for a fight, angry and confused, but she decided that answers would suffice.

"Yes."

Faith's shoulders moved in a small shrug. "Galen was already working for the company. I saw him at your graduation from Advanced DS Flight and told him to keep an eye on you. It was a good thing, since you had your...accident that very night." She looked away towards the vast expanse of the pool, the water as black as the night around it. "I didn't tell him to fall in love with you. That was his doing entirely."

Noel turned away and looked out through the wall of glass. Faith stared into the depths of the pool, mesmerized by the depth and the darkness, before pulling her eyes away and training them on the back of the Jordan.

"Is he...with you now?" she asked.

Noel shrugged, the movement throwing glints of light off her darkened form. "I wouldn't know."

"You haven't seen him since you...turned him off?"

Noel's face turned sharply, her blue eyes glaring at her sister, but Faith could see something else in those eyes. Guilt. Maybe even an edge of fear. "No." Her lip curled up away from her teeth. "Why? Did you want to speak with him?"

"No. I was just curious." Faith toyed with the rings on the index finger of her left hand, twisting them nervously. She cursed herself for being so nervous. For having any sort of hesitation to talk to this child. For feeling any sort of discomfort in her own home.

"Would you like something to drink?" Faith asked abruptly, deciding that she certainly needed something. Noel shook her head, making her blonde coils tremble between her shoulder blades. "What about something to eat? You look dreadfully thin."

Noel looked at her from over her shoulder, smiling with half of her mouth. "I could use a bite."

Faith ran a finger along the edge of the gold cuff on her wrist before bringing it up to her lips. "Penny, please have Mari make some sunbutter sandwiches. And send down some champagne for me."

Noel smiled at her again from over her shoulder. "I like champagne too."

Faith returned her smile. "I know."

Noel grunted and turned back towards the outer darkness.

There was a clatter of footsteps and Geary came down the stairs carrying a bottle of champagne and two glasses. Faith couldn't help but smile, knowing he had probably been in a near fit without being able to see her or hear what was going on. Faith realized he must have been waiting for any excuse to come down and check on her and had probably snatched up the bottle and glasses and ran before Penny could utter a word. He watched Noel warily as he loosened the wire cage and uncorked the bottle. When it popped Noel shot him a quick glance.

"One of his guys took my sidearm," she remarked.

"How do you know it was one of his guys? Maybe he's my butler."

Noel snorted. "Please." She turned her face away again. "What's with them, anyway? Do they think I want to kill you?"

"They assume that everyone is trying to kill me. It's one of the reasons that I am still alive."

Geary filled a glass and handed it to Faith. He raised the empty one with a questioning glance at his employer.

"Would you like a glass?" Faith asked.

Noel shook her head. "No, thank you."

Geary put the empty glass down on the table next to the lounger. "Mari should have the sandwiches done shortly. Is there anything else you need?"

"Thank you, Geary. That should be fine."

He gave her a slight nod and took the stairs quickly, leaving silence in his wake. The silence did not last long. In less than a minute Geary was again descending the staircase with a tray of sandwiches, sliced fruit, and glasses of water and milk. He looked questioningly at Faith as he set the tray down on a side table. Faith shook her head and waved him away. With a final glare at the Jordan's back, Geary turned and disappeared up the stairs once again.

"Please," Faith called to Noel, "sit down and have something to eat."

Noel turned from the glass wall, hesitated for a moment, then walked to the empty lounger and sat down on its edge, facing the woman she bore no resemblance to but supposedly shared some sort of background with, namely parental. She picked up a sandwich and took a bite.

"I'm sorry I didn't have peanut butter," Faith apologized.

The Jordan smiled around a mouth full of food. "How do you know I like peanut butter?"

Faith hid her smile in a sip of champagne before putting it down on the tray. "I have eyes everywhere."

The Jordan took the glass of milk from the tray and washed down a mouthful of sandwich. "Via Galen?" she asked, not attempting to keep the bitterness from her voice. She assumed it had to be the bright-eyed elfin doctor, since her penchant for peanut butter had evolved quite recently. The thought that her lover had been some sort of spy made a sick clamminess creep over her back. Faith shook her head.

"He refused to divulge any personal information about you, which I was not pleased with, but he did keep steadily reporting his progress on the Thermopylae, so I kept him employed."

Noel munched on her sandwich, thoughtful. "Did you want to speak with him?"

"At some point if you could...arrange a meeting, I would. Not right now. Tonight I'd like to talk to just you. I really am glad you are here, I wasn't just making polite conversation. I've been meaning to talk to you about something, something very important. This is just sooner than I expected."

Everything is happening sooner than I expected, Faith thought. *But perhaps that is a good thing.* She twisted the rings on her fingers nervously. Noel regarded her with an expectant expression above the sandwich that was half in her mouth. She tore off a bite and chewed it up, waiting.

"So, what the fuck is it?" she finally asked.

Faith laughed and picked up her champagne glass. She took a long drink and looked at the girl sitting across from her. They were almost knee-to-knee and Faith could appreciate how perfectly her eyes were matched.

"I want you to leave the IGC."

Noel choked, throwing a hand over her mouth as she coughed out half-chewed chunks of sunbutter and bread. Faith rose quickly to pound her on the back, or more if it was needed, but Noel waved her away. Faith realized the girl was laughing more than choking and sat back down, nonplussed.

Faith crossed her legs and waited for the Jordan's laughter to subside. The laughing died completely when Noel realized her sister wasn't joking.

"You're serious?"

Faith nodded.

"Are you insane?" Jordan Blue demanded.

Faith smirked. "More than a few people have asked me that before, but I doubt it."

"Leave the IGC and do what?" Noel asked her, grinning. "Retire?" She laughed aloud and stuffed the rest of the sandwich in her mouth, shaking her head. Faith waited until she had swallowed, she didn't want her choking again.

"No, but I think it's time you joined the company. Joined your family."

"You're crazy," Blue told her. "I'd never leave my Fledgling."

"I wouldn't want you to. I would want you to bring him. In fact, I'd like you to bring all the Fledglings." She watched her sister's face turn from good humor to confusion. Slightly frightened confusion.

"What do you mean, *all*?"

"The red one, as well as your own. I'm working on attaining the green one."

The Jordan's mouth sagged, her jaw hanging open. "You can't be serious," she whispered.

"I am."

Jordan Blue sat back so fast she nearly toppled over, keeping upright only by fastening a hand around her knee. "Fledge," she whispered. "*And* Verdana?" She took a deep breath and looked back at her sister, her blue eyes bright with curiosity. "And you think I could fly all of them?"

"You are already assuming control of the Red Fledgling, aren't you? In the absence of the Red Jordan, of course."

Noel blinked rapidly, surprised by what her sister knew and then her lip curled up in an expression of dry amusement. "I'm trying, but he is as stubborn as his mistress. I have gotten him to fly with me, occasionally, but only for training and growing while Scarlett recovers."

Faith waved a hand as she sipped her drink, signaling that the facts were inconsequential. "He will be yours soon enough. The green one as well, as soon as it can be brought around."

Noel was damned curious to know where her sister might acquire a Dragon Fledgling that had all but disappeared from the known universe but something else troubled her much more.

"What exactly would you want with a squadron of Fledglings?" she asked, her eyes narrow and her voice low.

Faith, not having the time she would have liked to prepare for such questions, answered directly. It was no time to mince words.

"The short story? To overthrow the IGC."

Noel stared at her sister in stunned silence before voicing a cackle of nervous laughter. "You *are* insane."

Faith shrugged and sipped from her flute of champagne. "Anyone might say so. But you do not know what I know, nor have you lived through what I have survived." She fixed her eyes on her sister. "Do you know what a Singularity is?"

Noel shrugged, the previous look of shock draining from her face as she considered the question. "It's a lot of things. In a black hole, it is where the spacetime curvature becomes infinite. It's also a mathematical term, having to do with a system breakdown. In the military we call it a goat-fuck."

Faith pressed her lips tightly together. "Lovely. I'll take your word for it. It is also a term used to denote a time when there will be an equal fusion of the artificial and the organic."

Frowning, Noel plucked up another sandwich and dug into it with small white teeth. It was clear that she was bright, but that she did not understand what her sister was getting at. Faith took a deep breath, carefully rolling the flute of champagne between the palms of her hands.

"A Singularity was reached on Earth in their recorded year of 2030, when artificial intelligence finally matched human intelligence. Once that happened, it passed human standards within seconds and then within minutes all hell broke loose. The result was almost the destruction of the human race – not by the machines themselves but by a war fought between the humans who thought that the machines should be destroyed and the humans who thought we should merge with them."

Noel listened, her blue eyes wide and interested. She had only the vaguest recollection of human history. She swallowed. "So who won?"

Faith shrugged. "Winning is only a matter of perception." She took a sip from her glass and continued. "Another Singularity was reached in the Year of the Third Dragon, as the elves call it. 3888, by human standard years."

The Jordan's nod was almost enthusiastic. This part of history she knew. "The Rebellion."

"Yes, when artificial emotion matched human emotion."

Noel took a bite of sandwich before pointing it at her sister in an accusatory manner. "When the life-forms *you* created realized what they were being used for, and decided to wipe out real humanity."

Faith shook her head. "They simply realized what they were, and what they wanted to be. I think every advanced life form, us included, reaches that at some point in their existence."

Noel sat back, commiserating with the constructs though she didn't want to – she had been fighting them since she had joined the IGC and the conflicting feelings roiled inside her. "They were being used." She shot an accusatory glance at Faith but the older woman only nodded, her face solemn.

"In the game of life there are only players and pawns. Whichever one you are is entirely up to you. Despite any background or circumstance, everyone must decide for themselves which one they want to be."

"Aren't some people born into it?"

"No."

"What about fate?"

Faith shrugged. "I believe in fate, but I think free-will is more powerful."

"That's ridiculous! How can you believe in both?"

Faith smiled. "I believe in gravity," she told the Jordan, "but that doesn't mean I think it should keep you pinned to the ground. You can rise of your own will. You can walk, you can jump. You can fly between the stars. You just have to decide."

The Jordan frowned. "What if there are people that don't decide? Or choose not to play?" she challenged, lifting her chin.

Faith sighed. "Then they are pawns by default, pinned by gravity. They constantly mourn their fate and play the victim, but it is still by their own choice that they are the victim."

Noel's sandwich had been worn down to the crust and she turned it around in her hands before tossing it back onto the plate. She brushed her hands on the thighs of her black flight suit, dusting off crumbs.

"What does any of this have to do with me or the IGC?"

"A Singularity is coming again. Intelligence, emotion, technology, desire – it is all reaching a breaking point – critical mass, if that is the term you prefer - and nothing is going to stop it. The Council will fight it and, for the first time in my life, I will fight the Council."

The Jordan's eyes grew wide as she listened. "When you say fight, do you mean voicing your opposition or actually fighting?" she asked.

"Why do you think I want a squadron of Fledglings?"

Noel's mouthed opened and closed uselessly for a moment. She looked away, breathless. "You are suggesting treason," she whispered. "I could be sentenced to a firing squad if I ever even related this to anyone."

"One of the reasons I know that this conversation will remain private."

Blue glared at Faith. "Still," she argued, frowning. "You think having a handful of Dragon Fledglings will give you control of the universe?"

Faith wasn't after a handful, she was after the whole damned rainbow, but she declined to say so at present.

"I don't want control of the universe, I just want to see that control change hands. The IGC should have been deposed half a century ago. GwenSeven already has more control of this universe than most people know. Hell, more than most people suspect. We do not have a military, however, though our allies are working on that."

"Allies?" Noel asked, startled.

Faith nodded. "I'm not just some raving lunatic. There are entire populations that have had enough of the Council and their tyranny."

Noel stared blindly at the woman across from her. She knew that not every species held a seat on the council, but she had never considered why. Tyranny? What did the IGC do besides fight the Chimera? Faith saw her confusion and continued.

"Having an elite force of fighters would make up the backbone of the new militia and put us on equal ground - give us a level playing field, as the expression goes. The Dragons have been the greatest military threat in centuries, but I don't believe they would attack their own children."

"Nor do I think any Fledgling would attack its own mother!"

Faith nodded. "That bond is what I am counting on. If I can create a stand-off of military power, or have a show of force that would prevent an offensive against us, the fighting should be minimal, the loss of life slight. It is actually what I would prefer."

"How do you know of the bond?" Noel asked suddenly.

"I have eyes everywhere," Faith told her again, but this time her voice was quieter, more somber.

The Jordan's mouth was suddenly very dry. She took a swig of milk from the glass, draining it, but held onto it, rolling it between her hands. "You want me to *fight* for you? What makes you think I even would?"

Faith's brow furrowed deeply in sudden anger, and though she kept her voice even and cool, her tone was sharp. "Who do you think paid for all of your schooling, including flight schools? Father never would, I can tell you that." She regretted her tone instantly, and could see that her words stung. She took a deep breath to calm herself. The younger de Rossi glared at her sister, her own anger rising.

"Are you the reason I made it through?" she demanded, seething. "You and your money?"

Faith closed her eyes as her anger dissipated, then opened them slowly.

"No. I covered all the costs but I never paid to have you accepted at any school or promoted to any rank. You got there on your own merits and earned all your own accolades." Faith saw the young woman relax noticeably though she was still unnerved and edgy. She reached out and placed a hand on the Jordan's knee and though the girl flinched at her touch, she did not pull away. "I care deeply for you," Faith told her earnestly, "and the ties that we have, that all us sisters have, it is *our* bond. It runs deeper than some loyalty to a council that cannot be trusted."

"You don't understand," Noel argued with a shake of her head. "The IGC is the only family that I have ever really known."

"You are *not* family to them," Faith said, her voice cold. "You are not even a person to them."

"I am a respected officer."

"Respected," Faith scoffed. "They don't respect you, only what you can do for them. You don't even have a name! You are a number and a color! You are a pawn in their game – they think nothing of you!"

"That's not true!"

"Don't fool yourself! I told you that in this universe you are either a player or a pawn, and right now you are the latter. The IGC is moving you like a piece on a holo board. You're going to have to decide for yourself if you want to keep playing their game."

"I'm a *Jordan* for Christ's sake!"

"Which is nothing compared to what you could be," Faith said, her voice cooling, becoming patient. "GwenSeven practically controls Galactic Commerce. Charity holds Universal Finance in her grasp. You would hold a position equal to ours in the new military. Not as a Jordan, or even a Captain, but as an Admiral. You and your Dragons."

"You're talking treason!" Noel hissed.

"I'm talking about the future," Faith said, perfectly calm. "A future that you cannot stop but one that you can participate in. As a player, rather than a pawn."

Noel stood up quickly, almost panicky, shaking her head. "I can't listen to this," she said, her eyes darting, looking for an escape. She placed her empty milk glass on the table and drew the back of her hand across her mouth. "Thank you for...for...for giving me so much to digest," she said, smiling awkwardly as she hurried to be gone.

Faith rose to her feet but her sister was already headed for the stairs. She called after her quickly, almost desperately. "Did you ever wonder who ordered the hit that cost Galen his life?"

Noel froze with her hand on the rail, her body tense. When she finally answered, her voice was heavy with emotion. "You were the only one I had considered."

"I would do no such thing!" Faith admonished. She looked at the slender form of the Jordan and sighed. "But the IGC would not think twice about terminating those they see as a threat, even a future threat, such as the people that are close to their key officers." Noel shook her blonde curls and started up the first few steps, deciding that she had heard enough. "They have done it before," Faith called to her retreating form, "just ask your fellow Jordan."

The Blue Jordan stiffened as if she had been given an electric shock, her mouth hanging open in surprise. She paused as the words sank in and then bolted up the stairs without looking back.

# ONE THREE

The crew, the damnable treacherous crew, that had transported seven cadets from the IGC Jordan Training Center to the Beryl Dragon, had massacred those cadets and then stolen that Dragon's eggs. They then, after having waylaid those eggs from the man who had hired them, scattered across the galaxy like a heard of antelope beset upon by pride of lions.

They had stolen four fighter jets from the Battle Cruiser *Resurrection* and, each taking off in a different direction, disappeared into the black with Alexander's Eggs and the Beryl Dragon's Engineer like thieves in the night.

JP had dispatched every jet at his disposal, and not just the ones from his own ship. He made sure that every Chimeran ship and pilot that could be spared was sent to hunt down the traitors. Every other soul had been commanded to find the missing eggs.

After seven days, just as doubt had began to gnaw at the nerves of the Commander and every other body aboard his ship, a call came through to the bridge of *Resurrection* from its very own Executive Officer, Jan Petrov.

The Commander met with the holo of his Second in Command in the bridge only seconds after it had been admitted through coms to materialize. Petrov stood on a holo-pad; a three-dimensional image of the officer in flickering yellow light nearly two meters high. His neck was streaked with dirt and sweat. His white-gold hair hung in damp clots about his face and there was a deep cut in his left cheek.

The glimmering image of the Chimeran officer showed that he had someone held close to his body. The person was down on one knee and had had their face turned away, but it was a female by the looks of the narrow face and long fall of brown hair. Petrov had her arm behind her back almost high enough to dislocate it, and his gun was pressed against the nape of her neck.

JP, dressed in a crisp blue cassock of heavy linen with cloth-covered buttons fastened by silk loops and his high round collar snug around his throat, faced the flickering image of his Executive Officer. The Commander's body was as taut as a strung wire, his bright blue eyes ablaze in his freshly scrubbed face.

"I couldn't find the pilot," Petrov said. "Or the coms man. They haven't regrouped. I was only able to get..."

"The Astrogator," JP said softly.

Petrov shrugged with only one shoulder, the one that held the Astrogator by the arm. The other arm remained frozen and the laser pistol in that hand was kept tight against the base of her neck.

JP cocked his head, looking at the woman that the Executive Officer had forced to her knees. By the look of Petrov, it hadn't been easy to do so. She didn't look like she was in much better shape than the tall blonde Chimeran, and trailers of smoke drifted into the holo like ethereal snakes.

JP didn't ask what had happened, where, why, or who was involved. He didn't even ask if any of the eggs had been found. The boyish Commander only spoke four words to his Second.

"Bring her to me."

Petrov gave a curt nod and jerked his head, motioning to someone out of view, and the link was cut. JP turned to his Communications Officer, a strikingly beautiful woman with raven black hair and large, dark eyes.

"Where did that transmission come from, Francesca?"

Francesca ran a hand over the upper right square of the sleek metal coms board. A holo formed over the steel dash of a rotating sphere of blue light. Holographic words streamed along over the dash, giving names and coordinates.

"D-799," Francesca said. "It's one of the unnamed moons of Jupiter."

JP's blue eyes flicked to the woman seated next to Francesca, who looked so much like the Communications Officer that they could have been twins. They had been cast from the same mold, which made them twins by manufacture, if not by birth.

Natalie, the Navigations Officer, turned her dark eyes to the coordinates streaming under the sphere of light over the coms dash and, after making a quick mental calculation, answered the Commander without him having to ask.

"Twenty-four to thirty-six hours," she told him. "Depending on how close he is to his craft and how fast he can get it out of there."

JP nodded, pleased. "Notify me when he is on approach."

"Of course, sir," they answered in unison.

★

Thirty-three hours later, Larissa walked briskly down the corridor towards the Commander's cabin. The pant legs of her blue coveralls made a swishing sound in the eerie quiet of the ship's dimlight. She wore a coms choker around her throat and a small audio transmitter in her ear.

Everyone had known for twenty hours that one of the traitors had been caught, and that Petrov was bringing her back to the Commander to answer for her crimes. The Lady Larissa had worked a double shift, and then two hours more besides, wanting to be the one to bring the Commander the news that Petrov had arrived.

As soon as notification of the impending arrival of the Executive Officer was announced over the ship's closed communication line, Larissa had responded immediately. She notified the bridge that she was close to his quarters and would go to him directly. She wasn't extremely close, however, and so hurried to close the distance.

Wisps of her dark hair had come loose from the bun she had tied and she pushed them away from her face. There was no longer a trace of the exhaustion that had been seeping into her bones only an hour ago.

She knocked softly at the Commander's door and then leaned close to the metal panel to hear his reply. The door swung open, startling her, and her hand fluttered up to her chest like a frightened bird. The Commander was wearing his formal cassock, rather than one of his coveralls he often favored with the high, round collars that mimicked the ones on his formal robes. The fabric was a deep Chimeran blue, his high collar enclosing a second ring of fabric that was a single shade lighter. The torso of the garment fit snug across his chest while the bottom of the priestly robe belled out, hiding the black boots that he wore. The colors accented the blue of his eyes perfectly.

"I'm sorry to disturb you, sir," Larissa stammered, but the Commander laid a reassuring hand upon her shoulder.

"There is nothing to be sorry for, Larissa," he told her, blinking slowly and tilting his head to one side while dropping his hand to grasp her upper arm. "Commander Petrov is on approach?"

Larissa nodded vigorously. "He should be here within minutes."

JP let his hand fall from her arm and turned his face away as he considered the arrival of one of those that had thwarted him. Larissa, still relishing the feel of his hand upon her arm, quietly admired his profile, inwardly swooning at the rosy color in his cheeks that stained his otherwise porcelain, if slightly freckled skin.

He turned his face back to Larissa quickly, having come to a decision. "Call the bridge, and the jet bay. Have Petrov and our guest meet us in the chapel, along with my other officers."

"Yes, sir," Larissa responded and, laying a finger upon the bead on the coms choker, relayed the Commander's orders even as she hurriedly followed his footsteps down the corridor.

The chapel was in the center portion of the massive Battle Cruiser, and was much farther away than the bridge from the Commander's quarters, but Larissa understood why it had been selected. What better meeting place for judgment?

Moving at a brisk walk, JP arrived at the chapel in just over a minute with Larissa right at his heels. The chapel, one of the few areas of the ship to be carpeted, was dimly lit by faux candlelight. On the walls to either side were sconces of wrought silver that held plastique candles. Eight rows of wooden pews were split down the middle by a narrow aisle. The aisle led to an altar that displayed the symbol of the Zealot Cassar Church on the far wall – two circles laid side by side, touching but not crossing.

The two circles signified the two faces of The One – the creator and the destroyer – but the way they touched made the symbol look like a more rotund version of the Chimeran logo – the symbol of infinity.

JP and Larissa arrived at the chapel to find the ship's ten highest-ranking officers, other than the two Commanders and the four officers on duty in the bridge, already there. They sat in the first row of pews, heads lowered in prayer. Each wore a gold necklace of finely linked figure eights. The delicate chains glimmered softly in the candlelight, throwing a luminous glow onto the perfectly sculpted face of each officer.

Eight of the ten officers were women. Likewise, a majority of the crew was also female. JP had a strong aversion to men, though it was worse for humans than the Chimeran males. Even so, there were few men he trusted. Petrov was one. The other, also an officer, was not aboard the ship but off on another mission. One of the female officers was missing as well but, thanks to Petrov, she was on her way back.

Larissa strode down the aisle with the Commander and was ready to slip into the second row of pews when he caught her gently by the elbow. She looked up, fearing that she would be asked to leave but humbly ready to do so.

"You may stand with me," he said softly.

Larissa bowed her head and, feeling exulted, accompanied him to the altar. No sooner had the Commander turned, keeping Larissa to his right and back just a step, before Jan Petrov entered the chapel, accompanied by his two personal guards and roughly escorting the prisoner in front of him.

As one, the heads of the seated officers lifted and turned, the way a congregation would turn to see the entrance of the bride at a wedding. Instead of a gown, this bride still wore a heavy canvas flight suit with IGC patches on the shoulder and over the heart, and was being frog marched down the aisle with a laser pistol jammed between her shoulder blades.

When they reached the altar, Petrov kicked her legs out from under her body and she fell in a heap at the feet of the Commander. She kept her head down, refusing to look at him.

Her hair, once a soft brown, was caked with grease on one side and matted with clumps of dried blood on the other. JP looked down at her, his shining auburn hair combed neatly to the side, his creamy skin glowing in the faux candlelight.

"Elanor," he said, his voice soft.

"I won't tell you where they are," she said defiantly with her head still down, refusing to meet his eyes.

"I know where they are."

Elanor looked up sharply. Even the officers in the chapel looked surprised. If the Commander had discovered the location of the missing eggs, he had not divulged that information to anyone.

Elanor's face, though it was streaked with dirt, dried sweat, and blood, was beautiful. Of course, it had been manufactured that way.

The woman was Chimeran, which was why Petrov had been able to find her. The other members of the treacherous crew were human, and he was unable to comprehend what a human might think. But he knew how a Chimeran would think, and he had tracked her down as easily as a predator would hunt down wounded prey by the trail of blood. Also like prey, she had fought hard when she was cornered.

Not that it will help her any, Petrov thought. *I don't even think that The One can help her now.*

The Chimeran woman's face was striking, in spite of the dirt, and her brown eyes were luminous in the glow of the chapel.

"You know where?" she whispered.

"I know where," JP told her. He stepped closer to the woman and reached down, his fingers caressing her neck as they slid between the heavy lapels of her canvas flight suit. His hand closed into a fist before he yanked it back out and stepped away so that he could see her better. A gold officer's chain dangled from between his fingers. "I know who and I know how. What I don't know is the why. Why Elanor? Why would you betray your people?"

"I did not betray my people," she said. "Only you."

The Commander let out a breath that was as gentle as a sigh. "What you have done to The Cause," he started but, to the shock of Larissa as well as everyone else present, Elanor interrupted him.

"What I did, I did for The Cause. Our people will be free, but you will not be the one to lead us. You are a madman."

"Elanor!" Larissa blurted out, unable to stop herself. The woman on the floor ignored the Lady Larissa and began to raise up, glaring at the boy-faced man in the cassock. Petrov took a careful step backwards.

"You are not Moses!" Elanor cried, her voice rising to a feverish pitch. "You are not Mikeal! You are not..."

Larissa's breath caught in her throat, unsure of what had been done to suddenly silence the brazen woman. It happened too fast for Larissa's eyes to follow. Even Petrov's keen gaze caught but a glimpse.

One second Elanor was rising to her knees, defying the Commander. Then there was a flicker of light and the next second a thin crimson line was racing across Elanor's throat. The woman's head slid forward off her neck and landed on its cheek with a soft thump, her mouth still open in defiance. The body fell forward as if in prayer, or secretly searching for its lost head. Blood poured from the severed neck, soaking the red carpet.

The Commander stood above Elanor's body. He held her gold officer's chain in one hand and a half-meter blade in the other, its tip pointed accusingly at the body on the floor. Blood ran down the length of the blade and thick drops fell from all along its edge.

"And you are not The One to judge me," JP told the still bleeding form. The gold chain disappeared into a pocket and with his free hand he held up two fingers and inscribed a circle in the air in front of his own visage. "May The One grant you peace in your next life. Or the punishment he sees fit."

"Amen," intoned the small congregation of officers. JP reached down, tore the IGC patch from the dead woman's arm and used it to clean the blood from his blade. When it was mostly free of blood he dropped the patch on the body at his feet.

"Put her in the incinerator," he told the small group. "Commander Petrov and Larissa, please come with me. I will see the rest of you at morning prayers."

Those seated bowed their heads as the Commander stepped around the body and left the chapel with Petrov and his bodyguards on his heels. Larissa followed behind them with quick, small steps in an effort to keep up.

When they were a distance away from the chapel Petrov politely cleared his throat to speak but JP made a quick gesture with his hand, silencing him. The Lady Larissa, along with Petrov and Petrov's guards, escorted the Commander to his cabin.

JP opened the door to his personal quarters and extended a hand, inviting them inside.

The entry room was monastic and sparse. A braided rug lay on the floor before an artificial stone fireplace. There was a single reading chair and side table on which sat the Commander's Bible. JP turned on the holo fire and paced in front of it, deep in thought. For minute there was only the sound of his robe, swishing around his feet. Petrov broke the silence.

"May I ask when were the eggs found, sir?" he asked.

"A few days ago," JP answered, still deep in thought, still pacing. Petrov looked at the floor and shook his blonde head.

"Sir, do you not trust me?"

JP stopped his pacing and looked at his Second in Command. With his head down and muscled arms out at his sides, he looked like a disheartened bull. JP could hear the hurt in his voice that he tried not to show and his own shoulders dropped in sympathy.

"Of course I trust you, my son," he assured. "But, you see, Elanor was not just a traitor. She was a message."

Petrov looked at him and cocked his head. "What do you mean?"

The Commander folded his hands and let them drop down

in front of his robes. "We have spies, an entire network of them, entwined within the enemy's ranks. Some are in very high places and close to important players in this war." JP lifted his chin and let out a deep breath. "Elanor was their message to us."

Petrov frowned, not understanding, but Larissa did and she spoke. "Their message was that they too have a network of spies. Ones that are in high places and close to important players in this war."

Petrov's face relaxed for a moment as understanding dawned on him, then tightened again in consternation. "Sir, you don't think that I..."

JP shook his head quickly, cutting him off. "No, Commander Petrov, of course not. But if we can be infiltrated by those within our ranks, by our very own people, then it is even more likely that we can be bugged – by cams, mikes, or worse."

Petrov nodded, understanding. "I'll have security sweep the ship. It will take them a few days."

"Even then," Larissa said, "they may not find all of them."

Petrov nodded, despondent.

JP was not discouraged. "Even so, we will take care of what we can, and let The One handle the rest." The other two nodded eagerly. "In the meantime, the eggs are safe."

Petrov gave the Commander a glance that was questioning, hopeful, and discouraged all at once. Smiling, JP put a hand on his shoulder and fished the mini-acrylic from a pocket in his robes and showed Petrov the last transmission he had received. The Executive Officer read the message and laughed aloud.

"They are safe," he agreed. "About the safest place they could be!" He threw back his head and laughed again, his elation only partly from the knowledge of the whereabouts of the eggs. His real pleasure came from the fact that his Commander trusted him, and only him, enough to share such critical information.

JP clapped a hand upon Petrov's muscled back. "Sleep well, my friend. In the morning..."

"The work of The One begins anew," Petrov finished. "Thank you, sir."

JP nodded. "But go to medical before you do. Have that wound cleaned."

Petrov's shoulders sagged and he gave his Commander a pleading look – that of a child being sent to bed early. JP gave him a stern look in return and the Executive Officer nodded, relenting.

"Yes, sir," he said, bowing first to the Commander and then to the Lady Larissa before he let himself out, his eyes still gleaming with pleasure.

JP turned to face Larissa, his robes swirling about his feet. "Well, my lady. It seems that I have an opening for an officer."

Larissa stared at him, her mouth slightly open. The offer, if that's what it was, caught her completely off-guard. Her mind raced as she went through what it meant for right now, and what it could mean in the future.

Her Commander, a man she would die for without a second thought, was telling her that he believed she deserved more. More status, more responsibility, more honor. Larissa did not fear more work, she would work her hands to the bloody bone for the man that stood before her, but she feared the status and where it would take her – away from the Commander. She would do anything he asked, but to be so far from him, to worry about him, would prove the greater task.

Larissa bowed her head. "I will do anything you ask of me," she answered, her voice husky. "And serve you in any way that I am able."

The Commander regarded her for a long moment and, looking so very young but being so very wise, sighed heavily.

"I can see that it is in your heart not to take such a position. If you are happy where you are, I shall not remove you."

Larissa felt tears spring to her eyes. She grasped his hand and kissed the platinum ring on his third finger. Then she knelt and kissed the hem of his robe.

"Thank you, sir," she whispered, looking up at him. He reached down and touched her cheek.

"Thank you, Larissa."

The Lady stood and bowed and left his chambers, closing the door quietly behind her. The Commander stared at the closed door for a moment and then sat himself in the reading chair, his hand pulling the gold chain from his pocket.

It was most likely for the best, he decided, running his thumb over the linked figure eights. Women were starting to appear as dishonest and as despicable as men. And not to be trusted.

# ONE FOUR

The day after her encounter with Bjorn, Scarlett put on her new denim pants and looked longingly at the crimson silk shirt. With a sigh, she tucked it into a drawer and put on a linen shirt. It was old and ill fitting, but certainly more practical. She wondered why it was that Elaeric even had women's clothes and how long they had been in the dresser. A long time, she was sure of that. She pulled on the new boots and then, with another sigh, decided just to put the whole business out of her mind.

Nothing good will come of me even talking to him, she thought. *Besides, he's just toying with me.*

After her morning chores and a longer than usual meditation, she rode across the southern fields and down to the river with its small fishing village to buy a fish or two for dinner.

Scarlett sat on an outdoor patio at an inn on the riverfront and had a cup of coffee while the mare rested, drank from the river, and munched at the new green reeds sprouting on the banks. Afterwards, she purchased two fresh rainbow trout and once they were wrapped in paper and tied with string she headed back towards the cottage.

As she crested a hill, the wind whispered in her hair, caressing her neck. Scarlett stopped the horse and turned, watching and listening. Atop the horse on the knoll, she could see the entire village and a great stretch of the river. It was wide and deep, though the current seemed mild enough.

Most of the fishermen were done for the day and tying their tiny boats to the smaller of docks on the riverfront, leaving the waterway to be dominated by two passenger ferries. One was arriving at the large dock with townspeople after fresh fish or possibly a chowder dinner at one of the village's quaint inns.

The other ferry was taking people back to Kayos, or farther.

He wouldn't come this far just to toy with me, Scarlett thought. The breeze blew Scarlett's dark hair away from her face and the horse snorted and stamped. The Jordan turned the horse away from the river and headed for home.

On the second day Scarlett's curiosity began to nag at her, and by the third day it had gotten the better of her. More, she realized that in the back of her mind she had already been formulating a plan.

"Master Elaeric?" she asked at dinner.

"Mmm hmmm." There was a small smile on the corners of his mouth that Scarlett eyed with suspicion.

"You already know what I am going to say, don't you?"

"Now, how would I know that?" he asked as he bit into the last biscuit, though Scarlett saw that it was to hide a smile.

"Fine," she said. "At least I don't have to lie."

"Why would you feel the need?" he asked. Scarlett shrugged off his question and continued.

"I am going to town tomorrow to have dinner."

"I do not see what might cause you to be dishonest about such a thing," he remarked, his almond eyes wide with innocent interest.

Scarlett huffed through her nose and ate her dinner, keeping a wary eye on her yellow-robed friend.

I think you see plenty, she thought.

Elaeric finished his biscuit, smiling to himself.

★

The next day, after lunch, Scarlett put on the black leather riding pants and the crimson silk shirt. A farm was no place for smooth silk and expensive leather, but a nice restaurant certainly was and Scarlett was glad for the chance to wear her new finery. She took a second to admire herself in the mirror above the dresser.

I look like my old self, she thought with a spark of pride. Then the spark blinked out like a candle in the rain. *Except that I am not my old self.* She knew that the realization should also give her a sense of pride. Instead, it had a haunting quality that filled her with unease.

Scarlett turned from her reflection and left her room.

Elaeric approached her as she was saddling the mare and Scarlett expected him to be smiling his little smile and have something suspiciously encouraging to offer, but the monk's face had no expression.

As Scarlett hauled herself up and into the saddle he placed a hand on her booted foot. "Be careful," he told her.

"With my friend?" she asked.

"With yourself."

Scarlett nodded. "I will."

Elaeric removed his hand from her foot and returned her nod. Scarlett guided the horse past the cottage at a slow trot and headed for the river, the dust puffing up around her hooves.

She stabled the mare at an inn at the fishing village. The innkeeper's wife, a portly woman with red cheeks and a white apron, took the horse and assured Scarlett she would be well taken care of and offered the Jordan a place to stay as well, though the day was still plenty young.

"Thank you, but no. I might be back late, however. Will that be a problem?"

The woman shooed away the question as she would shoo away a fly. "Of course not! The boys stay up till all hours. If I'm abed just ask for Tim. Mind you the last ferry leaves Kayos at midnight."

"I won't be that late," Scarlett assured her, "But thanks again."

She gave the mare a vigorous rub on the neck and pat on the rump and reluctantly turned away. The horse didn't seem to mind. She was eager for shade and could smell other horses. And oats.

Scarlett caught the next westbound ferry at the boat dock and found herself a seat. To her surprise there were very few locals. A majority of the other passengers were loud and garishly dressed foreigners. Mostly humans and elves, though there was a spattering of Triads and one small group of Gobli.

Tourists, Scarlett thought, amused. Her eyes fell upon a pretty young woman with dark hair pretending to read an electronic tablet. The woman looked up at Scarlett and the Jordan saw that the girl had strange golden eyes. She smiled at Scarlett and dropped her eyes back down to her tablet.

Scarlett watched the banks of the river flow by, keeping a wary eye on the woman while the tourists gushed and pointed and consulted the plastic map attached to the ferry's inner wall.

The ferry kept to one side of the river, close to the north bank, and Scarlett marveled at the yellow and green flowers that grew on impossibly tall stalks. The Jordan estimated that they would tower over her head had she been standing among them, quite possibly even if she were on horseback.

The banks of the river disappeared as they entered a grove of maldrove trees. The sky darkened slightly under the canopy of branches and the humidity spiked considerably. The tourists pointed at the maldrove trees and their colossal, unfurled leaves that normally sucked the moisture from the air but, being so close to the river, they were drawing it directly from the water.

Eventually the ferry passed through the grove and the tourists, fanning themselves with brochures, gave a collective sigh of relief as the humidity dropped back down to a bearable level.

The grove disappearing behind them, the riverbanks rose up into the countryside of East Kayos. Scarlett could see the bend in the river just ahead that housed the dock for east village.

The village itself was fairly quiet, not being a market day, but the tourists on the boat oohed over the countryside that sprawled up to the hamlet of houses and pointed at two dairy cows as they grazed in a field.

The ferry coasted to the dock for Village East and rocked slightly as it bumped into the wooden moorings. A deckhand threw a rope to a man on the pier who deftly caught the line with one hand and tied them fast. The Village East dock was nowhere near as busy as the one at the fishing village, but there was a small café and a few shops that sold refreshments or trinkets.

Businesses being set up for the tourists, Scarlett noted. *That's interesting.*

The deckhand lowered the passenger ramp and the few who stood up to depart were mostly the few locals on board along with the group of Gobli. Scarlett could feel the muscles in her back tighten, her instincts buzzing. She had originally intended to get off at the next stop – the dock on the west side. Decidedly, she stood up suddenly to leave with the other disembarking passengers.

The dark-haired young lady looked casually at her tablet but held very still. As Scarlett passed her the Jordan bent down quickly.

"You know," she told the young woman conversationally, "that works a lot better when it is on."

"Oh!" the young woman exclaimed, moving the tablet closer to her body. The brightly colored ferry walls reflected off her eyes, making them look like miniature twin kaleidoscopes. "Thank you!"

Scarlett smiled and moved away with the group leaving the ferry. The young lady had quickly moved the tablet to cover up a perismit, but not quickly enough for Scarlett miss it. The perismit was a device similar to a camera that was used to transmit video to another device. Scarlett knew that she was not only being watched, but monitored as well. The question was, by whom?

As she stepped onto the gangplank Scarlett looked back but the girl with the golden eyes was gone. The Jordan wondered if she had been from the IGC. She knew that she should be expecting a visit at any time. It was standard procedure for any officer on medical leave to be evaluated, usually via an informal interview by a junior medic. From there, the medic could recommend if it was necessary for a medical assessment to approve a return to duty or that it was obvious more time was needed.

The girl had been no one that she had ever seen before and, though she would rarely even so much as glance at someone beneath her – which she considered just about everyone aboard the Opal Dragon to be – her training would never let her forget a face. It meant that someone else was watching her.

Scarlett mentally ran through numerous possibilities and scenarios as she moved carefully around the Gobli that had stopped in the middle of the wooden dock to consult a maplet. After an excited bout of gurgling and pointing, they moved toward a trinket shop, their small round bodies jostling one another. Scarlett followed the small group of locals headed for Kayos.

The group of people split as some headed for the eastern gate in the wall that surrounded the town and the others headed for the southern gate.

Scarlett joined those that headed for the south side and went through the gate that, like the other three, could easily allow two carriages side by side to pass through - and always stood open. She began making her way up a cobblestone street past livestock stables and homes of townspeople. It was late in the afternoon when she reached the center of town. It was only the second time she had been to the village center, and it was a marvel to her now as it had been the first time.

The center of Kayos was a great, sun-filled plaza with a multi-tiered fountain at its center, surrounded by cafés and shops where Village East met Village West and a mixture of both sides clashed and mingled. Though all of the buildings surrounding the square were made of wood and stone, or some sort of facsimile, the feel coming from each side was distinct and different.

The smell of fresh herbs and baked bread rose from the air on the east to mingle in the square with smells of roasted sim-meat and synthetic sauces coming from the west. Though not obnoxious, the west side was distinctly louder - and boasted a younger crowd along with those that Scarlett could now identify as vacationers. People walked around in everything from country garb to casual flight suits, though Scarlett didn't see anyone sporting Mylar.

A group of long-faced teenagers from the east side sat joking and laughing outside of a sweetshop, eating marshmallow pies and drinking egg cream sodas through long silver straws.

Amongst the horses and carts were a number of air cabs, floating idly by the restaurants, waiting for fares. Along the outsides of their carbon fiber shells ran news headlines in a multitude of languages.

Scarlett watched the ticker along the side of cab that sported news about the InterGalactic Council and the Chimera.

Which one of you is watching me? she thought. *Could it be someone else?*

She looked at the sun, already on its course for the horizon. Pushing the thought of the girl with the golden eyes from her mind, Scarlett straightened her shoulders and headed for the closest taxi. She opened the door and was greeted by a cloud of smoke that came rolling out of the back of the cab, heavy with the sweet, heady smell of cannabis.

The Jordan stepped back, coughing and waving the smoke out of her face. She was about to close the door when a voice called out from inside the cab and all the windows went down at once.

"Wait, wait!" the voice called. "Get in, get in!"

After most of the smoke had boiled out, Scarlett could see the driver in the front. He had ebony skin and thick black hair pulled back in a braid. He had a thin but handsome face with big dark eyes and thin pink lips. When he saw Scarlett he pursed his lips and whistled.

"Oooo, pretty lady! Get in pretty lady! You don't like the smoke? I'll put it out."

"Smells like ganja," Scarlett remarked, waving it out of her face and squinting against the drifting clouds.

"It's better than the smell of horse," he argued amicably, indicating the horse drawn carriages that were available for hire.

Scarlett shrugged. "It's all a matter of tastes, I suppose."

The cabbie went off into gales of laughter as if it was the funniest thing he had ever heard. "Get in, pretty lady, I'll take you anywhere you want to go."

Scarlett glanced around the plaza and climbed into the back of the cab.

"Yes!" the cabbie exclaimed as if he had won a victory point. He eyed the Jordan in the mirror that ran along the top of his windshield. "Where you want to go?"

"Do you know the Huit?"

The driver whistled again. "Sure do. 'Spensive." The cab slid forward, slipping between two horse drawn carriages, heading east. "We picking up anybody else?"

"No, it's just me."

"Ooooo, maybe you take me then," he suggested, looking at her in the mirror with a huge grin splitting his face.

"Not this time, sweetheart."

"Maybe next time?"

"Maybe next time."

The cabbie went off into howls of laughter again. There were still wafts of smoke gathered inside the cab at the roof. Scarlett sank down in her seat. She didn't want to be stoned for her meeting with Bjorn.

"Just get us there in one piece," she said as the cab began picking up speed and darting west down a cobblestone lane made of composite plastic cobbles.

The driver laughed. "Honey, it's an aircab! Ain't nothing going to happen to you!"

Scarlett smiled and looked out the window. They passed through a residential district and though the houses were made of stone, Scarlett could see lights flickering through the glass windows that she knew didn't come from candlelight.

They passed through the entire Village West and out the west gate where the land opened up onto broad fields cut by irrigation streams and thickets of maldroves. The sun was a dusky rose husk above the horizon turning the northern sky pink.

The other side of town, past the wall, was empty save for the tents that were set up on market days. Outside the wall on the western side, however, were a spattering of expensive restaurants cleverly disguised to look like country farmhouses or medieval inns and the like.

The cab swung south and turned onto a lane of hard packed dirt. As it sped though a large space between buildings, Scarlett caught a glimpse of the sprawling wood and glass structure that was the Grande Edge Station. She knew that from there a steam-powered train took passengers north and south via a bridge over the river, while a hydrogen powered monorail took travelers west to the more modern cities on Adrogea.

"Is that how I got here?" Scarlett had asked Elaeric when he had shown her the station but he had shaken his bald head.

"A craft landed in my meadow," he had informed her. "Just a few hours before another craft arrived with the horse."

Scarlett could not imagine the state she must have been in, nor did she want to.

The cab made a turn sharp enough to spit up a scree of dirt and then angled slightly west before it came to a dust-raising stop in front of a wood and plaster crumbling château surrounded by hedged gardens.

"This is it?" Scarlett asked.

"This be it. Le Huit."

Now that she had arrived she found herself hesitant, unsure. It didn't look like a restaurant. But, then again, most places around didn't.

"Why is it called Le Huit?" she asked.

"It mean eight."

The Jordan felt a small shiver run up her spine. "Why is it called that?" she asked, though she thought the answer was obvious. The lazy eight, the symbol for infinity, was the mark of the Chimera. It must be a safe house of some kind.

The cabbie pursed his thin lips as he considered. "You know how a clock look?" he asked. "Old-fashioned kind?"

"The round kind? With a dial, like an old-style compass?" She knew that Grandpa had one, an ancient thing that was probably as old as the crest, but the look it had was somehow magical. It was a ticking device with beautifully scrolled numbers under glass. It closed like a clam with a carved golden shell.

"Yes, yes, pretty lady!" he exclaimed. "You berry smart!"

"I have my moments," Scarlett said with a smirk.

"Think of face of clock like face of compass. We exactly between south and west side."

Scarlett nodded, remembering the contrivance that Grandpa

had called a "pocket watch." If she thought of it as a compass and knew that she was at the point between south and west, it meant the tiny gold arrow on the watch would be pointing at the number eight.

Still, it seemed a bit too coincidental and she was about to voice her doubts when she saw the dark-haired young woman from the ferry come out the door and look around. The setting sun hit her golden eyes and they reflected pink and red and crimson. The woman saw her at the same time and spoke into a comset on her wrist. Scarlett was flooded with relief. She knew the young woman could still be IGC, but it was more likely that she was one of Bjorn's lackeys.

"This be it?" the cabbie asked, watching her reflection in the mirror that ran along the inside top of his windshield and seeing her indecision.

"Yep," Scarlett agreed, "this be it. How much do I owe you?"

"Two coppers."

Scarlett opened the leather drawstring sack that served as her purse. It was quite heavy tonight. Elaeric had made sure she had plenty of coins, including a number of gold ones she had never seen before, and for that she was grateful.

She handed the driver a bronze coin. "Keep the change."

"Thankya, thankya!" he told her as she slid across the seat and opened her door. "Do you need a ride home pretty lady?"

Scarlett paused. "I will, but not for a while. I'm not sure how long I will be."

"That's okay. I am Mica. You tell anyone who work here to call Mica for you."

"Alright, Mica. Thank you."

"Thank you, pretty lady. I'll be seeing you!"

Scarlett got out of the cab and it was away as soon as the door latched shut. The Jordan looked around and found that she was alone. She walked up a brick path towards the front entrance of the dwelling. There was a huge wooden door that had once been painted red but the color was now a faded memory. The weathered boards were bound with black iron hinges. She paused, not sure if she should knock.

Before she could decide the door swung open and she was greeted by the girl with the golden eyes.

"Hello, Scarlett. Please come in."

Scarlett walked into the château, taking her time to let her eyes adjust to the dim interior. There was a hostess stand, a room to either side with candlelit tables, and a noisy kitchen in the back.

"This way, please."

The Jordan followed the girl, taking in the surroundings with her dark eyes before they returned to the young woman.

"I take it you don't work for the restaurant," Scarlett remarked.

"That is correct."

Scarlett stopped as the girl's manner struck her, regarding her with a raised brow and a suspicious eye. Whether it was her training, her inherent senses, or the clarity from her meditations, the Jordan did not miss a beat. The young woman stopped as well, waiting patiently. "And something about you leads me to believe you are not human, not Chimeran even," Scarlett said.

"A Chimeran is as human as any cross-breed can be, such as human-elf, though those are quite rare."

"But you are a robotic."

"Correct again, and quite astute, I might add. Most humans never notice, and certainly not this quickly. Though, to be exact, I am a troll."

Scarlett looked again at the lithe body and dark hair and was suddenly glad that Calyph's troll didn't resemble this one in the slightest. She did feel a strange twinge within herself that Bjorn kept a droid that was so lovely.

Hmm, Scarlett thought as she noticed the twinge in her feelings. *I wonder what that feeling is all about.* She tucked the thought away in her consciousness to be examined at a later time.

"This way, please."

Scarlett followed the young woman through the restaurant and out a side door into a courtyard with a flagstone patio. There were elegant wood tables on the patio, each adorned with a small red globe that housed a flickering flambeau. The sun was setting in a bloody haze to the north.

The courtyard was enclosed on two sides by thickets of huge maldrove trees that were folding in their leaves for the night, releasing the moisture they had absorbed during the day into the evening air, watering themselves along with the parasitic flowering vines that spiraled up their trunks and snaked out over the ground. The release of moisture permeated the hot dusky air, making it heavy and humid.

Beyond the hedge on the northern side of the courtyard was a rolling meadow that afforded the patrons an excellent view of the enormous setting sun.

Swarms of aphids rose in great drifts from the clover fields and cloister flowers. The air smelled of lilac and thunder, though there wasn't a cloud in the sky that was now deepening from dusty rose to bloody red.

More than the lilac and thunder, Scarlett could smell Bjorn. He was sitting at a table and watching her, relaxed back in his seat and indulgently comfortable. Though Scarlett marveled that it could even be possible, the plain clothes he wore made his handsome face even more prominent, like a jewel against a backdrop of cheap velour.

The troll held out a hand, inviting Scarlett to go ahead. The Jordan did so, going straight towards the Chimeran Commander as the troll smiled and retreated back into the château.

Bjorn stood and pulled out the other chair at the table. "You look beautiful, Scarlett."

"Thank you. So do you." She looked at the proffered chair and bit her lip. "Do you mind?" she asked, pointing to the chair that he had been sitting in. Bjorn laughed and held out his chair.

"Of course not." Scarlett sat down and he took the other chair with a grin. "Old habits die hard, eh?"

Scarlett shrugged, trying to ignore the way his white teeth flashed in the light of the setting sun.

"Even though you don't have your back to the door," Bjorn said, "your blind is still against the trees, which could be a viable attack point."

"Unless everyone at this restaurant is one of your guards, and incredibly well trained – which I doubt on both counts - I will notice any commotion long before it becomes a danger to me."

Bjorn laughed. The sound was deep and melodious, and reverberated through her whole body. "And that was something you assessed and determined within the few seconds it took to cross the courtyard?"

Scarlett shrugged again. "I didn't really think about it." She glanced around. "Besides, of the guards that you do have placed around here, the only one who might give me a run for my money is the one at the table over there," she said, jerking her chin in the direction of a man sitting alone at a table behind Bjorn, pretending to read a menu. She smiled and shook out her napkin. "So, what's good here?"

"Everything," Bjorn told her, returning her smile as he motioned for a waiter. A small man dressed as a peasant hurried over and Bjorn favored him with his smile of even, white teeth. "A bottle of the Blackcuthre Syrah."

The waiter bowed and hurried away.

The Chimeran and the Jordan sat, watching each other with the pointed disinterest of a pair of predatory cats. Scarlett could feel the sultry air gathering on her body like drops of dew. There was a buzzing hum as a swarm of aphids drifted up and sank back down over another bed of clover.

Bjorn shook his head, laughing softly. "Scarlett," he finally said, "what are you doing here?"

Scarlett arched a brow at him. "At this café? I'm wondering the same thing myself. Or did you mean this planetary satellite?"

"Both."

"I came to this place to heal. I was in a flat spin towards losing my mind. Partly thanks to you no less." Bjorn waved a hand dismissively at this and Scarlett raised her shoulders in response. "I'm here at the café because I was hungry and, I'm not afraid to admit, curious as to what you are about."

The waiter arrived with the requested bottle and presented it to Bjorn. The Chimeran gave it a nod of approval and the waiter carefully placed the bottle on his knee before unfolding an old-fashioned corkscrew. Decorously, he placed the worm of the corkscrew against the cork and twisted it down.

Scarlett winced, for no reason she could place or understand.

The waiter poured a splash into Bjorn's glass and waited for him to taste and approve but the green-eyed Commander just waved at him to get on with it. When the wine was poured Scarlett took a sip and nodded at the waiter.

"Delicious," she told him. The waiter nodded approvingly and was about to speak when Scarlett quickly spoke first. "Why don't you give us a few minutes to enjoy the wine first, if you don't mind?" The waiter bowed, put at ease.

"Of course. Please enjoy."

Scarlett took another sip of her wine. It was full and rich and warm as blood. She could feel it travel down her throat in a hot and welcome wave before it hit her stomach with a spreading burn. She couldn't remember the last time she had a drink. She would have to be careful.

"So," Scarlett said after silent moments of watching the sun ease into the horizon, "what are you after? Besides me of course."

Bjorn laughed. "For a woman I found trouncing about a backward planet-moon far away from any real civilization and dressed like a peasant's wife, you think very highly of yourself."

Scarlett tucked a sly smile into the corner of her mouth but said nothing. Bjorn sighed and nodded.

"You are right. I am here for you."

"And?"

"Just you."

"I find that a little hard to believe."

"But it's true."

Scarlett placed her wine glass on the table and leaned forward. "However depraved you may be, I don't believe you would take a sideline from your war just to chase a piece of tail across the universe." She picked her glass back up. "You," she said, carefully poking the glass in his direction, "have an ulterior motive."

Bjorn laughed and leaned forward as well, placing muscled forearms along the table and resting his weight there. "I can't believe you would address yourself as a piece of tail." Scarlett shrugged and looked away as she sat back in her chair, sipping her wine. "And," Bjorn continued, "depraved I may be and ulterior motive aside, it is still just you."

Scarlett laughed softly and let the silence roll out once more. The sun disappeared, leaving a crimson slash against a lavender sky that eroded into layers of deepening violet.

Bjorn frowned. "You're different."

"People change all the time," she told him.

"No they don't."

"How would *you* know?"

"I've been around."

"I bet."

"Not like that. Well..." Bjorn sipped his wine and bobbled his head side to side. "Maybe a little like that." Scarlett laughed. "But that's not what I mean. I've been around a long time. More than twice as long as you."

"Gross."

"And I know that everything changes – except people."

"Of course they do," Scarlett remarked, her dark eyes still on the horizon.

Bjorn took a long drink from his glass and set it on the table. "They might change their habits – fat people lose weight, drug addicts stop using – but that doesn't change who they are."

Scarlett glanced back at him with an arched brow.

"Have you heard the story about the frog and the scorpion?" Bjorn asked. Scarlett smiled.

"Of course. Everyone has. And a tiger doesn't change her stripes. What's your point?"

Bjorn looked surprised. "My point? My point is – where is the viperous virago I once knew?"

The Jordan shook her dark hair. "First, you never knew me, but you are right in supposing that I am different. I have come a long way since I've been here. I *am* changing. Second, if I am different than the person you thought me to be, I should be of no more interest to you."

As she uttered the last sentence she felt a slight pang of regret, of loss. That feeling, too, she acknowledged and then tucked away to be examined later.

Bjorn sighed and shook his head. "I wish that could be so. Unfortunately, for me, it only makes you more intriguing."

Scarlett felt a rush of warmth that she hoped was coming from the wine. She placed the glass on the table and dropped her hand to rest next to it. Bjorn leaned forward and picked up her hand, examining the numerous scabs and welts, some healed and others that were quite fresh. His brows drew together and his green eyes flashed up to meet hers.

"What are they doing to you?" he demanded.

"It's not what you think," Scarlett told him, carefully removing her hand from his.

"I certainly hope not," Bjorn said, his frown deepening. "I don't like that they are trying to change you. And I would be furious to find out they have been hurting you."

Scarlett felt a deep swelling in her chest at his concern. She shook her head, resisting the urge to lay her hand over his in comfort. "It's from the chicken," she explained. She saw a look of puzzlement under his wrath and almost laughed aloud. "I'm learning control," she told him.

Bjorn sat back, relaxing after a long moment tight with suspicion and controlled anger. He took a sip from his glass and nodded. "Control is a good thing," he agreed. "An invaluable skill."

He remained silent, thoughtful. His eyes drifted across the fields towards the bleeding sunset. Scarlett sighed.

"This is getting weird. Cut to the chase, will you?"

Bjorn eyes came back to the present and he gave her an indulgent smile. "I told you – I am here for you."

"Not interested."

"I doubt that."

Scarlett forced herself to be still and hold his gaze, though her instinct was to look away. And cross her legs. "Order a bride via the galactic web. I'm sure GwenSeven has dozens of models."

"I'm sure they do. I don't want a companion, though I certainly wouldn't turn *you* down. I need an officer. I'm here to recruit you."

Scarlett jerked forward so fast that she almost spilled her wine. *"You're what?"*

"I'm here to recruit you," he repeated, obviously beginning to enjoy himself. Scarlett could do nothing but stare in shock before she managed to choke out a laugh. Bjorn's expression didn't change.

"You can't be serious!"

"Of course I'm serious. You don't think I would sideline the war just to chase a piece of tail across the universe?"

Scarlett laughed and shook her head. Bjorn leaned forward and put a hand over hers, sending a wave of heat rolling through her entire body.

"You are desperately needed, Scarlett. And not just to warm my bed," he added with his usual wolfish grin.

Scarlett looked away as the feeling he stirred within her boiled into a fever. She fought with her body not to shudder. Instead she pulled her hand away and used it to pick up the menu.

"You're crazy," she told him.

The waiter arrived at that moment, clearing his throat politely. "Perhaps you would like to..."

"I'll have the culotte steak," she interrupted, giving the menu a quick glance before looking back at Bjorn. "And the minted cous with rosemary."

The waiter nodded. "And how would you like..."

"Bloody."

The waiter smiled approvingly and turned to Bjorn.

"I'll have the same."

"Very good!" he exclaimed and, after a number of servile bows, hurried away.

"You are the perfect candidate," Bjorn continued as if they had not been interrupted. "And not just as a pilot, I'm taking about as a Commander in the revolution."

Scarlett laughed, putting an elbow on the table and placing a finger to her temple as if propping up her own head. "It's a rebellion," she corrected. "It's not a revolution unless you win."

"A semantic technicality," Bjorn said. "Because we will win. We want autonomy and freedom, and that is a fight that does not end until it is won."

"Why fight at all?" Scarlett asked. "Why not just leave? The universe is huge – you have the means to go anywhere."

Scarlett could see his hand tighten around the stem of his glass and she knew that she had struck a nerve.

"Some have chosen that path already," he told her with an edge to his baritone voice that she had never heard before. "But I will not be with those that run and hide."

Scarlett frowned, considering his words. Had some of the Chimeran done just that? Simply picked up and left? There were rumors that a great many of them had done so but, if that were the case, where they hell did they go?

Bjorn sighed, relaxing his grip. "We are not some power hungry race seeking to rule the suns and the seven systems. We are fighting for freedom. We are fighting against the tyranny of the Council. We are fighting for what is right. You could be integral in making that happen, Scarlett. I *want* you to be integral in making that happen, and I want to be by your side when it does."

"I would not be a good candidate, for any of those things," Scarlett told him, though it tasted like a lie.

I will have so much to meditate on, she thought.

"You would," Bjorn argued. "One of our greatest hindrances has been that we began a war and not a soul among us had any military training. Our second greatest constraint has been our limited range of imagination." Scarlett snorted but he continued. "You are a natural born leader, Scarlett, and you lack nothing to make you the greatest leader of The Cause."

Scarlett shook her dark curls, trying to mentally wring the heat from her heart and her body. "I hate the Chimera," she told him with all the coldness she could muster. "If you knew anything about me you would know that. If you had any idea what they have done to my family..."

"I do have an idea. In fact, I have more than an idea – I have more details than even you were ever given."

Scarlett looked back at him sharply and his green eyes bored into her. The wave of heat rolled through her again.

"What did you think, Scarlett?" Bjorn asked, grinning. "That I came chasing after you like some love-sick teenager? I did my research."

For the first time in a month, Scarlett felt her jaw tighten painfully.

Breathe, she told herself. *Breathe. Identify what you are feeling. Fear? There's no reason for that. Just breathe.*

"It was not an easy task," Bjorn continued, "considering your security clearance and the fact that the IGC keeps most of your records quite sealed." He took a sip of wine and Scarlett mirrored his movements, breathing slowly. "I thought it might be easier to research your family, and the events that have surrounded your life, but I found that most of those were sealed as well. Very intriguing."

"I'm sure," she said through lips that felt numb. Her mind raced like a wildfire. She tried to concentrate on what he was saying but she, in truth, was tantalized with the idea of being a true leader, a *Commander*, in the war. The thought of how closely she would be entwined with the green-eyed Chimeran made her groin ache. But her heart ached as well, her sense of loss was still too great.

The dark-eyed Jordan sighed and shook her head, summoning the resolve that had fueled her for the past ten years. "You said that you know what happened regarding my family history. If that is true, then you must also know why I could never, not ever, even consider what you are asking, nor could I stop until everyone in your rebellion has been blasted to nothing more than memory and ash." She took a long drink of wine and looked away, her chest filling with deep breaths in an effort to stay calm.

Bjorn kept his eyes fixed on her face until she looked back at him. "And I told you that I didn't just know about it, but that I have details, details that you have never been given. Ones that may do a lot more than change your mind."

Scarlett felt her body start to tighten in a strange way. She could feel the muscles in her body begin to constrict in a wave that moved up through her calves and thighs, then her back and her arms and she had to force herself not to let her hand convulse around the stem of her wineglass. She felt like a wire being twisted and turned and wound into a coil. She was about to start a mental calming exercise but Bjorn's next words belayed the need.

"The Amliss Attack was a false flag."

Scarlett stared at him, unmoving. Every muscle in her body that had been slowly winding into tight and lethal springs was frozen, pulled taut. Bjorn mistook her silence for lack of understanding.

"A false flag..." he started, but Scarlett cut him off.

"I know what a false flag is," she said abruptly. "But I don't think you know what you are saying."

Bjorn put his glass down and leaned forward over the table. "Your father and brother, along with their entire platoon, were not shot down by Chimeran ships."

Scarlett's lips moved but nothing came out. When she finally spoke she didn't recognize her own voice. It was so low that it could barely be heard above the soft voices and clinking silverware around them. "Of course they were Chimeran ships," she whispered. "Who else could it have been?"

Bjorn's eyes were as steady as his voice and, for the first time that evening, his face was devoid of emotion.

"Your father and brother were shot down by IGC ships, Scarlett. They were outnumbered and overrun and they didn't stand a chance. Moreover, it was no accident. It was a planned attack."

Scarlett felt everything in her body suddenly go slack.

* FROM
THE DREAM JOURNAL OF HOPE

The wet grit of mud beneath the leather sole. The waters opening up between the misty crested hills. Dark eyes that are shadow in the sun. Running, that hair, that flaming hair, like copper tainted with murderous blood, tied tight to avoid the winds of change.

The smell of blood, as dirty and biting as the taste of tin, a silver smoothness to make the roots of your teeth sing in quiet harmony. The smell of autumn leaves, wet and crushed and slightly decayed, like the smell of spice on a bloated corpse.

The pelting sound of rain like the drumming footstep of your hunter. The soothing sound of quiet fear like snow falling on a leaf.

And those eyes, those autumn eyes, so full of aching hope so cold in their knowledge, green on brown on gold on black. The sun and the darkness, life and death, the decay of mold upon new life. Those eyes, pulled at the corners, so old before their time, so sad.

White stockings with a rippled texture. Pigtails, curls and hair like silk.

A mountain split and consumed on three inner sides by a waterfall, like a cross-section of a bowl as water is poured through its rocky crags. A place where the leaves fly from the trees like memory fleeing before time and remembrance.

The silky golden shore where she leaves no prints. The blue sky that holds only the memory of clouds. Water like glass, its surface the reflection of that long forgotten sky where she could walk as if it were the ice of ages not touched.

The lighthouse, that phallic symbol of hope in the night - telling all to stay safe by staying away. The hammer of the heart - like a rabbit kicking against the wet earth, its final attempt at escape, beating at the earth like its own heart, pattering like the rain. The lighthouse holds the truth and shines it out into the night, the light that some will follow and some will shun for the fear of destruction. The candle and the vigil. The breath of the dead and the reflection of hope and her eyes, those dark autumn eyes. The rose that opens but all it offers is the promise of snow.

Apples and rain and fine links of gold, red autumn leaves, too stubborn to fall, edges of thick paper and close cropped nails, passion, obsession, and the fervor of spring in the grass and the flowers that grow wild in the field.

The lighthouse that stands alone in the field like a scarp of land in the sea and a wilting rose seen through a melting chunk of ice, both embracing the death they fear but cannot deny and the sound of rain and the deep autumn of her eyes.

A steel door. So new that the traces of the hammer that pounded it flat are still evident upon its surface. An artful staccato of a workmanship battle of man against metal where man is gleeful in his imagined victory and the metal, cold and smug, waits.

The wilting rose.

The loss of hope only because hope itself is glimpsed for one exquisitely painful second.

Bursting anger and splintering wood, misty moors and fields of wet corn.

The lighthouse shines but it is shunned, people only see what they want to see, and they turn from the light like it is a demon or a curse.

The smell of rotted fabric. The smell of wet pavement and the glint of a golden ring. Those leaves that smell like spice and garbage. The floating smell of the drowned, of the already dead body floating amongst the algae like an unwelcome guest.

Peeling wallpaper and clouded glass. Boots with heels. Copper hinges and handles, ornate as the workings on a cowboy's prized saddle. Dusty shoes sinking into swampy water, wading through the scrim of slime and oily decay. Blackened branches reaching through the water like the fingers of the dead trying to grasp at any life through their watery grave. Faces sinking away into memory - into the water and away from time.

Pewter emblems and glasses rimmed with gold wire, hiding the eyes of the damned.

The grit of mud caught between heel and glove.

The house so immaculate, the soul so filthy.

The energy so dark that it despises itself.

The sound of skin sliding against the linen of the paper and the lock of hair, that bloody copper hair, the terror of the truth, the thin white nail. Shirts of colors in the colorless canvas bag and garnet boots coming home in trepidation and hope. Hope for those eyes of autumn, like a gracious war that has first seen the sun and reflects its light with its color. The autumn leaves and the wet sticky mud.

Sad eyes and golden fields, the fields of wheat rolling into the hills of green and promise and a horizon of rainbow colored air. The golden sky crouches before the dead like pagans before an altar.

Kohl rimmed eyes and collar of fur. Flower dresses and smooth white skin. A golden chain with a delicate heart. Quilted blue collar wrapped about a dream, born upon the touch of the living; the sisters and their idea born of childhood secrets and whispers and a dream and love joined by those autumn eyes, the heaven of the golden fields of wheat and held down by the anchor of steel and blood and death, freedom delayed by the promise of love's first kiss.

She comes for you, she comes to be you, to save you and protect you. Those autumn eyes, eyes of mulch, eyes of lichen on stone that hold death and life. Eyes that see what is to come. Rubber tires, twisted steel, dirt and redemption. The promise of the future, the promise of the sky, the light of hope in those autumn eyes that assure you gently of your own death.

Promise slides away from everything you are able to hold with hands slicked with blood. Can you hold the word like you hold the smell of snow as an icy thrill on the edge of your nose? As I lay broken in the snow, my heart realizes that it can forgive anything, and it does. Thoughts fly as real and as uncatchable as butterflies chasing the autumn wind.

 ONE FIVE

Torches around the courtyard were lit as the sunset faded into lavender. Violent streaks of purple reached skeletal hands up into the darkening blue.

The combined light of the dying day and the flickering torches reflected off Bjorn's eyes and they shone like glass.

Bottle-green, Scarlett thought. *That's what Grandpa would call them,* though she had no idea why or where the thought came from. Never in her life had she seen bottles made of that color.

Their dinner arrived and Bjorn, seeing the state of shock that Scarlett was in, was ready to send it away.

"No," she said, taking a deep breath. "Let's eat. It will give me time to think."

Bjorn nodded approvingly as the waiter set down their plates. "You are learning quite a bit, I see."

"Thank you." Scarlett picked up her utensils and dug into her steak.

She thought that her mind was going to be too far away to enjoy her dinner but she was wrong. She didn't realize how much her body, not to mention her taste buds, had been craving red meat.

After a few heavenly bites she let her mind start to turn over what Bjorn had told her, both about herself and about the Amliss Attack. He was right about one thing - she *was* different. Two months ago she would have laughed in his face. Now that she had acquired an inner calm and an ability for contemplation, she turned the idea around in her head, examining it from different angles.

Her first thoughts took her back to the day of the attack. It had been twenty-five years ago but Scarlett could remember the day with perfect clarity. She had been away at college and had woken up to a beautiful day and a brutal hangover. Hell, she had still been half drunk when the IGC Agent knocked on the door of her podment. She had stuck a syringe of A-solve into her upper thigh and had been quite sober by the time they reached the secure IGC Thermopylae.

She could remember the fluorescent lights of the hospital and its acrid sterile smell. She could see John, distraught with indecision and loss. Becca's round belly and Sean clinging to her side. Grandpa's brooding silence.

The clearest part of it all, ringing like a bell of ultra-glass, were her father's words when she had entered the room where he had spent his last few minutes of his life. *I'm telling you it was an ambush!* he had told the IGC agent that had been debriefing him from his hospital bed. *They came streaming from behind that IGC freighter like water breaking around a dam. How could no one aboard the Amliss have seen them until it was too late? It was a goddamned turkey shoot! We didn't have a chance!*

Scarlett thought about the moment with perfect clarity, something she had never been able to do before. Pain and anger and loss had always clouded the memory, but now it was clear.

And that smarmy IGC agent, she thought. *Had I seen him before? Or since?*

Too many things didn't add up. But trusting her sworn enemy was not something she was ready to do. She wiped her mouth with a napkin and took a sip of wine. "Why should I believe you?"

Bjorn swallowed his food. "I think you already do."

"I don't care what you think I think, I want to know what you know. What did your research turn up?"

"Not much. Like I told you, almost everything encompassing your life or the life of your family is sealed. So I simply read the public records of the attack and recounted what I knew firsthand of that day and the events that followed."

The waiter appeared but Bjorn waved him away and refilled their glasses himself.

"We knew that we had staged no attack and that the reports were false. But who would we tell, and why should we?"

"How do you know it wasn't some rogue team within the Chimera, initiating an attack without your knowledge? I know another setback you had faced in the beginning was disorganization."

"True," he agreed, putting down his knife and fork. "But that is something we would all have known of, and we certainly never had any rogue factions. Disorganized, yes – but we were all united in The Cause."

"And?"

Bjorn smiled, appreciating that she knew he had more to offer. "And we had just secured our first platoon of fighter jets forty-eight hours before. But they were not weapons-ready for another week, five days after the attack at the *Amliss*."

Scarlett swallowed hard and pushed her plate away. She took a long drink of the wine and felt it burn going down. She put the glass back on the table and Bjorn refilled it as she sat back in her chair and crossed her arms over her chest, trying to hold onto the burning. A few moments passed before she could speak and, when she did, she didn't look at the green-eyed Chimeran.

"So it wasn't you, if what you are telling me is true. It doesn't mean it was the IGC. It could have been a stray tribe of Golgoth, or some subversive organization..."

"A Golgoth tribe would not have stopped with one attack, a subversive organization would not have gone without the credit. And neither would have just disappeared into the ether."

"But the IGC! Why?"

Bjorn favored her with a look that bordered on tenderness. "They are a governmental entity, Scarlett. They need money. Where do you think the money comes from?" She opened her mouth to answer but he continued before she could. "It comes from the people. And do people like to give up their money? Especially to a government or an enterprise where they will have no say in how it is used? No. People don't give up money unless it is for their own pleasure, which they don't get from the government, or unless they are being robbed - which is closer to the truth in this case. And when people are being robbed, it is not usually by a nice man in a tasteful suit being polite. Even an imbecile would argue with a non-threatening robber. People give up their money a whole lot faster when they are afraid. So if you want that money, it is much better to be a monster or have a monster that is so terrifying that you fear for your life and soul. When people are threatened with losing their life or, much worse, all their worldly possessions – they will give you whatever money you ask and not ask for an explanation in return. All they want is a promise of safety, no matter how false that promise may be."

Scarlett put her hand on the bottom of her wine glass though she didn't pick it up. "Thank you so much for the lesson in government-sanctioned terrorism," she said softly.

Bjorn leaned forward and put one of his hands over hers. "I can't imagine how it must be for you to take all of this in."

Scarlett offered him a wan smile. "Were you expecting me to leap into your arms?"

Bjorn returned her smile. "Hoping. Certainly not expecting." Her smile widened but it was merely reflexive. She turned her face away and looked out over the dusky fields.

"Even if what you are saying is true..."

"It is."

"I'll check."

"I know."

Scarlett sighed. "Even if it is true, my first duty is to my family."

Bjorn sat back, taking the warmth of his hand with him. Scarlett felt a twinge at its loss. The Chimeran cocked his head and looked at her, his green eyes suddenly sly. "And how will you serve your family by having no family of your own?"

Scarlett's eyes narrowed and he nodded.

"I know that as a Jordan you are forbidden to marry or have children." Scarlett looked away. "I am one the First Seven, Scarlett. We were not denied anything, including the ability to procreate."

Scarlett burst out laughing. "Jesus!" she exclaimed, "Is that how you are restaffing your troops? I can just imagine hundreds of horny little green-eyed psychopaths swarming about the galaxy!"

Bjorn threw back his head and laughed heartily. Their combined laughter broke the tension that had slowly been filling the air around them.

"No, Scarlett. I have not fathered any children. Not yet, anyway." As his laughter dwindled he took a few minutes to compose himself and the look of tenderness returned. "But just think," he continued, "of the child we might conceive, not to mention the fun we would have trying."

Scarlett shook her head at his wolfish grin, though her mind and heart were both racing at the thought.

Bjorn leaned over the table conspiratorially. "Oh, the temper he or she would have!" Scarlett laughed and tossed her dark curls away from her face, though the image, which should have been awful to her, made the breath snag in her chest and invoked a feeling of endearment and softness inside her.

"A tempestuous child with dark hair and bright green eyes," the Chimeran offered seductively. Scarlett's eyes met his as she measured the idea. Bjorn gave her a secretive smile. "And, I'm not sure yet, but I think I might know where I might find a green Fledgling for that green-eyed child to fly."

Scarlett's face contorted with pain, as if she had been physically slapped. She lost control of her emotions for the first time that night as they boiled over inside her. "From the Jordan that you killed?" Her accusation was sharp, hurt, and angry.

Bjorn frowned. "I did not kill him. That was his own doing. I never intended for him to die, or any of you for that matter. It was the Dragon we wanted, you know that."

Scarlett looked away, quelling the fury that had risen inside her with a deep and even breathing exercise. Bjorn leaned forward, placing his forearms along the table.

"For some time, drawing the Dragon had been my objective. It was the only thing I wanted." Scarlett looked back, returning his frown.

"For some time?"

"For the past two decades that had been my objective, my only objective. Until I met you," he told her. "After that, you were all I wanted." Scarlett looked back towards the open fields but they were now mostly hidden under a cloak of darkness. Anger and pride warred within her heart.

"Jade," Scarlett whispered. *Joe,* she thought. *Dad.*

"He chose his own path, Scarlett."

The Jordan was startled, thinking that he meant her father, but she realized that she hadn't said his name aloud. He was speaking of Jade.

"It is time for you to choose your own path, unless you intend to be propelled down one by force for the rest of your life."

Scarlett shook her head, unable to find the words.

Bjorn reached out again and put his hand over hers. The warmth returned in a welcoming rush. It burned, like the wine. Also like the wine, Scarlett knew that too much of it would be a dangerous thing tonight. "The universe lies at our feet, Scarlett."

Scarlett gently removed her hand and leaned back in her chair. She tipped her head back, her dark eyes searching the night sky. The constellations had a familiar quality but were still so odd to her.

"This is a lot for me to take in," she said.

"The stars?" Bjorn asked, looking up. His eyes fell back down as Scarlett lowered her own gaze to meet his. "Or the fact that the people you swore to kill to avenge your father's death are the same people to whom you have dedicated your life?" He grinned wolfishly. "Or, perhaps, just the thought of conceiving a child with me?"

Scarlett smiled. "Yes."

★

The waiter cleared their plates as they finished the bottle of wine and Bjorn ordered another. Scarlett sighed.

"Your group of rebels..." she started.

"Needs you," Bjorn finished.

"Doesn't have a chance, was what I was going to say."

"That's not true," Bjorn argued as the waiter arrived with another bottle of wine. "We are growing in strength. The war is escalating because of the assistance we are getting from non-Chimeran support and not just from the humans and the elves, but from other races as well."

That was a surprise to Scarlett. Many species had agreed with the Chimera that the use of manufactured beings was sanctioned slavery, but she didn't think anyone would stand up for them.

"Our leaders..." Bjorn started.

"Are lunatics," Scarlett finished.

"I hope you don't mean me," Bjorn remarked, picking up his glass as soon as it had been refilled.

"I wouldn't discount you," Scarlett told him, smiling. "But I meant the other ringleader in your circus. The Boy Butcher or Boy Vicar, or whatever the hell he is called."

"JP?" Bjorn asked, innocently. The green-eyed Commander shrugged. "He is a little fanatical, yes. But, you have to admit, that there have been many leaders throughout the history of every species that have been downright maniacal, and that hasn't negated the fact that they were great leaders."

Scarlett leaned forward over the table. "And them being great leaders does not negate the fact that they were downright maniacal."

Bjorn looked out into the darkened night and shrugged with only one shoulder. "I see your point," he admitted before taking a drink from his glass.

Scarlett took another sip of her wine and then set the glass aside. "And I hope you can see why I must decline your offer. As sweet as you make it, I just don't I see us landing on the same side."

Bjorn smiled as if he might have other ideas while the Jordan glanced about the patio, searching for the waiter. He spotted her the same instant that her eyes fell upon him. Scarlett held up a hand, signaling him. He came hurrying over, bowing.

"Do you know Mica?" she asked. The waiter bobbed his head.

"The cabbie? Yes. Would you like me to call him?"

"Yes, please." The waiter bowed repeatedly and scurried off.

"Can I tempt you with dessert?" Bjorn asked, his green eyes so bright they nearly glowed in the torchlight.

"I think you've given me enough to digest for one night."

Bjorn smiled, though his disappointment was apparent. "But you don't have to take a cab. Lucy can take you back to your cottage in our..."

"Lucy?"

"My troll. You met her on your way in."

"I certainly did," Scarlett smirked. "Since when did they start making such attractive historians?"

"Since GwenSeven started making them."

"Jesus. Is GwenSeven aligned with your Cause?"

Bjorn laughed. "I'm not ready to start giving you inside information until I know which side you are going to land on, though I really have high hopes. Ah! That reminds me, I have something for you." He reached into a pocket and pulled out a small blue box. He placed it on the table and slid it across the smooth planked wood of the table.

Not taking her eyes off of him, and unable to remove the smirk from the corner of her mouth, Scarlett picked up the box and opened it. She drew in a smooth, controlled breath and looked down.

There, on a bed of midnight blue velvet, was a necklace. A silver figure eight, the Chimeran double loop for infinity, the size of her thumb was held on either side by smaller links of infinity loops. It was an officer's chain.

No, Scarlett thought, *not just an officer's chain. It's not silver. It's platinum. It's a Commander's chain. He wasn't kidding around.* Her dark eyes flicked back up to meet his green ones.

"I can't take this."

"Of course you can," he said, his voice deep and soft. "Whether or not you decide to wear it is entirely up to you."

His eyes, his voice, his smell, the wine...Scarlett was suddenly hot all over. She stood quickly, pushing her chair back.

"I'm sorry, this is more than I can get my head around right now. I...I..." she stammered, finding herself at a loss for words.

The Jordan wanted to believe that it was entirely due to the information she had been given and not his presence that so easily rendered her speechless. So much about her was changed. She felt that her newly acquired inner calm had made her defenseless once again. She had always had a cutting retort for him before, now she had nothing.

"Thank you for dinner," she told him, feeling awkward and stupid. She bit her lip and, not knowing what else to say, turned and walked quickly back around the patio tables and towards the château.

Bjorn scooped up the box she had left and followed her, catching her as she entered the indoor section of the restaurant and falling in step next to her. He slipped an arm around her waist and, though her body tensed, she did not push him away or move to escape the embrace of his arm as he walked her through the restaurant's front door and outside to the waiting aircab. Headlines ran in a streaming ticker around and around on its doors and fenders.

The Chimeran opened the door for her and a cloud of smoke came billowing out. He waved it away and peered inside, frowning at the driver. He looked back at Scarlett. "Are you sure you want to get in there?" he asked.

Scarlett laughed softly. "Don't worry, Mica's an old friend."

"That's right!" Mica called from inside the cab. "Old friend!" His raucous laughter echoed inside the smoky taxi.

The Commander straightened and turned away from the cabbie with a dubious look. "You know they are planning a big celebration in town?" Bjorn asked.

Scarlett nodded. "It's the millennium celebration, though the New Year started over six months ago."

"They have been waiting for an alignment of planets, they are calling it the Synchronicity. Also, the eggs manifested by the Silver and Copper Dragons have been pulled. They should hatch within the year." He thought it prudent not to mention Alexander's Eggs for the time being.

"Really?" That was a surprise to Scarlett. She knew she was

cut off from the rest of the universe but she was sure that someone would have given her that news. The Opal Dragon, *her* Dragon, had been the first from the Third Generation Dragons to hatch eggs. Now, along with the Beryl Dragon, the Silver Dragon and the Copper Dragon were expecting Hatchlings. It truly was the Year of the Fourth Dragon.

The Year of The Rainbow, Scarlett thought.

"So," Bjorn continued, pushing a lock of hair away from her face, "I will be back for the big night. I will be meeting a contingent of others who are joining The Cause." He reached out and cupped her cheek with the palm of his hand. "I'd like to know that you have seen the light by then."

Scarlett tried to pull away but found herself too weak. Instead she just moved her jaw and hoped her lips would force the words. "I can't," she managed.

"You can," he told her, running his thumb gently across her cheek. "Think about your family. Think about your father. Think about Joey."

Hearing her brother's name was as much of a shock to her as the fact that Bjorn knew it. He cradled a jaw that had seemingly come loose at the hinges and fixed his green eyes upon her.

As the Jordan felt herself become more unraveled, she could see the Commander become more sure – he seemed to lock down on something, something that was important to him.

"Don't let them change you, Scarlett."

It was not a statement or a request. It was a command. Scarlett felt fragile and frail though she was determined not to show it - but when her lips moved, no sound came out. She could see the muscles in Bjorn's lean body go rigid.

"Never be anything but what and who you are," he said, his voice getting softer with every word. "But if you seek change, seek me." He leaned close, close enough for her to feel the warmth of his body though she did not back away. "I will change for you, Scarlett," he confessed, his voice barely above a whisper. "I will be anything you want me to be."

The Jordan was too astounded for words and looked doubtful. Despite the shock of the news he had given her over dinner and the offer he was making, she could not think clearly with his body and his smell so close.

"I don't know," she told him. "There are...people I need to talk to."

Bjorn smiled and leaned back a bit as he nodded in understanding. Scarlett almost heaved a sigh of relief, thinking that he was done giving her surprises for the night. But she was wrong.

"Of course," he assured her. "Be sure to tell Fletch that I said hello."

She frowned, thinking at first she that he had said Fledge, but then it hit her and her right foot fell back to support her as she reeled. He had not said Fledge but Fletch, short for Fletcher. Fletcher Mattatock. The man for whom her Fledgling Dragon had been named. Her Grandpa.

The Chimeran Commander leaned forward and left a lingering kiss on her cheek, but she was too astounded to feel the spreading warmth it made along her face until he had turned and walked back towards the restaurant.

"Hey pretty lady!" Mica called from inside the cab. "Save some for me!" He laughed uproariously and Scarlett climbed in the back, her head in the drifting clouds of his ganja smoke, though now she didn't mind so much.

As Bjorn moved away from the taxi the dark-haired girl with the reflective, golden eyes joined him. He stopped in the doorway and together they watched the taxi rise up and cruise away.

"Did it go as you expected?" Lucy asked.

"Pretty much," Bjorn admitted, watching the taxi dwindle in a plume of dust and then disappear into the dark as it crested a hill. "She's different," he mused, not for the first time.

"You told me before that people don't change."

Bjorn smiled distractedly, still watching the spot where the cab had vanished into the night. "She's the same inside," he said. "I can tell that just by her eyes. It's what's on the outside that is different. Like she is wearing a stranger's cloak."

"Does it alter your attraction to her?"

"Not in the slightest."

"And you think she would still be an asset?"

Bjorn grunted. "More than ever." He turned to face the troll. "She'll be different again after she's been shot, won't she?"

Lucy's voice was slightly metallic and matter of fact. "They always are."

Bjorn gave a resigned sigh and brought his strong hands together in a brisk clap. "Well," he announced, rubbing his hands together. "I'm going to finish that bottle of wine. Why don't you

THE MOONS OF JUPITER

join me?"

"I don't drink," Lucy notified.

"Then you can answer some questions for me."

"That is what I am here for."

Bjorn grinned and ushered the troll back into the restaurant.

★

Scarlett was already getting light-headed from all the ganja smoke. "Take me to the west-side ferry dock, please," she told Mica.

Mica babbled to her as the cab took them sliding over the roads on a cushion of ionized air. He never paused for an answer or input from his fare, but would erupt in gales of laughter whenever he said something he found particularly funny.

Scarlett barely heard him and was vaguely glad that most of the driving was automatized. She looked down at her lap and noticed that she was holding the box with the Chimeran necklace in it.

The ride was smooth and free of traffic – there didn't seem to be many people out and certainly no one headed for the eastward bound ferry in a motorized cab. They reached the west dock quickly and Scarlett paid Mica, politely declining a ride home – to *his* home.

"Maybe some other time?" he asked, laughing as she got out of the taxi.

"Maybe some other time," the Jordan agreed with a chuckle, shaking her head as she closed the cab's door. The taxi turned and sped away, trailing wisps of smoke and raucous laughter.

Scarlett's boots made hollow clunking sounds on the wooden dock that mirrored the strange hollowness she felt inside. She boarded the eastbound ferry and took a seat on a bench, trying not to control her train of thoughts but instead trying to let them flow around her like the waters of the river.

Well, my first instinct is to check out his story, see how much of it is true, or shows to be true. She sighed. *It would be a waste of time. He wouldn't outright lie to me, not about that. He would have to assume that I would look into it. Worse, if I did go snooping around I could leave an IGC inquiry trail, and they might want to know why I was looking into the events of the Amliss Attack. Not a good idea, especially if Bjorn is right.*

Scarlett looked out into the darkness, seeing the passing flow of the riverbanks only by the flickering reflection of the moonlight on the leaves. The ferry passed the walled city-town and stopped at the east-side dock where no one got on or off the boat. After a few minutes of creaky rocking and the ferry gently bumping against the small pier, it was on its way again.

I have to rely on what I already know. Which is what?

More than you think.

The voice that spoke inside her head was Master Elaeric, his tone as taunting and amused as always. She sighed.

I know that the attack was unexpected, out of the blue, and accomplished in one stroke exactly what some factions of the IGC had been after for a long time – the unification of all the councils on the matter of the Rebellion – along with a great deal of funding. Moreover, I remember what my father said right before he died.

He said they were ambushed. He said that the freighter supposedly hadn't seen the enemy fighters until it was too late.

Scarlett thought that something was beginning to smell fishy, and it wasn't just the approach of the fishing village ahead of the ferry. Ambush or not, it would have taken skilled fighters to take down her father and her brother, not to mention their entire team of trained f-jet pilots. Chimeran pilots hardly knew thrust from jettison, or their asses from their elbows as her father would have said. Even after a hundred years they only had a few squads of pilots that had the skill of a halfway decent IGC first year lieutenant. They only had a handful with real skill.

Dad and Joe alone should have decimated them.

The ferry nudged the dock and Scarlett disembarked at the fishing village on shaky legs. She found the inn where she had stabled the horse and, after paying a tipsy ostler, and refusing offers for drinks, she retrieved her courser. The mare snorted in greeting and Scarlett swung up into the saddle with a sense of familiarity that felt very comforting. She patted the mare's neck and urged her north.

The night was still warm but, as the mare broke into a trot, the wind blew through the Jordan's dark hair and cooled her skin. Scarlett was letting the horse find the way home at a brisk but easy pace when another thought raised chill bumps all over her arms and back.

Her brother John had arrived first at the hospital that night and had been told by the doctors that their father had been badly wounded but would most likely survive. John had been in anguish over the suddenness of his father's death and grieved by the fact that he was not given the chance to say good-bye. Johanna, still in shock herself, had told him that she had not really gotten the chance either and that the doctors had been wrong. It wasn't the first time and it wouldn't be the last.

Now she wondered if that were true. Maybe they had been right. Maybe her father should have survived.

She thought of the IGC officer. Not in a uniform, but in a suit. He had been young, but his eyes had the ferocity of a man that was determined to rise within the ranks. Looking back with calm clarity, Scarlett realized that there was definitely something familiar about that young man. It was the set of his eyes, she was sure. That dark glare. Had she seen him again since then? Where?

Her recall was quite clear, but she also recalled how drunk she had been. The shot of A-solve had killed her hangover and her father's situation had sobered her figuratively, but her brain cells were probably still pickled.

Unable to place the officer, she thought of how he had grasped her father's shoulder and how her father had winced in pain. Why? Had the man disturbed his wounds? Or had he pressed a derm-pin full of poison into Joseph Mattatock?

If Bjorn is right, she thought, *it's the latter. They wouldn't want him around, especially if he was voicing his opinions about the attack. They probably only kept him alive long enough to find out what he knew, and if anyone else was privy to the same knowledge.*

Scarlett felt her stomach clench at the thought and then swallowed hard and shook her head, letting the wind blow through her thick hair and cool her face. She let her shoulders relax as she bounced gently in the saddle, letting her breath fall in rhythm with the mare's easy gait.

The question now, she realized, *is what am I going to do about it?*

Her old self flared up at once, making her new self laugh out loud.

I'll kill every last one of them, the old self thought.

The new self laughed because she agreed.

It was hard for Scarlett not to urge the mare on - she was anxious to speak to Elaeric but was sure that he would be in bed and she would have to wait for the morning. As the horse and rider crested the hill and turned towards the house, Scarlett squinted her eyes, uncertain. She had expected Elaeric to leave a light burning for her but was surprised to see a shadow of movement coming from inside the cottage.

What is he doing up at this hour?

Scarlett rode the mare up the dirt lane past the cottage and towards the small barn, now sure that Elaeric was not just up but that he was in the kitchen. She unsaddled the mare and was giving her a quick rub down with a scrap of burlap when another thought occurred to her. It was the last thing Bjorn had said.

Tell Fletch that I said hello.

How in the hell does he know Grandpa?

Scarlett led the mare through the gate in the rail fence and turned her loose in the field. She carried the bridle back to the barn and tossed it inside on top of the saddle. She headed for the cottage at a brisk walk when she remembered the box Bjorn had given her and ran back to the retrieve it from her saddlebag.

By the time she came through the door, hoping to catch Elaeric before he went to bed, she was out of breath and the box with the Chimeran necklace inside was gripped tightly in her right hand.

The night seemed to hold no limit to the amount of shocks in store for the dark-haired Jordan of the Opal Dragon.

She swung the door open to the cottage to find Elaeric, looking at her with a mixture of surprise and delight, holding a steaming teapot in his hand. Sitting at the kitchen table, blue eyes shining at her, was Calyph.

# ONE SIX

Grandpa showered and shaved and, after he had dressed, brushed his teeth a second time. Not because he had forgotten that he had already brushed his teeth, which was often the case, but because he felt as if he had something lodged between his front two teeth on the bottom. It had been driving him crazy all night.

After a good deal of brushing and finally just mercilessly poking at it with his tongue, there was a small clatter in the sink. Grandpa reached down and pinched the object between his fingers and held it up to the light for inspection.

It was a tooth, what was left of it anyway.

Hardly a tooth at all, Grandpa thought, turning the small, yellowed bit of bone between his fingers. The nub, broken and worn down by time, was jagged and not much larger than the head of a pin.

He tossed it into the bathroom trash chute where it ricocheted around in the metal tube, chattering out a staccato goodbye on its way down. *Good riddance,* he thought, feeling a bit petulant.

Grandpa sighed as he left the bathroom, the light shutting off on its own when he was gone, knowing he shouldn't grouse. There was no reason to feel particularly down about the loss of the tooth. The thing had seen its share of meals and was down to nearly nothing anyway.

Besides, Grandpa thought, *I'm feeling much too fine to regret the loss of a little piece of mouth bone.*

Sean, true to his word, had come back the very next day after their discussion on Grandpa's health. He had brought with him some vitamin supplements that Grandpa didn't like but took anyway, nutrient shakes that Grandpa had found surprisingly tasty, and a new scrip from the pharmacologist. The boy had put the pills on the coffee maker so the old man would remember to take them, and the bottled shakes in the fridge next to his water pitcher.

After a week, however, Grandpa didn't need to see the bottles to jar his memory. He was remembering them on his own. His tremors had disappeared and, if he had been a swearing man, would have sworn that his eyesight was getting better too. He felt better than he had in years. He wasn't about to mourn the loss of a calcified nub of bone that had once, long ago, served as a tooth.

Grandpa went into his kitchen full of sunshine and took his pills as the coffee maker took care of business. He decided to skip his usual pastry and scrambled an egg instead. He ate it at the table in the kitchen's sunny breakfast nook and had a glass of juice as well. He smacked his lips in satisfaction as he put his plate and glass in the dishcleaner and then straightened up, putting his hands on his hips.

He looked at his chair in the living room where he usually parked himself for the majority of the day, watching programs or news on the flatglass. Then he turned his head to look out the kitchen windows.

More sunshine poured down onto the rolling green grass. He could see a bench in the sun that was partially shaded by the spreading branches of a full-leaf maple tree. The bench sat at the edge of the verdant lawn and faced a sandy playground where a mother pushed a toddler in some sort of swinging contraption.

His eyes caught the movement of a bird as it flitted from branch to branch but Grandpa was either too far away or too enclosed to hear its song. That decided it. He walked through his living room and out the door of his podment, something that he usually only did when he was being moved to the next one.

He paused with the door open as he tried to decide if he should lock it, then he remembered that it would lock automatically. Sean had told him that they don't use keys here – the door would recognize him and open for him. Experimenting, he pulled the door shut and let go of the handle. He could hear the lock slide into the jamb. Grandpa put his hand back onto the handle and heard the bolt retract the second before he lifted the handle up and opened the door.

He gave a satisfied grunt and closed the door again. *Might be the best piece of technology I've seen for decade,* he thought as his eyes searched the hallway for the exit. He found it immediately, not even needing the green holo letters that floated above it. It was a large glass panel that opened onto a paved walk that led to the park.

Grandpa strode down the hall and through the door that slid open for him with a soft whoosh. Standing on the smooth white path, he closed his eyes and turned his face up to the sky, feeling sunshine on his face for the first time in over a hundred years. For Grandpa, the feeling was like being reborn.

Grinning like a jack-o-lantern, Grandpa followed the path to the park and sat himself on the bench in the sun. He watched the woman with the child and thought of the children in his life. There had been many over the generations but now there were just two: Jeanette and Sean.

Despite how good he was feeling, he meant to stick to his guns and pass down everything he knew to one of them. There had to be someone in the family that knew their history. The whos, the whats, and the whys. The question he faced, was which child would it be? Sean?

Grandpa knew that he was a bright boy. Very bright. But how caring? How soft on the inside? Though he was growing fast, he still bore the gentleness of childhood, not yet jaded by the constraints of growing up and the mental burden of adulthood. Yet hope was slim, as it always was when there were siblings.

It seemed that when there was a pair of sibs, one would grow up sharp and the other soft. One a fighter, one a nurturer. Little Jean was already the latter, her brother the former. Jeanette was full of compassion and concern, for everyone. Sean was of a rougher cut, and was sure to hone that cut to a razor edge.

When more than one child was born by the same parents into the Mattatock family, there was always that inexorable splitting of traits. Grandpa wondered if it was the same with other families. Perhaps if Johanna had a single child...

Grandpa watched the mother in the park gingerly take her child from the pneumatic swing and cackled silent laughter at the thought. Johanna was strong and could pass down immeasurable greatness to a child, but she was no nurturer. Like a tiger, she might eat her young. Grandpa shook his head. It was funny even to think of Johanna as a mother. The idea was ridiculous.

Still, Grandpa thought as he drummed his knobby fingers on his thigh and his tongue poked around at the few remaining teeth in his mouth, *stranger things have happened.* He thought of the elf that had paid them a visit, trying to recall his name.

"Calyph," he said aloud, pleased that he remembered. "It was Calyph."

The Engineer of the Opal Dragon had paid the family a visit, personally informing them of Johanna's condition and whereabouts. John had thanked him and, after he had left, looked at Grandpa with eyebrows raised up almost to his hairline. There was something between the elf and Johanna, more there than just work. Even John could sense it, and was surprised by it.

It wasn't just that the elf had travelled all the way to Io to speak with them personally. Though the elf meant well, he was ill at ease and his speech was apparently well rehearsed. He clearly had strong feelings for Johanna and it seemed most likely that he was involved in some sort of relationship with her, though he only referred to her as Jordan Scarlett. When Grandpa called her Johanna he had blushed to the tips of his pointed ears.

John had been quite surprised by the elf, not the visit. He was certainly not the type that Johanna had ever had romantic dealings with in the past. She preferred men that were more like herself – strong-willed and fiercely competitive. The last man she dated, though he was an elf as well, had been a doctor and dangerously smart. Though John had found the relationship odd, Grandpa wasn't as perplexed by it.

Grandpa was more understanding. The Engineer was obviously socially uncomfortable, but in that way maybe he shared an orbit with Johanna. He had an aversion to society. She abhorred it.

Grandpa thought that a commonality such as that might be a stretch to base a marriage on, and the chances of an elf and a human having children were twice as unlikely.

Still, he thought again, *stranger things have happened.*

He watched the mother tuck her child into an airbuggy and glide it away down the walk. He was enjoying the feel of sunshine, the sound of the birds and the smell of the grass, when a voice shouted right next to him - practically scaring him out of his wrinkled skin.

"Grandpa! What in the hell are you doing out here?"

The old man cringed like he had been caught stealing candy, till he saw that it was his grandson. Sean, his blue eyes wide in amazement, stood with his hands on his hips as if he had caught the old man misbehaving. Grandpa straightened.

"Language!" Grandpa admonished. "And don't you yell at me!"

"I'm sorry," Sean apologized, dropping his hands to his sides. "But I was worried when I didn't find you in your pod. I was a little scared, even." He smiled sheepishly. "And I'm used to being loud when I talk to you." He cocked his head, looking at the man on the bench. "Your hearing is getting better, isn't it?"

Grandpa blinked in surprise. "Is it?"

"You tell me."

Grandpa thought for a few seconds. "It's possible," he admitted, thinking of the way he could hear the rustle of the wind in the leaves of the tree above him. Usually he couldn't hear the knock on his door. "You're home early," he said, changing the subject. "No arcade today?"

"No arcade today. I wanted to talk to you." Sean told him. What he did not share with him was that he wasn't going back to the arcade for some time.

The Skipper had handed him his ass twice already in two days. His friends had tried to console him, saying that the Skipper was probably hacking the game itself, that no one could anticipate fighter jet moves that fast. Sean let them commiserate, but he didn't think they were right. Nor did he subscribe to the rumors that maybe the Skipper was a highly experienced jet fighter that was just dicking around with the kids. Sean knew that adults didn't give a shit about kids and certainly never had time to dick around with them.

"Is that so?" Grandpa asked, his smile showing his yellow broken teeth.

"Yeah," Sean said, trying to smile back.

"Well?" Grandpa prompted.

Sean's young face took on a look of consternation. "Maybe we should go inside," he suggested.

Now it was Grandpa that cocked his head. "What exactly is it that you wanted to talk about?" he asked, his eyes narrowed a bit in suspicion.

"The First Seven," he said.

"Is that so?" Grandpa asked again, his smile fading. Sean nodded and Grandpa gave the park a parting glance and let out a deep breath. "Well!" the old man exclaimed, clapping his hands to his thighs before using them to push himself up. He straightened, stretching his back. "Maybe we should go inside."

Sean smiled and walked with Grandpa along the path and through the auto-slide door into their podment. When they reached Grandpa's pod the old man stopped suddenly, seeing something he hadn't taken note of when he left. Maybe the change of light now made it more noticeable.

There was a number seven on his door.

"I thought there were only four pods in this place," he told Sean gruffly, motioning to the number on his door with what felt like a very heavy hand.

Sean nodded. "There are, but it's a duplex, and we are joined to the quad of podments next to us, even though it's only by a short walkway. The pods on the other side are numbers one through four, and we're numbers five through eight."

Grandpa stared at the silver number seven imbedded in his door like it was the scarlet letter. *Scarlett,* he thought with a huff. *Seven.* "And what number are you in?" Grandpa asked without taking his eyes off his door.

"Eight," Sean told him as if it were the most innocuous thing in the world.

"Of course you are," Grandpa whispered, still staring at the number on his own door as if mesmerized by it.

Sean frowned at him. "Are you alright, Grandpa?"

Grandpa nodded and reached for the handle to his door. "I'm fine, son," he told him, offering the boy a bit of a broken smile. He led the way into the pod and went straight to his kitchen where he opened the fridge and took out his pitcher of water. He poured a glass and drank it down in three long swallows. It burned going down but he smacked his lips in satisfaction and then poured another.

Sean watched him from the wide and open doorframe that bridged the kitchen and living room. "Feel better?" he asked.

"Yes. Yes, I do."

Sean smiled. "Do you want to sit in the living room?"

Grandpa shook his head as he put the pitcher back in the fridge. "You're too big to sit on the rug. Let's sit in here."

Sean nodded and grinned as he took a seat at the kitchen table. "Am I big enough for a glass of water?" he asked, indicating Grandpa's glass as the old man sat down across from him. The answer was curt but given with a broken smile.

"Nope."

Sean laughed. "I didn't think so."

"So," Grandpa said, the mirth draining from his wrinkled face. "What do you want to know about the First Seven?"

Sean reached down by his hip and hefted his ac-bag up onto the table. He dropped his hand onto the canvas surface and drummed his fingers on the material. He took a deep breath as if summoning his courage.

"Do you know when they were made?"

Grandpa nodded. "Thirty-seven twenty-five. They spent three years training and undergoing tests, then they were sold in thirty-seven twenty-eight."

Sean nodded, relieved. When Grandpa had first told him and his sister about the First Seven, he had given them a different year – hell, he had told them it was in the 3600's. This week, Sean had come across the actual records and when the dates were so far off it made him worry. Either Grandpa had just been prattling on to hear himself talk, or he was outright bullshitting them. Now, something else occurred to him. Grandpa's memory, along with his hearing, was getting better.

The pills, Sean thought. *He must be taking the pills. Thank God.*

"Is that all?" Grandpa asked. "Seems like a lot of fuss over a couple of dates."

Sean shook his head, flipping the blonde hair out of his eyes. "No, that's not all." He drummed the pads of his fingers on his ac-bag while Grandpa waited. "You told me once that you knew Cronus."

"That's right."

"How?"

Grandpa took a sip from his glass. "When I was twenty-two, I got a job at a brand new company that was experimenting in cutting-edge biotechnology. The company was nameless and family-run, doing only research and development at the time. When they incorporated, that company became what is now called GwenSeven."

"Holy shit."

Grandpa smiled and didn't bother to reprimand the boy on his language. "That's right," he agreed.

"Were you there when the first constructs were made?"

"I was."

After gaping at his grandfather for a few seconds, Sean leaned forward. "So why are they called the First Seven?" he asked. "IGC Annotated History only names six, and there are only six records of sale for the first run of GwenSeven constructs."

"You looked up the sale records?" Grandpa asked, though he was more impressed than surprised. "You can do that?"

Sean shrugged as if to indicate that it was the most natural course of action. Grandpa lifted his chin, stretching his neck and then pursed his lips, thinking.

"Well," he said finally, "you first have to consider what the first run was made for, their original jobs, so to speak. It's not like the third run of manufacturing when they were being mass produced for a multitude of occupations."

Sean wiggled around as if settling in for a good story, something he hadn't done in a long time. "And?" he encouraged. "What were they first ones made for?"

Grandpa pursed his lips. "I think that originally they had planned to make them all to be companions, though for actual companionship – not for what Companion Constructs are mostly used for today. So they were all made as general humans, with the exception of one that was made an elf, and all were beautiful of face and body. Well educated and well cultured, and then fine tuned and trained for the services for which the buyers wanted them."

Sean nodded. "Protection, personal assistance, and companionship," he stated, matter of fact. Grandpa smiled at him and took a drink from his glass.

"That's right. One male was sold as a bodyguard, one as a personal assistant, and one as companion. Two females were sold as companions, one as a personal assistant." Grandpa finished his water in a series of gulps as if suddenly very thirsty.

"That's still only six."

Grandpa nodded. "One of the companions, a male, was pulled off of the line before talks of sale even began."

"Why?"

"We weren't given specifics. Ms. de Rossi announced that something had gone wrong and that a new construct was being made. Everyone assumed that the first one had been defective in some way."

"Which Ms. de Rossi?"

"I believe it was Faith, but I could be wrong."

"The defective one," Sean asked, "What did they do with it? Was it tested, or destroyed?"

"No one knows. I assumed yes."

Sean drummed his fingers on the canvas ac-bag. "The last one made was John Pierre," he said. "The one they call the Boy Vicar."

"That's right," Grandpa said. "He was even called Pious for a time, though it was more in jest." He tapped his fingers on his empty glass in the same manner that Sean tapped on the canvas of his bag. "What else do you want to know?"

Sean shrugged. "What else do you want to tell me? I was just curious about the numbers not matching up, six versus seven."

Grandpa let out a long breath that sounded suspiciously like a sigh of relief. He decided that maybe he wasn't quite ready to share *everything*.

"Are you sure you are okay?" Sean asked. "*Have* you been taking your pills? You seem a little shaky."

"Don't be ridiculous!" Grandpa told him. "I'm as fit as a fiddler!"

Sean cocked his head to the side. Though Grandpa was always full of crazy sayings, Sean was sure he had heard this one before. "Don't you mean fit as a fiddle?" he asked.

Grandpa scowled. "How on Io can a fiddle be fit?" he demanded. "It has to be the fiddler!"

Sean shrugged. "I don't know. I don't even know what a fiddle is."

Grandpa threw back his head and cackled at the ceiling.

★

Later that night, Grandpa went to work on his nubby teeth again with his toothbrush. He could feel something stuck in the spot where his bit of tooth had recently vacated. Not getting anywhere with the brush, he opened his mouth wide and tilted his head so the bathroom light would help.

In the divot between his remaining bottom teeth was a milky white gleam embedded in his shiny pink gums. Grandpa closed his mouth and frowned at the mirror. He went to bed, the light shutting itself off as he left the bathroom.

That can't be, he thought.

But when he checked again in the morning, the milky white gleam was still there, and slightly larger.

"I'll be god-damned," Grandpa whispered.

His old tooth hadn't fallen out. It had been pushed out. He was growing a new tooth.

# ONE SEVEN

Faith came down the lift into the foyer of the villa, stepping out before it had fully stopped and going straight towards her bedroom. She had been delayed on Io by an unplanned but important meeting that took up half the day. Solar winds from Jupiter had delayed the trip home even more.

She had planned on spending the day with Jasyn – maybe a trip to the Commons, an early dinner at a cozy restaurant or even in the dining room followed by dessert in the bedroom - but now there was no time for either.

To top it off, she was going to be gone nearly a week. She really needed the day to spend with Jasyn since she would be gone again and not see him for another seven days. She felt terrible. She pushed open the doors to her room and, seeing Jasyn, felt worse.

He was sitting in the wing chair, reading a book on his acrylic and sharply dressed for a night out. She supposed it could be worse – he could have been wearing less. Faith shook her head as he smiled at her and rose to his feet. He tossed his acrylic on the chair and came straight for her, his lips ready to greet her own. He wrapped Faith in his arms and kissed her.

"I missed you," he said when they finally broke apart.

Faith kissed his lips again and then his cheek. "I know," she sighed. "I missed you too." She pressed her forehead against his and closed her eyes. "I have bad news - I can't stay." Jasyn pulled his head away.

He blinked at her in surprise and then frowned. His disappointment was obvious. "You can't stay? What do you mean?"

"I'm sorry, I was supposed to be home this morning."

"I know."

Faith paused, struck by the tone of his voice. It sounded... almost angry. "Now I only have a few minutes," she apologized.

"Mostly just for Mari and Penny to pack the craft for my trip."

"Do you have time for me?" he asked, tightening his arm around her waist and taking a small step back towards the bed.

Faith kissed him and shook her head, carefully disengaging herself from his embrace. "Not this time. I'm sorry." She turned and walked towards her vanity to select a few pieces of jewelry that she wanted for the trip. His silence followed her, as heavy as his gaze.

When he spoke his voice was deep and flat and carried a strange tone of finality. "I could make you, you know," he said.

Faith, who was bent slightly over as she retrieved a necklace from a drawer, froze. A million thoughts raced through her head as she turned slowly to face him, drawing herself up. "What exactly do you mean by that?"

Jasyn walked slowly towards her until their bodies were almost touching. Faith was able to control her breathing but her heart was banging wildly in her chest. She unexpectedly felt like a caged animal.

Slowly, very slowly, Jasyn brought his head down and brushed his lips along her cheek. His mouth, slightly open, ran down the line of her jaw until he reached the side of her chin, and then ran the tip of his nose to the lobe of her ear. So soft that she could barely feel it, he kissed the skin just under and slightly behind her ear. Following her pulse, he let his lips slide down her neck and in the same way kissed the left side of her throat. He let his face fall until it was just above her shoulder, warming her skin with his breath.

His brought up his hand and with his thumb gently touched the hollow of her throat before his fingers spread out and slid down to graze over her right breast. She could feel her nipple tighten and her back start to arch. He slipped an arm around her waist and rested his hand firmly against the base of her spine so that she couldn't back away and brought his other hand down to her hip, holding her firmly in place.

Faith found that she could no longer control her breathing any more than she could control her racing heart. She leaned towards him, her mouth seeking his, but he pulled away just enough to keep their bodies from touching. She leaned forward again and again he pulled back.

With a wry smile, Faith snaked her arms around him and pulled their bodies close and tight. "Okay, smartass," she breathed, "you were right. You *can* make me." He laughed softly, burying his face in her neck and kissing it. Faith sighed. "But this time you might have bitten off more than you can chew."

He leaned back so he could see her face. "Meaning?"

Faith took a long look at him, pausing one last time before her indecision melted away. She thumbed the gold cuff she wore around her wrist and brought it up to her mouth. "Penny?"

"I'm right here," Penny said as she walked through the open doors of the bedroom. She was slightly breathless from dispensing orders as to the packing of Faith's craft as it was readied for the next trip.

Faith ran her fingers under the collar of Jasyn's shirt and spoke to Penny without looking away from her lover's face. "Pack Jasyn's things. He's coming with me."

Penny's brisk walk through the room pulled up short and a slight choking sound preceded her voice. "I beg your pardon?"

Faith smiled, seeing the surprise in Jasyn's hazel eyes and hearing the same shock in her PA's voice. "He's coming with me. And he'll need a tux. No, two tuxes, if memory serves. A gray vested suit and whatever Charity is insisting on for the dance."

"Ma'am?" Penny asked, stammering. "We are already running behind schedule. The soonest I could get a delivery would be in half an hour."

Faith turned her face so she could see her assistant and her smile pulled down at the corners of her lips, hardening her expression. "Then I suggest you hurry."

"Yes ma'am."

Faith turned her gaze back to Jasyn's face as a terribly flustered Penny hurried from the room.

"Where are we going?" he asked.

Faith tightened her arms around his waist and gave him a quick kiss. "To a party."

"Penny seems a bit frazzled over just a party."

Faith buried her face into his neck. She let the tip of her nose slide up to his ear, breathing in the soft scent that was his and his alone. "It's a ball that Charity throws every two years. It's held at her home, the Last Castle on the Distant Shore, and lasts for three days. Every head of the InterGalactic Council will be there. It's quite the party."

Jasyn pulled back slightly so he could see her face, thinking that she might be joking. "That is quite the party," he admitted. His face took on a look of consternation. "Are you sure that you want to take me to something like that?"

Faith reached up to run her fingers through his thick, dark hair. "I'm not just *taking* you," she told him. "I want you by my side the entire time."

Jasyn's mouth dropped open and he shook his head slowly from side to side before it was fully closed again. "Are you sure?" he asked again. It was not beyond him to understand what his presence at her side could mean, especially at such an important event.

"It's time," Faith said, her voice quiet but firm. She kissed him one more time before pulling away. "I would rather change before we go. Why don't you go let Penny brief you on what to expect over the next few days and board the craft. I'll get dressed and we should be ready to leave as soon as your clothes get here. You can change once we're spaceborne."

"Alright." He gave her a quick peck on the cheek and regarded her for a few moments without saying anything, maybe not knowing the right thing to say. Finally, he just smiled. "Thank you," he whispered before giving her another kiss and leaving to brave whatever storm Penny had brewing for him.

Faith watched him go and then turned and headed for her closet. It was large enough to be a room of its own – brightly lit and full of dresses and suits, shelves of neatly lined shoes, drawers of undergarments and more jewelry than the vanity could hold. In the center was a large pillowed bench covered in cream and gold fabric. On it was laid a sparkling black cocktail dress, black heels, an onyx chain necklace with matching earrings, and a tiny triangle of black silk that she assumed must be underwear.

Faith stared at the cocktail dress for a moment, noticing the similarity of the cloth to the flight suit that Noel had worn. Then she shrugged out of the white suit she was wearing, not wanting to waste time on useless contemplation.

Faith slipped into the dress and shoes then strode to her vanity and transformed it into her mainframe. She quickly finished up some work while Mari pulled up her hair and pinned it with dark barrettes set with shimmering jewels. Mari took up the onyx chain and carefully fastened it around Faith's neck. Faith handed her the one that she had pulled out a few minutes ago, the one Jasyn had gotten her.

"Please make sure this is packed with my things."

"Yes, ma'am."

Within an hour of arriving home, Faith was riding the lift back up from the foyer and boarding her personal spacecraft bound for another long journey. Exiting the lift she found herself on the top floor of her villa.

Much less cozy than the bottom floors of her home, the top third circumference was dominated by her security team, along with their offices and equipment. There were four bedroom suites for the live-in staff, and a long corridor with a sloping floor. The floor led up to the dock, where Faith's personal spacecraft waited. Stepping through the airlock was like stepping back into the living room that she had just left.

Faith's personal spacecraft was a replica, albeit much smaller, of her villa.

The living room of the craft – complete with black marble floor, white rugs, sofa and chairs – was bordered by a dining room and kitchen on one side and a bedroom on the other. There was no office and no guestrooms. Below there was a high-grade plutonium fusion drive instead of a pool, and upstairs housed the bridge rather than her security team, but the resemblance was more than uncanny.

When Charity had first seen the inside of the craft she had laughed, the lilt of her laugh carrying through the entire cabin. "A doppelgänger's doppelgänger!" she had exclaimed, partially doubled over with gales of musical laughter.

Even though they had been alone Faith had hushed her, blushing. Charity had kept laughing.

"What imagination!" she teased, delighted.

"I like the familiarity," Faith argued.

Charity only laughed harder.

Faith didn't care, much.

And now, as she spotted Jasyn already seated in a white leather wing chair, she felt something spark within her body, flaring at the sight of him. There was something about the way he watched everyone moving around him, his expression full of wonder, his dark hazel eyes all open innocence.

The craft was a bustle of activity as the crew, her security team, and her attendants prepared for the trip to the far side of the planet and nearly all the way to the next gas giant, Saturn.

The Captain winked at Faith as he made his way to the stairs that led to the bridge. Geary was rounding up his men and sending some of them topside along with the Captain. Penny ushered the attendants around, giving orders. Mari bustled by, assuring her employer that everything was all set and letting her know that all of her needs had been taken care of per her request.

Faith thanked her, only vaguely aware of what the woman was saying before she hurried off the craft. The housekeeper was no spacefarer, Faith knew, but she was unable to take her focus off of the one person already seated. He looked up and saw her standing in the doorway and smiled. Faith could feel the spark turn into a growing star of warmth that began spreading throughout her body.

It was more than just familiarity and comfort that was making her feel warm all over. Faith saw how Jasyn's eyes followed her as she moved through the cabin and knew that what she was feeling was the birth of joy. It was something she hadn't felt in a long, long time.

I'm in it now, she thought. The thought was a bit frightening, but the warmth that filled her quickly burned away any fear.

Penny held out a small silver tray and offered her employer a comset – a gleaming gold wire studded with jewels – which Faith took and hooked over her right ear as Penny hurried off to take her seat. Faith took the chair next to Jasyn.

"Did they brief you on what to expect?"

Jasyn nodded. "Yes. The Captain actually came out and told me. Does he always do that?"

"No, he only does that for special passengers."

"Did you tell him I was a special passenger?"

Faith smiled. "I think he figured that out on his own." Jasyn gave her a mistrustful smile as she ran a finger along the side of her seat and found the edges of the belt embedded there. She pulled out a stretch of the belt webbing and fitted the end to its mate on the far side of her lap.

She peeked over at Jasyn's lap to make sure he was secure.

"I'm all set."

"It's just a precaution," she assured. "We'll hardly move at all. Well," she corrected, "we'll move alright, we just won't feel it too much."

"I know, the Captain told me all about it."

As if cued, the Captain came over the intercom to let everyone know they were clear for departure. Everyone remaining on board moved quickly to take their seats and check their restraints. The crew attendants signaled the bridge once everyone was secure and the door to the craft slid closed.

There was a hiss of airlocks and a slight rocking as the craft disengaged from the villa followed by a few seconds of silence as they created a safe distance from the satellite city and amassed their momentum. Then the room tipped, tilting as the floor rose towards aft, as the jet shot out into space like a boat riding a wave. Unlike the villa, the furniture in the craft was bolted to the floor for just this reason. Three seconds later, the down compression found its medium and put the room and its occupants into a normal, if artificial, gravity.

A series of clicks and snaps followed and the craft was once again full of people moving all about. Penny was at Faith's side in an instant.

"We have coms," she announced with her usual crisp precision. "Mr. Canley has first, do you want to take the call?"

Faith sighed and nodded. A second later the gold wire over her ear was slushing out punctuated sounds of quiet conversation from light years away.

"I'm terribly sorry, Mr. Canley," Faith said, her eyes unfocused and downcast, "but that would be an issue you would need to broach with Charity."

She looked up and caught Penny's watchful eye. A glance, passed between the two and Penny nodded and moved away quickly. Faith looked away, returning to her conversation as a steward appeared, placing two fluted glasses on the slender table nestled between Faith and Jasyn's chairs. Another steward appeared with a bottle of champagne and a chill bucket.

Faith's eyes were far away, then abruptly focused on the present as the corked popped, her brown and gold eyes darting sharply towards the bottle of champagne. They lost focus again immediately as she looked away, returning to her conversation.

"I'm sure you are, Mr. Canley, but this is one area where I have no jurisdiction." She laughed apologetically, apologized once more, and said good-bye.

Jasyn was waiting with his glass slightly raised. Faith picked up her flute of champagne and gently touched the rim to Jasyn's. It made a delicate ringing sound.

"Cheers," he said softly. He took a token sip and then set the glass aside. He had found that he didn't have much of an appetite for drink.

Faith smiled in return and took a sip before she glanced up at

Penny. "Are all my calls like Mr. Canley's?"

"Not all, but most," Penny answered.

"Redirect them to Charity or her staff. I'd like to finish business for the day."

"Yes, ma'am."

Faith took only two more calls and then had Penny message the rest. She could feel Jasyn's gaze upon her body like a weight. She finally gave up trying to conduct business and handed the comset to her PA.

"Are Jasyn's clothes here?" Faith asked.

"Yes," Penny answered, taking the comset and placing it in a polished box lined with golden velvet. "They are laid out on the bed."

Faith turned her attention back to her companion. "Why don't you go get dressed?" she asked. "It's a long way but we'll close the distance pretty fast in this ship. We should be ready when we get there."

Jasyn ran the back of his hand down her bare arm. "Why don't you come help me?" he asked, his dark eyes shining.

Faith smiled, considering the idea. "Because the idea is to get you dressed. Not both of us undressed."

Jasyn gave her a look of over-exaggerated disappointment and trundled off to the bedroom. Faith motioned for Penny to take a seat so she could give her instructions on what needed to be done while she was occupied with whatever three-ring circus Charity had planned for this year. Penny had been taking notes on her acrylic for only a minute or two when the bedroom door opened and Jasyn stuck his head out.

"Penny?" he called out, surprising the PA.

Penny didn't know whether to answer him or go to him. She looked at her employer, questioning. Faith shrugged and sipped her champagne. Penny stood up and, after a moment's hesitation, smoothed down her brown skirt, tucked her acrylic under her arm and hurried to the bedroom door.

After a few words from Jasyn, to Faith's surprise, Penny went into the bedroom and closed the door. She emerged a few minutes later and came back to finish receiving her instructions.

"He needed help with the tie," Penny explained.

Faith nodded as her assistant sat down. She finished giving Penny her directions as Jasyn came out of the bedroom. Faith paused with her glass halfway to her lips, and then put it back down.

Jasyn cut such a striking figure in his tailored suit that it threatened to take her breath away. His smile was shy, like it had been in the first days of their relationship, or like it still was when someone was around that made him nervous.

"You didn't get that at Frederick's, did you?" Faith asked her assistant without taking her eyes from Jasyn, a curious smile tucked into the corners of her mouth.

"No," Penny replied, finding that even she herself could not help but smile at the dashing young construct. "I thought Iago's would be more appropriate."

"Good choice, Penny."

Penny beamed as if she had made the suit herself. "Thank you, ma'am." As Jasyn crossed the room she got up to make the calls that Faith had instructed her to take care of before their arrival at the party, flashing him a rare smile as she did so.

Even Faith, so moved by his elegant suit, rose to meet him. She took his hands and kissed him.

"Is everything okay?" he asked.

"Of course, why?"

"The way Penny was smiling, I thought maybe you had ordered for me to be thrown out of the ship."

Faith laughed. "No, she is just as taken as I am, for once." She ran a hand along the smooth cloth of his coat, feeling his arm underneath, and moved her body up against his. "It's almost enough to change my mind about us getting undressed."

Jasyn pressed his body against hers and placed a finger under her chin. Tipping her head back, he kissed her.

 ONE 8

"Calyph!" Scarlett exclaimed. She was both shocked and delighted, but not so much so that she didn't have the wherewithal to deftly tuck the blue box in her hand into the back pocket of her pants.

Despite any inherent shyness, Calyph was on his feet immediately and wrapping his arms around the Red Jordan who, also without pause, buried her face in his shoulder and squeezed him back tightly.

Though their relationship had been laced with sexual encounters in the past, his embrace did not arouse her or evoke in her the same feelings that the Chimeran Commander did with a simple touch of his hand. With Calyph it had always been different. Calyph's arms meant safety, security.

"I've missed you," he whispered in her ear.

Scarlett squeezed him tighter, clinging to his lean form with a feeling just short of panic. "I've missed you too."

Elaeric clucked a tongue at them and the pair reluctantly let go. Calyph sat back down as Elaeric poured them both tea and Scarlett retrieved a cup from the cabinet so that she could join them.

Elaeric hummed under his breath as he poured the steaming liquid into her cup and his eyes flicked up to look at her. Scarlett saw immediately that he wasn't looking at her face, but to the side of it.

He's looking at my aura, she thought as he straightened and gave her a knowing smile. He turned to put the teapot on the stove and Scarlett frowned at his back. *That little fucker. What did he see?*

The Jordan realized abruptly that Calyph was speaking to her and she blinked rapidly as she came back to the present, giving him her full attention.

"You look great, Scarlett," he was saying. "Really great."

"Thanks. You look great too. It's so good to see you." She sat down at the table and picked up one of his hands between her own. "And thank you for getting me here, it really was what I needed." She turned to Elaeric, who was just sitting down, and gave him a wry smile. "That's right, I said it."

The monk smiled and sipped his tea. "I did not say anything."

Scarlett snorted and turned back to the elf. "I'm getting stronger just by living in the higher gravity of this place, and I haven't eaten any simulated food the entire time. The meditations Elaeric has me doing are making me stronger mentally. I have a better connection with everything inside me as well as everything around me."

Calyph was silent for a few moments, watching her with a small, lopsided smile on his face as if he couldn't really believe what he was seeing.

"I can tell," he said, his voice soft. His blue eyes searched her face and Scarlett wondered if he could see auras as well, since it seemed like he was trying to read something about her. She dismissed the idea almost immediately. It was a subject that she was sure would have come up before. Still, the look he was giving her was strange.

"How is Fledge?" she asked, trying not to sound too eager.

"He's fine," Calyph assured. "He misses you."

Scarlett pressed her lips together into a tight line, looking away. She took a sip of tea in an effort to calm herself, but her hand was shaking. The Jordan felt that she had all that she could take for one night and it showed. Calyph watched her silently for a few moments, concerned.

"You're tired," he said. "You should go to bed."

Scarlett shook her head. "Not yet." She looked down and examined the inside of the teacup. "Has the Captain said anything," she asked quietly, afraid to look back at him, "about my return?"

Calyph squeezed her hand. "He talks of little else."

Scarlett turned her face back towards his eagerly, her dark eyes brimming with tears. "He does?"

The Engineer nodded vigorously.

He did not bring up the fact that the Captain hardly spoke to anyone about anything, that he was in a funk that some might consider dangerous, nor that the Executive Officer wanted Scarlett locked up. Calyph also thought it prudent not share that Jordan Blue was drinking from her own glass of crazy, now wearing a black flight suit in mourning for those she had lost, and that it was quite possible that she wanted to kill him. Facts that were just the tip of the iceberg on things he did not think would be a good idea to tell the Red Jordan.

With these things on his mind, the elf was uncertain as to what else to say.

"Well, it's late" he said decidedly. He picked up his teacup and drained it quickly. "And you are obviously exhausted. We should get some rest. We'll talk more in the morning."

Scarlett, surprised, rose as he stood up. "But, how did you get here? Is it just for a visit? Is anyone else here?"

Calyph leaned forward and kissed her on the cheek. Scarlett stiffened, feeling strangely relieved that he didn't kiss her on the mouth or, even more, that he didn't touch the same cheek that Bjorn had kissed just over an hour ago.

"It's just me," he told her. "I took a transport to Adrogea and the monorail to Kayos and a carriage from there. I have more to share, but nothing that can't wait until we have both had some rest. Let's get some sleep," he urged.

The moment took an awkward turn as Scarlett wondered if he was planning for them to sleep together. They had done so enough times in the past to make it a perfectly normal expectation, though Scarlett knew that she didn't want to. Part of her felt like it would be betraying Bjorn and she tried her best to crush that feeling.

I don't owe him anything, she told herself, trying not to think of green eyes and golden hair. *There is nothing between us!* Scarlett bit her lip, tired and confused. *Maybe I should sleep with Calyph,* she thought, *though what would that prove?*

"I brought a cot," Calyph said, dissolving the issue by pulling a hinged metal disc from his pocket. "I'll set it up in Elaeric's spare room."

"Spare room?" Scarlett asked, trying not to breathe an obvious sigh of relief.

"The meditation room," Elaeric said, so she would understand. "And I will get you a blanket," he told the elf.

"Thank you," Calyph said. He pulled Scarlett close again, holding her so tight that she thought he might be changing his mind about the sleeping arrangements. But he kissed her on the cheek again and reluctantly released his hold. "It really is good to see you," he whispered into her hair, his voice husky.

"You too."

Calyph let her go and, with a shy smile and one last kiss,

disappeared down the hall and into the empty room on the left. The two still in the kitchen could hear the snaps and clicks as the disc he had brought expanded itself into a bed.

Scarlett looked at Elaeric, who had remained silent. "Well?" she demanded.

The monk smiled into his tea once more and once more assured her, "I did not say anything."

Scarlett harrumphed and took herself to bed. She wanted to meditate – to clear her mind of the thoughts that whirled through her brain so that she could find clarity in both her life and her decisions - but she was just too damn tired and confused.

Her mind was a jumble of thoughts and time and events as she slid under the pilled coverlet of her bed. There was so much to try to work through; Bjorn's offer of a command, her father, the IGC, Calyph's arrival. But the only thing she could think clearly of was Bjorn. His flashing green eyes and lean muscular form. The feel of his lips pressed against her cheek. His wolfish smile and the smell of his skin, and the fire that all of those things ignited inside her.

*

That night Scarlett dreamt that she was in a jungle.

Moss covered trunks rose into a canopy of green mist and vines hung like snakes from unseen branches. Leaves as big as shields bobbed upon long stalks and ferns birthed low-hanging feathery leaves from the wide bases of the trees.

Birds and animals tittered and scurried, heard but unseen.

Scarlett took a few hesitant steps, the floor spongy with decayed vegetation and dangerously uneven with hidden roots and stones.

The air was humid and muggy, making sweat gather on her neck and chest and run down her body, making her clothing cling to her form.

She looked down and realized with a start that the cloth that stuck to her damp skin was a shimmering green flight suit, similar to the one that Jade used to wear.

Just as the thought of the green Jordan was beginning to make her throat constrict, Scarlett was distracted by a rustling in the jungle. She turned and dropped into a slight crouch, defensive, expecting to see an animal push through the broad leaves, but the verge parted to pass a small and rather slight elfin woman -

Jordan Blue.

The other Jordan wasn't wearing a flight suit at all this time, but some sort of coverall that was torn and filthy and the color of dried blood. Her pale skin showed through the tatters of her ragged clothing but her white blonde hair was pulled back into its usual, perfect pompadour, trailing large white-gold coils over her shoulders.

She gave Scarlett a disinterested glance and kept on her way, pushing her way through the jungle.

Scarlett followed, stepping carefully over the exposed roots of the colossal trees. Blue scanned the ground as she walked, slightly hunched over. She pushed aside leaves and stopped to peek behind rocks and roots. It was obvious that she was searching for something.

Scarlett trailed the other Jordan, her body becoming slick with sweat in the humid air as she ducked under hanging vines and dodged the broad leaves that swung back at her as Blue pushed them aside before letting them go.

"What are we looking for?" Scarlett asked.

"Eggs," Blue told her without stopping or turning around.

"I get the eggs every day. Why are you getting them?"

"Not those eggs. Different eggs."

Scarlett frowned, puzzled. "Is this a hunt? An egg hunt?"

"Yes," Blue said, her smirk distorting her scarred face. "An Easter egg hunt."

Scarlett's body straightened, her expression one of puzzlement. "The kind hidden in a computer program?"

Blue snorted. "No, the other kind."

"Real eggs?"

"Yes, it's a tradition of the humans."

"But isn't your mother an elf?"

"Yeah," she said, poking her narrow face behind an enormous fern. "But she's a Zealot, and the Zealots love all the traditions that have to do with the messiah."

Scarlett found herself helping, looking behind a grouping of rain forest shrub. "I never understood what hiding eggs had to do with the messiah."

Blue answered without turning around. "Eggs are considered a symbol of resurrection. Dormant life." She stopped and, with a hopeful look, stuck a foot covered with a crumbling gray boot into a round patch of thistles. A small animal came trundling out, chattering curses at her for being disturbed. Blue's shoulders dropped in disappointment before she continued on her way.

Scarlett ducked under a vine as thick as her arm, "Why are Easter eggs always painted with different colors?"

Blue shrugged. "They weren't always that way." She stopped and gave Scarlett a sly look. "They used to all be painted red."

"Red?" The significance wasn't lost on Scarlett and the Blue Jordan nodded as if seeing the other woman's understanding.

"To signify the blood that the Christ shed for humankind."

"Really?"

"Yes. But colors change. Traditions change. Religions change. All things change." Blue straightened, throwing back her shoulders. The coveralls hung on her like rags and seemed to grow thinner and more ethereal by the second.

The jungle was thick here, a mass of green blades and ropes and petals so thick that it had become a wall of foliage. Treating it like a drape of velvet in a holo-theater, the tattered Jordan stuck her arm right through it and pulled it aside so that Scarlett could walk through.

Scarlett walked past Blue's thin form and found herself in a clearing. There was a waterfall plunging into a small pool and sending up a steam of swirling mist to mingle with the humid air. Sunlight came pouring in from a break in the tree canopy. The golden beams streamed down into the forest and hit the motes of water, making them reflect the light in a rainbow of color.

Blue let the green curtain drop behind her and watched the sun dance and play off of the swirling mist. "Look at the light," she commanded.

"It looks beautiful," Scarlett told her, mesmerized by the dance of light and color.

Blue gave the other Jordan an impatient sigh. "*Look* at it. What do you see?"

"It looks like detfleck," Scarlett said.

"Yes, yes, yes. But what *don't* you see?"

Scarlett's brows drew together. "If I don't see it, how do I know what you're talking about?"

"It's what you don't see that's important," said a voice that did not belong to the other Jordan.

Scarlett spun around.

Elaeric was there in front of the green curtain wearing sage-colored robes and slippers and his bald head was reflecting the green of the tropical forest, but it was not his voice nor Blue's that she had heard. It was the voice of her dreams; the one she thought might have belonged to her mother.

"She knows what isn't there," the voice said gently, "but she doesn't know what it means."

"Do I know what it means?" Scarlett asked, but the voice didn't answer. The dream broke apart like the mist in the jungle, becoming a jumbled mess of meaningless faces and tribulations.

★

"You want me to drink his blood?" Scarlett asked, horrified.

Calyph choked with a mouth half full of juice and tried his best not to spit it out on the table. "No! Jeez, Scarlett," he said, wiping his mouth with a napkin.

They sat at the table in the kitchen before breakfast, Calyph sipping juice while Elaeric boiled water for coffee.

"It's not his blood, and you won't be drinking it."

"Then what is it and how exactly do you plan on getting it into me?" the Red Jordan demanded.

"Well," Calyph started, "it's a biologically safe solution infused with the metallic hydrogen that was drawn from him," he told her. He didn't want to tell her where it came from exactly, knowing how much she cared for Fledge. Scarlett might be more than a bit angry about the elf tapping into the hypothalamus of her Fledgling Dragon and, though she seemed much more in control that she had a few months ago, Calyph was not about to risk his own life.

"I don't know," Scarlett said, skeptical.

"It's perfectly safe," Calyph assured. "It's been SOP for new Captains for hundreds of years."

"It has?" Scarlett asked, surprised. "I'd never heard of it before."

Calyph grinned. "Well, I'm sure the IGC doesn't give you a full run down of everything in their arsenal of surprises on your first day. I'm betting there's a lot more information that they withhold than they give out. On a need to know basis, of course."

Scarlett gave a short grunt to insinuate agreement. She knew what Calyph meant by new Captains. They were the officers that were given command of a Dragon when its original Captain, the one that had flown with it since they were Fledgling and Jordan, had died. And she was indeed starting to learn that the InterGalactic Council was an expert when it came to releasing information only as they saw fit.

"What will it do to me?"

"It will give you a closer connection to Fledge," he told her. "They began using it in the last age of Dragons. The Fledglings have always reached Dragon maturity about the same time their original Jordans died, the human ones anyway - since even with hormonal replacement humans don't seem to make it far past five hundred years."

"Wow," Scarlett said thoughtfully as she added up her own years. "That means I'm over twenty-five percent there."

Calyph smiled, "For now. But medicine is advancing all the time. Who's to say that in another century they haven't doubled it, or more?"

Scarlett snorted. "Easy for you to say. You'll live for a thousand years without so much as a vitamin C supplement."

Calyph laughed. "Doubt all you want, but there was a time when the life expectancy of a human was only a hundred years."

Scarlett chuckled and leaned back gratefully as Elaeric leaned over the table to fill her cup with hot coffee. "Thank you," she told him earnestly. He nodded in acknowledgment before pouring a cup for Calyph and then himself. "So why did they inject the newly appointed Dragon Captains?" she asked Calyph. "What exactly does it do?"

Calyph's tongue poked thoughtfully at the corner of his mouth before he answered. "Jordans, I'm told," he said looking at Scarlett, "form a bond with their Fledglings over the years that strengthens to the point where they can read each others thoughts."

Scarlett shook her head. "Not thoughts," she corrected. "Not exactly. More like shared feelings."

Calyph bowed his head and held out a hand palm up as if to indicate he was expressing the same thing but if she preferred a different method then that was okay. "Possibly. But you've only been a Jordan for a few years," he told her. "That bond is only going to get stronger."

"I suppose."

"Either way," he said, "as you already know, when a Captain that has been with a Dragon since they were Fledgling and Jordan dies, a new one is given command. The new Captain, most often an Executive Officer that has been through Jordan Training, is given an injection of the Dragon's fluid. It hastens that connection, that bond."

Scarlett dropped two lumps of sugar into her coffee and poured in a bit of cream. Usually she would use more but they only had what was left from yesterday. She and Elaeric had not yet done their usual morning chores.

"So Brogan did this," she mused, taking a sip from her mug. "When he took command." Though her Captain had commanded the Dragon for only a century, Scarlett had been amazed by his intuitiveness. Now she wondered if it was due to the infusion that Calyph was now presenting her with. It had to be.

"In your case," Calyph said, dropping sugar lumps into his own mug, "we just want to make sure the bond stays strong. A Jordan has never been separated from their Fledgling like this before."

A derisive burst of air was expelled from Scarlett's nostrils. "I'll bet." She took a long drink of coffee and looked out the window as Elaeric joined them at the table. "Whose idea was it?"

"Mine."

Scarlett regarded him affectionately. "You're always looking out for me," she said, making him blush and look away. She took a smaller sip from her mug and thought of all the Captains that had undergone the simple procedure, which was most of them. There were only two Captains that had been with their Dragons since Fledglinghood, and they were both elves. "Condliffe, too," she said absently, thinking of the young Commander of the Beryl Dragon.

"And Blue," Calyph added, his tone cautious. Scarlett's dark eyes flicked to his blue ones and he braced himself inwardly for the acid retort he knew would be coming. She surprised him.

"Blue," she said softly. "How is she?"

For a few seconds, Calyph could do nothing but blink. "She, she's fine," he stammered. "Different, though. Like you, I guess."

Scarlett nodded and looked away as if it was what she expected. Then she looked quickly back at Calyph as if she had just processed what he had told her.

"You injected Blue? Why? Is she not with Cyan?"

Though Scarlett seemed concerned rather than angry, Calyph was clearly uncomfortable with the discussion. He tried not to squirm but he couldn't help it. "Well," he confessed, "it was kind of an experiment, never having done it to a Jordan before."

"So you used Jordan Blue as a Guinea pig. And?" Scarlett asked. "What happened?"

"What we expected – it strengthened the Jordan-Fledgling bond," Calyph told her, keeping his voice steady, with an effort.

"And?" Scarlett prompted, sensing there was more. Seeing the way Calyph shifted in his seat confirmed her suspicions. She pressed her lips together, trying not to scowl. "What did it do to Blue?"

"It's hard to say," Calyph told her, his blue eyes darting to Elaeric but there was no help from that quarter. The once-monk was merely a happy observer. "Like I said, she's been different."

Scarlett bit her bottom lip. "Because of me."

Calyph stared at her for a moment before shaking his head. He had never seen the Red Jordan show remorse before. "I don't think so. Jordan Blue is…is a lot tougher than she looks. I think it was more because of the loss of Galen and Jade."

Scarlett looked away, unable to meet the elf's eyes any longer. She decided that she didn't want any more explanations and for that Calyph was glad. "Let's get on with it, then," she said hoarsely.

"Are you sure?"

Scarlett nodded and watched as Calyph, after throwing her one more questioning glance, reached into the satchel he had left hanging over the back of the kitchen chair last night. He pulled out a small, square packet and then withdrew a long, stainless steel injection gun and laid it on the table. The Jordan held still to keep from flinching at the sight of it. She saw that it had been pre-loaded.

Elaeric took a seat at the table, watching eagerly.

"Where does it go?" Scarlett asked with a nervous laugh.

"Your non-dominant arm." Scarlett nodded and rolled up her right sleeve to the elbow. "Higher," Calyph instructed and she rolled it as high as it would go, and then pushed it up to her shoulder.

"Should I stand up?"

Calyph shook his head emphatically. "Definitely not. Stay sitting."

"Great." Scarlett took a deep breath and let it out slowly, grounding herself, finding her center.

Calyph tore the packet open with his teeth and shook out the small, alcohol soaked cloth that was inside and rubbed it over the Jordan's upper right arm. He dropped the cloth and picked up the injection pistol, placing the smooth square muzzle of the gun against the triceps muscle the way Doc Westerson had shown him.

"Ready?"

"Ready." The Jordan turned her face away, towards Elaeric who was watching everything with eyes pushed round in anticipation. Scarlett couldn't help but smirk at him. Then Calyph squeezed the trigger.

The hypodermic shot deep into her flesh and slowly released its contents there before snapping back into the pistol. Calyph carefully put the gun back on the wooden table, his almond-shaped blue eyes fixed upon the Jordan.

For Scarlett, after the initial feeling of being skewered, it felt as if her arm was full of microscopic bugs, all hell bent on a migration to her nearest vein - which, in essence, was exactly what was happening.

Searching for her bloodstream, Fledge's metallic hydrogen compound found her axillary artery first and shot into it like liquid lightning. Scarlett gasped so loud, sucking in such a great gulp of air so quickly that it was almost a scream in reverse.

Her right arm jerked out in front of her, her fingers both spread out yet clenched - like the talons of a hawk.

"Scarlett?" Calyph asked after waiting a few moments while the Jordan remained frozen. "Are you okay?"

"C-c-c-cold!" she stuttered.

And it was. Like ice it shot down her arm to her digital artery before jacking out into every capillary and cell in her hand where it came back up through her veins as it raced for the cardiac organ that was pumping the blood throughout her body the same as it had been for over a hundred years.

She had less than a second to consider what the compound would do to her heart when it reached it and then it was already there, exploding into her right atrium, and then dumped into her right ventricle before firing off into her pulmonary system.

The cold spread through her lungs, down into each miniscule alveoli before racing back to her heart, filled with oxygen now, and being pumped towards and into every cell in her body. No place was safe from the invading hydrogen; not the molecules of her fingernails nor the fine hairs inside her nostrils. The cold went everywhere.

Scarlett's cheekbone hit the table as she fell forward, gasping for breath and shaking as the cold took over her body, obliterating all her senses. The Jordan felt as if she had been dumped into a cryo-freeze without being put under, much less sedated.

The whole ordeal of the bitter cold racing through her body only lasted a few seconds but to Scarlett it felt like an eternity. The thought of eternity, of an endless chain of linked figure eights, was her first coherent thought. Cold silver, cold *platinum*, linked in an endless icy chain.

Forever, she thought. *Forever.*

Reality came back to her in a dizzying *whoosh* of cold air, spiked with icy shards that she recognized as her other functioning senses.

The first of her five senses to return was her olfaction. The sensory cells of her nasal cavities were bombarded with the ability to accept and recognize a billion more molecules than she was used to, swelling until they felt like they might burst. And, at first, all she could identify was the green-eyed Commander, Bjorn van Zandt.

His scent filled her nose and then her head. Rushing through her, his sensual smell filled her entire being. Unexpectedly, her blood that had been freezing only a moment ago was now burning. She could *feel* his smell all around her, caressing her like warm vapor. And where he had touched her – her hand, her arm, the place on her cheek where he had pressed his lips – she could feel a burning that was not unpleasant.

Her gasping became panting and Scarlett, her cheek still against the smooth wood of the kitchen table, moaned.

Soon she could smell Calyph's scent, overlapping Bjorn's but not overpowering it. She closed her eyes and tried to get control of what was happening to her.

The Jordan took a deep breath, a grounding breath, and found that she could smell the table. No, not just the table. She could smell the forest from where the wood of the table had come. The fresh, piney scent of the needles that had once clung to the tree. The fur of the squirrels that had nested there.

She could smell the chickens in the coop and the mare in the field. She could smell the dust on the road.

The dust on the road.

Eyes still closed, Scarlett listened.

Outside was the rustle of leaves, the beating wings of a jay as it swooped down and into a tree, and the soft sigh of the branch that it landed on. Scarlett squeezed her eyes tight, reaching further.

She could hear the turning wheels of a wagon as it approached the village, then she could hear the far off village itself - a bustle of happy activity – its war against the spread of technology, patient and jovial. Frowning deeply, her face drawn tight into a mask of concentration, Scarlett reached out.

Reaching out with her newborn sensory tendrils, she could feel the mental equivalent of heads turning in her direction.

The first head she could sense was covered with platinum blonde hair and it turned sharply towards Scarlett in sudden realization - violently, as if startled by a stranger, but it quickly turned to a recognition that was as cold and clear as it was immediately and undeniably smug. An astute awareness of her own awareness.

Her consciousness passed the smirking blue and went into the deepening twilight where it saw a flash of green that stopped her heart, making her mouth open and close as uselessly as a shark on the bottom of a boat.

The streak of emerald light was there and then it was gone, leaving Scarlett to wonder if it was only something that she had seen in the universe of her own imagination.

She blinked, taking herself past the horizons of all the planets, past the rising sun and far into the deepening twilight of indigo where it deepened to black. In the night of space, diving between stars and brimming with joy at her sudden presence, was what she sought. The beat of the Fledgling's heart.

The Red Fledgling, the Crimson Fledgling, *her* Fledgling - they were all the same.

Fledge, she thought as hot tears filled her eyes.

Scarlett, came the reply.

The Red Jordan choked and the tears, locked away for so many years, streamed down her cheeks.

I am so sorry, Scarlett told him. *So sorry for so much.*

Shhh, he consoled.

Scarlett could feel his consolation. His heartbeat, like the sound of rushing water, joined with the sounds of other Fledglings, of Dragons, of stars, of the universe. It rose above Scarlett like a wave and threatened to crush her like the insignificant speck of life that she suddenly felt that she was.

Enough!

Another voice, feminine but with the commanding, reverberating calm of a bass drum, rose above all the others.

Scarlett recognized it immediately as the voice from her dreams. The Jordan had been right, in a sense, about it being the voice of her mother. She knew now that it was the voice of the Opal Dragon. Her mother Dragon.

Slowly, feeling like she was growing, her spirit swelling within her body, Scarlett pushed herself up from the table and looked at the men seated on either side of her. To her great surprise, she could see an aura around each of them. Elaeric sat in a halo of bright green light, watching her with intense interest. Calyph was surrounded by a haze of silvery gray.

Scarlett felt as if her body was being stretched painfully to encompass the world around her while at the same time being compressed, feeling intensely small in the great scope of it all.

Scarlett blinked the tears from her eyes and wiped the rest of the moisture from her face with her fingertips. When she looked again at Calyph and Elaeric the auras were gone. Her frighteningly sharp senses softened and ebbed away until they were almost normal. Almost.

★

Shortly after what Scarlett thought of for the rest of her life as 'the procedure' was done, Calyph had to go. He remained at the table with Scarlett for as long as he could, watching her and asking her the questions Doc Westerson wanted to know. He was reluctant to leave but had orders to be back at the capitol by noon for transport back to the Dragon.

"Really?" Scarlett asked. "Won't you at least stay for breakfast? I don't know about you, but I'm starving."

Calyph smiled at her. "I bet you are."

"You can't stay any longer?"

Calyph looked sheepish, as if his quick departure was his own fault even though there was nothing he could do. "They don't want to keep the Dragon in one place for too long. You know how they are," he told Scarlett, standing up and slipping an arm through the strap on his satchel.

Scarlett, having more years in the IGC military than Calyph had as an Engineer, nodded. "Yeah," she said. "I know."

She stood and hugged the elf, not knowing what else to say. He, too, seemed to be searching for words that he could not express but seemed even more nervous than usual. He clung to her in an almost desperate embrace.

Scarlett pulled away from him and looked at his face, searching. "Is everything okay?" she asked.

His mouth opened as if he wanted to tell her something, but couldn't. He smiled nervously. "Of course. Everything is okay. I just miss you."

Scarlett smiled at him, though his words made her feel strangely uncomfortable. "I miss you too."

"Maybe when we are both back on the Dragon, we can…"

"Of course," Scarlett said quickly, not letting him finish. "Come on," she said, wrapping an arm about his waist. "I'll walk you to the road."

"Alright," Calyph said, putting an arm around her shoulders and letting her escort him from the cottage. He turned his face towards Elaeric as they reached the door. "Thank you."

Smiling, the monk that was no longer a monk bowed his tonsured head in response.

As soon as they were outside Scarlett stopped short. "Jesus!" she whispered, her hand going to her throat as she drew back.

Calyph glanced around the yard fearfully, looking for whatever had startled the Jordan, but saw nothing out of the ordinary. He looked at Scarlett, who was staring out towards the horizon.

"That explains it," she said softly. "The light, the pull, the constellations that were so similar and yet so different. I can't believe I didn't see it before. I've been blind, to so many things, it seems."

"Explains what?" Calyph asked. He followed her gaze to the glowing orb that was ascending in the morning sky.

The Jordan had thought that the orb was a sun, a red giant in a binary system with a white dwarf. Now, with her senses sharpened by the blood of her Fledgling, the scales had fallen from her eyes. Her crisp vision saw the orb for what it was.

It was a giant, all right. But it was no sun. And more orange than red, now that her ego was removed from it.

"It's Jupiter," Scarlett said in wonder, staring at the swirling patterns drawn across the colossal ginger globe that was rising into the sky. Calyph's almond-shaped eyes widened in surprise.

"You didn't know?"

Scarlett shook her head. "I had no idea where I was, just some guesses that were wrong. But I do now."

I'm close to home, she thought. *So close to home.*

The Jordan looked about the yard, wondering what else she might see. Everything stood out in stark clarity, yet nothing held the surprise of the planet she saw hanging in the lower part of the sky. The planet in whose orbit she had been born.

"Are you okay?"

Scarlett nodded and started walking again, throwing glances at the gas giant rising above the fields in the bluish sky. After a moment's hesitation, Calyph slipped an arm around her waist. Scarlett, just as hesitant, wrapped an arm around him in return. The Jordan and the Engineer headed down the path together to the road where he knew the coach would be arriving to take him away.

The oddly matched pair walked along in silence; Scarlett listening in amazement to everything around her while Calyph searched for what to say. When they reached the dusty lane that led towards the village he stopped and turned her so they were facing each other. He titled his head and the breeze blew his sand-colored hair around his pointed ears.

"You haven't said anything about coming back," Calyph said, his tone curious. "Other than asking about the Captain, you haven't asked about how long you'll be here or when you will be done."

Scarlett looked at him for a few moments, surprised. "I guess I was waiting for someone to tell me."

Calyph's brows drew together, though his expression was one of amusement. "That's not like you."

Scarlett laughed. "I know, I know. I'm different."

You have no idea how different, she thought, thinking of Bjorn and of her father, of the IGC. She considered the metallic hydrogen of her Fledgling that was now pulsing in her cells. *I have no idea myself.*

"Different," he agreed. "And the same."

The Jordan barely had time to voice a nervous chuckle, remembering how Bjorn had said almost the same thing, when the elf pulled her close, kissing her deeply. His hands traveled down the outside of her body, his thumbs brushing against the swell of her breasts before wrapping around her waist, holding their hips close together.

Either because of the Dragon blood or because of the other changes happening inside her, Scarlett felt strangely detached

232

from the kiss and the feel of Calyph's hands upon her body. She pressed against him and, though she felt her heartbeat quicken, it felt more like she was watching, rather than participating.

Will it be the same with Bjorn? Scarlett mused, even as she cursed herself for thinking it. *Here,* she told herself, *is where you are supposed to be. With this man who has saved you in so many ways. Safe. Fighting for the good guys.*

But she no longer knew what was safe, or who the good guys were.

"Do you know about the Synchronicity?" Calyph asked. "The big party that they are having to celebrate the New Millennium?"

Scarlett smiled. "Yes."

"I'll be at the village for the Festa."

"Of course you will."

Calyph cocked his head, not understanding how she could know. "Anyway, Elaeric thinks you should be ready by then, or close enough. I think my report will be enough for Doc Westerson to give the Captain his approval for you to return. If so, I'll be here to take you back. If you think you are ready."

Scarlett pressed her forehead against his shoulder. "What's left of me," she said, disconsolate. Never before had she felt as different as she did at that moment. So not herself.

Calyph leaned back and took her chin in his hand, tilting her face up to meet his gaze. "You are who you always were, Scarlett," he told her as if reading her doubts.

Scarlett stared at him and he kissed her again as the horse-drawn carriage came clopping up the road. The driver reined the horses to a stop, raising a plume of dust that billowed around the Red Jordan and the elfin Engineer.

They each broke the kiss at the same time, laughing and coughing and waving away the dust cloud. Calyph reached out and touched Scarlett's face one more time in longing and good-bye.

"I'll be seeing you, Jordan," he said.

Scarlett's rueful smile held a ray of hope. "Yes," she said.

★

Her stomach rumbling, Scarlett strode back to the cottage to get her basket for the eggs. Every step she took, every breath, felt like her first. She could feel a growing within her, as if she was seeing everything for the first time, or seeing the world through new eyes. It was a feeling she meant to discuss with Elaeric the first chance she got.

But first, breakfast was long overdue.

She nabbed her basket from the cottage and walked briskly through the mid-morning air to the henhouse. She looked towards the meadow, her eyes seeking the horse. The mare, her brown coat shining in the bright light, whickered and tossed her head in greeting. Scarlett lifted her own chin in return.

The Jordan could smell the earthy scent of the vegetable garden, and each particular root and bean and leaf as it pushed its way through the dirt and opened its leaves to the sun. The coop had an intensely earthy reek and Scarlett burst into it, leaving the wooden door swinging wildly in her wake.

The chickens, which usually raised a reproachful cacophony when she was this late, all fell silent.

"That's right, bitches," Scarlett told them. "You smell that? That's Dragon blood. A Dragon that would cook and eat the lot of you," she warned. "And not necessarily in that order!"

Their heads bobbed and twitched in their normal manner except for the gargantuan hen in the last box. The one that liked to take a meaty chunk out of the Jordan's hand every morning was holding perfectly still.

Scarlett hummed and smiled, enjoying her chore for the first time as she plucked eggs from under the warm bellies of the chickens. She got to the last box where the hen was so ridiculously large that she all but hid the crate in which she nested.

The monstrous chicken eyed the Jordan, motionless, sizing her up.

"How do you like me now?" Scarlett asked the hen as she reached for the egg she knew was waiting.

Elaeric, at that moment, was sitting on a wooden stool and milking the goat when the henhouse shook as if with thunder and curses came flying from between the gaps in the boards. The furious shouting was loud enough to rattle the wooden planks of the coop, sending dust sifting down into the yard and chickens flapping out its small door in a screeching whirlwind of dirty feathers.

Elaeric, though he kept silent and kept milking the goat, laughed so hard and so much that tears ran from his eyes. Still milking, his whole body shook with the effort to constrain the noise from his laughter – so much that he nearly fell from his stool.

 ONE NINE

The Captain of Faith's spacecraft announced over the com system that they were rounding Jupiter's far point moon and would soon be decelerating as they turned their course towards Saturn.

The Distant Shore was an aquaformed moon rather than terraformed, though it had significant masses of land that might equal large islands on a normal planetary system. Three large islands and four chains of smaller islands made up the main atoll that stretched from one end of the small globe to the other.

Should the truth be told, The Distant Shore had been a terraforming project the IGC had funded that had gone terribly wrong. The Terrageniers had done everything according to the normal terraforming blueprints they had used for all of Jupiter's inhabited moons turned planets, which is where they went terribly wrong.

The Terrageniers had not taken into account the size of the object that they were working with compared to the moons that had already been habitated. The sphere, at the time simply named EG-877, was hardly large enough to be called a moon. At only 500 kilometers across it was, in fact, the smallest a space-born mass could be that would enable gravity to crush it into a sphere.

To add insult to anomaly, it was one of seven satellites that circled the gas giant in an arbitrary orbit. Its pathway was sometimes elliptical, sometimes spherical, and sometimes neither. In its known history of circling the gas giant it had never traveled the exact same path twice.

Also, whereas the other moons and satellites of Jupiter held a predetermined orbit and were arrested deep within the massive magnetic field generated by the gas giant, EG-877 drifted on the cusp of the field, like a puny fighter jet drafting a Battle Cruiser.

The end result was a minimally inhabitable world that was mostly covered with water and erratically buffeted by solar storms. In general, a horrible waste of time and a deplorable waste of money. The only hope the IGC had was to use the area for training or testing, should they have any takers, which was unlikely given the location of the disreputable moon.

Charity de Rossi saw the hapless and inundated moon during a terrible storm and looked at it in the same manner Faith had done when seeing the skeletal beginnings that would some day be her villa. The InterGalactic monitorial branch was incredibly relieved and delighted when GwenSeven offered to step in and buy out the whole project. Though the company acquired the new world for a galactic song, the IGC was glad to be rid of it.

The name of the tiny water world was shortened to G-7 though it became commonly referred to as The Distant Shore. Of the three large islands, two were free-floating. One of the floaters held the headquarters for the GwenSeven Corporation. The other floater was home to the Last Castle, the home and grounds to Charity de Rossi.

Faith was just finishing her second glass of champagne when the Captain came on again over the com, letting the passengers know that they would be starting their deceleration within the next few minutes.

There was a great bustling as the crew moved to get everything and everyone secure. An apologetic steward relieved Jasyn of his unfinished glass as well as the bottle and the chill bucket. Another steward made sure they were comfortable and had their safety webbing securely across their laps.

No sooner was everyone seated and secure that the room once again rocked up, this time towards what Jasyn assumed must be the front of the craft, before settling back down. He reached over and enclosed Faith's hand in his own. Though he was controlling it well, she could tell he was very excited to be going with her.

Within moments the crew was up again and moving everywhere. Faith undid her webbing but remained seated and Jasyn followed suit, waiting to see what would happen next. Penny came and stood before them.

"Your car is here, ma'am," Penny informed her, bowing ever so slightly.

"Thank you, Penny."

"You have a car here?" Jasyn asked.

"No, she just means the car meant for me. For us. Are you ready?"

"Yes."

"Then let's go." Faith stood and smoothed her black dress down over her thighs as the airlocks around the door hissed. The door to her craft was located where, in the villa, the door to her office would have been. Geary was already waiting there, talking quietly but rapidly into the comset hooked over his ear. He either cut the link or simply stopped talking as Faith approached.

Faith held out her arm and Geary fastened a smooth black bangle bracelet over her wrist. He ran his finger along the inner edge and a green light blinked from the bracelet. Jasyn noticed a similar green light blink on Geary's comset.

"Anything," Geary said to Faith, "anything at all, and I'm there."

"I know," Faith answered, her voice barely above a whisper.

Geary gave her a smile of resigned exasperation that for once bordered on amusement, but then nodded, opened the door, and led the way out. Jasyn followed them out through the door and onto a flight of metal stairs that had opened out from the bottom of the doorway from the aircraft to the ground.

The first thing that struck Jasyn was the air. It was surprisingly warm, and humid. The sultry atmosphere was unexpected, something that he could not remember ever having felt. But before he could give the thought even a moment of contemplation, he saw the castle.

Half a kilometer away it rose like a giant's toy in a burst of colors. Walls, towers, turrets and spires encircled the keep and stretched high into the night as if trying to touch the stars.

The grounds were vast, much more than he had anticipated, and that was only considering what he could see. Hedges, gardens, and manicured lawns all lay down before the immense edifice that reared above the rolling landscape in a reach of brilliance in the bright colors of the rainbow.

Jasyn realized that he was alone and still standing at the top of the metal stairs and hurried down to join Faith, though his eyes were drawn back to the fairytale stronghold up on the rise.

The car waited for them at the bottom of the stairs and Jasyn hastened to catch up with Faith. The conveyance was an elongated glass globe, hovering half a meter off of the road. The road itself was more of a path, broad and clear, the grass cropped so close to the ground that it made a thin carpet between the wide-spaced hedges. Geary held the door open for Faith, also holding firmly onto one of her hands to steady her as she carefully climbed into the glass carriage. He closed the door.

"Jasyn!" Geary barked as he circled the car and opened the

door on the other side. Jasyn hurried to the other side and then stopped – Geary had never held a door open for him. Trying not to look as confused as he felt, Jasyn ducked inside the car and seated himself next to Faith on the blue velvet bench. The steel-eyed security man dipped his head so that he could see inside and fastened his cold stare upon the construct. "Keep her safe," he ordered. Jasyn's reply was so automatic that it surprised him.

"Yes, sir."

Geary shut the door and the car slid forward, accelerating. Jasyn craned his neck looking back, more surprised than ever. He could see Faith's ship; smooth white beryllium shaped like a diamond with rounded corners - and her obviously displeased head of security, glowering as he stared after the moving car. As he dwindled into the distance behind them Jasyn turned his hazel eyes to Faith.

"He's not coming with us?" Jasyn asked.

"No, only guests are allowed." Faith had a bemused smile tucked into the corner of her mouth. Jasyn tried to keep the shock from his face but failed miserably.

"No Penny? No Geary?"

Faith shook her head, her smile widening. "They will be there, just not with us. Geary will keep an eye on us via security monitors and he and Penny will both be available over a com-link, but Charity is extremely strict on keeping her parties personal."

Jasyn stared at the floor for a few seconds before he looked back at her. "Isn't that dangerous?" he asked anxiously. "For you, and others, I'm sure. You said a lot of important people would be here."

"There is danger in everything I do and everywhere I go," Faith acquiesced. Jasyn looked alarmed but she laid a reassuring hand upon his leg. "Just being able to find this place and get here will get you through most of the security that has been posted. The only real danger at this point is a Rogue Aridian."

"A doppelgänger."

"Yes, though the security we will go through would identify one."

"Security?"

"We will pass through a body scan, and we'll have to give a gel scan."

"But aren't there Aridians on the IG Council?"

Faith smiled and nodded. "Yes, and they have to have a DNA sample extracted to make sure they are not Rogues. Doppelgänging is strictly prohibited by even their own race, for obvious reasons."

"What will a body scan show? Does an Aridian have a different bone structure than... than us?"

"Yes. Their skeletons look like a body of shattered glass. Their bones are small, and not fused together. The DNA scan will show, hopefully, only one strand of DNA. Rogues store the DNA of anyone the have copied. It's a dead giveaway, no pun intended."

Jasyn looked out of the window on his side of the car. It was moving smoothly over the green carpet of grass that ran between lawns and hedges. The castle grew before them like a dream in vivid color.

"It's a rainbow!" he exclaimed, suddenly seeing the range of the colors.

Faith smirked. "It's actually just different colors of light being shot up against the walls of the castle. The structure itself is made of obsidian, and invisible both to the naked eye and to radar."

"It's invisible?"

Faith's head rocked back and forth between her shoulders. "Not really invisible. Camouflaged would be a better word."

"It's so big," he whispered without taking his eyes from it. "I don't know how anyone could miss it."

"You can see it if you're within a kilometer. Any farther and it looks like a shadow, or a hole."

"Does she always light it up like this?"

Faith shook her head as she peered through the glass. "This party is to celebrate the new millennium. The new age of Dragons is being called The Year of the Rainbow."

The Year of Promise, Faith thought. *The time that was promised to me.* She could only hope that those promises would be fulfilled. She remembered when Charity had first told her of the new age of Dragons and what it was being named. Faith had fallen to her knees and wept.

Jasyn nodded as if it made perfect sense. "There are seven colors in the rainbow," he said softly, as if realizing it for the first time.

"Yes, there are seven."

He looked at the large round towers that dominated the skyline of the castle walls. Three tall towers in the front and three even taller towers in the back guarded the smooth wall that surrounded the castle proper.

To Jasyn they looked like rocket ships, stretching up into the darkness and ready to take off. The six of them rose so high that the colored light shining from the ground didn't reach the tops of their conical roofs.

"Which one is yours?" he asked softly.

"What do you mean?"

"Which tower is yours?" he asked, still looking out the window.

Faith closed her mouth and bit down on her bottom lip, unsure. Then she let her eyes look out the window to see the castle and her expression softened. "The one in the middle," she told him. "In the back. The one that the yellow light is shining on, making it look golden."

Jasyn nodded again as if it was what he had expected and then turned to Faith. He put a hand on her leg well above her knee and gave her a wicked smile. "And I finally have you all to myself, don't I?"

Faith laughed, her chin tilting up, carefree and girlish. "Only for the moment. We'll have plenty of company soon enough."

As if to prove her point, the car began to slow as it pulled into a wide curve, bringing them to the front of the castle under a porte-cochere. The entrance was thrown open wide and brightly lit. The car slid to a stop, bobbing slightly only a few inches over the grassy drive.

Valets appeared on both sides to help them out. After Faith was securely on her feet, Jasyn offered her his arm. She slipped her arm inside his as the glass car closed up and slid silently away.

They were courteously ushered into a hallway of black marble where Faith's black heels tapped out echoing clicks upon the floor. They could hear the noise of the party that had already begun coming from the far end of the hall.

Jasyn turned his face slightly so that his mouth was closer to her ear. "When do we go through the body scan?" he asked.

"We're going through it right now."

Jasyn looked up, surprised. His eyes darted about the wide and brightly lit hallway expecting to see security men and radio panels but there were none. The corridor was polished stone that reflected the soft light coming from globes that hung from the vaulted ceiling.

The noise rose in chattering waves as they neared the room beyond, which was separated from the hall by a semi-transparent, flickering field.

"What is it?" Jasyn asked as they came closer to the field of flickering light, his hazel eyes transfixed on the moving lines of gold and color.

"Detfleck. Don't touch it."

"Don't worry."

A small man with black hair and black, almond-shaped eyes stepped out of an adjoining hallway. He wore loose fitting black pants and black silk shirt that fastened together down the front by satin loops over silk-covered buttons.

His skin was a golden tan and, though he smiled and seemed friendly, Jasyn could sense an edge to him that he knew Geary would appreciate, and quite possibly envy.

"Good evening," the man said, bowing. "Please." He offered Faith a black box a little less that half a meter long with no lid. The inside was filled with a silver-colored gelatinous material.

Faith reached out with her right hand and sunk it into the box, the gel closing over her fingers. The man produced a miniature acrylic from the folds of his shirt and, after examining it with a critical flick of his black eyes, smiled at Faith.

"Thank you, and welcome, Ms. De Rossi," he said, bowing.

Faith bowed in return as she withdrew her hand from the box. The man offered it next to Jasyn.

"Please."

Jasyn raised his hand and hesitated, looking at Faith. She nodded encouragingly and he put his hand into the gel and held it there. What surprised him first was that it was warm. Second, it moved as if it were alive.

The man once again produced the miniature acrylic, though it seemed to Jasyn that he studied it a little longer and a little more closely than he had for Faith. He could feel the gel move under and between his fingers, over the back of his hand. He knew it was reading, testing, gently extracting. After what felt like minutes but was probably no longer than a few seconds, the man smiled at him.

"Thank you, and welcome, Mr. de Rossi."

Jasyn pulled his hand back quickly, startled. Faith laughed softly at his side. He looked at his hand, expecting to find some of the gel clinging to it, but it was clean and dry.

The man bowed again and placed his thumb and forefinger at two corners of his acrylic and the wall of detfleck disappeared.

There was a murmuring roar, like the rise of a cresting wave, as the people on the other side of the defunct barrier turned to see who was joining them. The sound grew, the wave rolling and breaking as people recognized Faith and identified her to whatever people were closest to them.

Faith slipped her arm back into Jasyn's and together they stepped into the room at the edge of the tide. Immediately, the detfleck snapped back to life right behind them. Faith could feel the energy of the fence hum on the back of her neck and she stepped away from it, drawing Jasyn along with her.

The murmuring tide of people parted to let their hostess, Charity, pass by unscathed and without having to push her way through. The younger de Rossi was already calling out to her sister and clapping her hands in delight.

She was dressed in a sparkling black dress as well, though hers was much more complicated and flamboyant than Faith's simple cocktail dress. Jewels sparkled from her throat, ears, wrists and white-gold hair.

"Faith, darling!" she gushed.

Faith let go of Jasyn long enough to take her sister's hands as they exchanged a kiss on each cheek.

"Charity, you look gorgeous, as ever!"

Charity laughed as if it would be ridiculous for her to look any other way. "Of course!" she agreed. "And you as well!" She looked at Jasyn with theatrically feigned surprise but real delight. "And you!" she exclaimed. "You look positively scrumptious!"

Jasyn couldn't help but smile. He took Charity's hand and lightly kissed the back of her fingers. "Ms. De Rossi."

Charity laughed. "Jasyn! You know you can call me Charity, we're old friends!"

Jasyn found himself wearing much the same smile that Faith often wore – slightly secretive and tucked into one corner of his mouth. Faith slipped her arm back inside the bend of his elbow once more and they followed Charity as she moved through the parting crowd, chatting at them from over her shoulder while simultaneously talking to the guests she passed.

"Some people you must meet! Hello, Mr. Resnick. Faith, you wouldn't believe...yes, yes, I'll be right back...how worried Barin... hello, Shayna, darling...was about you not being here yet...of course, of course! If weather permits, that is!" Charity laughed and glanced over a bare shoulder to make sure they were still behind her.

Jasyn smiled, noticing the incredible variety of people as they passed through them, most of them greeting Faith with a short word or a polite nod. People of all colors and almost of all species.

They passed through a large hall with wood paneled walls,

each with a long fireplace, and hung with heavy tapestries. The floors here were rough-hewn gray stone, covered with thick hand-woven rugs.

They crossed under a broad arch and into another room, this one plaster and stone and hung with framed paintings on canvas. Jasyn could tell in a glance that they were art from another age, another world. They went through another wide opening and into a room that seemed all wood (floor, walls, and ceiling) and cloth (rugs, tapestries, chairs, and couches).

"Here we are!" Charity announced and stood aside for a small group of people, two men and one woman, all holding drinks. The men couldn't be more different, though they both looked pleased to see Faith. One was tall and lanky and gray-haired. The white of his eyes had begun to yellow with age though the irises remained a brilliant blue. The other was a handsome, trim and athletic, man with salt and pepper hair and dark eyes. The woman was bird-boned with a long, stern face.

Jasyn didn't know if the woman had looked so dour before their arrival but she certainly was less than pleased now.

"Ms. de Rossi," she acknowledged before she turned up her nose and promptly walked away before her greeting could be returned.

Charity laughed, dismissing her with a wave of a jeweled hand. "Here she is!" she exclaimed to the two gentlemen. "Safe and sound!"

"Ms. de Rossi," the older one greeted with a short bow.

"Faith!" the other exclaimed, taking her elbow and leaning in to kiss her cheek. "I'm glad you made it."

"Glad!" Charity laughed. "He was worried sick!"

The man laughed complacently. "I've never seen her late before!"

Faith smiled at them. "There's a first time for everything." She turned slightly towards the young man who had escorted her. "Gentlemen, I would like to introduce you to Jasyn." She looked at Jasyn. "Jasyn, this is Dr. Silas," she said, inclining her head towards the older man.

"Jasyn, it is a pleasure," Dr. Silas said, offering his hand. Jasyn reached out his own hand and the doctor grasped and shook it enthusiastically.

"The pleasure is mine," Jasyn replied, grinning.

Faith nodded to the other man. "And this is Barin Trey."

Barin gave Jasyn a begrudging look laced with suspicion and

shook his hand, though much less enthusiastically. "Jasyn."

Jasyn simply nodded, not knowing how to respond to such a curt and cold greeting. Charity looked about the room, a crease between her brows.

"I know I have circulating trays," she said, her voice pouty. "Oh well!" She smiled broadly, beguilingly optimistic once more. "There is always the bar! Jasyn?" The construct looked at her with raised brows. "Come with me, will you?"

He smiled, obliging. "Of course." He turned to Faith. "Can I get you something to drink?"

She let go of his arm and rubbed the edge of his elbow. "That would be wonderful. Thank you."

He gave her a smile and followed Charity through the crowd. Faith turned back to the two men. "It's good to see you both. How are we progressing on the latest prototype approval?"

Barin laughed. "Faith! It's a party! Do you always have to talk business?"

Faith's smile might have been coy or embarrassed, had she been younger by a hundred years or two. Instead, it was an expression of forced patience. "It's all I know," she admitted.

"I'm doing what I can," Silas told her while making incriminating motions with his head towards the younger man.

"And I refuse to talk business at what Charity demands to be a strictly social event," Barin declared, fixing his dark eyes on Faith.

Dr. Silas laughed good-naturedly. "Well, in that case, I need to find the bar myself!" He gave Faith a crisp bow and with a slightly dark look at Barin, turned and followed the path Charity and Jasyn had taken.

Barin glanced after him and turned to Faith, giving her an incredibly charming smile. "Who is he?" he asked. Faith laughed.

"I love how subtle you can be, Barin."

Barin sipped his drink. "He's either awfully young," he said critically, "Or way over-fixed. Don't you think?"

Faith smiled. "Actually, I think he is quite perfect." Her smile widened as she saw Barin's square jaw clench. His dark eyes looked away, trailing across the top of the murmuring crowd.

"How do you know him?"

Faith almost laughed aloud, hearing the vein of jealousy in his purposely casual tone, but knew it would make him angry. "I know him because I made him."

Barin, who had been taking a sip of booze, nearly coughed it back into his glass. He swallowed hard and the alcohol went down his throat like a squash ball set on fire. "He's not real?"

Faith laughed. "He is as real as just about everyone here, I imagine," she said indicating the crowd. Charity herself had often remarked that the InterGalactic Council was full of nothing but phonies and cronies, and enough implants and prosthetics that they could aptly be called, and possibly even be managed, as virtual robotics.

Barin tipped his head back, tilting his face towards the ceiling, chuckling. He took a tentative sip from his glass and gave Faith a sly smile. "I don't remember approving his prototype," he teased.

"He was grandfathered in to the new clause, abiding by all regulations, of course. His proto is actually too old to have passed over your desk."

"He doesn't look old."

"That's half the point."

"What's the other half?"

Faith smiled her tucked-away smile. "He doesn't act old."

Barin straightened as if stung. "And that's why I am not approving your latest proto. It's immature, in every manner of the word."

"Dammit, Barin," she said softly. "You're being unreasonable!"

Jasyn returned at that moment - without Charity, the hostess undoubtedly detained by another guest. He handed Faith a flute of golden champagne, while he held a heavy crystal glass of dark, amber liquid.

Faith gave him a questioning look, wondering what he might be drinking, since he usually forwent alcohol. Jasyn smiled at her and took a sip from his glass. She turned her attention back to her argument.

Barin reached out and touched Faith's arm just above the elbow. His fingers traveled up the side of her bicep to just under her shoulder, before sliding back down again. "I know I can be unreasonable at times," he admitted. "But I can also be persuaded."

Faith gave him a suspicious look. "Hasn't Silas made any attempt to persuade you? He seems to always see the things you so casually overlook."

Barin's smile was charming and sly. "I don't want Silas to persuade me," he whispered to her, leaning close.

Faith rolled her eyes and sipped her champagne. A log in the fireplace behind them broke, sending a plume of sparks up the flue. Barin's glance flicked to the dying fire before settling on

Jasyn.

The construct was completely still and quiet, probably not knowing what to do or say. Barin looked at him with open disdain before turning his gaze back to Faith.

"And how much are you throwing yourself into your work?" he asked, indicating Jasyn with an inclination of his head.

Faith shrugged. "You know how I am."

Barin smiled, running his fingers along the inside of her arm. "I do."

Jasyn cleared his throat. "Excuse me," he said, placing his drink on the mantelpiece. "I need to find a restroom."

"Over there," Faith told him, pointing with her glass to the far side of the room where it intersected with the next.

"Thank you. If you will excuse me?"

"Of course."

Faith and Barin watched him go, attracting looks as he went and leaving a trail of whispers in his wake.

"Is that because of how good he looks, or because they know what he is?" Faith asked, almost to herself.

"Maybe both," Barin answered, putting a hand on the small of her back.

Faith watched Jasyn disappear through a door and then, before she had time to look away, come back out. Confusion was plain upon his face as he looked around until his eyes settled on her, questioning and unsure.

"Excuse me, Barin," Faith said quickly, placing her glass on a side table and hurrying away.

Barin rolled his eyes and shook his head, though it was all with good humor.

Women who worked so much. What could you do with them? The damned construct probably had the sense of a child, though he suspected that the droid's confusion and current situation was probably due to Charity.

The hostess had always been inclined to have a queer sense of humor, especially where the lavatories were concerned. Though the castle itself was an ever-changing structure, Charity really delighted in throwing in a surprise or two where the facilities were concerned.

Barin remembered that at the last party the lavatory was constructed to resemble a forest, requiring the guests to relieve thamselves in the burbling stream that passed through the moss covered rocks and stunted trees that graced the small room. He, along with most of the male guests, had been delighted in the naturally simulated environs. The women, of course, seemed to have taken offense at the situation.

Barin thought of Faith as he often did – undoubtedly the most powerful woman in the civilized galaxies – completely under his thumb. As always, the thought was accompanied by the reflection of what it would be like to have her in bed. His erection was surprisingly immediate, which caused him a hitch of irritation as he saw her construct appear and then stride quickly away down an adjacent hallway.

Faith appeared in the hallway only moments later, troubled and anxious.

She stood next to the wall, touching her fingers to her forehead and then placing her hand on her chest at the base of her neck. Barin didn't know if it was from having to care for a robot but not wanting to admit any shortcomings in her product, or some unsavory surprise that Charity had waylaid in the lavatory.

He downed the rest of his drink and set the empty glass on a passing hover-tray. He could see one thing for certain and that was that Faith needed him –needed loving, *human* support.

As he reached her she jumped as if startled to see him. He brushed a stray lock of hair away from her flushed cheeks and frowned, seriously concerned for the first time.

"Are you all right?" he asked.

"No," she said, shaking her head. "I suddenly don't feel well." Her breathing was uneven and he could feel her body trembling. She took a deep breath, trying to compose herself. "It's probably from the flight," she said quickly. "I'm sure I will be fine."

Barin drew her body close to his own in a gentle embrace. "Of course it is," he said over the top of her head. "I can't imagine the state you must have been in, late as you were. You probably just need a little rest."

Faith sighed. "Thank you. If you will excuse me, I think I will go lie down for a while. I'll see you at the brunch. I'm sure I will be fine by then."

"Get some rest," he advised. She gave him a grateful smile and hurried away.

Hmmm, Barin thought. *First time in the hundred years that I've known her that she has been ill. But, like she said tonight, there is a first time for everything.*

# TWO ZERO

The monorail picked up speed as it left the pseudo-crumbling city of Kayos behind on its route to the modern city of Nysordia on the far side of the moon. Like a slender, metal snake it slid smoothly and silently through the bright rosy morning across the grass-covered moonscape until it disappeared into a range of green and violet hills.

Bjorn looked out the window from his first class seat in the private car, watching the scenery turn into a blur as the train reached maximum speed. He touched a small panel under the window and the blur disappeared and was replaced by an image of jungle riverbanks. He touched the panel again and the next image was the inside of a steel tunnel. The next showed blackish space, dotted with stars.

He scrolled through the images until he found one that was a simple map showing the train's route and progress. As the holographic image of the train moved away from the raised image of the medieval-looking town, the Chimeran could feel something tugging deep inside him. He hated leaving Scarlett behind but he knew that taking her by force was not the answer.

Lucy sat in the chair across from him, her multi-colored eyes turned away from the map, not looking at anything. Bjorn had selected her because, of all the trolls offered by GwenSeven, she had looked the most like Scarlett. He soon discovered that more unlike the Red Jordan, she could not be. True to her nature, she was a well of knowledge and would not speak unless spoken to, and Bjorn found her dreadfully dull.

A knock sounded on the metal door of his car.

"Come in," Bjorn called.

A handsome black-haired Chimeran, one of the Commander's personal bodyguards by the name of Diego, stuck his head inside the cabin. "Sir?"

"Yes?"

"JP, the Commander of the *Resurrection*, is on the satellite link - demanding to speak with you."

"And?"

Diego cleared his throat. "He seems furious, sir."

Bjorn sighed. "JP is always furious," he told his guard. "That's what makes him JP. I'll open the link," he said, waving him back through the door. Diego bowed respectfully and the door slid shut against the wall once his head was clear of the frame.

Lucy turned her face towards the green-eyed Commander and he gave her a curt nod. "If you don't mind?" he asked.

"Of course not," she answered. "Why would I?"

The troll placed her hand on the table that separated them, palm down. It began to glow as different colored lights danced beneath her manufactured skin.

The map disappeared from the window to reveal the image of an auburn-haired young man, examining a thumbnail. His blue eyes snapped up to find the other Chimeran Commander.

"Bjorn," he remarked curtly.

"JP."

It was all the greeting the two felt they needed.

"Well?" JP demanded once they had dispensed with the pleasantries. Bjorn cocked his head.

"Yes?"

"It's about time!" JP hissed.

"Time for what?" Bjorn asked, nonchalant.

"For a report!"

Bjorn's green eyes narrowed. "The day I owe you a report is the day I resign."

JP let out burst of exasperated breath and looked away as he composed himself. He looked back at the other Commander, his blue eyes sharp and cold. "I'm not saying that you have to report *to* me, but an update would certainly be nice."

Bjorn smiled indulgently. "I can be nice." While JP seethed, he turned his green eyes to his troll. "Why don't you be nice and get me a glass of Varti?" Lucy lifted her hand slowly and checked the window to make sure the connection stayed. The auburn-haired boy, who was actually well over a hundred years old, still loomed in the glass.

Lucy bowed her head, stood and left quietly. Bjorn turned his face back to the image of the young man fuming in the window.

His slightly freckled face was just regaining composure.

"Well?" he demanded again. "How about some 'nice' news? Do you have the Jordan?"

Bjorn smiled. "Of course. She is sitting right here."

The look of surprise on JP's face was so comical that Bjorn had to laugh, though he knew it was not a wise thing to do. The look of astonishment on the Commander's young face melted into a scowl as he realized Bjorn was joking.

"Where is she, then?"

This time it was Bjorn who scowled. "It's not like going to the market to fetch a liter of milk. Recruiting someone to The Cause is not always an easy task, and it's a lot more complex if that person has already devoted their life to the other side."

Nor can I imagine that person is likely to trust someone who has tortured them in the past, both Commanders thought, though neither said so.

"Do you have anything to share or not?"

"Well, I'm not in the Red Fledgling." Bjorn told him. *Nor in the Red Jordan,* he thought disconsolately.

"I can see that," JP told him. "Were you able to meet with her? Can you at least tell me how it went?"

"About as well as could be expected," Bjorn said. "Maybe better."

"Truly?"

"Yes. I was worried that what might be happening to her here would be detrimental to our ability to recruit her."

"Meaning?"

"That she was learning to still her emotions. Learning acceptance. She is learning meditation."

"That heathen monk!" JP cursed.

"Mmm," Bjorn mumbled. He knew who JP meant and why, though he didn't necessarily agree with him. "Anyway, I think he has her headed in the right direction. This might be easier than we thought."

The young-faced Commander was instantly piqued. "Really?"

The door to the car slid open and Lucy's slender form walked in holding a short glass filled with equal amounts of ice and dark amber liquid. She placed it in front of Bjorn without a word before she sat back down. He picked it up, giving her a nod of thanks before turning his face back to JP.

"Yes. I had expected much more resistance."

Had I wanted more? he thought, questioning himself. *Of course I had, but only if it was physical.* He snickered and took a snort from his drink.

JP stared at him. "And? Do you think she will be easy to turn?"

Bjorn contemplated the dark liquid in his glass and nodded. "She will be now. And much sooner than I had hoped."

Really? he asked himself. *Hadn't you really been hoping that she would go home with you that night?*

"I'll be back for the Synchronicity. I'll get her then."

JP relaxed visibly, looking pleased for the first time since he appeared in the com window. "That is good news."

Bjorn took another long drink from his glass, feeling the liqueur work its way into his system with effective speed. "And you?" he asked with an insolent grin. "Do you have a report for me?"

"Don't be pert!" JP reprimanded.

Bjorn laughed, feeling the Varti warm his blood. "Very well. Do you have anything you want to share?"

The corners of JP's full lips pulled down. "Elanor betrayed us."

Bjorn winced. "And we put her there because we didn't trust the humans on the mission. The irony."

"The humans aren't to be trusted either!"

"Elanor," Bjorn said, shaking his head and taking a long drink, "Still, when you say she betrayed us, was it to the IGC?"

"No. It looks like the other player we have suspected for some time has finally joined the game."

Bjorn nodded. The Chimera had known for some time that another faction was secretly opposing the Council. "That doesn't necessarily mean she betrayed us. She could have..."

"She betrayed us!" JP shouted.

Bjorn looked at Lucy but the troll had nothing to offer. "Do you have any other news?" Bjorn asked, changing the subject.

JP's expression changed immediately. The Commander was unable to contain his boyish smirk. "I might."

Bjorn shook his head, smiling. "Be nice," he scolded in good humor.

"My spies have informed me of where and when I can find Charity and Faith de Rossi. Together."

"The Last Castle?"

"Yes."

Bjorn looked away as he thought. "Do you think they are behind the other faction?" he asked, swirling his drink almost absently.

"Knowing them, I think it is quite likely. Either way, I plan to see them dead by the Synchronicity."

The smile drained from Bjorn's face. "You still think they are against us?"

"I think that if we don't know for sure, it's better to err on the side of caution. Even a human could see that logic."

Bjorn's eyes flicked over to Lucy who shook her head, meaning that JP's statement was more opinion than fact. Besides, Bjorn knew all too well that it was JP's opinion to err on the side of murder.

"Any other choice tidbits you would like to share?" Bjorn asked.

JP templed his fingers and touched the tips of them to his full lips, smiling delicately. "I know the location of the Lido moon."

Had he been able to whistle, Bjorn would have done so. The Lido moon was an uncharted IGC military base, which included their most intensive preparation compound - the Jordan Training Center.

"Faith and Charity," he mused. "If they are behind the other faction, do you really see the need to stop them? Let them usurp the IGC, it's what we have been trying to do for a century."

The pious looking face of the Commander contorted with a look of disgust so deep that it bordered on rage. "Only in part. Our main objective has been our freedom, and I will not trade one oppressor for another!"

"I don't really see two de Rossi women as oppressors," Bjorn remarked, the ice clinking in his glass as he took a sip.

"Maybe not them," JP agreed reluctantly, "but whatever government they instill will eventually strong-arm their own agenda, and it is high time we lived by our own rules and principles. Those of us that have them, that is."

"Are you implying I don't have principles?" Bjorn asked in mock surprise. He couldn't help but laugh at the real surprise on the young face of the other Commander. He chuckled into his glass, trying to hide his mirth, but it was too late. JP's expression dissolved and Bjorn could see the pulse in the other's smooth, freckled temple.

Stand back Petrov, Bjorn thought, though he could not see the Executive Officer. *Be wary of his blade.*

"Are you done?" JP snapped. "This is serious! We will be delivering crushing blows to both factions, taking out the directors of GwenSeven as well as destroying the primary IGC military base."

"Your spies have been quite active," Bjorn said, his voice impassive.

"Yes. And I pray that they have been accurate as well. I will send a team to destroy one, you will send a team to destroy the other, if you choose not to do it yourself."

Bjorn shook his head. "I'll do it myself."

JP nodded as if it were no more than what he expected and the smile began to return to his face. "I thought as much," he admitted. "Which one do you want?"

Bjorn swirled the dregs in his glass and then tossed them down his throat. The burn lingered as it wormed its way down. "The Last Castle," he said, his voice gruff.

JP gave him a boyish grin. "Again, I thought as much." JP signaled to someone out of view of the camera before turning his attention back to Bjorn. "The coordinates are being sent to Lucy right now."

The Commander turned his green eyes to the dark-haired droid. Her own eyes were alive with swirling color. She nodded at Bjorn and he turned back to the screen.

"Would you like the coordinates for Lido?" JP asked. Bjorn gave him a look of annoyance.

"Why would I?"

The boyish Commander shrugged. "I just thought I would offer. How soon can I expect you to carry this out?"

Again Bjorn looked to Lucy. She held out a slender hand and a holo of a small, rotating moon appeared a few centimeters above her palm. In the space between the glowing orb and her fabricated flesh were a glowing series of numbers – the astral coordinates. The Commander's green eyes narrowed as he scrutinized the numbers before glancing up to her lovely yet emotionless face.

"Seven days?" he asked.

She rocked her head back and forth in an attempt to mimic human indecision. "It's possible. If you hurry."

Bjorn turned back to the screen and the visage of JP. "I'll run the mission in eight days, if you can do the same."

"I can," JP intoned enthusiastically.

"Very well. Until then, you know where to find me."

JP smirked. "I certainly do. The One be with you, Commander."

Bjorn grunted. "And you as well," he obliged.

JP cut the link and swiveled around in his chair that was securely bolted to the floor of the bridge aboard the *Resurrection*. He fastened his blue eyes upon his Second in Command.

Petrov grinned and his ice-blue eyes shone. "And I shall take the IGC base at Lido?" he asked, as eager as he was proud.

"No."

Petrov's face fell in disappointment. "But..." he protested before falling silent under the glowering gaze of his Commander.

"I want you to accompany Bjorn on the mission for The Castle."

Petrov frowned as his mind shuffled through the possibilities behind his Commander's decision. It took less than a second.

"You don't trust him?" he asked, amazed.

"I'm not sure," JP said, putting his fingertips together once again and resting them on his full lips. "The fact that he did not care about the other coordinates is a good sign. As is the fact that he wanted make sure I ran our mission simultaneously. The destruction will be greater if neither side is on alert." He favored his Second in Command with a beatific smile. "Still, I trust you to make sure the mission is carried out. And to select a team for the destruction of Lido."

Petrov bowed deeply. "Yes, sir."

He turned and strode from the bridge beaming. His Commander trusted him. Trusted him even more than the Chimeran First Admiral, Bjorn van Zandt.

 TWO ONE

"Good lord!" Ruby exclaimed, fanning herself weakly with one hand. "The heat! Why doesn't she cool it down in here?"

"I'm sure she thinks it's hilarious," Dora replied.

"It's her subtle way of showing us the power she has over us all!"

Dora regarded Ruby's long and dour face with raised brows. "Charity? That's ridiculous!"

"What is ridiculous is this heat! She could turn on the fredo and make us all comfortable, but instead she hands out these disgusting party favors!" Ruby spat, her gray eyes full of righteous disdain.

At the entrance to the conservatory, which was now stifling hot, were trays of cunning paper fans that, when unfolded by the press of a button, showed different animal species engaged in sexual intercourse.

When Ruby had glimpsed the scene on her fan she quickly put it down, though most of the other guests had laughed or at least shown mild amusement for the quirks of their hostess.

Heathens, Ruby thought, her wrinkled face grimacing. *I'd rather sweat. My make-up is permanent anyway.*

The conservatory was a vast and circular room at the center of the castle, just over the ballroom. Its domed ceiling was made of a perfectly clear hyper-glass that let in streaming sunlight for what seemed like a thousand living plants. The potted plants, which ranged in size from tiny orchids to tall, tropical trees, had been imported from every planet in the seven systems. They encircled the room and stood in groups like miniature forests.

The center of the room was dominated by a fountain of boulders that were also in a multitude of shapes and sizes. The water bubbled and streamed over the rocks before gathering into a reservoir at the base.

Ruby's thin face was drawn down in a perpetual frown, her expression as dour as ever, and her gray hair was damp with sweat. Dora's shiny black hair fell straight down her back, clinging to her olive skin. The dark-eyed woman perspired in the most lady-like fashion, gently fanning herself with a picture of a bear species that hadn't been seen in the known universe for centuries, involved in an act that was natural for no animal.

Ruby glanced at the fan and quickly looked away in disgust. *No wonder they're extinct,* she thought.

"How dare she treat us like this," she told Dora. "It's humiliating."

Dora fanned herself and removed a cold glass of juice from a circulating tray and took a small sip. The juice was freshly squeezed from a blood-orange and spiked with a strong liqueur that made her tongue slightly numb. "You make it sound like you're being held captive. You could have gone anywhere this morning before the brunch. Didn't you get a cookie under your door?"

Ruby indeed, like all the other guests, had found a small metal disc on her bedroom floor that morning that had been slipped under her door sometime during the night. She had thumbed the inva-chip and had found a silver hologram of Charity de Rossi standing in the palm of her hand.

The hostess had given an itinerary for the day and had extended an invitation to tour the gardens or gather in the conservatory for special libations and special company before brunch. The disc had then flattened into a paper-thin sheet of metal, the itinerary printed on its surface in an iridescent, flowing script.

"Yes," Ruby said. "I got it."

"Then why did you come?" Dora asked, smiling elegantly as she sipped her drink and fanned herself. "You don't even drink."

Ruby's thin lips pressed together into an even thinner line. "I wanted to see what she was up to."

Dora laughed. "As did everyone else."

It appeared that every guest had passed on the garden for the antics of the pre-brunch cocktail party. With all the bodies and the greenhouse roof contributing to the heat, and the fountain and plants spiking the humidity, the room was stifling. No one, however, seemed as miserable as Ruby.

"There she is," Dora said, inclining her head towards the woman that was making her way around the room.

"Speak of the devil," Ruby muttered.

Dora laughed lightly, fanning her damp, olive skin.

Charity, wearing a slip of a dress - the fabric so thin and so pale that it almost appeared that she wore nothing at all - made her way through the crowd. She was as bubbly as ever, despite the oppressive heat, and holding the arm of an exceptionally tall man with blonde hair and a downy red-gold beard.

"And the devil's advocate," Dora chimed before sipping her drink.

Ruby's gray eyes scanned the guests until they fell on Faith de Rossi, wearing a dress almost identical to the one Charity wore, except that it was a pale gold instead of silver. She was hand in arm of a dark-haired young man who wore a shimmering white-collared shirt and metallic gray pants.

"He's a construct you know," Ruby confided with a tone of disgust.

"Oh, I know," Dora told her. "Barin has been sure to let everybody know."

"It's scandalous," Ruby remarked with zeal. "I can't believe she would have a manufactured companion in the first place, let alone be seen with one!"

"I think it's brilliant. I bet every woman here that can afford it will have one on order before they even get home. She's going to make millions just by having him here."

"She already has billions," Ruby sneered. "Why on earth would she want to embarrass herself for a few more millions?"

"Are you serious? Look at him. Look at *her*. She doesn't seem embarrassed. Quite the opposite, she seems thrilled – despite the heat."

They watched as the sisters encountered each other near the fountain. The water was rushing and bubbling over the stones so loudly that it almost drowned out their voices. Ruby took a few casual steps closer and Dora followed.

"Faith!" Charity called. She drew the blonde-haired man closer to her sister and her sister's escort. "This is Nathan," she said. "Nathan, this is Faith."

"It's a pleasure to finally meet you in person," Faith said. She moved to shake his hand but he took up her fingers and kissed them.

"The pleasure is mine," he said, straightening slowly and fixing his blue eyes on the older de Rossi woman. "And I thought the heat in here was from the greenhouse ceiling," he remarked, holding on

258

to her hand.

Charity gave a girlish laugh. "And this is Jasyn," she told Nathan.

The man barely gave Jasyn a glance. "Nice to meet you," he offered, his eyes already back on Faith.

"I'm sure," Jasyn said, his voice flat.

Faith gently pulled her fingers from Nathan's hand. He let them go but did not back away. Instead, he took a step closer and stood towering over her. Faith took a small step back and felt her calves smack up against the base of the fountain. The sound of the rushing water filled her ears and she could feel small splashes of it on the backs of her legs. With nowhere to go, she had to tip her head all the way back to meet Nathan's eyes.

"Has everything been taken care of to your specifications?" she asked, looking up at him. She tried not to sound anxious but the way he was looking at her, the way his eyes were devouring her, was making her breath catch in her throat.

"For the most part."

"Well, please let us know if any adjustments need to be made. And if you need any more assistance, just let us know."

"I'll take care of it personally," he told her. "I should certainly make a trip to your home," he added. "Charity said your villa is quite spectacular."

Faith laughed nervously. "That's strange. Charity doesn't like my villa." The way he was smiling at her was starting to make her feel peculiar. She had a sudden urge to reach up and touch his beard, to see if it was as soft as it looked. Either not sensing her distress or because of it, he leaned a bit closer,

"I'm sure it is as stunning as you are."

Faith twisted her hands together to keep from reaching up to stroke his face, and blinked rapidly, trying to recover her bearings. "I can guarantee that it is as stark and austere as I am," she said in her coldest tone.

"You are neither," Nathan said, his smile widening. "Just the same, I should come by to make sure you have everything that you need."

"That would be fine," Faith agreed. She threw a darting glance at Charity who laughed, completely aware of her sister's discomfort.

"Come on, Nathan," Charity said slipping her hand around his arm. "We should probably lead everyone out of here before they begin to melt!"

"Alright," he agreed, though his eyes and his smile lingered on Faith.

Faith caught Jasyn's arm and clung to it almost fearfully, letting her sister lead the tall gentleman away.

Charity caught sight of a butler droid and signaled for him to announce the meal before turning to make her way through the crowd. Turning, she caught sight of Ruby and Dora close by and watching their exchange.

"Ruby!" she exclaimed. "I thought for sure you would be in the gardens. And Dora! How nice to see you here as well."

"I wouldn't miss it," Dora told her. "And I love your dress!"

"I'm surprised you bothered to wear anything at all," Ruby said caustically. Charity gave her a demure smile.

"I wouldn't want to offend anyone."

Ruby snorted. "Which surprises me even more."

Charity laughed. "You know me so well, don't you Ruby!" She saw her tall companion eyeing the dark-skinned Dora and laughed again. Dora was openly returning his stare and his smile. "Come Nathan! Faith may by spoken for, darling, but Dora is quite free."

"Well," Dora remarked, "not free. But available."

A chime sounded though the thick air and the relief was palpable as the guests began to file into the much cooler adjoining room for a brunch that would last nearly half the day.

"Won't you ladies join us?" Nathan asked.

Ruby was about to decline but Dora fell in next to Nathan's tall and lanky form as they headed for the door. Ruby rolled her eyes and turned to join them, falling in step next to the incessantly chattering hostess.

She felt a breath of air, like a cool breeze, coming from the woman at her side. She looked at the shimmering slip of a dress that Charity wore and knew that it was coming from the fabric. Her gray eyes narrowed and sought out the woman's sister and companion.

Ruby caught sight of them and noticed without much surprise that even though the two did not carry the inappropriate and quite offensive fans that everyone else had delighted in, neither one of them was perspiring.

★

After a long morning and half a day of forced socializing, Faith and Jasyn returned to their bedroom in the castle to rest and bathe. They did both together.

The expansive bathroom of cream-colored marble, freestanding claw foot tubs, steam showers and gold-plated body driers, was the size of an entire podment for a large family and was entirely dwarfed by the bedroom.

The three-room suite had enormous closets and antique dressers along with a colossal four-post bed with an ornately carved headboard. There were two fireplaces, one close to the bed and another in the adjoining sitting room. High, vaulted windows of leaded glass looked out onto the gardens and were covered by heavy drapes of crimson velvet, similar to the ones that hung from the bed's canopy.

Jasyn stood under the rush of heated air from the bathroom drier and then wrapped himself in a heavy white robe. He returned to the bedroom to find clothes laid out for him on the bed. An outfit for Faith had been laid out as well.

"Does she always do this?" he asked.

Faith walked up behind him wearing a similar robe and, seeing the clothes, knew that he was talking about Charity. She ran her fingers through her hair, finding a spot that the bathroom drier had missed.

"Yes, though it is more of a suggestion than a request. Sometimes I wear what she picks out for me, sometimes I wear what I brought."

"Well, I'm glad we wore the ones she gave us this morning. Could you believe how hot it was in there?"

Faith looked away with a knowing smile. "You know how Charity is."

"No, but I think I'm getting a pretty good idea." He looked at the clothes on the bed that were obviously for him. The tuxedo looked like an average formal suit, narrow and fitted. The shirt was white and the tie and jacket black, though they both had an iridescent sheen, as if the fabric had been layered with holographic rainbows.

Faith looked at the elaborate gold dress that had been set out for her. Next to it was a golden eye mask. Closer inspection showed that it was actually just half of a mask that would cover only one eye, the side of it attached to a long, golden wand.

Jewelry had been laid out for her as well. Instead of one large gold chain, like Faith preferred, there was a necklace made out of dozens and dozens of tiny gold chains. The earrings were simple studs, though each had a single strand of the same diminutive gold links.

"Doesn't look so bad," Faith remarked.

"Do I have to wear a mask?" Jasyn asked, looking at the black eye mask on the bed next to his clothes. The mask looked like it would cover both eyes and a portion of his face. Instead of being secured to a wand, it had ribbons that would tie around his head.

"Of course not," Faith told him. "But it is a Carnivale party. Most people will have masks." She wrapped her arm around him and peered at his face, concerned. "Are you worried about something?"

He smiled and pushed the top of her thick white robe down over her shoulders. "Only that Charity might have cameras in here," he said and kissed her neck.

Faith smiled, letting her head fall back. "How worried?"

"Not enough to stop me."

★

Downstairs from their bedroom, out of the tower and towards the center of the castle, was the grand ballroom. The room, large enough to hold an army, was complete with a parquet dance floor made of imported wood and an orchestra before a stage that was mostly hidden behind curtains of heavy red satin.

Small, round tables were draped with white linens and laden with food. Circulator droids swept slowly around the room in lazy circles carrying trays of drinks, napkins, and plates. Most libations were the bright colors of the rainbow and poured into intricately shaped flutes and beakers of blown glass.

Jasyn retrieved a flute of champagne from a passing tray and handed it to Faith without comment, almost without thinking about it. Faith accepted the glass and took a sip as her eyes traveled over the guests.

They were all lavishly dressed, and many wore the masks that Charity had supplied. Others, in the spirit of the party, had brought their own. A few were simple gilded eye pieces tied with ribbon, but many were elaborate and bejeweled and covered half, if not the whole, of the wearer's face.

Despite the masquerade, Faith could tell who most of the guests were with a glance. She spotted her younger sister immediately, decked out in an emerald silk ball gown with a hem so wide that Faith suspected that Charity must be wearing a field generator underneath the skirt.

Charity's mask was just an eyepiece much like the one that Faith held in her hand. It was perched atop a slender wand as well, though Charity's wand was silver instead of gold and the mask itself was studded with emeralds and lined with diamonds. Also, it covered both her eyes instead of just one.

Charity spotted Faith and Jasyn and quickly excused herself from the group of guests she had been chatting with, going to them in such a rush that she nearly tripped over her own skirts.

She reached them, breathless and laughing. "Faith! You look gorgeous! Do you like your gown?" she asked but continued speaking without waiting for an answer. "Do you like mine? Do you recognize it?" she queried in earnest, her smile sly.

Faith began to shake her head, having never seen Charity before in such an outlandish dress, but then her breath caught in her throat. "It isn't!"

"It is!" Charity gushed. "And not a copy! It's the actual gown from the holo!"

A grimace of disgust warred with a smile on Faith's countenance. "My God, Charity!" she said, keeping her voice low. "That's in horribly bad taste!"

Charity had the decency to look shocked, or at least feign it. "What in heaven do you mean? After all, the character played in the movie was *me*!"

The smile won over the frown and Faith shook her head, hiding the smile in her champagne. A holo film had been made years ago, a remake of a human movie about slave owners. The de Rossi family had made up the core of main characters and by the time Faith had seen the feature, an hour after its release, it was too late to quash it. It went virally through the galaxies. She found it best just to dismiss it with a grunt of disgust, though she did feel a bit of satisfaction when the director of the holo died in a horrible sporting accident a few days later.

"I even have the pett-coats and corset!" Charity informed them. She leveled a lecherous stare at her sister's companion. "Would you like to check, Jasyn?"

Jasyn did his best to tuck his smile into the corners of his mouth as he often saw Faith do. "I'll take your word for it."

"Odd that the character in the first movie was called 'Scarlett,' don't you think?" Charity asked. "If you pay attention you will see that there also was a Blue, though much different than ours!" She trilled laughter while Jasyn and Faith gave each other a look so knowing that it made both of them smile.

"There's Barin!" Charity announced as the IGC Director entered the room in an all white tuxedo and pearlescent mask that covered both his eyes and half of his face. "I'll take care of him for you," she said throwing Jasyn a conspiratorial wink. She raised her emerald-studded mask to cover her eyes and waved at Barin, calling his name as she hurried away in a rustle of layered silk.

Faith and Jasyn looked at each other and laughed.

The music, which had been playing when they entered the room, wound down and then picked up again as one song ended and another began. A woman with golden brown skin and an elegant dress of flowing copper stepped in front of the orchestra, carefully fastening a microphone over her ear, preparing to add vocals to the next piece.

Jasyn cocked his head at Faith. "Would you like to dance?" he asked. Faith was unable to keep the shock from her face.

"Do you know how to dance?" she blurted in surprise. Jasyn gave her a look of amused exasperation and she laughed into her glass of champagne before draining it. She gave him a guilty smile and placed the empty glass on a circulating tray. "*Of course* you know how to dance."

Jasyn held out a hand and she slipped her fingers inside his. He led her out to the parquet floor and turned her, placing a hand on the small of her back and pulling her body close to his.

"Sometimes I forget what you were made for," she confessed with a wry smile. "Though I shouldn't, after last night. And this afternoon."

The smile drained from Jasyn's face and was replaced by a look of serious concern. He reached up and held the curve of her cheek in his hand, forcing her to look up and meet his hazel eyes with her own eyes of brown and gold. She stared into them, nonplussed.

"I was made for you," he told her, his voice firm. If his hand hadn't been under her chin, Faith was sure that her mouth would have dropped open. She could feel the breath leave his body in a deep sigh. "I know you don't believe that," he told her, "but I do." Jasyn dropped his hand from her cheek and she opened her mouth to speak but he shook his head slowly, silencing her. "I don't have any illusions about what I am, Faith. I know full well. But I also know, somewhere deep inside, that I was made for you."

He picked up her hand again and stepped slowly to the right, drawing her along. She followed his movements, realizing that they had been standing still on the dance floor for some moments. She let him guide her across the floor, her eyes fixed on his perfect face, feeling his dark hazel eyes bore into her depths.

Faith felt herself overcome with weakness, something that she had fought against almost all of her life. The elder de Rossi sister unexpectedly felt everything that she had been holding inside of herself for so many decades rise up like a burgeoning storm. Suddenly, all of her fears built on the past and all of her plans that hinged upon the future no longer seemed to matter.

For just over one hundred years she had built walls around herself, each brick and stone cemented together with the mortar of her soul. Now those walls that she had so carefully constructed came down, not crashing and tumbling with a deafening roar as she had expected they might someday, but simply vanishing into the ether, like mist evaporating in a bright ray of sun.

She thought of the two lives she had been living over the past month; one was a life of work and plans and determination that she had been trying to force together with a life of love and forgetting and now she realized that it would never work. Her only choice was to abandon both lives and make a single new life, one of fulfillment – for the both of them.

She thought of all the risks she had taken to get where she was. She considered the one she was about to take. Her body trembled with what she was contemplating but she knew that she would never shut Jasyn out again, never leave him behind. It was like waking from a dream. The only thing that mattered to her now was the man she was dancing with and the way that he looked at her - like she was the only other soul in the universe.

They moved slowly across the floor, holding each other's gaze as if to look away meant to lose all that they had. Hand on hand and hip on hip, they clung to each other. Their bodies moved in unison to music they did not hear – moving together as a single current in the river that flowed around them.

*

The party was an outrageous success, as it always was, and goodbyes were long and overdramatic. Plans were made for another, more intimate, party at the Last Castle for the Synchronicity.

For Faith, it was the best time she had ever had at one of Charity's parties, but was glad when it was over. She was overcome with relief upon making the trek home and elated when they were finally back at the villa. She heaved a massive sigh of contentment upon walking into her bedroom.

"It's going to feel so wonderful to sleep in our own bed again," Faith said, kicking off her shoes. "Don't you think?"

"I don't care where we sleep," Jasyn told her as he shrugged off his coat and tossed it on the wing chair. "As long as we're together."

Faith smiled and, grabbing a handful of his shirt, pulled him close and kissed him. "That won't be a problem anymore," she assured, undoing the button on his shirt. "From now on, where I go, you go."

He slipped a hand behind her neck and kissed her. "That's the best news you've ever given me," he whispered in her ear before kissing the corner of her jaw.

A soft knock sounded on the bedroom door. Faith sighed, turning her face towards the door.

"Yes?"

"Barin Trey is on the s-comline," Penny's voice called from the other side. This time Faith's sigh was one of exasperation.

"I'll be right there," she called to Penny. She turned her face back to Jasyn, who was smiling.

"Do you want me to come with you?" he asked.

"Do you want to talk to Barin?"

"Not in the slightest."

Faith kissed his cheek. "I'll be back as soon as I can," she told him.

"I'll finish undressing."

"At least I have something to look forward to," she said, kissing him again. "But don't wait up if you're tired."

Jasyn put a finger under her chin and tilted her face up to meet his own. "Only if you promise to wake me if I'm asleep," he said. Faith beamed at him.

"I promise."

Jasyn kissed her and then began to undo the rest of the buttons on his shirt. "Give Barin my regards," he told her, grinning, as she headed for the door.

"I'll do that," she called over her shoulder as she entered the living room on the way to her office. Penny, waiting patiently in the other room, closed the door quietly behind her employer after she had passed.

Jasyn went to the closed door and paused, listening. He could hear Faith's fading voice giving Penny instructions as she headed for her office. Satisfied, he put a careful finger on the door handle and slid the hasp on the electromagnetic bolt.

Moving quickly and ignoring his open shirt, he went to the wing chair where he had left his coat. He picked it up and pulled his acrylic from the inner pocket before dropping the jacket back onto the chair.

Open shirt flapping, he strode across the room to the vanity and dropped down onto the velvet-covered bench. He reached out and pulled his hand down the side of the mirror that was farthest to the right like he had seen Faith do so many times – like he himself had done many times as well.

The mirrors did their dance, changing and shifting. Some became holoboards, while others turned into compute screens. Half a dozen were flatscreens with a video feed. A ghost pad appeared on the vanity's black, glassy counter. The GwenSeven mainframe was wide open.

Jasyn opened one of the vanity's drawers and was greeted with a metallic jingle. He plucked an earring at random and, holding it between the thumb and middle finger of his right hand, lifted his acrylic up with his left. He ran his right index finger along its side, looking for the sling pin. Once he found it, he placed the post of the earring against the small dimple on the surface of the sling and pressed it.

Looking back into the drawer, he found another earring – this one with a magnetic backing. He put the magnetic back over the sling depression in his acrylic, and put the earring itself along the edge of the ghost pad, where the transmit tooth would be on a normal, hardwired keyboard.

Laying the acrylic over the ghost pad, he began typing quickly on the acrylic. He knew that Faith would be occupied with Barin for a while but, as always, did not want to take any unnecessary chances. He also knew that he could message from the mainframe itself, but that was something he dared not risk. Though he had found that the computer itself was untraceable, he was quite sure that the user interface could recall sent messages even if they had been sent DOD - deleted on delivery.

Jasyn, his face drawn and intense, pecked out a quick message on the keyboard of his acrylic. As soon as it was sent, moving intently, he disengaged the acrylic from the mainframe and returned it to its former state as a woman's vanity. He returned each earring to its mate inside the jewelry drawer.

Crossing the carpet on cat's feet, he released the magnetic bolt with a barely perceptible sigh and then returned the acrylic to the wing chair, this time simply dropping it on top of his coat.

The construct kicked off his shoes and lay on the bed on top of the smooth, gold coverlet and reclined on the pile of gold and copper pillows. He crossed his muscled arms behind his head, lacing his fingers at the back of his neck. Staring at the ceiling, he thought of the message he just sent to his Commander, the Commander of the Chimeran Battle Cruiser *Resurrection*, John Pierre.

TWO TWO

Scarlett's dreams, already made vivid by her daily meditations, were given an especially acute jolt of reality after the injection she sustained of her Fledgling's fluid. It made the good dreams exquisitely intense, usually causing her to wake up panting, in a hot sweat and on the verge of a scream. The bad ones were made worse with their nightmarish reality, also often causing her to wake up in a cold sweat and on the verge of a scream.

But more than anything, she dreamt about Joe. Joe Junior rather than her father, Joe Senior. Her younger brother that everyone had lovingly called Joey. With his dark hair and sharp dark eyes, he was always ganged up on by his older brother and sister, which only made him fight harder. He had his sister's temper but his brother's cool head.

Little Joe always wanted to show that he was as tough as or as good as either of them and, before he had even made it all the way through adolescence, the youngest of Joe Mattatock's children had proved it again and again. By the time he was seventeen, Joey could out-fly and outmaneuver both of his older siblings. He graduated at the top of his class at eighteen. He received his gunner stripes by the time he was nineteen and was given combat status just before his twentieth birthday.

He was often remembered by friends and family for his accelerated career path and extraordinary skills as a fighter pilot, but Johanna always remembered him as a little boy. A little boy who believed in fairy tales no matter how much he was teased by his older brother and sister. A boy who at eleven years old would still search out a hand to hold when he crossed the street. The same one who had once crawled into a trash chute to rescue a litter of kittens.

The sack had been tossed into the communal trash chute and its mewling occupants left for dead, but the bag had snagged on a screw in the grimy metal tunnel only to be found later by the dark-

269

haired boy from pod number 108. Doing his only chore of taking out the garbage, Joey had heard the soft mews and had crawled into the chute to drag out the burlap sack full of tiny furry bodies.

Joe Senior had tried to be patient and explain to his youngest son that they were unwanted and would die anyway. Eight-year-old Joey had only looked at his father, his dark eyes round and sad. When he finally spoke, his voice was barely above a whisper.

"Somebody wants them."

Joe Senior had sighed. "You have until midnight to find out who."

John and Johanna had looked at each other and shaken their heads as the dark haired boy left the pod with six mewling balls of fur stuffed into the front of his shirt.

At a quarter past midnight Joe Senior went out with John and Johanna, looking for his youngest son. Though they lived in a safe neighborhood, there was a wire of fear wrapped tightly around his heart.

Why? he thought as he left the podment, his older children in tow. *What was I thinking, letting him go out so late?* Joe Mattatock sighed. *I guess I thought he would have given up by dark. I should have known better.*

To his great relief they found Little Joe immediately – curled up on a park bench across the street from their podplex, exhausted. His dark eyes were open and staring at a news holo that was playing repeatedly on a billboard at an airbus stop. A single kitten lay stretched across his neck, sleeping.

Joe knelt down in front of the boy, laying a hand on his arm.

"What does it mean?" Joey asked softly, not turning his head to look at his father. Joe Senior frowned.

"What does *what* mean, son?"

"What does it mean?" Joey simply repeated.

Joe Senior turned so that he could follow his son's gaze across the street to the bus stop. The billboard holo was showing a mug-shot of a Rogue Aridian, wanted for Doppelgänging. The holo constantly turned to show the face from every angle but the word underneath it stayed the same. Joe turned back to the little boy on the bench.

"Lichen," Joe told him. "It's Elfin for 'most wanted'."

As if this answer was all that he had been waiting for, Little Joe sat up stiffly with a hand over the kitten so it would not fall. The tiny ball of gray fur stretched and yawned, sticking out a small pink tongue. Joey wrapped careful fingers around it. Cradling it in his hand, he held it out to his father.

Joe Senior pushed the small hand holding the kitten back towards his son.

"I think that one is yours," he said, his voice low.

Little Joe brought the ball of fur back under his neck where it settled in comfortably. He nodded gratefully at his father, his eyes large and dark and full of tears. Thirteen-year-old Johanna looked at her older brother and rolled her eyes. Fourteen-year-old John simply shrugged. Joe Senior wrapped an arm about his youngest child's shoulders as they headed for home.

"What are you going to name her?" he asked.

"Lichen," he answered, as if it should be the most obvious thing in the world.

Lichen.

In Anglicus is meant some sort of moss that grew on trees or stone. In Elfin it meant most wanted. To Joey, it meant that every living being deserved a chance.

"Lichen," Scarlett whispered, opening her eyes, her body damp with sweat. She had been dreaming about Joe again. Little Joe, the IGC fighter pilot who had rescued kittens from a trash chute when he was just a tenderhearted boy.

In this dream he was flying a jet. He was flying a jet on a sortie with her father and enemy ships were swarming out to ambush them, strafing them with laser fire. Scarlett wanted to call out and warn him, warn them both, but there was something covering the lower half of her face.

Besides, what was her little brother doing flying fighter craft when he was only eight years old?

She tried to scream at him to get out of there, that he was going to get killed, but there was something over her mouth. She reached up with a gloved hand to pull it off when she realized it was the oxygen mask attached to her pilot helmet. She was in a jet herself, wearing coveralls with the bars of a Lieutenant. There was a piece of black tape over the IGC patch on her shoulder to disguise who she was, just like there was paint streaked over the numbers and the logo on the jet she flew.

She pushed the jet down, finding her target even as she screamed from behind her mask for him to get away. She tried to pry her left hand off of the yoke but something made it clamp down on the metal rod, pushing the jet faster on a collision course with her little brother.

Scarlett screamed at him to get out of the way. Her mutinous hand tightened on the yoke and her index finger found the trigger, sending deadly pulses of light gashing out into the black, tearing apart the jets coming towards her.

She could see him in the cockpit, made tiny by the huge controls, his skinny body practically swimming in an adult-size flight suit. His eyes were large and dark but his lips were pressed tight so they would never tell his big sister that he was ever afraid. Peeking out of the neck of the too-big flight suit was a gray kitten. Both Joey's face and the kitten's fur lit up, turning pink as their jet was hit with a barrage of red laser fire.

Scarlett awoke, trembling, in her bed in Elaeric's cottage. Her body was damp with sweat and her hair clung to her face.

"Lichen," Scarlett whispered again. Every muscle in her body had contracted painfully in her sleep as she had fought for control, leaving her waking form tight and tense and afraid to move.

The terror of the image filled her body. All she could do was try to still her trembling body as the room began to brighten around her and wait for the feelings to ebb away. The dream had seemed so real that everything she had felt in the dream remained - soaked into her conscious body like water into a sponge.

As the horror dried out it was replaced by anger. Just when she felt she was getting better, maybe even healed, that strong grip on reality became tenuous once again.

Don't be stupid, Scarlett told herself, closing her eyes. *It was just a dream. It's not real. This is real. My room is real. The bed is real. I am real. Fledge is real. Elaeric is real. Bjorn is rea...*

Her eyes flew open as the thought snagged in her mind like a woolen sweater on a rusty fishhook.

Scarlett closed her eyes again and turned her face so she could bury it in her pillow. After a few smothered breaths to steady her mind, she stopped for the first time to consider how real her enemy might be.

Though the rebellion of the Chimera had been going on for over a century, The IGC had only viewed it as a war after the Amliss Attack that took the lives of her father and brother and their entire platoon, ten years ago. Since then, Scarlett had been doing everything in her power to destroy those she had thought responsible for the deaths of those she loved. She had always thought of them as nothing more than psychotic robots. Monsters.

She wondered if she had told herself that they were monsters so it would be easier to kill them. It would make sense – she would certainly consider anyone who would kill a member of her family a monster – and objectifying them hardly made it killing at all.

The IGC had always denied that the GwenSeven constructs were real people. Their definition of real was an organic reproduction via a male and female of the same species that resulted in the birth and growth of the offspring. The Chimera defined a real person as a living creature of any species capable of decision-based action, either by coherent thought or pure instinct.

For the first time since she had gotten involved in the bloody war, Scarlett could see both arguments.

The IGC had always maintained that the Chimera was an army of bloodthirsty aberrations that were after control of the civilized galaxies. Bjorn told her that they were simply fighting for their autonomy. Who to believe?

Believe your heart, the Dragon whispered.

Scarlett closed her eyes and sought out the soothing swish-swish sound of Fledge's heartbeat. Hearing it, she could feel his warmth reaching out to her. After allowing herself a few moments of comfort, she got up to begin her day.

She gathered the eggs, her mind so preoccupied that she hardly noticed the compulsory divot of flesh the fat chicken took out between her left thumb and forefinger. She made the morning coffee as Elaeric scrambled the eggs in a pan with some chopped green onions and a small hunk of leftover white cheese from his small refrigerator.

Scarlett dropped some sugar into her coffee as Elaeric put the plates on the table. He handed her the cream pitcher without needing to be asked and she did likewise with the sugar bowl.

"Do you know the story of the frog and the scorpion?" Scarlett asked.

"Of course. Who doesn't?"

Scarlett smiled. "What's your take on it?"

Elaeric gave an exaggerated shrug. "Don't be the frog."

The Jordan laughed, shaking her dark hair. "Do you think a person can change their character?"

"Why would a person want to?"

That question surprised her, but she persisted. "Do people really change?"

Elaeric's brows drew together, making a tiny line between them. "People change all the time. You are not the person you were five years ago. You are not the person you were five minutes ago."

"What worries me is that I don't know who I am anymore."

"Then the question is, who is the person you want to be?"

Scarlett looked away. "I don't know that either," she said softly.

Elaeric sighed. "Finish your eggs and go to town for some pearl onions and I will make a stew tonight with the rest of the lamb in the icebox. The ride will do you good. It always does."

There was no need to tell her to meditate; she would do that on her own.

Scarlett nodded and dug into her breakfast. She ate quickly without tasting much of it, trying not to think about her dream, but the feelings that it had produced still haunted her. She tried to think about the other people in her life besides her father and little brother, but those thoughts gravitated to the lowest level, haunting her even more. She pushed the plate away in exasperation when she was done.

"Master Elaeric?"

"Yes."

"How is it that the only other woman in history to be chosen as a Jordan, happened to be involved with the same man as I once was? Was it just a coincidence? It seems so unlikely."

"Bah!" Elaeric spat. "Coincidence is a word used by cowards and fools who don't know its meaning. They think it means an unexplainable accident, or chance occurrence. It *really* means two or more things happening at the same time. But I can assure you there are no accidents. Nothing is random, not even chaos."

Scarlett toyed with her fork. "I'm not so sure," she said. "I can accept that Galen fell in love with someone else. I just have a hard time believing that out of all the souls in the universe, the one he found was my worst enemy."

"Was she really your worst enemy?"

Scarlett laughed. "No," she admitted. "I was. I made her my enemy. Still, what are the odds?"

"Odds? Greater than you know. Much more than Spade Poker," he added with a smile. "The universe is a web, Johanna, of space and time – like a fisherman's net. Each strand is a life or a song or a breath, and they cross more often than you can ever imagine."

"Don't any strands cross just once?"

"Occasionally they do. But, even then, they are part of your web forever. Even if the strand breaks, it leaves a mark on the place where it touched."

"Those spots are on our hearts," Scarlett whispered. "Like the sticky strand of web you can't shake off your hand." The old monk regarded her silently but with infinite compassion.

"Yes."

She looked up at him. "Some of those...strands...feel a lot stronger than just gossamer webbing," she said, thinking of not just Galen and Blue, but of Calyph and Bjorn as well. Elaeric nodded.

"The ones that cross again and again are usually more than strands - they are cords. When those cords cross your own more than once it is called entanglement, and they are quite likely to cross again."

Scarlett eyed him nervously, noting how the mirth had drained from his smooth golden face and his voice had gone solemn. "And when that happens?" she asked.

"Make sure those cords aren't around your neck."

The Jordan nodded. "I'll do my best."

*

It had been a few days since the injection Calyph had administered and Scarlett had spent the entire time looking and touching and listening.

The world around her, already made closer and clearer by her meditations, was now razor sharp. When she looked at a meadow her eyes now saw every individual blade and stem. Moreover, she saw how they sank their roots into the soil and how that soil stretched out over the surface of the elf-made moon. She saw the moon like a horse, one she was riding through the stars in its orbit around the gas giant.

Every breath was sweet with the feel of the world around her and she savored every breath as if it were her first, or her last.

She saddled the mare, her nose full of horse and leather and history. Scarlett swung up into the saddle and headed for town, taking to the open fields rather than the dusty road.

She hadn't ridden since her 'procedure,' and found the experience was exhilarating. She leaned forward as far she could, pressing her cheek into the rust colored mane and closed her eyes, listening to heartbeats and hooves as the wind whipped though her hair and whispered secrets in her ear.

Upon reaching town, Scarlett picked her way through the people that were there for market day. She turned the mare over to the mop-headed boy at her favorite stable and made her way back through the town wall to the market beyond. She took her time, seeing everything with her new eyes, touching everything with her new hands.

She lingered in a spice stall that was as dark as a fortune-tellers tent. The Grevin Spicer claimed to have a bit of every spice from every inhabited planet in the seven systems – including ones that originated on Earth and ones from Elbuelver, the first planet of the elves.

She closed her eyes and could smell every herb as it had been when it was fresh on the stem. She could smell each hand that plucked and dried each spice. She could smell the blue-fire used to blow the black glass of the bubble jars that housed each variety of seasoning.

Scarlett turned her head and her eyes popped open, her nostrils picking up the scent of the aphrodisian herbs usually bought by apothecaries for sexual stimulation. Unintentionally she thought of Bjorn, wondering for the hundredth time what produced that scent of his that managed to arouse her without warning. Even now, just thinking of him made her cheeks flush.

The Jordan bought a small jar of minted salt, thinking of the lamb stew Elaeric had promised for dinner. The Grevin wrapped the small bottle in a twist of paper and handed it to Scarlett along with her change. She thanked the Spice Grevin and tucked the wrapped jar into the purse on her belt.

Scarlett finally turned and headed for Arwa's stall, though she took her time in hopes that most buyers would be gone, especially the annoying babushka that always seemed to precede the Jordan's arrival.

Her eyes traveled over rings and amulets as she passed between a number of tents displaying gemware, while her fingers trailed over bolts of velvet as she passed the clothier's stall.

The clothier, a human woman getting on in years, came to the front of the stall wiping her hands on a bright red apron. She saw the longing in the Jordan's eyes. "Are we thinking of a dress?" she asked.

Scarlett laughed. "I don't think so, I'm not really the dress wearing type."

"I have Mylar as well!" the woman confided. "I can make you a flight suit, like a real Jordan!"

Scarlett's light laugh was full of mirth. "Is that so?"

"Yes, yes!" the woman assured, her voice deep. "In fact," she said, brightening, "your looks favor the Crimson Jordan! You should wear a red flight suit to the Festa! You would knock all the men dead!"

Scarlett laughed. "That might happen anyway," she told the woman. "Thank you, but no. But if I do decide on a costume," she added quickly, "I promise you my business." Scarlett touched her chin with her index finger and extended it towards the clothier in the local custom of showing a pledge.

The woman nodded, pleased. Scarlett gave her a nod in parting and continued to the area of the market taken by the produce stalls, keeping her eye out for Arwa's blue and white striped silk tent.

"These tomatoes are too expensive," the woman was complaining as Scarlett arrived. "They get more expensive every week!"

Arwa's long white linen robes were dusty by this time of day but his patience was as immaculate as ever. His black eyes caught sight of Scarlett and he grinned, showing rows of square white teeth. He winked at the Jordan and turned his attention back to the pinch-faced woman dickering over the vegetables.

"Madam," he offered the woman apologetically, spreading his hands. "I have not raised my prices since the first drought. My vegetables are only slightly more than farmer Whey's, and they are twice as big!"

How the hell is it that she is always the one in front of me? Scarlett thought, shaking her head. *Coincidence?* The Jordan chuckled and looked away as the babushka continued to haggle over the tomatoes.

"But I want to buy meat this week," she argued. "I promised my husband a roast for the Festa. If I pay that much just for tomatoes, I will have none left for meat!"

"But Madam," the trader whined gently, pleading, "if I give you the price you are asking, I will have to give the same price to everyone. I will go broke!"

The woman snorted. "Extortionist! You will never go broke – you make more than anyone here!"

Bjorn's assumption just might hold true for some, Scarlett thought as her eyes fell on the scarf-wrapped head of the woman. *Some people never change.* Of course she was thinking of the babushka, not herself.

The Jordan began tapping her foot impatiently, the tip of her boot sending up little puffs of dust on the hard-packed dirt road that encircled the town. She looked away again and drew a deep breath into her lungs in an effort to clear her mind and her emotions.

"What will I tell my husband if he does not get his roast?" the woman demanded of Arwa. "That he is the only man in Village East that does not get to celebrate the Synchronicity?"

Maybe you should tell him he should have chicken, Scarlett thought caustically. *Or better yet, just vegetables. It would do him good.* She had seen the husband once on a market day. He was as fat as the babushka was thin. Maybe more.

Arwa was as apologetic as always, but the woman was relentless. "Maybe I should treat him like a prisoner? Just throw him a crust of bread?"

Maybe you should save your money and get him some wine, Scarlett thought, *he probably needs it, listening to you day in and day out.* She bit her lip and looked away again, listening to the rising sound of Fledge's heartbeat in her ears. Abruptly she realized that it wasn't Fledge's heartbeat, but her own. She looked inward and could feel her blood warming. *Breathe,* she told herself. *Just breathe.*

"Madam," Arwa offered, "perhaps potatoes would be better. They cost less than the tomatoes."

The woman looked at him as if he had slapped her. "Potatoes! Are we to eat like paupers?" she demanded.

"Maybe some squash would be better?" Arwa suggested.

"I don't like squash!"

"Some onions? Onions give flavor to any meal! If not roast, then a stew!"

Scarlett's stomach gave a little growl, thinking of the stew she would have tonight and then onions she wanted for it, if this crazy woman would just get her shit together and her whiny ass out of here.

"Onions upset my stomach," the babushka whined.

"My garlic then!" Arwa suggested. "They are small and quite affordable. Just one bulb will give you a flavor you will not believe!"

"But I want tomatoes! I came here for tomatoes!"

The Jordan could feel her blood getting hotter and hotter. Silver hydrogen raced through her veins, a tide of burning fire that she could feel rising up within her like a flood against a dam.

"Then you should get the tomatoes, I am sure you can afford them," Arwa consoled.

The flood rose, a burning rage of red and silver...

"I could afford the tomatoes if you did not raise the price every week!"

...and the dam that had been holding it back burst.

"Godammit you imbecile!" Scarlett shouted. "Those tomatoes are the same fucking price every week!"

There was a moment of shocked silence that filled the entire section of the produce market as the woman drew away from Scarlett in terror, but it only lasted for a second. Then, as the other stalls recommenced their murmured haggling, and with a dignified harrumph, the woman took the tomatoes from the table, dropped the appropriate coin in Arwa's dumbfounded hand, and stalked off with her back straight and her narrow and pointed chin high.

Arwa, hardly aware of the coin as it disappeared into his robes, continued to regard the Jordan with an expression of shock. He held out his hands as if to beseech her. "Scarlett," he admonished. "Why do you shout at the babushka? She means no harm."

Scarlett, however, was beyond reprimand. She could feel her blood boiling through her veins and knew it was the best she had felt in months. Her grin, already shark-like, widened. Arwa saw it and took a step back, his own smile faltering. Scarlett saw his reaction and her grin widened even further.

"I'd had enough," she said, her voice low.

Arwa again was taken aback and again Scarlett was surprised with the satisfaction it gave her.

"Well," he said, forgoing their usual flirtations. "What can I do for you today?"

Scarlett grinned her newly found shark-like grin. "I think you have already done it," she said. "But I'll take some pearl onions, please."

Arwa nodded solemnly and, though he had rehearsed a dozen offers to entice Scarlett to join him for the Synchronicity, he wrapped the onions in a small paper bag and handed them to her without another word.

"Keep the change," Scarlett told him as she handed him a coin. He nodded, his large dark eyes watching her carefully.

As they should be, Scarlett thought. She gave Arwa a quick nod and turned to make her way back through the market so she could retrieve the mare and head for home.

The produce trader watched her head back toward the town and heaved an audible sigh of relief when the beautiful dark-haired woman had gone.

★

Scarlett rode home, giving the mare her head. The charger could feel the ire of her mistress and, once clear of the town, bolted down the dirt road. After an entire kilometer at a hard gallop the horse pulled up into a sharp trot, waiting to see if it was the right thing to do.

The Jordan leaned down and gave the horse a number of hard pats on the neck. "You do what you want to do," she told her. "We'll see if I can do the same."

The mare edged sideways along the road for a few steps, kicking up dust in indecision until she settled into a comfortable trot.

I've changed, Scarlett thought, watching the horizon, waiting for the cottage to appear. *Of course part of me will always be the same. But how much? How much do I keep? How much is safe?*

When the cottage materialized in the distance she kept her eyes trained on it, watching it grow in her field of vision. She considered the questions that had bothered her for the past many days. One question, however, loomed above all others.

What am I going to do?

The Jordan was so intent when she arrived that she simply removed the saddle and turned the mare loose in the field without rubbing her down. The horse didn't seem to mind.

Scarlett found Elaeric just outside the cottage, tending to the herb garden with a watering can. He looked up from a thick bed of basil and offered her a silent greeting with a nod and a smile as he went about his work.

"Master Elaeric, I am torn."

The monk straightened and raised his eyebrows, piqued. "Indeed?"

Scarlett cleared her throat nervously. "I feel that being here has helped me – not just healing my...ahem...condition... but in more ways than that. But I feel that what I am learning is pushing me to make a bad decision."

Elaeric waved a hand at her, the sleeve of his yellow robe giving a soft flap as if to dispute any nonsense as he bent back down over the thick rows of green herbs. "Then you should know by now that there are no wrong decisions. There are just decisions. The consequences of those decisions may have outcomes you favor or outcomes that you do not."

Scarlett frowned. "So if I make a decision that others think is wrong, but it makes me happy, then it is the correct one."

Elaeric turned his head and his dark almond-shaped eyes fixed upon her own. "You are not listening," he said, his voice firm. "There is no wrong decision, so there can be no correct decisions. Never will *everyone* agree on what is right. The difference is not between right and wrong, the difference is only a matter of opinion. People must always hang the sign of 'wrong' about the neck of someone else's opinion if it does not agree with their own."

"Is it wrong that I want to hit you with a stick?" she asked sharply.

Elaeric looked as surprised as if he had been struck. "Wanting is not wrong. Hitting is not wrong." His voice dropped, becoming grave. "I will not condone killing, but even I know that sometimes it must be done. But decisions have consequences both great and small, and you must live with them all. The effect of your actions – you must ask yourself: how will those actions affect people? How will they affect you? How will they affect the fabric of the universe?"

Scarlett blew a burst of air through her teeth and rocked her head back as far it would go. "That is exactly what I am asking myself!"

Elaeric turned back to his plants. "If you ask, the universe will answer – if it has not done so already."

Scarlett bit her lip. "I am being forced into a choice."

"Bah!" Elaeric cursed. "You are not forced into anything. Trust the universe."

"Are you saying I should do nothing? That I am not in control of my own fate?"

"Do you never listen to what I tell you?"

Scarlett stamped a foot, another habit that had not surfaced in a while. She took a deep breath and sat down on the ground. "Could you please be a bit more clear?" she asked when she had calmed herself.

"The universe knows what is in your heart, it will show you the path. It is up to you to walk it. Most people try to follow their head, rather than their heart, and stubbornly choose another path. It is like trying to swim upriver to catch a fish, instead of floating along with the current, to where schools of fish wait." He reached down and pinched a newly sprouted weed between his thumb and index finger and pulled it out before moving on to the next bed of greens, slowly making his way back to where the Jordan sat.

Scarlett remained silent for a while and then sighed, resigned to ask what she must – knowing that Elaeric would not answer anything but a direct question and even then it was iffy.

"Master Elaeric?"

"Mmm hmm."

"You were around for the Age of Creation, weren't you?"

He didn't turn but she could hear the smile in his voice. "Does it show?"

Only in the way you act, Scarlett thought. "Do you know much about the creation of the first constructs?"

Elaeric paused, the watering can hovering above a thirsty mure-plant. "What is it you want to know?"

"How was it that the first constructs were programmed to have that compelling sort of effect on people? The First Seven in particular?"

Elaeric turned and gave her a blank look. "Compelling effect?"

Scarlett sighed impatiently. "You know," she urged. "The voice, the touch, the smell. The..." her eyes searched the air for words that wouldn't embarrass her but didn't find any. Her shoulders dropped in resignation and she met his dark eyes with her own. "That effect, the sort of... sexual shockwave they produce."

Elaeric regarded her with his almond-shaped eyes opened wide. "Sexual shockwave?"

The Jordan sighed again. "Yes. What did they program into those first constructs to trigger that sort of response in a person?"

Elaeric pursed his lips and looked away, thoughtful. When he spoke his voice was soft, as if he were talking to himself. "The voice...yes, I remember. It was pure genius of Cronus to use a baritone orchestra, but..." he frowned and then looked back at Scarlett and shook his head. "There was no trigger programmed into them. The response - that was programmed into you."

Scarlett stared at him in shock.

"Not like a computer program," he told her quickly, remembering the tenuous hold she had on her reality when she had first arrived. "Your DNA. It is something unique in you that produces the effect."

Scarlett closed her eyes. "Shit."

Elaeric, smiling, leaned forward and laid a gentle hand on her shoulder. "Yes."

TWO THREE

Grandpa finished his morning routine in the bathroom and headed for his kitchen. His tongue naturally sought out the space in his gums between his bottom front teeth. He had lost another jagged stub of a tooth, only to find it had been pushed out by a shiny new replacement.

There was no doubt about it. Two new teeth were growing where two old ones had given up. He could see it with his own two eyes, which had been surprisingly clear of late. His hearing was rather clear as well. And his thinking, too. And right now he was thinking that there was something fishy going on.

He had a pretty good idea what it was and who might be responsible. He also had a pretty good idea on how to find out and that was on his morning agenda as he started up his coffee maker. While it steamed and hissed out a cup of coffee he went into the living room to retrieve his acrylic.

The device, something Grandpa had always thought of as a fancy toy, had been a gift from John and Rebecca some years ago at Christmas. Rebecca had known that he loved to read but that his eyes were going. She had told him that he could have any book he wanted right there at his fingertips, even the Bible, and make the letters as large as he liked. He had thanked her, the gesture having been so kind, and then tucked the thing away in his closet. He didn't have the heart to tell her that his eyes were past any resizing of the letters.

Last week he had gone to look for it and there it had been, in his new closet just like it had been in his old closet at the last pod. He had pulled it from the shelf and taken it from the box – it looked like a square pane of clear glass with rounded edges. He had asked Jeanette to show him how to use it and she did, with surprising alacrity.

Grandpa had watched in amazement as her fingers, once chubby but now to his dismay growing long and delicate, moved deftly as she showed him how to turn on the device and make it work. Activating the thing made the glass turn a dark, smoky color.

"This is a really nice model, Grandpa," she told him. "I'm glad you're finally going to use it."

"Do you have one?" he asked.

"No," she told him, her eyes moving as fast as her fingers as she opened and closed different windows of light and color. "I'm not old enough yet."

"Then how do you know how to work it?"

She shrugged. "Mom lets me use hers for some things. School projects, or to take pictures when we are someplace special, or to play games on when we're waiting somewhere."

"You can do all those things on this piece of glass?" Grandpa asked. "I thought it was just for reading books."

Jeanette giggled and shook her head, her fingers dancing across the darkened glass. "You can do just about anything with an acrylic. A good one, anyway. Here." She held the glass in front of her chest, turned so that he could see its face. "I've loaded the things I think you might want. Someone should have done that for you in the first place – it would have made it easier for you to use."

If I could have seen it in the first place, Grandpa thought, *I might have asked.* "Okay," he said, "show me what you got."

Jeanette tucked her chin down so she could she what she was demonstrating. "If you tap this," she said, pointing to a blue square on the face of the device, "you can get the local news. If you tap here," she said pointing to a red square, "you can get IGC news and events. If you open this..." she tapped a green square on the pane and a window opened up with more squares. "You can play games. I know you used to like crosswords so you can get them here." She indicated an icon of black and white squares.

"Really?"

"Really. These are some other games I thought you would like. They involve words or history or trivia. If you want something different, maybe some serious war or strategy games, I can show you the best ones."

"I don't think that will be necessary," Grandpa told her, beaming at the young girl that seemed to grow before his eyes.

"I didn't think so," she said with a smile. She closed the game window, taking him back to the first screen. "And this," she said as she pointed to a multi-colored square, "is if you want to ping anything."

"Ping?"

Jeanette's lips scrunched to the side as she thought. "What did you used to call it in school?" she asked. "When you wanted information on something?"

"We Googled it," Grandpa said without hesitation.

Jeanette nodded quickly, her dark curls bobbing about her face. "I've heard that term," she said, excited. "This is the same thing. When you want to know something, open this browser and type it in. Tap on this picture up in the corner at any time, and it will bring up the keyboard."

"That's it?"

Jeanette giggled again. "For now, unless you want something else."

"What else can it do?"

Little Jean rolled her dark eyes. "Just about anything. What do you want, Grandpa? Music? Holos?" She laughed suddenly. "A calendar?"

Grandpa frowned at her, knowing what she was implying about his memory. "I most certainly do not," he said.

"Then what? I can show you how to order groceries and have them delivered."

Grandpa tapped a finger on his lip, thoughtful. "Keep that in mind for later," he told her. "But I was thinking about a journal, or a notepad. Someplace where I could write things down."

Jeanette gave a quick nod and turned the face of the acrylic around, her fingers once more dancing along its glassy face. "Here," she said, showing it to him. "Open this yellow box..." she demonstrated by tapping the yellow square on the glass and the screen was filled with the image of lined yellow paper, "and type in whatever you want. Over here you can make tabs for different years or subjects, or start a whole new notebook."

Grandpa, thoroughly impressed, beamed at his dark-haired granddaughter. "Thank you," he said. "You are a genius."

Jeanette smiled. "That is yet to be decided," she said, planting a kiss on his cheek. "But I have to run – I have dance class." She scooped up a black shoulder bag with a holo of pink slippers dancing along the sides. "If you need help, just ask Sean. He's turning into a real ac-worm," she said with another giggle.

"I think I'd rather wait and ask you," Grandpa said.

Jeanette beamed proudly. "See ya, Grandpa," she said before flitting out the door, her dance bag slung over a shoulder that still seemed so tiny.

"She is nine, now," Grandpa had said to the empty room after the door had slid closed behind her.

Today he was ready to try it out by himself. He carefully placed the acrylic on the kitchen table and poured himself a glass of water. Real water, not the watered down moonshine he had always kept in the fridge – he gave it up last week when it started making his throat burn.

Grandpa grabbed his coffee and his pill bottle, and settled his narrow butt in a kitchen chair at the table. He opened the scrip bottle and washed a single lavender pill down with the cold water from the tap.

He took a drink of hot coffee from his mug and turned the scrip bottle in hands. The words used to be nothing but a dark blur, but now they were crystal clear – sharp black print standing out on the white-capped tube. The logo of the pill manufacturer was there as well. Two weeks ago he had thought it was the yin-yang symbol, but now he could see that it was an oval G7 logo.

The logo did not surprise him the slightest. After all, GwenSeven had started out in biotechnology. No reason why they wouldn't keep it up. But when he turned on his acrylic and opened the application to 'ping' the name of his medication, what he saw surprised the hell out of him. So much so that he turned off the device and laid it back down on the table with a trembling hand.

He drummed his fingers on the surface of the table, thinking. The first thing he thought was that he shouldn't have thrown out that moonshine water. He could use a drink, burning throat or not.

Finally, he got up and scrambled an egg and made a piece of toast. After breakfast he sat at the table, waiting. He didn't feel much like eating when lunchtime rolled around, so he just peeled a violet banana and munched on it while he waited.

He was still there in the kitchen nook when Sean came home, startled to see Grandpa sitting there and doing nothing.

"What's going on, Grandpa?" Sean asked, dropping his ac-bag onto an empty chair.

"You tell me."

"Excuse me?"

Grandpa tapped a finger on the pill bottle that was sitting on the table. Sean had the decency to look a bit guilty.

"Oh, those. Well, you needed a new scrip, so I got you one."

"Mmmhmm. Did you know what they would do?"

Sean shifted his weight from one foot to another, making him look much younger than he was. "I know what they are supposed to do."

"Are you trying to turn back the clock on me?"

"Yes."

Grandpa harrumphed. "At least you're honest." The old man sighed. "Son, it's not your job to save me."

"I'm not ready to let you go," Sean said quietly.

Grandpa felt his heart clutch in his chest. *And all this time I thought it was Jeanette that was the nurturer. Could they both be so caring? Maybe the boy is the one that should be handed our history. Or maybe I should just write it down in the damn acrylic.* The thought of the acrylic brought him out of his short reverie.

"That's awfully kind of you son," he told Sean. "And we'll talk more on that, but later. Right now I want you to explain something else to me."

Sean shifted his weight again. "Yeah?"

Grandpa turned on his acrylic and rotated it so that Sean could see. "What in the Sam Hill is this?"

"You're using your acrylic?" Sean asked, surprised.

"Yes, yes, yes. Little Jean showed me how." Sean smiled approvingly but Grandpa seemed less than pleased. "Tell me what's going on here."

"It's a search window."

Grandpa scowled at him. "I know it's a search window boy!" he scolded. Sean had to bite his lip to keep from laughing – he could see Grandpa was getting mad. "What I want to know is how it knows my name, and why it says GwenSeven."

"Ohhhh. It has your name because this acrylic is registered to you – probably something Mom or Dad did when they bought it."

"Alright. And the GwenSeven?"

Sean shrugged. "This acrylic was manufactured by them, it's only natural that it automatically defaults to their browser. You can change it if you want to. I use..."

"This thing was made by GwenSeven?" Grandpa interrupted. "When did they start that? I thought they were strictly bio-tech."

Sean shook his head slowly. "They expanded around two centuries ago, Grandpa, and have been expanding ever since."

Grandpa sat back in his chair, his blue eyes clear and thoughtful. "What else do they do?" he asked. His voice was both quiet and expectant, as if he was afraid of what the answer might be.

Sean looked away as he tried to reel in an easy answer, but he couldn't think of one. "I wouldn't say they own everything, but they certainly own part of everything – at least everything I can think of right now. If they didn't make your flatscreen, they made the fiber optics that are in it." Sean gestured about the kitchen. "They didn't make your appliances, but they made the circuit boards that make them work."

Grandpa looked out the window. "What about fuel?" he asked, his eyes far away. "Transportation?"

Sean nodded and took a seat in a kitchen chair. "What they don't own I'm sure they have a hand in – I think they do refining."

"The InterGalactic Council has three branches," Grandpa said, still looking outside. "Industrial Development, Economic, and Military. Does GwenSeven have a hand in all three?"

"No, not the military."

"Are you sure?"

Seam tapped a finger on his lips, thinking. "No, you're right, possibly. She's not GwenSeven technically, but the youngest de Rossi sister is the Blue Jordan."

"What?" Grandpa asked, fixing his blue eyes on the blue eyes of his grandson. "Are you serious?"

"Yeah. She's on the same Dragon as Auntie Jo."

Grandpa let out a long, low whistle. "I'll be damned."

The boy waited for him to say more but the old man remained silent. As usual for him these days, Sean had come with some questions of his own and fidgeted with his canvas bag on the chair next to him as he summoned the courage to ask them.

"Grandpa?" he started.

"Mmm?"

"You've never taken pills before to stop or reverse your aging?"

"No."

"Well, then how...I mean...I don't want to be rude but..." he looked at the old man for help but Grandpa only smiled, waiting. Sean cleared his throat, "I know you're not really *my* grandfather. Dad's father died in the Amliss Attack. Are you Dad's grandfather?"

Grandpa nodded slowly, considering. "Yeeesss...but there are probably a few 'greats' in there somewhere."

"How many greats?"

"Son, I don't really know."

"How many grandchildren have you had?" Sean asked.

"Many," Grandpa told him, looking a little sad. "I couldn't tell you how many, though. Maybe if I keep taking those magic beans you brought me, I might remember."

Sean didn't know what beans he was talking about – maybe he meant the pills. But he wasn't getting the answers he was after. He decided to take a different track. "The last time we talked, you told me that you worked for Cronus and the de Rossi's before they had incorporated as GwenSeven."

"Yes."

"Well, that would make you close to three hundred years old."

"I'm pushing the big three-oh-oh," Grandpa confessed. "I'll beat Charity de Rossi there by three years."

Sean nodded as if he had assumed as much, but was still impressed. "How?" he asked. "How have you made it so long? That's a long time to live without any sort of hg-supplement or biological enhancement. Are you part elf?"

Grandpa threw back his head and cawed laughter. Sean hadn't heard him laugh like that for some time and had no idea why his question struck Grandpa so funny, but he bore it patiently.

"Heavens, no!" Grandpa finally said. "Like I said, I was in my early twenties when I worked for Cronus and the girls." Sean could only blink in response, his blue eyes wide as he tried to imagine what it must have been like. What Grandpa must have been like, when he was young.

"Wow," he managed.

"Wow is right," Grandpa agreed. "Back then, shortly after the creation of the First Seven, something happened to me. Something that altered my biology and slowed down the natural decomposition of my body."

"What was it?" Sean asked, almost breathless.

Grandpa frowned as he considered the question. "A story for another time," he told him. "Suffice to say that my aging slowed. It was quite drastic for the first hundred years – I didn't change at all in that time!" Grandpa threw back his head again and cackled at the memory. "After that, the maturation process kicked in again. Slowly at first, then picking up as the years went by. The last 'unert years or so I started to lose my memory, and show my age." Grandpa had another cackle at that one.

"Whatever was done to you has been wearing off," Sean realized out loud.

Grandpa nodded. "Until a few weeks ago."

Sean smiled sheepishly, but this time when he spoke his voice was firm. "Like I said, I'm not ready to let you go."

"Good. 'Cause I'm not ready to go."

"Does that mean you'll keep taking your pills?"

Grandpa took a deep breath, considering. "Yes."

"Good."

"How did your games go this week?" Grandpa asked, changing the subject.

Sean wished he hadn't. "Terrible," he admitted. "Each time I get killed faster than the last."

"The Skipper?"

"Yes! And it's as if he knows it's me every time I strap in! I'd be ashamed to play again in front of my friends except that it happens with them too."

Grandpa laughed. "What game is it?"

"All of them!"

Grandpa cackled. "Are they all the same type of game?"

"No," Sean admitted. "Chimera Battle is a simulated jet fighter game, so is Golgoth Invasion. But IGC Commission and Lost Earth are both strategic games, and the Skipper dominates those as well."

"The whole Sphere?"

"The whole Sphere."

Grandpa gave an appreciative grunt. "So the Skipper has learned to read your moves, and the moves of the other players in order to beat them. What have you learned about the Skipper?"

"Nothing!"

"Bah! Nothing!" Grandpa scolded. "What does he always do or, at least, what does he do consistently?"

Sean frowned, not ever having really thought about it before. He gave Grandpa's question serious consideration before he answered. "He never does the same move twice."

"That's all?" Grandpa scowled at him. "Forget game strategy, think about real life. Any coincidences occur to you?"

Sean thought about it. "He does have certain game times, at least so I've heard. Despite the game, it is never before two in the afternoon or past nine at night."

Grandpa smiled. "So what does that tell you?"

Sean smiled back. "That it's a kid. Definitely a kid, but not even a teenager! One that has to be home at first curfew."

Grandpa nodded. "And?"

Sean smirked. "That he's smart – not just smart enough to play, but smart enough not to get caught."

"Those are usually the smartest," Grandpa told him.

 TWO FOUR

Scarlett sat on the top rail of the fence that enclosed the meadow, looking at a strange sight. In a grassy field on the far east side of a medieval town, where there was usually nothing but a chestnut mare along with a dozen butterflies dancing and bobbing among the wildflowers, sat a hulking metal spacecraft.

It had arrived the day before while Scarlett was out riding the mare. She knew when the craft was on approach and took the horse out in an effort to keep the animal from getting spooked. Once it had landed, the Jordan had returned and rubbed her down and turned her loose in the field, giving her time to get used to the foreign object that had taken up a temporary residence in her home.

All through the night the mare stayed clear of the metal beast that had invaded her yard, but by morning her curiosity had gotten the better of her and she began trotting to and from the craft, sometimes daring to touch it with her nose before giving it a snort and galloping off again.

Now the ramp was down and the mare stayed well away, keeping close to her mistress perched on the fence. Scarlett held out an apple and the horse trotted over. The mare gave the apple a sniff and then shied away, giving Scarlett a rather reproachful look.

The Jordan laughed under her breath. "I know, I know," she admitted, "it's drugged. But it'll make your ride a whole lot more comfortable."

The mare paused and then, either understanding Scarlett's words or just giving in to the treat, came over and began munching away at the proffered fruit. When the apple was gone the horse stepped nearer and nearer to the Jordan until they were nose to nose.

Scarlett carefully reached up and put a hand on either side of the mare's head and pulled her even closer, until their foreheads were touching.

"You be good," she told her. "Be happy."

The horse whickered but did not pull away.

The Jordan dropped her head and planted a kiss on the mare's nose at the tip of the white streak that nature had painted there. In return, the mare gave her a shove that almost knocked her backwards off the fence.

Scarlett laughed and held on, pushing back as much as she could. There was a whistle and she looked up to see the transport crew motioning to her. They were ready.

Elaeric came up behind her and climbed the fence in emerald-colored robes and slippered feet. He sat on the rail and held his hand out to the horse who obligingly nuzzled it with her soft nose, her velvety lips searching, hoping for another treat.

Scarlett leaned out from the fence and wrapped her arms around the mare's neck. She put her cheek against the smooth chestnut hair and closed her eyes.

"What is the horse?" Elaeric asked, his voice gentle.

Scarlett answered without opening her eyes. "She is the grass that she has eaten and the birdsong she has heard. She is the sunshine upon her back. She is stillness and motion. She is a whisper that fades in the wind. She is me and she is you and she is every speck of fleeting dust that drifts through the universe."

"And will you be sad that she is gone?"

Scarlett pulled back and gave the mare's neck a vigorous rub. "No. I'll miss her, but there will always be a part of her inside me."

"And part of you will always be in her," Elaeric assured her.

The thought made Scarlett smile. She buried her face in the mare's forelock so that their foreheads were touching and inhaled deeply before drawing away and peering at the monk perched upon the fence.

"When we first began, I asked you if there was a shortcut to enlightenment."

Elaeric chuckled. "Yes, I remember. But the thought of a wormhole is misleading. Think of the way to enlightenment as more of a long path set with four large stepping-stones and filled with pebbles in between. Each stone, each pebble, is a lesson. Some must walk step-by-step, pebble-by-pebble, learning every lesson diligently, but even then there is no guarantee for inner peace. Some hop from stone to stone, attaining enlightenment quickly. Still others fly like a dragon, not touching anything but encompassing all as it soars, and enlightenment is theirs."

"I like the dragon part," Scarlett said, "but I know my limits. I'll settle for jumping. What's the first stepping stone?"

Elaeric laughed softly and for a few seconds Scarlett thought he wasn't going to answer, but he did. "Forgive the past completely."

"And the next?"

Elaeric laughed harder. "It took me a hundred years to do that! You think you have already done so?"

The Jordan smiled and shook her head. "No," she admitted. "That will be a tough one for me as well. But I thought maybe I could plan ahead."

"Work on number one. I will tell you the next when you are ready."

"Alright."

Elaeric smiled and looked at the handlers waving from the transport. They held their arms out palms up, silently questioning. "They are ready for her."

"Well?" Scarlett asked the horse. "Are you going to go on your own, or do I need to take you?"

The mare edged away and then back again, again almost unseating the Jordan with a hefty shove.

"I believe that is your answer," Elaeric told her.

Scarlett chuckled. "Alright. One last time."

The mare moved close to the Jordan who stood up on the fence, wrapped her hand in the rust-colored mane, and threw a long leg over her back. Scarlett clucked her tongue and the mare trotted into the meadow, letting Scarlett guide her towards the craft.

The Jordan realized that it was the first time she had ridden without a saddle and wished she had tried it sooner. The mare whickered and jerked her head as they approached the craft, but otherwise did not balk.

Scarlett eyed the ramp but doubted that her head would clear the top if she tried to ride in. She slowed the horse to stop and dismounted, sliding smoothly off the mare's backside. Two lean human men with calloused hands greeted her.

"Thank you, ma'am," one said, holding out a slim silver bit to the horse. His Anglicus was heavily accented by a dialect Scarlett did not recognize.

The horse jerked her head away at first and then, almost

daringly, sniffed the metal rod. Hoping that it might be a treat, she bit it.

The mare had no sooner taken the metal rod between her teeth before light shot from both ends, followed by metallic tendrils that snaked around the mare's nose, up the sides of her face, across her brow and behind her ears.

Dancing light traveled around the holo bridle and the first man handed the luminous reins to his partner. The partner simply gave Scarlett a quick nod of acknowledgment before trying to lead the horse away.

The mare balked and Scarlett gave her a heavy swat on the flank.

"Go on!" she urged, smiling. "Get your ass up there!"

The horse stomped her hooves a bit more and then obligingly let the man lead her up the ramp. Scarlett watched them go, noting the stable that had been secured inside the craft. It was duro-plastic instead of wood, but complete with straw on the floor and alfalfa hay in the food trough. There was even a small sack of oats.

The Jordan shook her head at the strange sight of hay inside a spacecraft. It was as odd as seeing the craft sitting in the field. She considered asking to speak to the Captain of the ship to find out how fast they would be going, by what course and drive – then dismissed the idea as quickly as it had come.

The mare would be fine. It was time to go and let go.

Scarlett gave the handler a nod and he waved in return as he went up the ramp and into the craft to help his partner in making the horse comfortable. The Jordan sighed as she turned away and started back across the meadow.

The grass was a vivid green with thick bladed leaves that came to tops of her boots. Heavy wildflower blossoms bent their stems and bobbed in the breeze. Butterflies whirled, chasing each other. An occasional bee droned by on its way to the hive. It was a perfect day.

Scarlett plucked a long blade of grass that had bent halfway to the ground, drooping with a heavy seed ball. She joined the monk, resuming her perch on the wooden rail of the fence. The Jordan placed the long grass stem between her teeth, enjoying the clean, earthy flavor. She knew that she looked like a perfect hick, and didn't care in the slightest.

"Great progress," Elaeric said.

Scarlett did not need to ask if he meant her or the horse. She simply answered as he would. "Yes."

They watched the craft in companionable silence as it made ready to depart.

"I wish they had come," Scarlett finally said. "The owners."

"Why?"

Scarlett shrugged. "I don't know. I suppose in the same way someone wants to meet the family of the person they love."

Elaeric laughed softly. "No sane someone."

Scarlett chuckled. "I guess I just want to see what they are like. If they love her, or if she is just some sort of prize."

"I don't think they would have sent her here if she was just a trophy," he remarked. Scarlett nodded in agreement as Elaeric reached into his robes. "That reminds me." He drew out a small leather bag. It was the one he always gave her when she went to town. "This is for you," he said, handing her the pouch.

"What's this?"

"Money from the owners. I want you to have it."

Scarlett smiled. "You keep it."

"I already took most it," he confided.

Scarlett laughed. "Keep it all. I don't need it where I'm going and I don't expect to be back this way anytime soon."

"Keep it as a souvenir then. Besides," the monk added with a wink of one almond-shaped eye. "You never know."

Scarlett accepted the pouch with a grateful yet suspicious smile. "But you do know, don't you? You wily bastard!"

The monk took her playful accusation with a smile and gracious bow of his bald head.

"The universe is a holographic tapestry, Johanna. So complete and so profound that even the tiniest fleck of thread contains the whole. Just as you are a part of the universe, the entire universe exists in you. The answer to your question, of course, is yes. I think our threads will cross again."

The Jordan regarded him with a rueful smile. "Well, when that time comes, your thread better not be around my neck."

Elaeric laughed and both their heads turned as one as the craft rose from the field. Looking like a giant metal insect, it rose silently as it folded in upon itself, raising a huge cloud of dust under its belly.

Something about that dust cloud struck a chord inside of Scarlett and she watched the motes swirl over the waving field of grass, mesmerized. She felt a tickle on the back of her neck and she tensed, expecting to hear the voice of her mother Dragon. Moments passed and no voice came, from within her head or without.

The two on the fence watched the craft rise higher and higher as it shrank into the sky above them, growing smaller by the second, dwindling until it disappeared altogether. After a heavy sigh, Scarlett jumped gracefully to the ground. Elaeric climbed down with a bit more care.

"Well, Johanna," he said, brushing his hands together. "Now it is time for us to say good-bye as well. Or, as I prefer, until next time."

He began to bow in a respectful farewell but the Jordan surprised the old monk by suddenly embracing him and holding him close. There was too much to thank him for but he seemed to understand, as he always did.

"I know," he told her, patting her back.

"Yes," she whispered.

*

Scarlett returned to the cottage to collect her things, the only two things she would be taking with her besides the leather pouch. She opened the top drawer of the chest in the room that had served as her bedroom these past months.

Beneath her undergarments were the items she was after. Her family crest, suspended from a wide black ribbon, and the chain of platinum figure eights that Bjorn had given her. The Chimeran Officer's chain.

She slipped the chain into the right pocket of her black leather riding pants, and tucked the crest into her left pocket with the leather pouch. That was it. The only other thing she was taking with her was the silk shirt on her back, the crimson one. Another gift from the Chimeran Commander.

She reached into the drawer and touched the folded linen shirt on top of the small pile of clothes that had been hers for a while. She ran her fingers over the cloth, looking at the faded pink flowers that had undoubtedly been red poppies at one time, wondering again what Elaeric was doing was doing with women's clothes.

Maybe, Scarlett thought as she shut the drawer, *from time to time he gets other victims to torture.*

297

As she reached the door she turned and looked into the room with more nostalgia than she had been capable of when she had arrived. Her eyes fell on the red clogs next to the bed.

"There's no place like home," she said softly.

She closed the door and, as she did, her eyes fell on the near empty room that Elaeric -and herself as well these past few months - used for meditating. Curious, Scarlett approached the room and pushed open the door.

As always, clean sunshine streamed through the windows. The sitting pillows were two puffs of canvas fabric. The wooden floor was immaculate. And, for the first time, the Jordan *saw*.

"There's no dust," she whispered.

Even if Elaeric cleaned, which she had never witnessed, and even if the floor had just been swabbed with alcohol, it would never be so sterile. Especially considering all the dust kicked up in the field by the mare, the powdered earth raised in the yard by the chickens, and the simple dirt she dragged into the cottage on her boots.

But it wasn't the floor on which her eyes were fixated. It was the light. The light streaming in through the windows, so clean and fresh and bright. Not a single mote stirred in that precious beam of rosy gold.

No dust. No dust at all.

Now the voice of the Dragon came. *Remember,* the voice whispered in her mind. *Remember for Blue.*

"I will," Scarlett answered softly.

She closed the door behind her, her emotional thread feeling strung out and tight. As she walked out of the cottage and into the warmth of the morning she found Elaeric waiting for her on the path that led to the road.

"You might get hungry on the way," he told her. "And thirsty too, with no mare to carry you." He held out a scarf containing an apple, a pear, a leftover biscuit and a leather flask. The scarf was just like the one Scarlett would take into town every week except that this one was new. The fabric was silky, and a dark red.

"Thank you," Scarlett said. "What's in the flask?"

"Water," Elaeric told her, sounding surprised. "What else would it be?"

Scarlett laughed and, taking the scarf, put her arm and head through the tied ends so she could wear it like a sling. As she secured the makeshift garment, the fingers of her right hand

298

touched the rippled skin on the back of its counterpart, and something else suddenly occurred to her.

A day of revelation, she thought.

"Master Elaeric?"

"Yes?"

"What was the lesson in gathering the eggs?"

Elaeric grinned. "No lesson. I hate the fat chicken. It always pecks me."

Scarlett pressed her lips together and bowed to Elaeric who courteously returned the gesture. There was no more to be said. The monk turned so that she could pass and she walked by him towards the road, overcoming the urge to hug him one more time.

He expects I'll be back. Well, who knows? He's been right about everything else.

Scarlett turned right on the main dirt road and headed for town on foot. She expected to walk most of the way and, normally, she would be right.

With the Synchronicity, however, there were many wagons and horses headed towards town and most were offering rides to those using their own legs. Scarlett accepted a ride from a drawn carriage of dark-skinned traders that reminded her of Arwa.

They were in high spirits, and passing around a bottle of high spirits, as they made their way to the Festa. They offered Scarlett the bottle and she good-naturedly toasted them and took a drink. The raw alcohol burned her throat and chest and she coughed, making the traders laugh heartily and thump her on the back.

The next time the bottle came by she politely refused, throwing them into more gales of laughter. Instead, she ate her apple and offered her pear to the one boy that was obviously too young to drink. He accepted it with a huge grin, his head bobbing and nodding his thanks.

They reached Kayos Proper a little past noon and all the men vied for the chance to help Scarlett down from the wagon. She thanked them in Anglicus and then in Swathi, bowing to them with her hands clasped in front of her forehead.

There were jeers of surprise as they saw she knew something of their customs and speech. Then she blew them a collective kiss and they all went wild. The one who spoke a bit of broken Anglicus begged her to stay with them for the Synchronicity Carnivale.

"I'm sorry," Scarlett apologized with a gracious smile, "but I have other men to both disappoint and delight this evening."

"Ah!"

The man bowed, Scarlett bowed, and the other men along with the boy bowed. Scarlett bowed once more, chuckling and backing away.

She finally turned and, seeing the medieval town like she had never seen it before, gasped in delight.

There were banners and flags, pennants and trailers in every color of the rainbow. They waved and snapped in the breeze from the tops of the conical towers of the government buildings, as well as from the rooftops of inns and restaurants. Multi-colored streamers fluttered from flagpoles as well as from the hair of young girls. There were brightly colored lights on the stone buildings and holo lights along the walls of the village with pale projected scenes of horses and riders jousting. As the day dimmed to darkness the scenes would be projected onto the night sky for all to see.

Scarlett felt like clapping her hands like a child, but instead simply grinned and headed for the center of the town. Feeling nostalgic once again for her new and short-lived home, Scarlett changed direction and headed toward the stable that she had used to house the mare on their trips to town.

She found her favorite café and, though it was much busier than usual with the throngs of people arriving in the Village, she was able to find a small table outside. She ordered a coffee and brioche and watched the people arrive as the sun began its descent towards the horizon.

The people, trickling in at first, soon became droves and as the crowds grew thicker she could see why the Chimera had chosen this spot for their meeting.

A large number of the growing crowd wore masks and nearly everyone was in costume, many of which were flight suits and space wear. People were dressed like Dragon Captains and Chimeran Commanders. Some wore fancy dresses and harlequin masks, while others wore swampy rags and frightening Golgoth masks.

Scarlett was even surprised to see a number of young women, and some men she realized, dressed in the shimmering flight suits of the Jordan. A few of them were sporting crimson along with masses of dark hair that Scarlett suspected might be wigs. The others wore blue flight suits and had platinum hair so perfectly sculpted that they *had* to be wigs, maybe even plastic ones.

The ones in emerald green tugged at her heart until her eyes found a platinum blonde in a black flight suit. There were a number of people around the young woman making a fuss about her black flight suit and the real Jordan could only suppose the clothiers ran out of blue Mylar.

All Scarlett could do was shake her head and smile into her coffee. She sipped at her second cup as the sun began to set and realized that Calyph hadn't told her why he would be in town for the Synchronicity.

Coincidence? she thought wryly, and then put her cup own as she remembered his words. *Well, that's not entirely true. He said he was going to be here to get me. But, now that I think about it, it sounded like he had another purpose here and I was secondary.* She tried to remember what else he might have said but the memory evaded her.

The sun was a dull band of yellow and orange, under a wide swath of bloody red. The red gave way to a strip of blue atmosphere that was topped with a strata of indigo and violet. Scarlett was startled as she contemplated the fact that the sunset displayed the colors of the rainbow. Minus the green.

Her eyes blurred and she turned her thoughts from the lost Jordan to the choice that lay before her.

I could never hurt Calyph, she thought with stout determination. *There is no way that I can. He has done too much for me. He is everything in my life that is steadfast and secure. Still, I can't be dishonest about my feelings for Bjorn. Those feelings are there, and too strong to be ignored.*

The Crimson Jordan considered the two paths that lay at her feet and looked at both of them with fear and longing. The hardest thing was always to choose just one.

You don't need to choose, she heard Elaeric say. *The universe has already chosen for you.*

That may be the case, she thought. *But I know my heart. And I will choose my own path.*

Still, for a second, she wavered. Then the Jordan straightened her back, lifted her chin, and chose her path. The choice having been made, she brushed the crumbs from her hands with three quick resounding claps. She smoothed her shirt and stood up, leaving a coin on the table. It was time.

Scarlett joined the stream of people headed for the center of the darkening town, glad to be swallowed in the mass and simply part of the whole force that moved eagerly towards the same goal.

Some that were more eager, and most that were drunk, pushed past her – clapping her on the back or even stopping to hug her or plant an occasional sloppy kiss on her cheek.

Scarlett took it all in good humor and thought, *if they had done this just a few months ago the streets would have been filled with blood.* Her smile widened into a grin and she shook her head.

She was different now. Some things might never change, but the old Scarlett was dead, she realized. Not lost forever, but reincarnated into the new person she was becoming.

No, not reincarnated, she thought. *Resurrected.*

I can't change who I am.

But I can be better than I ever was.

Just don't be the frog.

Finally, she reached the square at the center of town where Village East converged with Village West. The place was alive with color and packed shoulder to shoulder with revelers. The sun had gone but had left a crepuscular light to settle over the land and the mini metropolis that had grown large upon it.

Lights in all the colors of the rainbow shone upon the walls of the town hall as well as on all of the IGC and non-denom government buildings. Holographs of Dragons now swooped through the skies above.

Scarlett entered the expanse of the square not by her own will, but by the will of the crowd pressing against her back. Despite the throng of people that already crowded into the square, she was propelled forward until she met with some kind of equilibrium where the crowd ahead pushed with the same intensity as the crowd behind.

There were many Jordans there, in costumes and wigs, but the true Red Jordan wiggled her way sideways until she found a space at the entrance to a restaurant where she had at least a few centimeters of space around her so that she could move a little more freely.

Scarlett turned this way and that, scanning the crowd, taking inventory and cataloging it all in a military manner.

As her eyes traveled across the droves of people oohhing and ahhing over lights and costumes and banners, they finally found what they sought. When they did, her dark eyes felt hot and swollen, like balls of lead trapped within her skull.

She expected that she would see them both that night – in fact, she intended to see them both – just not at the same time. And what stopped her heart was that they were standing right next to each other, making them impossible to miss.

An unusually tall elf with blue and slightly slanted eyes, his pointed ears hidden in his sandy colored hair, stood close to a stall that was selling grilled ears of corn dripping with butter and sugar. His head turned as if he felt her sight upon him and as those blue eyes met her own that were dark and still edged with crimson, his face lit up so bright that it tore at her heart.

Safety, Scarlett thought as she looked at him. *Someone who will stand by me till the very end. The end that I planned out so many years ago. Who will listen to my secrets and love me all the same.*

Next to him, even taller, stood a man with golden hair, glinting green eyes, and a jaw line so sharp that it looked as if it had been chiseled from stone. He stood with his arms crossed across his lean but athletic body, his eyes already fixed upon Scarlett as if he had been waiting for her.

Danger, Scarlett thought. *Desire. Someone who already knows all my secrets but would take me down a different path. Force my eyes to look at the unbearable. Is it the truth that is the hardest to bear?*

The Jordan looked at the two men standing so close to one another. The only thing that separated them was a banner of green silk. A thin wisp of cloth undulating between the choices she must make.

Coincidence? Scarlett thought wistfully.

In her mind she heard Elaeric laugh. *Coincidence is the word of cowards and fools,* he had told her.

How right he was.

I may be a coward, Scarlett thought, *or I may be a fool. Either way, I've made my decision.* She took in both men at one glance and, flashing them a predatory grin, turned on her heel and walked away.

Come and get me, she thought. *My choice was made by the universe, but I have chosen as well.*

Come and get me.

 TWO FIVE

Faith was true to her word. Though she didn't drag Jasyn into the numerous meetings she was required to attend, meetings that she found more and more pointless these days, he accompanied her every time she left the villa. They no longer spent so much as a single night apart.

They slept at home, in the spacecraft, in hotels and at embassies. It didn't matter where they were, they slept in each other's arms.

Their current place of residence was the Last Castle on the Distant Shore, on the charity of Charity for the last few days while the sisters attended board meetings at the GwenSeven Headquarters.

The compound that housed GwenSeven Headquarters took up a continent-sized island on the watery planet-moon of the Last Shore. The complex included offices, labs, an enormous medical center, housing for employees, and the GwenSeven prototype factory.

Faith had arranged for Jasyn to receive a tour of the compound to keep him from getting bored at the Castle, though he had assured her with a long and sensuous kiss that he didn't need looking after and would be just as happy to wait for her in bed. Faith had laughed but urged him to go, saying they could have lunch together as soon as she was out of her first conference, and he agreed.

He and Faith, along with her small escort that included Penny and Geary and Geary's smallest security contingent, had traveled from the Castle's island on a high-speed hydrofoil that could easily fit a small army – which was proportionate to the size of the entourage that constantly accompanied Charity.

Jasyn found the compound both fascinating and terrifying, from seeing where constructs were made from design to release, to the way the company was run down to the last detail. And everywhere he looked he could see Faith's hand.

His escort returned him to the main office building where the door was flanked on one side by Geary and by a portion of Charity's security team on the other. Jasyn joined Penny and a number of other assistants, mostly Charity's, in the plush lobby decked out in varying shades of gold and silver.

The assistants, usually quite chatty when left to themselves, talked in hushed and hurried whispers. Jasyn's eyes flicked to Penny, her brown hair pulled back as tight as her brown suit, and could see that something was up. He could see the tension in the brown eyes behind the square black frames of her glasses.

He watched as her eyes moved in tiny fractions back and forth and knew that she was reading the ticker on the inside left lens of the eyeglasses. She touched the comset on her ear and began speaking but her voice was too quiet for his ears to pick out what she was saying. Jasyn looked outside and saw Geary speaking discreetly into his own comset.

Whatever was going on, it was serious enough to make Jasyn nervous. He forced himself to take a deep breath as he looked out the window, watching and waiting. He didn't have to wait long.

The double doors to the boardroom swung open on silent hinges and the de Rossi sisters emerged, leading a smartly dressed group of humans and elves, two Gobli males and a single Aridian. Charity was laughing and talking loudly, as she usually was, but Faith looked away from her as soon as they entered the lobby, noting how the waiting entourage had gone suddenly silent.

She touched her sister's sleeve gave a slight nod toward Penny and the others. Charity stopped mid sentence, startled. She excused herself from the group and walked over to Aide who leaned close to her employer, whispering intently.

Penny's brown eyes looked longingly at Faith as if trying to will her over so they could speak. Faith knew this and gave her PA a slight shake of her head before she turned her attention to the group, picking up where Charity left off, just not quite as loud. She thanked the others for their time as they crossed the gleaming lobby and then gently ushered them out the door so they could be escorted to their departure transportation.

Charity gave Aide a curt nod and turned back to bid all those exiting through the doors a final goodbye. Jasyn could see that the tension had found its way into even the younger de Rossi. When the door closed behind the last boardroom guest, she fixed her green eyes on Faith.

"She's here," she announced, one corner of her mouth twitching up into a diminutive edge of a smile. Faith's eyes widened just a tiny bit but for less than a second.

"Noel?" she asked.

Charity nodded.

"See that she is made...comfortable," Faith said, the corner of her own mouth twitching. Then she clasped her hands in front of her and bowed her head, her eyes making quick, miniscule movements as she thought. "You have a jet here at the compound?" she asked without looking up and already knowing the answer.

"Of course."

Faith nodded. "I want it outside this building in thirty seconds." Charity lifted a hand and one of her assistants hurried away, already chattering into her comset. "Send everyone else back to the Castle in the hydrofoil," Faith instructed.

Penny stepped forward, but Faith spoke before she could utter a word. "Penny, you'll come with me. Have Geary accompany everyone else on the hydrofoil."

Penny bit her lower lip. "Ma'am, Geary isn't going to..."

"I know he isn't going to like it," Faith finished for her. "But it's what I want and it might help if you remind him where we are. No one can even land on this moon without security clearance and there is still a security detail at the Castle."

Penny nodded her acquiescence though her lips were pressed together in a tight line. "Yes, ma'am."

"Besides," Faith said, slipping an arm inside Jasyn's elbow as Charity was motioning for her crew to get moving, "I have Jasyn to keep me safe."

Penny looked doubtful but kept her opinions to herself, which was what she was paid to do. "Yes, ma'am," she repeated as she followed the others out the door.

"And I'm sure," Faith said once she was alone with Charity and Jasyn, "that I can handle a one-eyed Jordan that hardly weighs eight stone."

She didn't know how wrong she was.

★

Scarlett made her way through the crowd, though it was no

easy task. Everyone was going in the opposite direction – and they all seemed to want her to join them. Twisting from side to side, always leading with a shoulder, she began to make her way across the square.

The Jordan slipped through a party of reveling Gobli women decked out in holographic streamers and little else. They shouted drunkenly for her to stop and dance, waving their flabby arms at her, but Scarlett never slowed more than necessary. Their shouting picked up again behind her a few seconds later, angrily this time as if someone had bowled into them.

Scarlett pressed on, keeping her eyes fixed on her destination that, for now, was the east side of the square. It was all she could do not to look back over her shoulder. He would get her, she was sure of that – but not yet. She had to get clear of the crowd.

Her sharpened senses were frantic with the copious amount of input that was being dumped into her nervous system. The smell of so many close-pressed bodies and of such a variety of species. It seemed each group of the reveling humanoids shared a common, distinctive aroma, though each one had their own unique odor, like a fingerprint. Most bodies were infused with various drugs or such an abundance of liquor that she could almost taste the intoxicants in the air as their essence was released from the pores in the skin of each partygoer.

She could feel the weave of their clothing as she brushed and bumped against them and the flesh of their bodies underneath - some were sinewy and hard muscled, but most were as soft as dough. The sound of the tumultuous crowd as they undulated like crashing waves in a tidal pool was a continuous roar punctuated with shouts and howls that she could feel upon each delicate bone in her inner ear.

The Jordan also could sense her followers as they kept a determined pursuit. She felt as if the revelers were all intent on keeping her from leaving, but knew that her pursuers were having the same difficulty. Those on her trail hurried but, like her, were constantly bumped and pushed and harried.

Scarlett paused midstride and closed her eyes. Letting her breath come and go as if she were in deep meditation, and let her mind and body go still.

Do not fight the current, she thought. *Let the current take you.*

She opened her eyes and the path became clear. She could now see the way through the crowd as her newly honed eyesight predicted its ebb and flow and Scarlett moved into it, becoming one with it. The Jordan kept her pace quick yet even as she moved with a gentle yet steadfast purpose and the revelers parted for her and then closed behind as she passed. She could feel the frustration of her pursuers as she quickly widened the distance between them and herself.

Come and get me.

The air was filled with explosive cracks as a few premature fireworks were ignited. They fractured the growing darkness with ribbons of colored light. The crowd went wild every time, roaring drunken approval.

The Jordan could feel the excitement of the party along with each participant rising to a feverous pitch. She could feel the communal heat of bodies mix with the cool evening air as the violet sky faded to black. She could feel the push and pull of the crowd that became more riotous by the second. More than anything else she could feel a burning within her.

Her skin burned and her blood boiled as it roiled through her veins with the same increasing frenzy of the crowd.

I won't be what I was, she thought. *But I cannot change who I am.*

The Crimson Jordan felt truly crimson, as if she had been engulfed in flames. She felt herself being burnt away and reduced to ash. She felt like the legendary phoenix rising from those ashes.

Don't be the frog.

Scarlett laughed aloud as she was propelled towards the east side of the square, feeling overwhelmed with ecstasy. Feeling larger than life.

Suddenly, she could sense that the number of pursuers had grown. The number of those that were after her doubled at first, then trebled. She had the feeling of slowly but carefully being surrounded, and the surrounding forces were closing in. Scarlett's smile widened.

Come and get me.

The Jordan stepped and sidled and twisted through the heaving mob with the grace of a dancer and found herself near the edge of the town's open center. She was about to squeeze herself out of the main crowd and make her way through the masses in the cobbled streets between the cafés when she abruptly came face to face with Bjorn's beautiful dark-haired troll, Lucy.

Lucy smiled, pleased as a non-human could be, that her calculations of Scarlett's movements had been correct. But then the Jordan did something that the troll had no way to predict.

Scarlett, recovering immediately from the surprise of the confrontation, returned the young woman's smile. Then she grasped the lovely figure by the shoulders and planted a firm kiss on her cheek.

Lucy's eyes widened and every color of the rainbow swirled across their glassy globes as she attempted to process what had just happened and what it meant, both in course and consequence. While the troll attempted to deduce Scarlett's actions and their implications, the Jordan let go of her shoulders and walked right by her, tossing her own dark hair in gleeful satisfaction.

She squeezed between a crowd of drunken partiers and twirled her way through a group of dancing horse traders before heading down a side street packed with people waving holo banners. Behind her, she could tell that her pursuers were closing the distance again, and attempting to encircle her.

Scarlett stopped brusquely and the crowd moved around her like a single living organism. She closed her eyes and breathed deeply. He was close. She could feel him. The feeling he gave off awoke everything within her that cried out in need – safety, security, desire, power.

He was coming for her, she could feel it.

The Jordan felt her face nearly split in half with an ever-increasing smile. She opened her eyes to see a woman – petite and thin with a perfectly round head, white skin, and dark eyes so large that they took up half of her face. Her smooth, black hair was parted down the center of her round head and fell straight down on each side of her face.

Scarlett faltered, startled to see an Aridian. The Jordan paused, trying to politely discern if it was really an Aridian or simply another merry-maker in costume. She had no time to decide because suddenly he was there.

The one she had called to with her heart and soul had responded. He had come for her, like she knew he would. Her back arched in anticipation and her lips parted as her head tilted up. Ghostly light emanated from the three moons that hung in the darkened sky like mismatched globes.

The air above the town was ripped apart with sound and light as it was torn asunder by a silver Fledgling Dragon, trailing crimson light as it crashed into the atmosphere over the town.

The moving mass of life within the town went crazy at the

sight – jumping and cheering at what they thought was an illusory vision put on for their benefit. Scarlett knew better. She knew how real he was. She knew he had come for her.

Like everyone else, Scarlett's face was turned upward to watch the apparition as it swooped across the sky and then circled back in a wide turn. Then, quite unexpectedly, something was drawn across her neck in the manner of a blade slitting her throat, though it only felt like it was a finger or two and the touch was a gentle caress.

Scarlett dropped her chin and clutched her neck, looking around. She saw only bodies and faces and limbs and hair and streaming cloth, all jumping up and down and screaming in feral excitement. There was no sign of the Aridian.

Other hands clutched at her arms, other bodies pressed hard against her own from every direction and she had to continue moving just to keep from being knocked over. It was utter madness.

I guess that's my cue, Scarlett thought, her hand still at her throat. It felt wet and clammy from whatever creature had touched her but the Jordan's smile barely faltered in a momentary grimace. Fledge had come. That was all that she cared about.

She closed her eyes and she could see what he saw – a Dragon's eye view of the town and its surroundings. She could see every building, tower, and spire; each one made of fabricated stone and roofed in plastique clay tile. Surrounding the village proper were the synthetic wattle and daub café's, stables and inns, roofed with blue slate, dried sod, or faux thatch. The cobblestone streets were hidden under the seething mass of people that had flooded the town.

Keeping her eyes closed, she fixed her vision on the meadows to the north. Nearly flat grassland, and the closest open point to where she was now.

There, she thought.

Fledge wheeled away to the north and Scarlett opened her eyes, absently pawing at the wet gleam that clung to her neck as she made her way through the crowd. They still oohed and ahhed over the sight of the Fledgling Dragon that they thought was a holo, conjured up for their entertainment.

She made her way down the Street of Souls, realizing that she could not have chosen a worse course. Every fortuneteller's shop was open and, on a night like this, was doing a booming business. Everyone wanted to know what the new millennium had in store for them.

The Jordan could see an abundance of black elves, sitting in silk tents set up along the walks for the special event. Their ebony skin gleamed in the moonlight as they touched their patrons and told them their future.

She had been pressing through a throng of fortune seeking tourists when she suddenly realized that she was no longer moving. It was only the crowd that was moving. She was just simply standing in the street, staring at a flower like a mindless idiot. The flower, a red poppy, stood alone in a vase on a table in front of a tent. Behind the table was a silk-robed, black elf.

Smoke crept like searching fingers from the striped silk tent at his back. He smiled at her and his teeth shone as white as beacons. "Pretty lady!" he sang out.

"Mica," Scarlett whispered, feeling the crossing of threads in her heightened state of awareness.

"Come!" he called. "Let me tell your future!"

The Red Jordan shook her head slowly, feeling as if she were in a dream. "I will make my own future," she said, almost to herself. "I will choose." But she was feeling horribly tired.

Drowsy, she thought. *I feel so drowsy.*

Mica was saying something but she couldn't seem to understand his words. Her eyes traveled over his tent, realizing in a sleepy dreamy way that it was the same white and blue striped silk that Arwa used over his vegetable stall.

Mica. In Arwa's tent. Even the flower – Scarlett was sure that she had seen it before somewhere.

The universe is reusing the extras in my life, she thought, and a low, drunken chuckle escaped her lips. *But they are out of context. That's why I can't place the flower. Because it wasn't just one flower – there was a whole field of them.*

The gossamer strands of the universe thickened into threads and, even as drowsy as she now felt, Scarlett could feel those threads around her grow thick and turn into cords. She jerked reflexively.

When those cords tighten, Elaeric had told her, *make sure they are not around your neck.*

Her neck. Her right hand came up and touched her neck where it still felt clammy. She looked at her fingers and could see an iridescent shimmer there. She held her fingers to her nose and she reeled, falling onto the table and knocking the poppy to the ground where the glass vase shattered on the cobbles.

Chlorforgel, she thought, trying to regain her balance.

She stumbled into a woman and grabbed the hem of her shirt and used it to wipe her own neck clean. The woman snatched her shirttail from Scarlett's hand, laughing and shaking her finger at the Jordan.

Naughty me, Scarlett thought belligerently. *Naughty me.*

Mica was calling to her but she ignored him. She shook her head in an effort to clear it and continued on her way, pushing weakly against the crowd. She knew that Fledge had landed, that he was waiting for her.

Trying to keep her sense of direction, she pressed on. She knew that she didn't have much time. The gel had been mostly absorbed into her skin and she would pass out soon. She also knew that she was close. So close and yet so far.

She pressed and pushed and stumbled, finally making it to the outer wall of the village, though there was no opening. She had misjudged the angle and had come upon the wall too far to the south.

The Jordan turned away from the opposing force of the revelers and put her hands out against the wall that encircled the town and began to feel her way along to her left. Relying on her sense of touch as her eyesight began to darken, she crab-walked and stumbled sideways, her fingers and sometimes her forehead scraping against the rough stone as she made her way.

At one point, she stumbled and fell forward and would have smacked her head a good one on the hard rock before her, but the blow was cushioned by a gray patch of

Lichen

moss that was growing along the stone wall. As it was, the blow sent her reeling back into the crowd before she was pushed in the opposite direction.

Lichen. Most wanted. Who do I want most? Scarlett shook her head. *What do I want most?* she thought, correcting herself. *What do I want most?* She sighed heavily, tired. *I want him to come get me.*

The Jordan came to the vague realization that she was no longer moving. She was leaning against the wall, her forehead against a streak of moss. She pushed away just enough to get going again.

He's here, she thought, stumbling. *He's come to get me. I just need to get out.*

Just when she thought she had misjudged where she had started, and that she should have gone *right* instead of *left*, there was a rush of cool air and she almost fell on her face as the wall opened up and she found herself staggering through the eastern gate and out of the city.

The earth was trampled here from the market days that came every week, but just a few meters past the rutted and flattened ground the land dipped and rolled into the grassy hills beyond.

On the first rise of hills to the north, looming and brilliant silver in a luminescent glow of crimson light, was Fledge.

He was bigger than the last time she had seen him, but there was no doubt that it was her Fledgling. He had come for her. She could hear the swishing beat of his heart in her ears and her heartbeat fell into a matching rhythm.

One of her knees gave out and she pulled up reflexively, locking the knee and making her leg ramrod straight. Despite the deadening effects of the Chlorforgel, she could see him and feel him and...

Scarlett.

hear him. Scarlett felt her eyes well and her throat close up, hot and tight. Choking on emotion as much as the Chlorforgel, the Jordan tried to make a last dash for her Fledgling but her legs refused to comply.

She swung her right leg forward first, then her left. She repeated the process as her vision began to dim.

Faster, she thought. *I need to go faster. Fledge is not the only one who is here for me.*

She swung her legs, one at time, building the momentum she knew she needed to make it up the rise just ahead.

I'm almost there. He's almost here. Do I want him to get here before I make it? Do I want to choose? Do I have to? Has the universe already chosen for me?

Fledge loomed on the rise above her. He was so close that she could have wept. The ground sloped upward and she knew that she would have to bend her knees if she was going to make it.

She leaned into the hill and, as she staggered drunkenly up the rise, both of her knees buckled, sending her tumbling forward. She tried to flail her arms in an effort to regain her balance, or at least protect her face, but the appendages could have been shackled to the earth since they seemed even less compliant than her insubordinate legs. She would have crashed to the ground, smashing her face and who knows else, save for the arms that caught her at the last second.

Despite the grogginess that was overcoming her - she knew instantly that those arms had caught her before, but she couldn't remember where or when.

I hope, she thought. *I hope it's you.*

She tried to open her eyes to see if the man she had hoped for was also the one that the universe had chosen, then wondered if it even mattered.

It does matter, she thought, her eyelids fluttering. *I need you. I know that now.*

She thought of what Elaeric had told her about the threads of the universe.

Some threads are woven together, she thought. *Some are knotted.*

She found her eyelids too heavy to open. Her head lolled to the side as she was lifted off the ground and she thought of what Elaeric had said about coincidence. There were no accidents; nothing was random.

Scarlett felt every thread of her being begin to unravel as everything went black.

 TWO SIX

Faith walked through the double glass doors of the office building and out onto the paved courtyard with Jasyn on her right side and Charity on her left. Penny followed her employer at a brisk walk while two nervous personal assistants skittered along in Charity's wake – the only bit of her own entourage that she felt she could not do without.

Up ahead, almost every one of the IGC ambassadors and directors was already departing via secure hydroids or escorted to air cars that would take them to the GwenSeven private spaceport.

Behind her and to her left, Faith could hear Geary issuing orders to the rest of the staff to get to the hydrofoil and, despite how quickly they were moving, it was not quick enough for him. His speech was calm and deliberate but there was an intense undercurrent in his tone and Faith could feel the grip of his tension even at a distance.

She smiled, knowing that he was usurping Charity's security team with his orders and that he didn't give a damn. She also knew that he was inwardly furious at her for going off without him and he was determined to meet up with her as soon as possible. She could almost feel him seething at her impudence and his own imposed impotence, even if the situation was only for a matter of minutes.

He would make a great Commander, she thought. *Though it might be more prudent to keep him by my side.* Her eyes narrowed in deliberation as she strode from the path and onto the field of genetically engineered grass. *When the time comes*, she decided, *I'll give him the choice. He's earned it.*

Jasyn caught Faith by the shoulder, holding her back as a jet descended less than twenty meters in front of them, blowing her brown and gold hair away from her face and whipping it wildly.

You too, she thought, looking into his hazel eyes and feeling her heart fill with love. Her chin lifted and her chest swelled as her lungs pulled at the air like a diver just risen from the depths. She could feel everything around her begin to build, like the first breath of wind that would grow into a deadly storm. *This is it,* she thought, feeling that she might burst with ecstasy. *This is where it all begins. Again.*

★

The three aides, two sisters, and single Companion Construct boarded the plush jet that was obviously a pleasure cruiser. It was normally a craft used for giving tours of the compound and its environs. Charity used it often and even Faith had ridden in it a number of times.

It was made for recreation rather than security or speed, with wide velvet benches and chairs that would swivel so that one could take in the views. Instead of the usual number of small windows, the jet had a single great, long curved window of ultra-glass from floor to ceiling on either side. The effect was that of a jet without walls, minus the wind.

Faith imagined she could hear Geary's teeth grind as he caught sight of her through the window while he boarded the hydrofoil.

The Captain greeted them cordially and began with introductions of the crew in a heavy Europan accent. Faith cut him off as she directed everyone to his or her seats with a brusque and businesslike attitude.

Faith spoke a few words to the Captain in fluent Europan and he gave her a curt nod and turned on his heel to head for the cockpit as everyone fastened their safety webbing. Only moments later they were airborne, the jet rising up and banking to the west.

Like an enormous gull, the jet dove towards the choppy waves and leveled out as it gained speed. The craft flew so low that it was practically skimming the water that separated the island of the GwenSeven Compound from the island that housed Charity's castle. The force of its engines carved a great concave tube in the ocean below, sending up torrents of water on either side.

As soon as the castle was in sight, the jet began to brake, reversing its thrust. Faith watched through the glass wall as the island passed by on their right, its rolling grasslands and rivers rising to the center where the obsidian castle reached up like a broken chunk of night, its black towers stabbing at the sky.

Faith gripped Jasyn's arm as the jet tipped, circling the island, and went straight back towards the land from the other side. Jasyn leaned close to the glass, trying to see where they were headed. His dark brows drew together over his hazel eyes, concerned because it appeared that they were set on a collision course for the castle itself. The jet crossed low over the manicured lawns and gardens as the looming black fortress grew and grew.

From the perspective on the backside, the construct could see that the castle rose up out of a magnificent outcropping of the lava rock from which it was built. It was for this mountainous base of obsidian that they were headed and, though the jet was still braking, Jasyn could see that they would not stop in time to land before the outcrop of rock and within another few seconds they would not be able to avoid it.

Unable to drag his eyes away, he stared at the wall of ebony as it grew and grew until it took up his entire field of vision. His body tensed and he involuntarily squeezed Faith's hand as the darkness swallowed them whole.

There was a silent vibration that ran through the bodies of everyone on the jet as they passed through the electrical field that both protected and camouflaged the base of the mountain. Dim lights came on in the cabin and he turned his hazel eyes to Faith but it was Charity that answered his unspoken question.

"There's always more than just the front door, Jasyn!" she exclaimed, laughing. Faith gave her sister a good-natured glare in the semi-darkness.

Everyone on board was caught deftly by the safety webbing in their seats as the velocity of the jet rapidly slowed, though nothing but shifting darkness was visible through the glass for a number of seconds.

Faith felt a flutter in her stomach as the jet dropped straight down before landing gently on the tarmac. Through the long glass walls they could now see that they were in an immense cavern, so well lit and well staffed that it could be a military-grade hangar.

The eldest de Rossi woman quickly undid her safety webbing and was on her feet in a blink, Jasyn following as close as he could. Two crewmen were immediately at the door, releasing the locks. They pushed open the door and a stairway unrolled and locked into position, leading down to the tarmac. Two more crewmen were on the ground, waiting to help the passengers off as they hurried down the steps.

A security contingent of four lean men in smart black suits and sleek black comsets tucked into their ears appeared from seemingly nowhere and fell into step on either side of the group, escorting them through the hangar and into a series of wide corridors. They entered a lift large enough to hold twice their number, and rode it up fast enough for Faith to feel the flutter in her stomach once again.

When the doors opened, two of the suited men stayed to guard the entrance to lift. The other two entered the elevator to ride it back down and guard the bottom.

"Thank the Captain for me," Faith instructed them.

They both gave her a brisk nod in unison as the doors closed. Faith turned and strode down the corridor with the rest of the party on her heels. The entire group was silent, save for the footfalls that echoed through the marble-floored hallways. Though it was not her home, Faith led them quickly through the castle, taking twists and turns past room after room with a haste and grace.

They finally entered a part of the castle that Jasyn recognized by the wide staircases, elegant rooms, heavy tapestries and rich carpets. These expanses seemed warmer to him, not just by the many burning fires in the hearths, but by the abundance of rich cloths and dark, polished wood rather than the smooth gleaming stone that dominated so much of the castle.

Faith brought the group to an abrupt halt in front of an enormous pair of closed mahogany doors that were intricately carved, the raised areas gilded in silver. Jasyn recognized it as the entrance to a large sitting room. He had been here many times over the past few nights, pretending to be absorbed by his acrylic while he listened to Faith and Charity talk an almost unending stream of bullshit.

Faith turned to Penny first. "Please wait here," she instructed. "When Geary arrives, have him wait here with you."

Penny nodded quickly and stepped demurely to the side while Faith turned to face her sister.

"Something to drink?" she asked.

Charity grinned. "But of course." She turned to Jasyn, much to his surprise. "I think it's time we celebrate, don't you?" When he only blinked at her in puzzlement she laughed. "Would you be a darling and get us a bottle of champagne? Aide will help you."

Jasyn smiled. "I know the way."

Charity could not contain her smirk. "Aide will go with you

anyway. You too," she said motioning to the other assistant. "Though Jasyn is the only one to return." She eyed her two top aides, making sure they got her meaning.

They nodded in assent, letting her know that they understood, and turned to head for the supt-kitch, the closest room that had a full bar - it was closer than the kitchen and much closer than the only room on the ground level that was an actual bar. Jasyn threw a glance of concern at Faith and then followed Charity's assistants down an intersecting hallway.

Alone, except for Penny standing quietly to the side, the sisters looked at each other with expectant eyes.

"Do you want to hold hands?" Charity asked. Though her tone was light, she was completely serious.

Faith smiled. "Yes, but we'll save that for another time. I think we might need it more then."

Both of the sisters, each after taking a deep breath, put their hands on the carved wooden doors in front of them and together they pushed them open.

The room that opened before them was bright but softly lit. Faux candles burned in the sconces upon the wall and real fire burned in the hearths that dominated two of the soaring walls made of stone.

Ancient tapestries hung from the walls and the floor was covered with rich burgundy carpet. Most of the furniture - small tables, chairs, and sofas - consisted of antique carved wood and velvet-covered cushions of crimson and gold.

Upon a long and priceless couch, sprawled as carelessly as a cat, was a woman who looked very young and very thin.

Her form, that looked near emaciated, was clothed in a shimmering, black, flight suit. The dark cloth was just loose enough to allow movement, but clung to her thin form and reflected flecks of light with every move. Her platinum blonde hair was done up in a high pompadour that was gathered at her neck and separated into three large and perfect coils that fell haphazardly over her shoulders.

Her face sported a scar that ran raggedly across the right side. One streak of puckered flesh fled from her blood-red lips to her pointed ear and another, smaller scar shot down across the line of her jaw like a ripple of shiny pink lightning. Her left eye was a bright and sparkling blue, a shimmering black eye patch made from the same fabric as her suit covered the other.

Next to her was a wooden table on wheels and on it were platters laden with round fruits and crisp vegetables. There were tiered plates of hot savories, miniature tarts, and delicate cookies. In the midst of the diminutive feast was a chilled bucket full of ice, cradling a tilted bottle of champagne.

The Jordan held a flute of the golden liquid in one hand, the tiny bubbles streaming like mad in their endless race to join the atmosphere. In her other hand she held a petite slice of filled bread.

Her ravaged face split into a grin as Faith and Charity entered the room.

"My sisters!" she greeted, her voice high and mocking, though she made no move to rise from the couch. "How lovely it is to see you!"

Faith's smile was small and forced at the Jordan's insolence but Charity, who was usually full of mirth and delight, clasped her hands in front of her body and straightened as she sucked in a deep breath between her teeth.

Noel cocked her head playfully, eyeing the two women. "I know what you're thin-king," she teased in a singsong voice. Charity, already taut, stiffened a bit more.

"Is it to get your boots off of that sofa?" she demanded, her voice icy. "It's from Earth, you know."

Noel lifted her boots from the fabric of the couch and swung her legs over until her feet were firmly on the floor. "Better?"

"Better," Charity agreed, relaxing. She cocked her head and a small crease appeared between her perfect brows as she eyed the Jordan's narrow face. "Wouldn't that have sufficed on its own?" she asked, motioning to her own eye but indicating the patch that the Jordan wore.

Noel jerked her head and shoulder in a dismissive manner. "I don't want to be one of your pawns," she remarked, throwing a cold glare at Faith with her single eye before taking a long drink of champagne.

Faith was not put off in the slightest. She sat down in a straight-backed, carved wooden chair with her hands clasped in tight fury. "You fool!" she hissed. "What were you thinking?"

"I just told you," the Jordan said with a scowl. "What were *you* thinking? How dare you use me? Did you think to make me your spy without my knowledge or consent?" The young woman's wrath slowly evaporated and she sat back, crossing one leg over the other and throwing a slender arm covered in sparkling black fabric along the top of the sofa.

Faith relaxed and crossed her own legs. She had not been ready for their last meeting, but this time she was prepared – despite the turn of events that had surrounded her youngest sister so recently.

"Would you have consented, had I asked?"

The Jordan looked at her from the corner of her eye as she sipped her champagne. "Probably not," she conceded.

Faith smiled as if it were the answer she had expected, though she cocked her head, examining her sister in a curious manner. There was something different about her. Not just in her eye but also, Faith realized, in the way that she breathed. Like she was tasting the air – and, by that, everything and everyone around her.

"You said you knew what we were thinking," she reminded the Jordan. "Please be so kind as to enlighten us."

Charity plucked a small bunch of dark purple grapes from the cart and took a seat in another of the high-backed chairs. She placed a grape into her mouth and watched the other two with a sly smile as her right canine teeth split the skin of the fruit before it was crushed by her molars. The juice was as sweet as the scene before her. Charity knew that Faith had come to this meeting with her guns loaded this time. She doubted Noel was quite as prepared.

"You're thinking that you are pretty damned smart," the Jordan told Faith, though her blue eye flicked to Charity as well, including her in the accusation.

"Yes," Faith agreed. Noel scowled at her.

"You think you can steal Alexander's eggs and win some sort of revolution. But you are going to need a lot more than just Hatchlings and Fledglings."

Faith resisted the urge to roll her eyes. "The moons weren't settled overnight," she said, quoting an old saying. "What's your point?"

"My point is, you have no idea what kind of military it is going to take. Even if you steal all the eggs of the rainbow, you're going to be horribly outnumbered and undertrained. The First Dragon, Old Ferrous, would most likely be next to useless in a fight, but the Second Dragons, along with their children, would decimate you."

Charity ate another grape and glanced at her older sister, watching the poker match unfold and wondering how much Faith would reveal. Faith uncrossed her legs and then crossed them again, switching her left leg from the bottom to resting atop her right. She was wondering the same thing but, like any novice player, Noel continued to lay down each card she had.

"Oh, you might be right about the Dragons not fighting each other," Noel informed them. "But they will still be used to incinerate any base of operation you might have, along with any and all armies you can put together – those on the ground and in the air. To the point," and here she smirked and raised her glass towards Faith as if toasting to her health, "you're going to need more Dragons."

Noel selected a piece of herbed bread filled with creamed white cheese and chopped chives and popped it into her mouth and chewed, her expression triumphant. Faith regarded her for a few moments before speaking.

"How about an answer to my offer," she said. "Are you going to join us?"

The Jordan shrugged and washed her food down with a long swallow of champagne. She placed a fist on her sternum and belched, making Charity's green eyes widen. "I'm still considering the *offer*," she replied, smirking at Faith and her own choice of words.

"I thought you might," Faith replied. "Especially with what is going on aboard the Opal Dragon."

The Jordan's single blue flickered in surprise and anger. "That doesn't concern you."

Faith shrugged. "Maybe not directly. But if it concerns you, it concerns all of us."

"Well, right now, it doesn't look so good for all of *you*. Family or not, I don't think I want to join a lost cause. And you should really consider what I told you, without more Dragons, your cause is most surely lost."

Charity delicately placed another grape in her mouth and chewed slowly, her gimlet eyes fixed on Faith. The older sister smiled and tossed her gold and brown hair back over one shoulder as she regarded the young woman on the couch.

"And you should consider this," she told her, "if you haven't already. Why have the missing eggs been named 'Alexander's' Eggs?"

Noel gave a small approximation of a shrug, her thin shoulders pulling up inside her sparkling black suit. "It was just a nickname that stuck. The dark colors are supposed to represent Alexander's

Band."

"And what *is* Alexander's Band?"

Again the tiny shrug, though it was accompanied by a fine line between her blonde brows. "It's the dark space between a double rainbow."

Faith laced her hands together upon her lap and watched her sister carefully, waiting to see if the youngest was as sharp as she was reported to be. She must have been, because her already drawn face turned a whiter shade of pale as the realization sank in. Her blue eye looked at one sister and then the other, and her mouth opened slightly, as if she needed just a little more air.

"There's going to be a second rainbow," Noel breathed, her voice quiet and doused with wonder. "The Third Year Dragons are going to manifest a second set of eggs." The Jordan's sapphire eye traveled across the room before it came back to rest on her oldest sister. "Is that what you are saying?"

Faith gave her a single nod, pleased. "And what has to happen for a Dragon to manifest eggs?" she prodded. The question caught the Jordan off guard, even more so than the others her sister had been asking.

"I...I'm not sure," Noel said, but Faith could see the flicker of fear in her sister's eye and knew that she might have an idea.

"I know that the IGC strictly limits the information you are given," she said, lifting her chin. "The same way they limit all that you do and all that you can have." She narrowed her brown and gold eyes at the Jordan. "For a Dragon to manifest eggs," Faith said, drawing herself up, "the Captain of that Dragon must die."

Noel sat frozen for a moment, and then shook her head slowly from side to side, thinking about all of the Dragon Captains, thinking about her own Captain, Commander Brogan. "That can't be true," she whispered.

"But it is," Faith assured. "Though no one speaks of it, you must have noticed how one event always follows the other."

Noel had not noticed. Or had she purposely ignored it? She wasn't sure. It seemed glaringly obvious, especially now that it was brought to her attention, but something else lit up inside her memory and she shook her head, shaking the blonde coils that fell on her shoulders.

"Not Ferrous," Noel said, indicating the First Dragon, the Iron Dragon. "Ferrous has always had one Captain."

Faith nodded slowly, her smile grim. "That's because, when

the time came, the Executive Officer took his place." Noel's blue eye widened as her sister continued. "And I don't think it was necessarily by choice. It might be one of the reasons that the XO's are circulated between the Dragons. They say it is so they can't form any bond, but most likely it is because they are safer that way."

The Jordan's sparkling blue eye was positively round with shock as her sister's words sunk in and took hold. "I won't kill my Captain," she said finally, her voice quiet. "Nor will I lead a mutiny against him."

Faith's expression softened. "I wouldn't ask you to."

As the quiet settled around the women Noel's head jerked up and Faith looked around to see what had startled her. Charity's expression of surprise and expectation mirrored her older sister's. After a moment Faith realized that she could hear voices on the other side of the closed door – they were heated but quickly hushed. The tension ebbed away from the Jordan's body.

"It's your security man," Noel told Faith with a wry smile. "Pissed, as always."

Faith's eyes narrowed. "How do you know that?"

The Jordan smiled but didn't answer her question. "And your champagne is almost here," she told her. Charity regarded the young woman, astonished.

"And how do you know *that*?" she asked.

The Jordan's smile didn't waver but her voice lowered, became more breathy, almost dreamy. "Because I can hear it," she said slowly, "inside the bottle. Uncorked champagne has a very special sound. And glasses, two of them. I can hear them touch with every step. And..." Her next words, unspoken, were replaced by a puzzled expression.

Faith looked at the girl, who was looking away.

"What is that?" Noel asked softly, though it did not seem that she was speaking to the other women in the room. The way her expression changed, however, suggested that she got her answer.

Again there was a heated but quiet discussion on the other side of the door, but it was brief and fell silent as one of the doors swung open.

Jasyn entered the room, carrying a bottle of corked champagne in one hand and two glasses held upside down by their stems in the other.

"Here we..." Jasyn started but stopped abruptly as his eyes

fell on the Jordan in shimmering black, half sprawled in a languid fashion upon a couch. Both of them froze as his hazel eyes met her single eye of sapphire blue.

After the second it took for their shared gaze to lock, the Jordan moved with no hesitation and uncanny speed.

In a single fluid motion she pitched forward, rolling over her shoulder and coming up on a single knee, pulling a slender object from her boot and aiming it at the dark-haired young man that had brought the champagne.

Faith let out a strangled cry and made a lunge for her sister, but she was not as fast as the Jordan.

EXCERPT FROM
THE DREAM JOURNAL OF HOPE

The constellations war
Over the galactic bar
The gunfighters are there
With their heads shaved bare
In an empty house
The assassin waits
Crosshairs of his laser travel across the wall
I summon my courage and stand in the dark
He takes his time he knows
He has me. I take my time
My last chance, last breath
A flash of light
And the hilt of my knife stands in his chest.
From the other room someone gives chase
I open the front door
And hide in the closet.
Footsteps rise and fall
Silently, the closet door swings open
Johnny is there, with his close-cropped hair
His eyes as blue as my frozen heart
Stopped in time.
He joins me in the confines and whispers
"He is not the one."

# TWO SEVEN

Faith had no idea what the object that the Jordan had produced actually was, but the intent made it clear enough. It was a weapon of some sort and Blue had already leveled the glassy wand at Jasyn.

Her brown and gold eyes widened in horror. The next moments only lasted a few seconds but Faith saw them as if watching a recording in slow motion, seeing each movement frame-by-frame and powerless to stop any of it.

"No!" she screamed, though it felt like the word was lodged in her throat. With what seemed like agonizing slowness, her limbs suddenly awkward, she lunged for the Blue Jordan. The older de Rossi closed the distance quickly, but not quickly enough. She crashed into her youngest sister as a flare of white light shot from the end of her weapon. Her shabby tackle took both of their bodies rolling towards the couch even as Jasyn's form crumpled to the ground.

There was a crash of metal and glass as their bodies hit the wheeled cart the Jordan had been feasting from. Trays and glasses and food went in every direction before raining back down on the floor and furniture. Faith was vaguely aware of Charity calling for the security team that was already pounding down the hall.

Jordan Blue was trying to shove her sister's weight off of her body while at the same time trying to fix the shimmering, black eye patch on her face that had come askew.

"Get off of me!" she hollered, struggling, but the woman on top of her seemed to have as much determination as she had years. "He's Chimeran!" Blue shouted in her own defense but her sister's weight still refused to budge, pinning her down.

"I know that!" Faith hissed in her ear.

Noel's single blue eye widened but, before she could voice another word, security teams for both of her sisters were pouring into the room. Faith pushed herself roughly away from Noel's body and scrabbled across the floor to where Jasyn was lying on the plush carpet, bleeding from a hole blazed into half of his ribcage.

Chaz, the head of security for The Castle, hauled Jordan Blue to her feet where she quickly adjusted the black patch on her face. Geary immediately confiscated her weapon and made it disappear. He pulled a pair of restraints from the back of his belt and held them up.

"Don't you dare even try!" Jordan Blue hissed at him.

He looked to his employer for instruction, even a nod of her head would suffice, but Faith was occupied with the injured construct and didn't look like she had any interest in what happened to her youngest sister.

It's alright, Geary," Charity said, "Chaz will take her from here." She looked at the head of her own security. "Take her to the conservatory," Charity instructed Chaz. "I'll be there shortly," she said, her green eyes fixing upon Noel.

Chaz roughly turned the Jordan to frog march her down the hall but she shook her arm free of his grip.

"I can walk myself," she said, angry. With a final, albeit confused, glare about the room she stalked off, escorted by half a dozen of Charity's security men. Two more stayed behind.

Geary's steel eyes followed the ones leaving the room, undecided for only a second if he should follow and make sure the prisoner was guarded, then electing immediately to stay with Faith. His head swiveled around to see her kneeling by Jasyn's body, slipping an arm under his neck so that she could cradle his head.

The construct opened his eyes and, seeing her, managed a grim smile. Faith looked up, her brown and gold eyes searching.

"Penny?" she asked. Her PA was already close by, her brown eyes wide behind her square black frames.

"I'm right here," she assured.

"My surgeon," Faith instructed in a pleading tone, but she knew even before Penny began to shake her head that Dr. Rawling was light years away. She looked at Charity, the question already in her dark eyes. "M-cen Five?" she asked, her voice hoarse with desperation.

Charity nodded quickly. "I'll call personally and have them ready." She turned to find her own PA who quickly handed her a glittering com-set. As she put it over her ear she noticed a butler, his shaking hands trying to gather slices of cheese and errant red grapes. along with broken glass and dishes onto the tray. "Leave off," Charity told him, motioning to the remaining guards.

The security men helped the butler to his feet and, carrying the tray for him, escorted him from the room.

Faith's eyes found Geary. "Secure my jet. When medical gets here give them any help they need to get them moving as fast as they can." He gave her a curt nod and rushed off to execute her bidding. Faith jerked her head, motioning for Penny to go with him. After an anxious glance her employer, Penny turned and hurried after the lean man that was the head of de Rossi security.

"I'll take care of Noel," Charity said to Faith, who acquiesced with a nod. Charity turned away and looked at the remaining aide. "Ping the main Medical Center at the compound," she instructed as she strode from the room, the PA following close behind. "I want whoever is in charge on the line."

Except for echoing footfalls and the ragged breathing of the last two occupants, the room fell silent. Faith and Jasyn, for the time being, were alone.

She laid a cool hand along the side of his face. "You're going to be fine," she assured him, her voice soft.

He shook his head slowly, his lips pressed tightly together, before a spasm of pain crossed his face. When it had passed, his fixed his eyes on Faith.

"You knew," he whispered.

Faith paused, then nodded.

"When?" he asked, his dark brows drawn together. "When did you know?"

Faith pressed her own lips together and shook her head slowly back and forth, a frown creasing the brow above her gold and brown eyes. Jasyn closed his own eyes, realization making his expression grow slack.

"From the beginning," he said, then a wheezy chuckle escaped from his lips. "You knew the whole time."

Faith nodded slowly and her expression was that of strain and guilt. Jasyn tried to shift his weight but pain tore up through his side, making his body jerk convulsively. Faith saw his face twist with the effort and helped him move so that he was lying slightly on his uninjured side, facing her, his head cradled in her lap. She kissed the ridge of his brow and he reached out, wrapping an arm around her.

'The messages," he said.

"Shhhh," Faith told him, laying two fingers across his lips and looking into the hazel eyes that had beguiled her from the very first time she had looked into them. "Don't say anything. This place is too secure."

"The messages to JP?" he whispered.

"Yes?"

"You saw them?"

Faith sighed. "Yes."

Jasyn closed his eyes and spoke, keeping his voice as low as possible for her to still hear him. "Did you destroy them before they could be sent?"

"No."

His hazel eyes opened, surprised. "You let them go through?" Faith nodded, gently pushing his dark hair away from his face. A face she had always thought of as perfect. "Why?" he asked.

"Because I trusted you."

His face contorted, this time in guilt rather than pain. "You can. You can trust me now."

"I know."

He tried to take a deep breath but his ribcage screamed in protest. "I love you," he said as earnestly as he could.

"I love you, too."

"I want you to believe me," he whispered.

Faith smiled down on him, her fingers tracing the edge of his chin. "I do believe you," she whispered back.

His face pulled together in a grimace of pain. Whether it was physical hurt or mental anguish, Faith did not know. She winced as well, only able to imagine his suffering as his blood soaked into the cream-colored fabric of her suit. She could smell burnt hair and burnt flesh, mixed with the spilled champagne that had soaked into the carpet.

"Be honest with me," she coaxed, cupping his chin with her hand. "Have your feelings for me really changed since we've been together? Would you really protect me?"

Jasyn, his hazel eyes lucid though full of pain, nodded. "I would protect you," he said without hesitation.

"And I will protect you," she said softly. "Your secret is safe with me."

Jasyn closed his eyes and turned his head, hiding his face in her chest.

Faith leaned down, covering his upper body with her own. She brushed her lips against his soft dark hair, inhaling deeply. She enveloped his body as much as she could, bringing her lips down to the edge of his ear.

"And now that we are sharing secrets," she whispered, "and being honest with one another, there is something that I should tell you."

Jasyn managed to pull himself closer to her slender form, though he shuddered at her word *honest*, and wrapped his arms around her waist as he felt the blood seep in slow rhythmic waves from his body.

Her lips brushed his ear and her voice was just a breath.

"I am not Faith de Rossi."

TWO 8

Sean let his ac-bag fall onto the rough fabric of Grandpa's couch. The old man, seated in his old favorite chair, looked at his grandson. His eyes were not quite as bleary as they used to be, but they were just as blue as they had ever been and, for the moment, full of questions. Outside of Grandpa's podment, from across the hall, could be heard the sounds of a heated argument.

"Is it something I did?" Grandpa asked, anxious. He couldn't remember doing anything that might get him into trouble and, though his memory was getting better all the time, he suspected that he might be the cause for the shouts that carried across the hall and through the walls.

Sean laughed and shook his mop of blonde hair. "No, Grandpa. Believe it or not, it's Jeanette. For once."

Grandpa frowned, the scowl hardly showing in his wrinkled face except for the movement of his white eyebrows. "Little Jean? I don't believe it!"

Sean collapsed onto the pilled fabric of the old couch. "Believe what you want, but she's in deep shit."

Grandpa glared at the boy but did not reprimand him for his language. "I haven't heard your mother shout like that for a decade!"

Sean shook his head and laughed. "That's only because your hearing is getting better."

The old man grunted, knowing that the boy was probably right and was glad that he had missed what might have been a decade and a half of heated marital arguments.

"What in heaven's name did she do?"

Sean gave an exaggerated shrug. "Something about dance class. That was all I heard before my presence was noticed and I was ordered over here." He laughed again and Grandpa glared at him.

"Why are you so darn gleeful?"

Sean grinned. "Because I've been telling everyone for years that Jeanette isn't so damned innocent as you all seem to think, yet all of you have always treated her like she's some kind of prima donna."

Grandpa's face scrunched to the side as he considered Sean's words. "Possibly," he admitted. "But I still don't see how a nine-year-old girl, especially one as sweet as that, could cause such a commotion."

"Honestly," Sean admitted, "I don't either. And I don't think I have ever seen my Mom this mad. She's absolutely furious."

"Is that so?" Grandpa asked. He stroked his wrinkled lips with a knobby finger as he considered what could make Rebecca so furious. The only thing that he could think of was her sister-in-law, Johanna. He cackled as he wondered if his wayward Dragon-flying granddaughter had anything to do with the trouble that the youngest granddaughter of the family was in now.

"What's so funny?" Sean demanded.

"I'm thinking how funny it is that the little tiger might have teeth and claws like the big one!"

Another voice joined the shouting coming from the other podment, causing the other voices to fall silent, but only for a second.

"And boy can she roar!" Sean said

The old man lifted his chin and cackled at the ceiling.

Sean looked at him and shook his head. Then, for no reason he could understand, he started laughing as well.

The two, one so old and one so young, laughed and cackled until they were holding their sides - tears streaming from their equally blue eyes, eyes full of hope.

★

The figure on the bed shifted slowly, the pilled blanket that may have once been black twisting and bunching in a slow-motion tidal wave of cheap cotton.

She felt heavy. Compressed - like she might be strapped to a bed. She could see bright light through her eyelids and her first thought was that she was in her bed at the cottage and that the bright light was from the sunshine streaming in through her window.

Squinting, Scarlett cracked her eyes open and saw that light was simulated, most likely fluorescent. She moaned and turned her face away.

She could feel someone close to her, moving in response to her sound. When the voice spoke it was as warm as the light. Also, like the light upon her face, it had a peculiar quality, like a gentle weight.

"Scarlett? Jordan Scarlett? How are you feeling?"

She tried to laugh but all that came out was a hoarse gargle. Her throat felt like an ancient and rusty hinge. She tried to swallow but only succeeded in making a sound like sandpaper being pulled across a rock.

A cup of water was held to her lips and, though she normally despised help, she opened her mouth eagerly. The water was cool and welcome as it poured into her mouth and dribbled down her chin.

She tried to sit up but again felt as if she were being held down by restraints. She looked down her body to find that, instead of restraints, she was covered with a blanket that was thin but felt achingly heavy, as if it were made of lead.

"Jo," she croaked.

"Hmm?" The voice asked, leaning closer. "What was that?"

"Johanna," she said, her own voice thick and heavy, like the light and the air. "My name is Johanna."

The voice that was close to her laughed softly.

With an effort she rolled over, turning away from the voice and the light, and did not fall back asleep as much as she was pushed down into it.

# AUTHOR'S NOTE

Winston Churchill said, "You create your own universe as you go along." It's one of my favorite quotes, along with "life is but a dream," and "button, button, who's got the button?" (though I don't think I can credit the second two quotes to Churchill).

I really do believe that we create our own universe as we go along, yet in storytelling I think that the universe we write about creates itself, and - if we are lucky – we can share what we are witnessing with others.

Alright, now the questions.

Where was Blue in this book, other than a few honorable mentions because she is tied to Faith's story? Where was everybody for that matter? What's going on aboard the Opal Dragon?

Alas, my writing skills are not yet up to the task of a Stephen-King-sized novel. I hope that someday they will be, but - for now - I had to divide the book to keep my mind whole. The next book *(The Moons of Jupiter, Redemption)* is the same story happening at the same time (so save your money if you think you will be bored) but from different points of view. It covers what is going on with most of the characters missing from this book, but certainly not this tale.

As for the eggs, you know where they are.

CPSIA information can be obtained
at www.ICGtesting.com
Printed in the USA
LVOW04s2248230816

501568LV00029B/779/P